THE SONGBIRD'S SHADOW

J.F. PAGE

For my father, who is nothing like any of the fathers in this book.
Dad, since the day I could hold a pencil, you told me that I could be an author.
You always said my stories could give people nightmares. I'm starting to think you were right.

For my mother, who listened to me ramble about this book for over a year on never-ending phone calls.
Mom, I'm sorry if you fall for the good guys that I'll likely kill in every book.

And for anyone who has ever felt broken, who has found themselves frozen with fear. This one's for you.
You are so much stronger than you realize.

Author's Note

The Songbird's Shadow is a dark romance meant for adult readers. It contains content/themes that may be upsetting for some readers. Reader discretion is advised.

For a full list of sensitive topics included within this book, please visit the author's website at jfpageauthor.com or use the QR code below:

This book is a work of fiction and as such, it is not meant to be a realistic depiction of a healthy relationship. The actions of the characters in this book do not reflect healthy, realistic behavior.

Contents

Chapter 1	1
Chapter 2	7
Chapter 3	13
Chapter 4	17
Chapter 5	23
Chapter 6	27
Chapter 7	33
Chapter 8	41
Chapter 9	47
Chapter 10	55
Chapter 11	63
Chapter 12	71
Chapter 13	77
Chapter 14	85
Chapter 15	97
Chapter 16	101
Chapter 17	107
Chapter 18	113
Chapter 19	119
Chapter 20	125
Chapter 21	129
Chapter 22	137
Chapter 23	151
Chapter 24	155
Chapter 25	161
Chapter 26	169
Chapter 27	175
Chapter 28	181
Chapter 29	195
Chapter 30	201
Chapter 31	209
Chapter 32	215
Chapter 33	231
Chapter 34	239

Chapter 35 247
Chapter 36 255
Chapter 37 265
Chapter 38 273
Chapter 39 277
Chapter 40 285
Chapter 41 293
Chapter 42 301
Chapter 43 309
Chapter 44 311
Chapter 45 317
Chapter 46 321
Chapter 47 327
Chapter 48 333
Chapter 49 337
Chapter 50 341
Chapter 51 351
Chapter 52 355
Chapter 53 359
Chapter 54 367
Chapter 55 373
Epilogue 381

Acknowledgments 387
About the Author 389

Chapter One

I t's been days since I've had blood on my hands. Days since I've felt it dripping from my fingers like wet silk. An excited tremor ripples through them at the thought.

My phone vibrates through the pocket of my jeans, and I open it to find a text message.

> Barry Nielson, warehouse 156, Filchon Street

Another vibrate and a photo appears on the screen: a picture of a man who looks to be in his late thirties. The guy looks like shit. His hair is disheveled, the gray, greasy locks flopping over his wrinkled brow. His eyes are sunken and tired. It looks like what I'm about to do might be a relief for him.

I'm an independent contractor, performing wet work for numerous entities, local and otherwise. I don't concern myself much with details—that's Shawn's job. He deals with the customers and makes sure the money is green before sending me the information I need.

This guy Barry stole from the Volkovs, a local branch of the

Bratva. Not a smart move for anyone wanting to stay alive in this city. I may not have any allegiances, but I know who the players are around here, or at least enough to keep myself alive.

I park my black Ford Taurus next to an industrial dumpster behind the Filchon Street warehouses. It's not a flashy car, but it meets my needs; something that's common and doesn't call attention to itself. In the dark, it's barely noticeable.

It's been idling for the last twenty minutes, as I wait for darkness to blanket the city. The wait and the numbing hum of the engine make my palms itch with anticipation. Luckily for me, it's September, so the sun is almost down by 7:30 p.m. After the sun dips below the horizon, I switch off the ignition.

Grabbing my black duffel bag from the passenger seat, I make my way toward the back entrance of the defunct warehouse. Like a lot of the buildings in this part of the city, it's been abandoned and neglected for a few years. Forced to step around broken beer bottles and used needles, I slowly approach the gray giant. The building is structurally sound for now, but you can see the concrete beginning to crumble around the corners and seams. The hard walls climb upward to broken windows where shards of glass stick out like dirty icicles. What a shithole.

Pausing at the door, my ears prick up, listening for movement or voices, but find only silence. The rusted, metal door squeals as I shove it open. Immediately, stale air hits my face with the fragrant bouquet of piss and vomit. The building is almost empty, save the remnants of squatters and drug addicts. The room is littered with old sleeping bags, broken crack pipes, and garbage.

Still and silent, I scan the area from the dark edges of the room. It's only a moment before my eyes lock on my target, crouching next to an old filing cabinet, Glock in hand. Given his options, the cement-lined fireproof cabinet isn't a half bad spot to hide from a mob gunman. Unfortunately for him, I'm not one.

Our eyes meet, and panic whirls through Barry's eyes as he starts shooting haphazardly. I step back into the shadows, tucking my body behind a rusted, metal barrel.

1, 2, 3, 4, 5.

He makes quick waste of his bullets. Grabbing the closet empty beer bottle off of the dusty floor, I huck it across the room. It explodes with impact just yards away from him and he lets out a shriek.

6, 7, 8, 9, 10, 11.

A laugh pulls itself up from my belly, but dies in my throat. He's making this too easy. I grab another piece of trash, a crunched up Pepsi can, and throw it against the wall twenty feet to my right.

12, 13, 14, 15, click, click.

A grin spreads across my face. It's my turn now.

Stepping out from the shadows, I move quickly toward the puddle of a man huddled on the floor. He jumps up, swiveling his head around, seemingly deciding on his best exit strategy before making a beeline for the nearest door. He pushes it open, and the sound of his feet hitting the concrete echoes as he pounds up the stairs. A light chuckle escapes my lips; it's so much more interesting when they run.

My duffel bag is deep and holds everything needed for a job: a folded up tarp, a few knives, a small ax, and more. I feel my way through the bag before settling on a piece of nylon rope about five yards long. I listen to his footfalls and the crashing of a door opening on what sounds like at least two floors up.

"There's no way down from there, Barry," I call out, my voice dripping with glee.

The sour air blows over my face as I charge up the stairs. The scent of damp and rust flood my nose until I stop on the third flood landing. The thick coating of dust on the door is smudged, revealing a sweaty handprint on the metal bar handle. The door is heavy as my shoulder shoves it open. My duffel falls to the floor with a light clap. I ready the rope in my hands, stretching it taught and wrapping each end around my knuckles.

There's just enough light struggling through the busted windows to reveal the room beyond; the floor is mostly empty. Rusted chemical drums and rotted wood pallets are stacked in high columns around the perimeter, the only remaining evidence that this used to be a bustling commercial operation. Out of the corner of my eye, there's movement. I whip my head around just in time to catch sight of my target hurtling toward me, a shard of broken glass in hand.

Barry barrels toward me, forcing me to pivot and throw my elbow out, protecting my head. Sharp, hot pain surges down my arm as the glass slices my skin. Warm blood spreads over my skin and the anger rises in my throat like an exhale of hot smoke.

"You fucker!" I yell, throwing the full weight of my body into him, smashing him into the concrete wall. With my shoulder against his chest, I snatch his wrist in my hand, twisting until he cries in pain. The glass shard falls to the ground with a clink that rings out against the emptiness of the room. The rope, still wrapped around my hands, pulls tight in my grip, ripping at my skin. In a flash of movement, the rope is against Barry's neck and my hands are grasping both ends from behind him, forcing him to spin around until his back is against my chest. One swift kick to the back of his left knee sends him crashing to the floor.

Pulling the rope tight, he thrashes his body against me, wheezing, choking, grabbing desperately at my jeans. He gasps loudly as I loosen my grip, giving the rope slack around his neck. His body eases and his muscles relax. The hope flooding through him is palpable as he breathes deeply. He rolls his eyes upward and turns his head toward mine to search my face. His expression begs for mercy that I won't give. Beaming down at him, my eyes are bright and my smile is wide before my face dissolves into laughter. The optimism drains from his eyes like water dribbling out of a broken bucket.

It reminds me of that old children's song. "There's a hole in the bucket Liz-a, Liz-a," I hum, pulling the rope taught around his neck again. He grunts and gurgles as his body convulses. He lingers there a moment, in that place between life and death, listening to my song until the weight of his body falls forward, collapsing against the rope. I let the rope slip out of my hands and watch his corpse thud against the floor.

My boot shoves against his torso, rolling him over. I pull my phone out of my pocket, snap a quick photo, and text it to Shawn. He'll send it to the customer as evidence of a job well done before they wire the remainder of the money. It's good that he handles that end of the business—customer service isn't exactly in my wheelhouse.

My duffel is still lying next to the door. I pull out a tightly folded plastic tarp and lay it down flat on the floor before rolling Barry's lifeless body into its center. I fold the sides over his feet and head before enveloping him entirely, then fastening his plastic tomb with rope. After throwing the duffel over my shoulder, I grab the foot-end of the tarp. Dragging Barry with me, we haul down the stairs, Barry's body knocking against each step.

Thunk, thunk, thunk.

The sky is dark when I exit the building, towing the body back to my car. The trunk opens with a click, allowing me to throw my duffel into my backseat. Barry isn't a terribly large man, allowing me to hoist him into the trunk before slamming it shut. Walking around to the front driver's side door, I take in my reflection in the dark windows. My hair is disheveled, making me rake my fingers through it, calming it and wiping away any remnants of the dusty building. The forearm of my black, thermal shirt is ripped and hanging in two long strips around my wound. Damn, I really liked this shirt.

Climbing into the car, it's time for me to plan the remainder of my evening. I'll need to wrap my wound with the gauze that lives in the glovebox; a standard hazard of the job. The heart of the city is close to the warehouse district. I'll park my car in the garage on Hart Street and walk the few blocks to the men's clothing store to replace my shirt. It's cool enough outside to leave the corpse in the trunk for an hour. Plus, it's not like he'll mind.

I'll dispose of him tonight, just pass the witching hour, when the world is quiet and no one is around.

Chapter Two

The old grandfather clock chimes to signal the top of the hour as the minute hand rolls over. Its tall, pearwood frame stands ostentatiously in my front room; the only nice thing my father left me from my mother's estate. It sticks out like a sore thumb in the modest fixer-upper that was once my childhood home, but it reminds me of her. It's 4:00 in the evening, so there's enough time for me to finish my work before I have to get ready.

Last week, I received a new manuscript from Jessica Shore, an author I work with regularly. She writes mystery novels with a romantic flare. Editing her work fills me with such an incredible range of emotions—fear, hope, lust, longing. She weaves fantastical stories with imagery so powerful, you can feel, see, and touch every piece of them.

Today, I've been lost in the busy streets of mid-century London, following an ambitious young woman on a mission to solve a series of ritualistic murders. My heart pounded as she uncovered tantalizing secrets buried deep in the fabric of society. The clues she'd collected seem to suggest that the killer is closer than she realizes.

Normally, I'd let her words consume my day, right into the late evening hours, but not today. Emily texted early this morning asking me to meet her for dinner. It's been a few months since we last got together, so I agreed to make the almost hour drive into the city.

I let myself be enveloped in the suspense of the tale for a few more minutes before jotting down some notes about minor grammatical issues and a spelling mistake. The cushion of my chair sighs softly as I push myself away from my work and trudge up the stairs.

My bedroom is one of three rooms that branch off from the short hallway on the second floor. It's the larger of the two bedrooms, but it's nothing grand. The doors of my reach-in closet open to a full, but organized collection of clothes and shoes. Running my hands along the wall of fabric, I think about the image I want to present to the world. What costume will I wear today? Outgoing and available? No, that's not me. Available, sure, but not outgoing. Cute and bookish? Yeah, that's more realistic.

With that in mind, I settle on dark blue, skinny jeans and a burnt orange, cable knit sweater that falls just below my shoulders. To finish the outfit, a pair of brown, leather ankle boots, a delicate, gold chain necklace and small gold hoop earrings. Releasing the clip from the back of my head, my thick, brown hair falls to my collar bones. A swipe of brown eyeliner makes my eyes pop and apricot lipstick makes my lips look soft and full.

My car weaves through desolate backroads, autumn trees looming overhead with gold and crimson leaves flickering in the wind like holiday lights. The warmth of the heater and the soft narration of an audiobook hypnotize me until the road begins to change into a bustling freeway. By the time my car pulls off onto the busy downtown streets, I'm fully aware, if not a little anxious.

Having never been particularly comfortable with street parking, I pull my car into the garage on Hart Street. The restaurant where I'm meeting Emily is only a couple of blocks away. The short walk gives me time to prepare myself for her typical bombardment of stories and questions.

Emily and I met when we were in college, in a way that created an instant friendship—regardless of how different we are as people. It was my first and only frat party. I was shocked when Billy Hensley, the captain of the football team, offered me a drink and asked me to dance. I sipped the sickly sweet mixture of fruit punch and tequila while he twirled me around a crowded living room. I felt like the prettiest girl in the room with his eyes on me—until my head started swimming. My vision narrowed and the room began to fade to blackness. He ushered me upstairs, cooing sweet words in my ear.

Laying on his bed, the whooshing sound of my blood pumping in my ears was deafening. I watched Billy peel off his t-shirt and unbuckle his belt. Just before my vision went dark, a thin slip of a girl with flowing, blonde locks popped up behind him. She pulled her arm back through the air, cracking him over the head with a lamp.

After I woke up in her dorm room the next morning, we became inseparable opposites. Emily has always claimed it was purely coincidental that we ended up living within an hour of each other after we graduated, but I suspect that she was afraid to let me out of her sight. I can't change what I am—the mousy girl who shrinks away from conflict, too afraid to speak up, too afraid to run. She knows it, too.

The street-facing wall of The Cedar Grill is a row of crystal clear picture windows. The amber glow of the spun glass pendant lights hanging over each table flows through them, falling over the sidewalk. Looking through, I catch a glimpse of Emily sipping a martini.

Dodging patrons awaiting their reservations, I make my way to the table. When our eyes meet, her face cracks into a toothy smile.

"Babe! I missed you," she squeaks. Her dusky, blonde hair bounces against her shoulders, surrounding her heart-shaped face with bright blue eyes shimmering like moonstone.

I reply in kind, "I missed you, too." Our server arrives just in time for us to order drinks before Emily launches into a lengthy history of the last few months of her dates and sexual escapades. She's an uninhibited extrovert, and I love that about her.

"Well?" She looks at me eagerly.

"Well, what?"

"Come on, Ava. Seeing anyone? Dating?" She wiggles her perfectly plucked eyebrows. "Fucking?"

This is the part of the conversation I dread. The part where I tell her that there's no man in my life, that no man compares to the strong, dreamy lovers in the manuscripts I pour over each day. The only crumb of news to pass on is that one boring date I went on last month. I met Mr. Tall, Blonde, and Average during my Tuesday night yoga class. We had dinner, during which *he* talked. He talked about work, about his mother, about his exes—everything I didn't care to hear about.

I narrowly avoided his sloppy kiss at the end of the night. His slimy tongue popped out of his mouth before his lips were even near mine. Bobbing my head to the side, I dodged mouth-to-mouth contact and instead had his drool on my cheek. I've since started going to Thursday night yoga.

"Did you at least get *something* out of it?" she asks, her eyes pleading.

I scoff. "He didn't exactly sweep me off my feet, Em." Her forehead wrinkles in frustration as she rolls her eyes. "I'm doing just fine on my own, you know." A line that always seems to gratify her inner feminist.

Her face softens into a small smile. Immediately, her eyes light up like nightlights and her mouth opens, ready to speak, surely preparing to persuade me to let her set me up on a date with "this guy she knows". With impeccable timing, our server is back to take our dinner order. I use the interruption to segue into more palatable topics for the remainder of our meal.

Around 8:45 p.m., we say our goodbyes and I begin the walk back to the garage. Meandering slowly down the block, I take in the sights and sounds of the city at night. Street lights sparkle in rows down seemingly endless stretches of pavement. The sounds of music and chatter seem to bounce between towering buildings, only interrupted by the whoosh of passing cars. People like Emily love it here; they crave the chaos, the frenzy of this place. I feel small, like an ant trapped in a tunnel of noise and lights. It makes me long for the quiet of my home.

But I can't deny the benefits of the city as the smokey scent of fresh ground coffee fills my nose. Across the street, the coffee shop aptly named City Coffee is still open and buzzing with late-night coffee goers. I can practically taste the pumpkin pie spices as I dash across the street, ready to fill myself with the warmth of autumn special blends.

Chapter Three

A bell tinkles lightly as I push open the door at Murphy's Men's Wear. Behind the counter, a young blonde looks up and smiles widely, giving me her best flirty grin. She bounces quickly across the floor, her tan stiletto heels clicking against the linoleum. Her eyes are wide and sparkling when she stops, barely six inches away from me.

"How can I help you?" she coos sweetly.

"I'm fine. I'm just here for some shirts." My words are hushed, pushed out between my gritted teeth.

She blinks at my reply and her lips press together in a tight line. I set my eyes on a circular rack of shirts a few feet behind her, then back to her before raising an eyebrow questioningly. Catching my meaning, she hastily moves out of my way, eyes cast downward, as if she's admiring her shoes. Her cheeks pinken with embarrassment as I step past her.

I thumb through the items on the rack. A couple of thermal shirts to replace the one that got trashed tonight and two black button-ups end up hanging over my arm. I don't need to ask the still red-faced clerk where the dressing room is, I've been here before.

Her eyes burn against my back as I make my way to the far end of the store and step into the small booth, pulling the thick, polyester curtain shut behind me. As I peel off my spent shirt, crusted blood sticks and pulls at my bandaged forearm. Dropping it to the floor, the sound of a small gasp catches my attention. Around the edges of the dressing room curtain, the shop girl is watching. Her eyes rake up and down my torso, filled with awe and hunger.

I'm not a nice looking man. I'm hard and scarred with hardly an inch of me that isn't tattooed. Some women go for that, like her, if the way she's looking at me is anything to go by. Her attraction to me, the ravenous look on her face, makes my lip curl and a pit form deep in my gut. I don't have time for this. I don't want her. I'm not enticed by her bottled-blonde hair, her pink, plastic fingernails, or her beige, suburban beauty.

Frankly, if she knew anything about me, she wouldn't want me, either. If she knew there was a body in the trunk of my car right now, she'd run as far and fast as her skinny legs could take her.

I pull a black, button-up shirt over my broad shoulders and rip the tag from the sleeve. I can't wear my old shirt out without drawing some attention, and with Barry still in my car, that's not ideal. Throwing the remaining shirts over my arm, I push the curtain aside and head for the counter.

The hungry clerk seems to be putting in effort to make this transaction last a painfully long time, delicately folding and bagging my purchase, giving me my change along with a small piece of paper. I unfold the paper to find her name and phone number scribbled on it. I grab the change and drop the paper back on the counter. I look up at her face, which is drawn with disappointment, before whirling around to leave the building.

A surge of white hot anger pumps through me, like fire. I fucking hate her desperation, her want for me. I find her interest intolerable, like her eyes on me should burn holes through my skin. She doesn't know who I am, what I am. She doesn't know that I'm a broken thing, a monster.

As I step out onto the sidewalk, the cool air calms the fire inside me, pulling me back to myself. It's dark outside, but it's city dark. Light pours from street lamps and shop windows, setting the streets ablaze. The familiar buzz of the city hums around me, dazing me as I make my way down the sidewalk toward the parking garage. About a block in, something stops me. Through the window of a coffee shop, I catch sight of a woman. If I had a heart, I think it would have stopped at that moment.

Her hair is the color of earth after rain. It flows by her face, the silken waves stopping just above her collarbones. Her orange sweater is pulled low below her shoulders, revealing milky, pale skin that gleams under the shop's harsh fluorescent bulbs. She looks like a sunrise, like the place where warm earth and cool skies meet. The curve of her full hips press tightly against her jeans, while her short heel boots lift her perfectly round ass. I watch as she shifts impatiently and her delicate fingers fidget with the straps of her purse.

Behind the small cafe tables that line the perimeter of the shop, hang large window-shaped mirrors, giving me the perfect view of her face from multiple angles. She's fucking gorgeous. Her wide, moss-green eyes shine sweetly amid her perfectly round face. Her lips sit full and pink below her narrow nose. There's a quiet seductiveness about her. She's beautiful, but I doubt that she knows it. There's something sad about her, too. Something that lingers behind her eyes that calls to me. It feels like it's asking, *are you broken, too?*

My spine tingles; I need to get closer to her. I slip into the shop through the partially opened door, careful not to make any noise that would draw her attention. My shoulders tense as I step into the line, directly behind her, keenly aware that my body is only inches from hers. Fuck, she smells like strawberries. *Does she taste as sweet?* The thought sends lightning through my veins straight to my cock.

"A pumpkin spice latte, please." Her feathery voice is suddenly the only thing I can hear amongst the sounds of the busy shop. She fumbles clumsily through her purse for a moment. The sight of her credit card appearing in her hand thrills me. She's making it so easy for me to find out who she is.

Without pause, I wave my hand forward just enough to bump her elbow, and we watch as the card falls to the floor. She has no time to retrieve it, it's already in my hand. Her eyes go round as I straighten myself, towering over her small frame. Holding it out for her, I read the name embossed across the front:

Ava Moore.

"Thank you," she murmurs, staring directly ahead at my chest. She's shy. Fuck, I love it when they're shy. The smile forming on my face is unavoidable. After she pays, I order the quickest thing on the menu—a black coffee. The barista hands me the small travel cup just as my new interest walks out the front door. I trail behind her, leaving enough space to not draw her attention, but not enough to lose sight of her.

She's anxious now, walking in the dark. The sound of her heels clacking quicken as she moves further from the busy storefronts. She clutches her purse tightly under her armpit and glances warily at men who walk past. She doesn't know it, but she doesn't need to worry about them. I won't let anyone touch her.

After a few minutes, she turns off the sidewalk and enters the parking garage. It's a convenient coincidence that we're parked in the same place. She pauses at the entrance of the stairwell, eyeing the near-vacant lot cautiously before walking up the stairs. I watch her plump ass swing from side to side as she moves, her heels slowing her considerably. Slowly and quietly, I ascend the staircase behind her.

When she reaches the second floor landing, she looks around anxiously as she continuously presses the button on her key fob. It's not until a familiar beep sounds and headlights flash that she moves. Shit, she doesn't even know where she parked her car. Why do I find her absentmindedness so enthralling? I watch from the dark corner of the lot as she gets into an unremarkable, dark blue Honda Civic. The few minutes before she pulls away gives me ample time to memorize her license plate.

I'll come find you later, Ava. For now, I have to deal with the corpse that's waiting in my trunk.

Chapter Four

I call Shawn from the car as I drive out of the city.

"What's up, Gray?" His voice reflects his irritation with the late phone call.

"I need you to trace a name and plate. Get me all the information you can. Ava Moore. Plate number FR58602."

He sighs audibly. "I'm tired, man. You need this tonight?"

"I need it yesterday," I bark.

He grumbles his agreement before the line clicks dead.

It's a forty minute drive to my makeshift graveyard; a secluded spot deep in the forest. The terrain is rough enough to keep hikers out, and there aren't enough animals for hunters to bother with it.

It's dead silent in my car. Usually, the radio would be tuned into a local rock station, but not tonight. I don't want the music to distract me from the sound in my head—her hushed thank you, the quiet, breathy way she says please. I white-knuckle the steering wheel, imagining that *please* being directed at me. I bet she begs so sweetly.

At the edge of the forest, I maneuver my car around a dark wall of looming evergreens and into a small clearing. When the engine clicks off, the only sounds remaining are the soft hush of the wind and the chirping crickets. I give myself a moment to savor the night air before hauling the tarp-wrapped corpse out of my trunk. With a shovel in hand and a body over my shoulder, I make the half-mile trek into the woods to the place where I dug a grave early this morning before the sun came up.

There's just enough moonlight spilling through the heavy tree cover to light the ground with thin, silver beams. The air is thick with the musk of damp soil. This place would seem beautiful, if I didn't know that it was littered with the graves of my former targets. Grunting with effort, I heave the body from my shoulder and into the deep hole. The damp earth is heavy on my shovel, but I'm glad for it. I need some heavy labor to work out the frenzied energy that's been lighting my nerves on fire since I laid eyes on her. Filling in a six-foot hole should work for that.

After Barry's good and tucked in, I pull my phone out of my pocket and find an encrypted email from Shawn that reads:

Who's Ava Moore?

I've been asking myself the same question—who is she? There's something different about Ava, something special. There's something deep inside of me, gnawing at my insides, demanding that I make her mine.

There's a large file attachment entitled *Ava Marie Moore*. The wind whips at my back while I make my way back to the car. As I walk, I flip through the files of the carefully compiled dossier. The moment I get into my car, I plug her address into my GPS. A smile creeps across my face as the navigation system informs me that I can be there by midnight.

The country roads are dark and empty, winding and curving around dark bends and deep forests. Stars sparkle through my windshield in a way they can't in the city. It's picturesque, if you like that kind of thing. The longer you drive, the further apart the houses become. I know based on the land survey and deed in her file that there isn't another house within a mile of hers, and that her property sits in the middle of several acres of woodland. The setting couldn't be more ideal for my purposes.

The car slows to a crawl as I pass by the entrance to a hidden driveway. The only indicator of its presence is a black, metal mailbox on a slanted, wooden post. With my foot pressing steadily on the brake, I cut the headlights and roll to a stop in a clearing at the edge of the woods. Stepping out of the car, I grab a few fallen spruce branches and lay them over the hood. It's unlikely that a car will pass by, but I'd rather be sure no one will see me, including her. She's not ready yet.

Gravel crunches lightly and shifts under my boots as I walk the long, winding driveway that leads to her home. It's a small split-level perched on a hill. A steep sloping metal roof tells its age with thin lines of rust. Nestled low beneath the center of its apex, is a wooden porch with jagged edges and a mismatch of new and rotted floorboards. The dark brown wood siding is a similarly ill-matched mixture of newness and decay. If she's doing the updates herself, I'm impressed. If not, she needs to fire her handyman.

The first floor is dark. The only light in the house is a soft, yellow glow spilling from the second story windows. My blood is pounding in my ears, threatening to burst my eardrums. My mouth is so dry, it feels like it's full of flour. What the fuck is wrong with me? I don't get unnerved like this. Why am I so affected by this mousey little woman?

I round the corner, going up the hill behind the house. There's a clearing between the house and what looks to be another couple of acres of woodland. The ground is blanketed with fallen leaves. They crunch under my boots, upheaving the musty scent of the death of summer. I've always liked autumn for that; it kills slowly, just like me.

From the edge of the clearing, every aspect of the second floor is clearly visible. A pale green bathroom sits empty at the far end of a short hallway. There's only one toothbrush on the edge of the green, porcelain sink. Her name was the only one on the deed, but there's always some chance of a live-in boyfriend. It'd be a messy start to our relationship if I had to kill her lover. I ball my fists as the thought of her having a lover threatens to send me into a rage. I shake my head, willing it away.

The second window is only dimly lit by the light in the hallway. It's a small bedroom with light blue walls. A twin-sized bed with a white comforter and way too many pillows sits in the corner. A plain white dresser takes up most of the opposite wall. It doesn't look lived in, probably a guest bedroom. I don't like the idea of her having overnight guests; I'll have to put a stop to that.

In the third window, I catch sight of her earthy, brown hair. There's a small alcove with a cushioned bench directly in front of the window where she sits. Her back is pressed against the wall, propped up with a small pillow. An oversized, pink t-shirt hangs loosely over her body, ending at the tops of her bare thighs. Her pale legs are pressed together, a book resting on her bent knees. Her fingers twirl absentmindedly around the strands of hair that fall beside her face as she pours over the pages.

I lean against a wide-trunked oak tree and watch her. Every few pages, she reaches over to the windowsill to pick up a large mug. The steam cascades over her face, momentarily fogging her thick-rimmed reading glasses as she sips the hot liquid. When she pushes them back higher onto her nose with her middle finger, she looks like a librarian straight out of my best wet dream. She's fucking gorgeous.

At least half an hour passes as I study her, barely stirring, entirely engrossed in the book before she looks up. Her chest rises steeply and her mouth parts as she sighs deeply. She presses the book closed against her knees before dropping it onto the cushion beside her. My pulse quickens as she turns her head toward the window, right in my direction.

For a second, I think she's spotted me, but it's too dark. She can't see me here, hidden under thick tree branches. Her eyebrows lower and pull closer together, and her rosy lips lower at the outer corners. Her arms snake around her knees, pulling them close to her chest as she stares out into the night. Those bright eyes are filled with long-ing. What's she looking for? Fuck, I'll give it to her, whatever it is.

That searching look in her eyes is too much; it's too heavy, too thick with need. My chest pinches with an unfamiliar feeling, a need developing inside me. I have to get away from it before I do something stupid like break into her house in some misguided attempt to comfort her. I push myself away from the old oak tree, feeling the ripples it's left on the skin of my back before making a full circle around the house to scope out her security.

There are two entrances—the porch door at the front of the house and the door off of the kitchen, each with a single lock. There are no deadbolts or chain locks on either. She feels safe here, in her seclusion. The monstrous thing inside me perks up. It whispers in my mind, *she won't for much longer.*

Chapter Five

I press my eyelids closed tightly in an attempt to avoid the light spilling through my bedroom window, my body begging for a few more minutes of sleep. It's no use though; the day is calling. I crawl out of bed and make my way to the kitchen to pour myself a bowl of cereal. I've always loved breakfast—eggs, sausage, pancakes, the whole lot—but I'm not much of a cook. Mom was, and she had promised to teach me one day. Neither of us realized that we wouldn't have the time.

Cancer took her from me in the first months of my senior year of high school. I went to college in another state, as far away as I could get—from my father, from this town, from the awful memories it holds. After graduation, when I came back, my father had already left with barely a word spoken. I prefer it that way. I don't know where he went and I don't want to. I'm not really sure why I came back here. Maybe to reclaim my home, to face my demons.

So here I am, the embodiment of the story we all hear about—the girl who goes away to find herself and make her career, only to come back to her podunk hometown with nothing much to show for it other than a moderately-useful degree. I've made it work, though. It took years and a lot of work, but at thirty-three, I can now say that I run my own small business. I don't make a lot, but it's enough for me.

I bought this house from my father with the money Mom had left for me. It's not much, and it needs work, but it was hers and now it's mine. Despite the terrible memories it holds, I couldn't let it go. I couldn't let her go. Breathing deeply, I push the thought of my mother out of my mind. It's been nearly sixteen years since she passed, but thinking about her still makes my heart ache.

"No, no, Ava, not today. You've got work to do," I console myself, willing myself out of the funk my brain has dug me into. After a few more deep breaths and some fumbling around the kitchen, I head into my office with a heaping bowl of Lucky Charms and a full cup of coffee.

Sitting down at my desk, I glue my eyes to an author's first draft manuscript. At the first word, I leave my world behind and fall into the world she's created.

I yank my hood over my head, avoiding the heat of the sun that prickles my scalp. Sand scrapes against my toes within the confines of my boots. The scratchy rocks slide in from the holes worn in the soles. Kicking my toes into the dirt, I watch as pieces of earth flake and crumble. I wipe the sweat from my brow and scoff. That's why they call this place "the crust".
Folks say it's because the earth is so dry here that it flakes like the dough of a fancy pastry. Not that any of us would know, since no one here can afford pastry.
My grandma used to say that travelers would speak of it when they passed through, but that was years ago. Nowadays, the only people who come through the crust are the guards.
Once every five years, they come. When they do, it's chaos. Women hide their daughters away in any place they can—cupboards, closets, even burrows beneath the dirt beside their homes. Not that it ever matters. One by one, girls of the right age are dragged from their homes. Their wrists and ankles are locked in shackles, their emaciated bodies stuffed into great wheeled cages lead by black stallions.
I turned twenty-five last week, so the next time the guards come, they'll take me. I have no family to hide me, no loved ones to grieve for my loss. I prefer it that way.
There's no point in opening my heart when I already know my fate. Death awaits me at the other end of the Earth, and that's exactly where they'll take me.

The alarm on my phone howls next to me, signaling that it's time to call it quits and get to yoga class. Brushing the tears from my eyes, I quickly draft my notes from the day. I breathe out a sigh before closing my laptop and making the short drive into the center of town.

There's only one yoga studio in Greenwood, and frankly, I'm surprised that we have one at all. My town is small, the exact opposite of Charlton, the city where Emily lives. It has a local kind of charm where everyone knows your name.

Arriving a few minutes late lets me avoid mingling with the other locals—a lesson I learned after my entirely uninteresting date with one. I sneak in just as the instructor calls for the first downward dog of the evening, the sea of asses in front of me making me chuckle as I plop my mat down at the back of the room. By the time we reach shavasana, the stress of the day has melted away and fallen off of my skin in the droplets of sweat that land unceremoniously on my mat.

Having had my fill of reflection and quiet for the day, I flood my car with whatever the latest pop hit is on the local radio station and make my way home. I put my car in park at the entrance to the driveway to check the mail. The latch sticks and metal creeks as I pry open the small mailbox door. I thumb through the pile of envelopes in my hand. Junk, junk, bill, junk—and a small black card envelope. There's nothing written on the outside and no postage stamps adhered to it. It's not even sealed.

Using the edge of my fingernail, I pull the flap open before removing its contents, a small piece of paper with ripped edges and handwritten, black lettering. The words are legible, but written with a hardness that gives them an air of aggression. The words are written so forcefully that they indent the paper beneath.

Do you know that your name means bird in Latin? I can't wait to make you sing little bird.

My head swivels left and right, searching for whoever is playing this weird joke on me, but I find myself alone, freezing in my sports bra and yoga pants. It's too cold to stand out here while I figure it out. I drop the mail on my passenger seat and let my mind sift through the possibilities as I make my way down the driveway. Emily wouldn't have driven all this way just to prank me with a cryptic note and then leave. If this was her, she'd have stuck around to laugh at my reaction. Maybe I have a neighbor with a strange sense of humor. It can't be anything more than that, right?

Pausing on the porch, I search the edges of the property. Scanning the tree line, I see nothing. The near-bare trees give way to more trees behind, their trunks buried in red and gold leaves. The dusky light makes everything look calm. My ears strain, listening for something, anything, but it's quiet. Even so, I'm relieved when I find my front door still locked up tight, just as I left it.

Once inside, I tuck the note between the pages of my most recent read, and leave it on the coffee table in the living room. I should crumple it up and throw it in the garbage, but something in the back of my mind tells me to keep it. Perhaps because it's the most interesting thing that's happened to me in months, or maybe I just want it to be more interesting than it is.

Dropping myself onto the couch, I chastise myself for thinking this could be anything more than a simple misunderstanding.

Chapter Six

I waited for her at the edge of her property, crouched beneath the trees. I knew she'd check the mailbox when she got home and find my note. My breath catches in my throat as she gets out of her car. She looks absolutely fucking edible. Her forest green pants hug her tightly, outlining the curve of her hips and her hourglass waist. A sliver of her exposed skin peeks out from under the matching sports bra that squeezes her breasts. She hugs her arms tight to her chest as she hustles from the car to the mailbox, her tight ponytail swinging behind her.

She opens my note right away, too curious to wait until she gets inside. Her wide eyes move around wildly, searching for her anonymous admirer. She sucks her lower lip into her mouth and chews on it nervously before getting back in the car. She's anxious, but it's not enough. I want her scared. So scared that she finds solace in the thing she fears most—me. I want to infect her with my darkness until she craves it. Until she craves *me*.

When I lose sight of her, my body, without any direction from my brain, pulls me in closer, walking around the house until she's in my line of sight again. Pressing my body against the house, I crane my neck forward to peer through the window of her living room and watch her. As she nestles my note between the pages of a book, I'm dumbfounded and left sucking in air like I've never breathed before.

She sits for a while, her face is contorted, struggling to brush off what's happening. Her head shakes from side to side, as if she could shake away her thoughts. After a few deep breaths, she settles, grabs a large stack of printed pages from the table, and pulls her legs up to lay on the couch.

Her eyes dart back and forth as she reads and furiously flips through the pages. Something on the current page is different for her, though. A pink hue creeps up from her neck, blushing over her cheeks as her breath quickens. Her lips part with a gentle sigh and her hand releases, dropping the pages to the floor.

Hooking her thumbs into the tops of her pants, she pushes her hands down her thighs, peeling them off. With one hand, she bunches them up and tosses them to the floor. The sight of her immediately makes my cock stiffen and press uncomfortably against the zipper of my jeans. Silky panties hug her soft curves, riding high on her hips. Her wetness darkens the pale, purple fabric between her legs.

Her delicate hand pulls her full breasts up from beneath her sports bra. My mouth waters when I see her nipples, hard and reaching. Her mouth falls open as she rubs her thumb in small circles around the hard nub before pinching it gently. I can't tear my eyes away from her body as her right hand caresses down her sternum, over her stomach, reaching her soaked panties. Her outstretched middle finger rubs circles around her clit, forcing a soft moan from her lips. Even muffled through panes of glass, it's the sexiest sound I've ever heard.

"Fuck," I grunt under my breath, rubbing my hand over the length of my cock through my jeans. In one swift motion, she jerks her panties off and tosses them aside, revealing her pink folds dripping with need.

My cock presses harder against my zipper. I can't contain myself watching her like this. I unzip and free myself from the rough fabric. She moans loudly as she plunges her finger inside of her sweet cunt.

My fist encircles the tip of my dick, mimicking her motions, envisioning myself between her thighs as I press inside her. I jerk the length of my cock, increasing my pace along with hers, imagining how her tight cunt will feel wrapped around me. Her back arches as her fingers move in and out, while her thumb rubs circles around her clit.

She cries out as the orgasm hits her. The sound makes my balls tighten. "Fuck yes, come for me, little bird," I growl as I fall over the edge of my own orgasm. I spatter the leaves beneath her window with my cum.

She's beautiful, basking in her post-orgasm haze. Eyes closed, thighs quivering, her hands shake as her chest heaves up and down. Her soft hand brushes away the hair that's fallen into her face as her breathing steadily slows. In that moment, she's mine. No matter what I have to do, she's going to give herself to me completely, body and soul.

Even if I have to force her.

My eyes stay on her as she collects her discarded clothing and makes her way upstairs. The sound of old pipes hums through the walls, telling me that she's turned on the shower. This is my chance. I quickly tuck myself back into my pants and move around the house to the kitchen door. The lock is simple, and I pick it easily with the kit I keep with me. The moment I push open the door, the smell of her hits me like a rush of strawberry wine. It's intoxicating.

I make a beeline for the room she was in. The sweet musk of her sex still hangs thick in the air. Blood rushes back to my cock as her scent fills my nostrils. A gray couch sits against the wall that separates the kitchen and living room. I press my face against its arm, breathing in the scent of her hair. My finger traces through the damp spot she left on the cushion beneath her before I suck it into my mouth, tasting her. She tastes like Heaven, or as close to it as I'll ever get.

The stack of papers lays on the floor, held together by paper clips—it's a mess of sticky notes and highlighted pages. A fingerprint from her sweaty hands leads me to the page I need. What's got my little bird so bothered?

Jonathan's breathing was ragged. The waves of heat danced along the side of Christine's neck. His strong hands gripped her waist firmly, using the full weight of his Herculean frame to press her against the door. She tried to hold back the moan that fell from her lips, but the feel of his body on hers was too intense. She had craved his touch since all of this began. It wasn't right, but she couldn't escape the feeling that overcame her, that begged her to close the distance between their lips.

She felt his dark eyes on her face, but she couldn't meet them. Her own eyes remained fixed on his chest. Her voice came out as a shaky whisper, "We can't. Not here, not like this."

Jonathan's hands grabbed at her hips. He whipped her around and pressed her face roughly against the wooden door. She hissed in pain, but was pinned, unable to move while his fingers skimmed along the back of her thigh, tracing a line up to the top of her stockings where he lingered. Her breath caught in her throat as his knee jutted out between her legs, forcing them apart.

The shredding of fabric tearing echoed in the cold, empty room as he ripped them from her body. Christina gasped, feeling the cool air play along her sensitive folds. He let her dwell there for a moment, dripping and panting before she felt the heat of his hardened manhood pressed to her opening. Her mind was a tangled web of confusion and lust. The only word she could muster up repeated uncontrollably in her head until it tumbled out of her mouth, "Please."

Sharp, burning pain seared through her core as he plunged inside of her. She screamed, feeling his enormous shaft impaling her, stretching her wider than she thought possible. He held her roughly, bruising her skin while his hips slammed against her in unrelenting thrusts. Loud, husky moans reverberated through the room, like the sound of some feral animal. The sound was so foreign to her that she didn't realize it was coming from her own body.

Her legs trembled, threatening to give out as he thrust in and out of her, his pace increasing. A need crept up inside her like she'd never known before, like a fire building inside her belly, ready to engulf her in flames at any moment. Jonathan growled behind her, a low, wicked sound that made her sex twitch in anticipation. His shaft pulsed inside of her as a rush of warmth spread through her core. A wave of unimaginable pleasure crashed into her, buckling her knees as their intertwined bodies crumpled to the floor.

A dark grin spreads across my mouth. Maybe my little bird isn't as sweet and innocent as she looks. I tilt my ears up, listening for her, but I'm only met with the pattering sound of water hitting tile. Looking around, I notice a bookcase in the corner of the room overflowing with haphazardly stacked novels. I drop the manuscript and run my fingers along the fore-edges of the books, finding indentations where she's dog-eared the pages. Skimming through the books, I find that every folded page is a sex scene. But to my surprise, none of them are romantic, storybook love-making. There are no gentle princes in these stories—they're fucking and it's rough.

My poor, desperate little bird. She doesn't know how badly she needs my darkness or the shadows I'll cast over her. I'll wrap her in them like a blanket before she even realizes that she's cold.

Chapter Seven

I would have stayed with her tonight, hidden until she went to sleep—my need to watch her threatens to overpower my will to do much else—but tonight, I have a job to do. And it's not one I'm looking forward to. Shawn had texted me earlier this evening.

> She wants to meet.

She, meaning Bianca Rossi. Most clients are willing to work with my associate to set up jobs. In fact, they find it significantly more appealing to meet with my assistant instead of the murderer. That's not true for her. Bianca likes to be more involved, and Shawn is more than happy to avoid interacting with her.

Despite his generally nervous disposition, Shawn's not afraid of thugs. He grew up in the criminal underbelly of Boston, working tech and surveillance jobs for the Irish. They snatched him up straight out of high school for his particular skill set.

He was clueless about what he was getting himself into until he was in too deep. When some big players in the family went down, they got suspicious. He had nothing to do with the arrests, that was just bad business, but they didn't know that. He knew too much about their organization for them to let him leave, so he ran. The kid was clever—he erased his entire digital footprint and built a new one with a new name.

When he arrived in my city five years ago, the cocky little shit sent me an encrypted message, telling me that he was the best guy to help me with my work. Of course, I considered killing him just for figuring out who I am and what I do, but he was right. He's been good for business since then. The kid may not be afraid of murderers, but anyone in their right mind would be afraid of Bianca. I, myself, am obviously not in my right mind.

Bianca is the head of the Rossi crime family. Their business is trafficking women; selling them to the highest bidder or forcing them into prostitution. When I first heard about a woman running a sex trafficking ring, I thought she must have inherited or been forced into the business. But that's not the case. In fact, the business has thrived under Bianca's rule.

The girls were hard to control before she ordered that they be forcibly drugged with narcotics, regularly. It also made them less credible witnesses, should they ever escape. Bianca isn't some pawn in this—she's the queen bee. She enjoys her work and the profits that come from it. I'd bet if you were to look up *soulless bitch* in the dictionary, you'd find her picture.

Her business is disgusting, but I learned a long time ago that you can't stop the monsters in this world. After that lesson, I became one, instead. Not the same kind as Bianca, but I'm still a monster, nonetheless. I wonder if my little bird will be able to see the difference.

There is no difference, the little voice in the back of my mind whispers.

Balling my fists and clenching my jaw, I force the voice away. It's wrong. I would never force a woman to endure the horrors of Bianca's world. I would never force Ava to do anything that she doesn't want, even if those desires are buried deep inside of her beneath a layer of the things society has taught her she *should* want.

"You've got to be kidding me," I grumble as I round the corner to State Street. The address Shawn sent me for the meeting is a high-end Italian restaurant, La Stella Della Sera. The hostess looks me up and down as I enter, seemingly unsure of what to make of me. Just as I open my mouth to tell her who I'm meeting, a smokey, feminine voice sounds from behind me. "This one is mine, Cara."

The meek hostess' eyes widen as she nods frantically. Bianca slips a thin arm under mine, like a snake wrapping itself around its prey. It takes every bit of my willpower to not pull away from her grasp as she leads us through the busy restaurant.

Her eyes sparkle as she saunters around tables, meeting the gaze of every male diner who turns away from his date to gawk at her. We stop in front of a table in the back; an intimate, small table lit by candlelight, nestled between two place settings. My eyes roll as she sweeps a hand in the direction of the chairs, indicating for me to sit. I indulge her, taking the chair against the wall. She chuckles knowingly, sitting opposite of me.

She crosses her ankles, her expensive heels clicking together under the table. Her hands press down her thighs, smoothing the wrinkles on her red, designer dress. Its plunging neckline highlights her long neck and substantial cleavage. Her olive skin gleams in the low light, the flicker of the candles shimmering against her long, brown hair. Sitting across from her, she's undeniably alluring. A sly smile pulls her plump lips upward, accentuating her high cheekbones. Her thin eyebrows rise questioningly while her deep, brown eyes stare intently into mine.

Her hand reaches across the table as one long, cherry-red fingernail traces gently across my knuckles. "We can skip dinner and go back to my place for dessert," she offers in a hushed, sultry tone.

"I'm not here for that," I retort quickly, pulling my hand away, as if her touch burned.

"Hmmm." She runs her finger along her lower lip suggestively. "Someone special you're saving yourself for at home?"

I harden my features, keeping my face devoid of the emotion that churns in my gut. The thought of the boogeyman, or *woman*, as the case may be, knowing about my little bird sends fire burning through my veins. I envision her chained, forced to serve the disgusting excuse for men at Bianca's clubs. I will carve up the flesh of anyone who touches her. I'll make them beg for death. I ball my fists under the table, my fingernails carving into my palms. The pain calms me, pulling me back from the brink.

"What I do in my home is none of your concern."

Her wicked smile widens. "For now."

I'm not interested in playing games with Bianca. As I begin to stand to leave, she huffs out an exacerbated breath before shoving a manilla envelope across the table.

Her once sultry tone turns cold and monotonous as she describes the job. A former employee of hers fell for one of her girls. He grabbed her and they escaped. She wants him dead and the girl returned.

As she speaks, my mind wanders back to my little bird. I can imagine myself taking her to a restaurant like this, sharing a romantic meal. Her eyes would sparkle like emeralds in the candle-light. Under the table, I'd run my hands over her thighs and press my palm into her sweet pussy, until she begged me to take her. But realistically, I don't think the waitstaff would take too kindly to me carrying my date over my shoulder and tying her to a chair. I doubt that killing an entire restaurant of witnesses would endear me to her, either. I'm willing to admit that maybe we're not quite ready for public dates. Yet.

The snake's voice pulls me back to reality. "You'll find all the information you need in this envelope. Kill him and bring the girl back to me."

"You know how this works," I reply. "I'll end him, but I'm not taking girls for you."

She chuckles. "What a virtuous murderer you are. Fine, get it done."

As I stand to leave, she adds, "We could skip all of this next time, if you'd simply join my organization."

I roll my eyes at her as I walk back toward the door. She's been attempting to pull me into her business for years. If for nothing else, to ensure that I no longer accept jobs from her only rival.

There are two families that run this city—the Volkov and the

Rossi families. Mikhail Volkov, the head of the Volkov family's empire of narcotics and weapons, has been a thorn in Bianca's side for a long time. Driven by ambition, she'd rather see herself running all illicit trade in the area. At best, the relationship between them is an uneasy alliance. At worst, it's a slow boiling pot, ready to bubble over with any slight from one side or the other.

I do jobs for both of the families, but I don't accept jobs that go between them. I'm not dumb enough to pick a side that would pit me against either of two of the most ruthless crime families in the country.

Just as I reach the door, Bianca's voice calls behind me, "Oh, and Gray? I'll be seeing you soon." I exit the building, followed by an echo of devilish laughter.

My car idles in the parking lot of a seedy motel until just after midnight. The name of the motel, along with its address and photos of my target, were all included in the envelope Bianca gave me. The lights in room 17 went out nearly two hours ago, leaving me confident that its occupants are asleep. I pull a mask over my face, one of those Halloween Ghostface masks. It's the only thing I could find on short notice in a drugstore. I don't normally worry about hiding who I am, but I know that there are two occupants inside that motel room and I only plan on killing one of them.

The locks are simple in cheap motels; it barely takes a minute to get the door open. The room is quiet. The alarm clock on the nightstand bathes the room in a faint, red glow. On the bed, a small-framed woman lays sleeping. She looks rough. Her emaciated body sports large purple and green bruises that peek out over the neck of her t-shirt and along her thin arms. The track marks on the inside of her elbows are inflamed and badly bruised, like she'd tried to fight the injections.

Her frail fingers are wrapped around those of a man—the man in the photos from Bianca's file. He's sound asleep, snoring quietly next to her. Poor fucker did this all for a girl—his girl. Maybe that's why I'm making this quick. Or maybe it's because I'd hate to give Bianca the satisfaction of making him suffer before he died.

Keeping my eyes on my target, I pull my gun out of my pants and screw on the silencer. It's easy to shoot an unmoving target, but I want to be close enough that I don't risk hitting the girl. With careful steps, I inch closer to the bed until my knees almost touch it. My gun is aimed directly between his eyes as I squeeze the trigger.

This isn't like the movies—silencers don't make a gun quiet, just quiet enough to reduce the risk of hearing damage. And shooting a man at this range doesn't leave a small bullet hole, either. I watch as the impact craters his face, sending chunks of his skull and brain crashing against the headboard, splattering onto the face of his sleeping girlfriend.

The girl's eyes fly open, her hands pawing at the blood and brain matter splayed across her face and hair. She sucks in air with rapid, wheezing breaths while her chest heaves. Her eyes catch mine. I wait for her to scream, but she's silent, frozen in the bed next to a corpse.

"Run," I growl.

She remains unmoving, glancing at her now dead savior before staring back into my eyes. I wave my gun toward the door in an attempt to snap her out of her trance. Her hazy eyes follow its direction. When she looks back at me, her eyes widen with realization. She dives out of the bed so quickly that she falls to her hands and knees, the collision vibrating the floor beneath the threadbare carpet. She begins to sob as she jumps to her feet and runs out the door.

I snap a quick photo of the dead man and make my exit. There's no time to hang around since neighbors will undoubtedly have heard something. No one is going to sound the alarm for a body at a sleazy motel anyway. I send the photo to Bianca as I drive away from the motel. Within minutes, my phone is ringing.

I tap my knuckle on the car's touchscreen, accepting the call. My car is flooded with a deafening scream from a man. It surges through the speaker, hoarse and cracking. The man cries over and over in short bursts. I imagine the poor fucker attached to the sound, bloodied and tied up in Bianca's basement. The line goes quiet for a moment until I hear Bianca cooing in a voice as sweet as honey, "Now you'd better keep quiet, or I'll come back and cut something else off."

When the line is silent, I speak, "Job's done."

She chuckles lightly. "Of course it is with *you* on the job. It's a pity you didn't bring my girl back, but maybe next time."

I suck in a breath and press my lips together in a hard line.

"Your payment's been wired. Maybe next time we can tag-team it." She giggles. "How fun that would be! See you soon, Grayson."

I hang up, irritated. Crazy bitch.

Chapter Eight

With a warm mug of fresh coffee in hand, I push open the front door. It's cold outside, but I'm determined to enjoy the last autumn mornings of the year from my porch swing. I breathe deeply, filling my lungs with the crisp air. The scent of damp earth and leaves hangs heavy in the air; I wish I could bottle it up and infuse it into a candle. It wouldn't be the same as the real thing, but just enough for the days I really miss it.

Pulling my fleece bathrobe tight to my chest to stave off the chill, I shuffle my slippered feet over to the wooden swing that hangs from the corner of the porch. Nestled between the cushions is a small, black envelope. I hear the shattering of ceramic before I realize that my mug is no longer in my hand. A small yelp jumps from my throat as hot coffee splashes on my shins. I frown at the brown streaks on my favorite cornflower blue, flannel pajama pants and matching slippers.

I sidestep around the pool of brown liquid and brightly colored fragments of the once floral mug to grab the envelope. It's the same as before—a plain black envelope. Inside is another piece of paper with crudely torn edges. It's written in the same forceful handwriting as the note from my mailbox.

Realization hits me like a ton of bricks, almost dropping me to my knees. This isn't a joke or a misunderstanding; someone is watching me. Bile heaves up from my stomach, coating my throat with a familiar burn. I swallow hard, forcing it back down. My legs wobble as they drag me back inside where I sag against the door. I run my shaking fingers through my hair, pausing at the back of my head with my face between my elbows. Slow, uneven breaths vibrate through my chest.

I stare down at the message in my hands, reading it over and over until my eyes cross and the words bleed together. My mind fixates on just two words: *my pussy*. What the Hell does that mean? Why would it say *my* and not *your*? Could this be a simple mistake by the hasty writer, or something more sinister?

My voice is an octave too high as I console myself. "Okay, okay. It's okay. It's going to be okay. Just call the police and they'll handle it."

My breath catches and my eyes become wide as saucers as realization hits me. I can't show them this. It's bad enough that some creep has already stolen away the sanctity of my privacy. Someone watched me touch myself and I refuse to let everyone else know about it. The thought of the local cops reading about it makes my cheeks hot and my stomach knot. But I can't just do nothing and expect this to go away. I'll file a report, but only tell them about the note from the mailbox. It has to be enough for them to do something.

It's around 3:00 in the afternoon when three loud knocks startle me. Someone is at my front door. I grab the paperweight off my desk.

It's a heavy, gaudy thing—a clear, glass bauble with a gold-dipped rose floating in the center. The only thing that's kept me from throwing it away is that it was a Christmas gift from Emily. I never imagined I'd appreciate it as much as I do right now, if only because it's hefty enough to hit someone with it.

Tiptoeing to the door, I duck under windows and peek around corners. I wedge my face under the small window in the front door, peering up between the curtain and the glass. At the sight of the sheriff standing on my porch, I blow out the breath I'd been holding since I got the note this morning. The paperweight gives a hearty clunk as I drop it onto the small table next to the door.

I step out onto the porch and close the door behind me. Sheriff Lynnfield's eyes narrow under the thick brim of his hat. Small-town politeness would insist that I should invite him inside and offer him a cup of tea, but my privacy has been invaded enough today. I'm not exactly itching to give anyone a tour around my home. He pulls off his hat and holds it to his chest. The tan lines between the wrinkles under his eyes tells a story of a summer fishing on the lake. He clears his throat as he looks me up and down.

"Miss Moore," he says my name like he's spitting out spoiled milk.

I put on my sweetest voice. "Sheriff Lynnfield, nice to see you. I haven't seen you since my mom died all those years ago," I said, making sure to emphasize those last four words.

When I was a kid, the sheriff and my father were best friends. Almost every weekend, they went on camping, fishing, and hunting trips, or out drinking. Those weekends were a respite for Mom and I. We were safe. When she died, the sheriff and his wife were practically leading the parade of tuna casseroles and well wishes. Their attention faded after a few weeks. I don't know why, but Sheriff Lynnfield didn't come back after that. They abandoned their well wishes and sympathies when they left me alone with him.

He huffs out a little breath. "Well, tell me what the problem is."

Handing him the black envelope, I explain that someone is watching me, maybe even stalking me. He inspects the note, flipping it back and forth between his plump fingers. I scowl as I watch his ungloved hands shove it into his back pocket instead of putting it into an evidence bag.

"Any other incidents?" he asks.

The question flops around in my head for a moment. Should I tell him the whole truth? No, I can't bring myself to tell the man who once watched me play on the playground about the naughty note I found this morning. It's too personal. With my eyes turned down to my shoes, I shake my head.

His tongue clicks against the roof of his mouth. "Your daddy did always say you were dramatic. Seems like nothing to me, but if it'll make you feel better, I'll send one of my deputies to check on you for a few nights."

"I would appreciate it," I reply through gritted teeth.

He curtly nods back at me and the sting of forming tears burns in my eyes. I press my eyelids shut, willing them to stay inside. They remain closed as I listen to the creaking of the porch steps and the rumbling of the police cruiser as it pulls away. When I open my eyes, the tears fall. My legs tremble as I sink to my knees.

Jumbled thoughts spin around in my mind, a tornado of anger and regret. Why did I even bother? I should have known he wouldn't believe me. He didn't believe me last time, either. Memories flash behind my eyes—the night Dad beat me until I could barely move. It was the night I finally called for help, the night when nobody came. I cry until my eyes have nothing left to give. Sitting on the splintering wood slats, a breeze sweeps over my face, soothing my swollen eyes and raw, tear-stained cheeks. I suck in the cold air until my lungs feel like they might burst. Forcing it out in a shaky sigh, I collect myself, along with the remnants of my favorite mug. I have to keep going, I can't fall apart.

The parking lot at Greenleaf Grocery is nearly empty when I arrive. The usual afternoon rush died down hours before, leaving only a few evening shoppers scattered around the store. I tuck my head under an old ball cap and keep my face low. If my stalker is here, I have to make an effort to conceal my identity.

A shudder runs through me as the automatic doors open with a loud ping. My knuckles whiten as I grip the handle of my shopping cart like it's a rope tethering me to reality. As if without it, I would slip entirely into the madness of paranoia. My sneakers pad delicately over the checkered linoleum flooring as I make my way through the aisles.

Lessening my death grip on the cart, my hands shake uncontrollably. I move slowly, as if methodical movements will make me less noticeable. But the shaking in my fingers causes my hands to clumsily fumble and fail as I reach for my usual items, knocking them into my cart rather than grabbing them. I list them off under my breath like a calming mantra—bread, lettuce, macaroni and cheese, chicken nuggets, and chicken salad.

At every sound, every passing person, my head swivels and my grip tightens again. My mind races, tossing around the possibilities of who could be watching me—the middle-aged man in a ball cap browsing the cereal aisle, the security guard from the high school at the deli, the teenage bagger at the check-out counter. It could be anyone. How long has the stalker been watching? How many times have I been in this same store with them?

As a dizzy feeling washes over me. I realize that I'm breathing so fast that I'm starting to hyperventilate. I pull my cart into the aisle of wines and liquors and steady myself against a display. Three bottles of pink Moscato clink together as I set them down into the cart. If there was ever a night for drinking, it's this one.

As I approach the check-out counter, I feel a sense of relief when a white-haired woman behind the counter smiles at me warmly. She's not my stalker; not with her motherly smile and kind eyes. My face pulls into a frown as I lay the items onto the belt. This is why I like shopping when there's hardly anyone around. My pick of boxed, frozen, and premade food items fits the lifestyle of a young bachelor. When you add in all the wine, it just looks sad. The kindly woman seems to agree as she eyes my unfortunate haul.

The computer pings loudly as she scans each item. Grabbing the wine bottles she pauses. "Bad day, honey?" she asks with gentle concern.

I huff out a ragged breath. "Yeah," I reply softly as the tears threaten to fall again.

She nods knowingly while placing my things into a paper bag. She packs the bag gingerly, as if the slightest sound might spook me. And to be honest, it probably would.

I suck in a deep breath as I leave the store, walking out into the unknown darkness of the nearly-vacant parking lot. My nervous fingers stumble around, feeling for the electronic lock button on my key fob. I run the last few feet to my car and all but dive into the driver's seat, like a kid jumping into bed before the monster underneath can grab their ankles.

I drop the grocery bag into my passenger seat and drive home in silence. With every turn, I glance at my rearview mirror. I'd notice if someone were driving behind me, wouldn't I? Would I know if I was being followed? I've never thought about it before.

My breath falls out in a relieved sigh when I find that the house looks just the same as I left it—doors closed and a few lights left on. I rush inside through the kitchen door, locking it behind me. I wiggle the knob, ensuring that it's locked up tight.

The grocery bag plops onto the kitchen counter with a thunk and a clink. Once I've put everything in its rightful place, I feel lighter. The small sense of normalcy brings me back to myself. That is until my eyes shift upward toward the small table in the corner of the kitchen. There in the center, sits another small, black envelope.

Chapter Nine

I *inhale deeply, pulling the strawberry scent of her hair into my lungs. With her ponytail clenched in my hand, I pull, tipping her head back toward me. My teeth sink into the sensitive spot below her ear, forcing a whimper from her lips. It's the sweetest fucking sound. I know exactly what I need to do to hear more of it. I press my hips against her perky ass. She pushes back to meet me, rubbing herself against my cock. As my fingers curl around her throat, she moans and her hips pick up speed. I press my lips against her ear. "Tell me what you want, little bird."*

Her voice is strained under the pressure of my fingers clenching around her neck. "Please. I want——"

My phone vibrates against the bedside table, pulling her away from me. I pinch my eyes closed, hoping for another glimpse of her, but the buzzing continues. My hand slaps down onto the phone, causing it to bounce up, but silences it. The screen is lit up with Shawn's name sprawled across it.

"This better be good," I grumble into the speaker.

"I'm just following your orders, *boss.*" His voice drips with sarcasm as he throws extra emphasis on the last word.

"Alright, so spit it out. Why are you calling me at…" I glance toward the clock. "Nine in the morning?"

"I got an alert of a police call at Ava Moore's house."

My mouth pulls up into a smirk. How sweet. My delicate, little bird is begging for someone to save her from the big, bad wolf. Truthfully, I'm impressed that she's trying to protect herself. She seems so meek and quiet that I was half expecting her not to. I'm glad she is; it's much more fun this way. I wonder how long she'll keep this fight up. She'll learn soon that the cops can't protect her from me.

"So…should we maybe…do something about it?" Shawn questions anxiously.

"Don't worry about it. I've got it covered," I huff before hanging up the phone.

It's standard practice for Shawn to set up alerts of police activity in the places I've been. With this being recreational rather than work-related, he put up a bit of a fuss about it before giving in. In the end, he knows better than to stand in my way when I'm determined. He knows I'm not the kind of man you say no to if you want to keep all of your body parts intact.

I occupy my morning with research on my new obsession. The file Shawn pulled together covers the basics. It allows me to dig into her birth and medical records, family ties, real estate, and job history. The first layers of her paper trail indicate a woman who's decidedly normal, just a woman living an average life. She got an English degree out of state before coming back to her hometown to work as a book editor.

But I dig deeper. I know there's more to her than that. She has almost no family to speak of, her mother is dead and her father doesn't seem to be in the picture. Medical records from her childhood are littered with emergency care visits for broken bones, contusions, and various accidents. None of them were indicated as suspicious, just a very accident-prone child.

I comb through her social media, which is unsubstantial. From what I can gather, she has a number of acquaintances, but doesn't seem to have a lot of friends that she keeps in regular contact with. Her posts are similarly unforthcoming, limited to a few memes about work and life. She rarely posts photos of herself. The few she does post show a strikingly beautiful woman with a smile that never reaches her eyes.

By noon, I push myself away from my desk with renewed determination and head for the shower. I'll figure out what makes my little bird's eyes light up.

The shower knob is small in my hand as I twist it onto the hottest setting. Within minutes, the room is engulfed in steam. I swipe my palm across the mirror, wiping away the condensation before flicking the damp remnants into the sink. The reflection that stares back at me is menacing. I run my fingers through my thick, black hair, pushing it off of my face. The rose tattoo that covers my throat stirs as I swallow hard, taking in the harsh lines of my face. I wonder if my little bird will be afraid when she sees me.

As I step into the scalding water, the thought of her frightened eyes makes my chest tighten and blood rush to my cock. Standing under the hot stream, my mind replays the unforgettable sight of her full lips falling open while her pussy clenched around her fingers. The way my body responded to her needy moans was undeniable. I wrap my fingers around my shaft, gripping tightly as I envision those lips wrapped around me. I see the fear in her eyes as she chokes on me, unable to breathe. Her tears fall onto my cock as she gags and tries to pull away. I imagine holding her in place by her hair as I stroke my length.

I slam my hand against the tile wall to steady myself as my pace increases. My hips buck into my hand as I imagine rubbing myself against her slick, pink tongue. I erupt, spurting cum onto the tiles as she rubs her clit beneath me, staring up at me, begging for her own release.

Clearly, Ava is quickly becoming more than just an interest; she's becoming my obsession. I dress quickly, my excitement building. To blend in with the shadows that lurk around her house in the evening, I pull on a pair of black jeans and a t-shirt. My face is hidden under a black hoodie. Coupled with my leather jacket, it provides enough warmth for the autumn air.

The drive to her house is maddening; every traffic light and stop sign prolonging the time before I'm in her space, enveloping myself in her sweet scent. My fingers drum impatiently against the steering wheel. I feel like I'm in that Salvador Dali painting where the clocks are melting. The minutes dripping like a viscous liquid at a painfully slow speed.

Drip, drip, drip.

As I leave the city behind and drive along the quiet, country roads, I feel the tension in my shoulders begin to ease. The tight knots in my neck unwind and settle when I pull my car into the clearing at the edge of the woods by her home. Her car isn't in the driveway, leaving me free to walk straight to her door unnoticed.

Knowing she isn't home, I take my time. Stepping slowly into the kitchen, I breathe in the smell that is uniquely hers. My eyes wander around the room, becoming familiar with her belongings. Quaint, hideous, multicolored coffee mugs dangle on hooks above a run-of-the-mill Mr. Coffee machine.

Oven mitts made to look like cows flop over the edge of the stove, staring at me with beady, plastic eyes. I brush my hand over them as I walk by, eliciting a light jingle from their tiny bell collars. My lips pull up in a small smile. My little bird certainly has a sense of humor.

I pull open the pantry cabinet, finding that it contains more tea than food, but showcases her love of all things instant. My nose wrinkles as I run my hand over no less than five boxes of macaroni and cheese. I'm going to need to feed her better; she eats like a four-year-old.

In the corner sits a small wood table, barely large enough for two people to share. I drop a black envelope on it. She'll find my message when she returns home later, a warning against calling the authorities again.

I'm not a patient man, but I'm not entirely unreasonable, either. I need her to understand that her actions have consequences. I'm fairly certain she won't heed my warning the first time. In time, she'll learn that I don't make idle threats.

She needs to understand that the police can't help her. She needs to know, without a doubt, that no one can take her from me. When she accepts that she's mine, she won't want them to. She'll come to understand that I'm the only one who can protect her. She'll need that protection if I pull her into my life. A good man wouldn't do that to her. A good man would leave her alone to go back to her safe, boring life. But I've never claimed to be a good man. I'm a fucking monster.

I leave the kitchen and make my way through the house. Moving slowly through each room, I explore her home. In her office, my fingers wander lazily over the knick-knacks on her desk and bookshelves, as if my hands have the means to interpret the story behind them. I press my finger against a key on her laptop, springing it to life. My eyes roll when the screen unlocks instantly. My little bird is so sure of her privacy. I don't linger on the contents of her seemingly work-related laptop; I have much more important things to dig into while I'm here.

The steps creak beneath me as I climb the stairs to the second floor. My smile widens as I push open the door to her bedroom. As I stare at her unmade bed, images flood my mind. I think of her warm, brown hair splayed across the pillow, small strands streaking over her sleeping face. Her naked body barely hidden beneath her bed sheets where her pebbled nipples peek through the thin fabric.

I push my jacket off of my shoulders, letting it fall to the floor before kicking off my boots. I let gravity take hold of me, my body falling onto her bed. My body twists and turns, the sheets cocooning around me, enveloping me in her scent and replacing it with my own.

When I was a little kid, my family had a golden retriever named Max. Every week on laundry day, my mom would dump our laundry baskets into a pile near the laundry room. Max would roll around in the pile of our dirty clothes, looking happier than a pig in shit. Now, I understand why, and it's fucking worth it.

As I unwrap myself from the sheets, I notice the small drawer in her bedside table. My fingers curl around the bronze handle and pull it open. My mouth pulls into a wide, wolfish grin as I stare at the items inside. Amidst the mess of hair ties and lip balms, I find lube, a purple vibrator, and the note I left on her porch. It's not just the fact that she kept it that has my dick rock hard, but that she kept it *here*, hidden away next to her bed with her most private items. I groan, gripping my bulge through my pants.

The sudden sound of the clicking of keys in the kitchen door interrupts my thoughts. Grabbing my jacket and boots from the floor, I quietly exit and slip into the guest bedroom. I press my back against the wall, hiding in the shadows just beyond the reach of light from the hallway as soft noises float up from the kitchen. My neck cranes toward the door as I try to decipher the quiet sounds.

When the familiar creaking of the stairs resonates through the empty hallway, I move quickly. With my boots still in my hand, my feet pad quietly across the room where I flatten myself behind the open door. Peering through the small space between the hinges, I watch as Ava thumps into the guest bedroom, her steps loud and purposeful. She mumbles angrily to herself, "That fucking crazy bastard." A laugh builds in my chest, but I press my lips together to stop it from escaping. I know exactly to whom she's referring.

Her pale fingers wrap around the inner edges of the blue, polyester curtains, peering out the window. She snorts out a frustrated breath from her nose as she yanks them shut. She pinches her eyes shut and huffs out a guttural growling sound from between her downturned lips. She's so cute when she's pissed.

She spins on her heels, wrapping one ankle in front of the other and effectively tripping herself. Her body falls forward, crashing into the door. The force sends the door crashing into my chest, knocking the wind out of me. She rights herself and stomps out of the room. I stand there, pressed against the wall, slightly sore and flabbergasted as I listen to her footsteps stomp down the hallway and into her bedroom.

Reinflating my depleted lungs, I pull on my boots and stretch out on the small bed. With my arms crossed behind my head and my legs dangling over the edge, my mind wanders. It doesn't go far though, just into the room next door where Ava lays in her bed. Being so close to her makes my chest tighten with nagging need—to keep her, to possess her, to protect her.

The sound of soft snoring cuts through the silence, pulling me out of my daze. I swivel my legs off of the bed, standing up as quietly as the creaking bed frame will allow. My legs carry me, without any direction from my brain, directly into her bedroom. A small night light plugged into the wall next to her bed blankets the room in a dim, orange glow. Did she install that recently? Is she too afraid to sleep in the dark knowing that I'm out there? My dick responds immediately to the thought, hardening painfully in my jeans.

The warmth of the tiny light falls over her soft features, making her look impossibly delicate. Her arms are curled into her chest, pressing against her breasts and accentuating the cleavage above her thin, white tank top. I watch her chest rise and fall with her deep, steady breaths. The sheet is wrapped around her stomach and arms, leaving her legs bare. Her silky, white panties are pulled high on her hips, accentuating the mouthwatering curve where they dip to meet her soft thighs.

I inch closer, until my legs are pressed against the side of the mattress. As if controlled by anything other than my conscious will, my fingers reach out toward her. They hesitate briefly before brushing a lock of untamed hair behind her ear. She stirs with a small whimpering sound that forces more blood to rush to my already achingly hard cock.

The feel of her soft hair against my skin dissolves any remaining control I may have had over my actions. I let out a haggard breath as my hand travels lower, hovering over her pale legs. My fingers dip down, connecting with the soft skin just above her knee. They trail upward, stroking a gentle path to the top of her thigh.

A faint moan escapes her parted lips. A jolt of anxiety coated in arousal rushes through me, knotting my stomach. My hand freezes as I internally plead with her. *Don't wake up, little bird. I'm not ready to leave you yet.* Her eyes don't open and her breaths remain deep and steady. But she does move; she shudders and her thighs part, opening herself to me.

A slick spot of arousal spreads along the center of her panties. I suck in a breath and bite into my lower lip to stifle the satisfied groan building in my chest. I love how her body responds to me. My hand clenches into a fist as the temptation to touch her more becomes irrepressible. I give into the urge, just enough to run my thumb delicately over her panties, increasing the pressure just slightly as I reach her clit. Her hips lift, pressing her pussy further into my hand as her back arches, begging for friction.

"Fuck," I mutter, stepping back from her bed. Every nerve ending in my body screams at me, willing me to take more. They fight against the logical part of my brain that knows it's not time yet. I need to wait.

In my life, women have only been a means to get off; a quick transaction to ease the tension in my body. I fuck them and I leave them. I've never slept next to a woman, never held one after sex. But looking at my little bird, I feel my resolve slipping against the overwhelming urge to curl myself around her. What is she doing to me?

I force my legs to carry me further away from her, no longer trusting my usual ironclad resolve; the one that seems to dissolve rapidly in her presence. Stealing one more glance as I backstep through the threshold of her room, a voice in the back of my head screams.

Mine.

Chapter Ten

Noticing what's been left for me on my kitchen table, my breath leaves me all at once. Panic blooms in my chest, squeezing like a vise around my heart. I press my palm into the edge of the table, steadying myself against the wave of nausea that threatens to buckle my knees. Through gritted teeth, my breath comes in short bursts. My eyes flit wildly around the room, searching for any sign of the intruder. Everything looks the same; everything else is as I left it.

The black envelope glares at me, daring me to explore its contents. Its sleek, ebony lines taunt me, demanding that I open its elegant wrapping even though it promises to be filled with poison. I nudge it gently with my fingers, as if it might sting to touch it. I've clearly left my rational mind behind entirely, because I'm actually relieved to find that it doesn't burn my hand.

I expel a deep, shuddering breath and open it to find the scrap of paper that I already know is inside. I grasp the edges of the note, pulling it out slowly, hoping that somehow it will disappear from between my fingers. I suck in a shaky breath, readying myself for what horror I might find.

MY POOR LITTLE BIRD, THE POLICE CAN'T SAVE YOU FROM ME. CALL THEM AGAIN AND SOMEONE DIES.

The paper falls from my trembling fingers, fluttering to the floor. My thoughts race, desperately trying to navigate through the fear that's clouding my mind. *Shit, shit, shit.* He knows that I called the sheriff. He knows and he's been in my house. He's actually come inside my *freaking house.*

I'm suddenly struck with the awareness that I've decided my stalker must be a man. There's something about the handwriting and the possessive tone of his notes. That knowledge sends an increasing sense of dread flooding through me. Not that it would be much better if I was being stalked by a woman, but I might have more of a fighting chance against one.

A crushing weight presses down inside my stomach, pulling me to my knees in a crumpled heap on the floor. Hot tears prick my eyes. I blink rapidly, trying to force them away as my vision blurs. Still, they spill over and cascade down my face. With a clear goal suddenly forming in my mind, I crawl toward the cabinet under the sink. If he's going to kill me, I'm not going to be sober for the event.

My shaking hands fumble with the knob as I wrench it open and grab a bottle of wine. I drop down onto my bottom and press my back against the refrigerator, allowing myself to be soothed by the comforting, mechanic hum. Nearly an hour later, after draining most of the bottle of the sweet, pink alcohol, my mind descends into a cozy fog.

The tension in my muscles loosens as the fear begins to dissolve. I gulp down a few more swigs from the bottle. The room begins to spin, but that fear has disintegrated entirely, replaced by white hot anger. This is my home, my safe place, my freaking sanctuary, and some creep has been inside it!

I stand quickly, too quickly, in fact, which sends me toppling to the side. My hip crashes against the fridge, rattling the contents inside. I press my palms against my thighs as my vision settles and the floor unwinds into a mostly flat surface. With all the determination I can muster, I stumble through the house, closing every curtain on every window.

"Can't watch what you can't see, you freaking creep!" I exclaim triumphantly to the darkness beyond my living room window. Satisfied that all the windows on the first floor are sufficiently covered, I turn out the lights and set my sights on the second floor. On wobbly legs, I stumble up the stairs. The old, wooden railing groans in protest as I use it to anchor myself. When I reach the top, I press my hand against the wall in an attempt to reinforce that the room isn't actually whirling around me.

Reeling and angry, I march into the guest bedroom and stand in front of the window. I stare out into the darkness, where the psycho may be lurking. "That fucking crazy bastard," I spit venomously before pulling the curtains closed. I swivel my body back toward the doorway with enough force that I fall against the open door. An aching pain fans out across my chest as I stumble into my bedroom.

I frown at the small reading nook that sits just below the window. It's always been my favorite spot in the house, but now it feels tainted. Despite the nagging thought in the back of my head that he might be out there, I allow myself a moment to stare out into the night. On calm nights like this, the stars twinkle brilliantly like tiny lanterns floating in a black sea. With a heavy sigh, I pull the curtains closed, blocking out his view, and unfortunately, mine.

Sheriff Lynnfield promised to have someone from the station drive by the house tonight, so at the very least, I'll be safe while I'm asleep. That thought, combined with the mellow haze of the wine, comforts me. I shed my clothes and shoes, leaving only my tank top and panties before collapsing into bed.

I press my head into the pillow and wrap the soft sheets around me, pulling them to my chin. Rubbing my cheek against the plush pillow, I'm suddenly keenly aware of how drunk I must be. My bed smells different. It smells like vanilla and leather; a rich combination of sweet syrup and warm earth. I pull the sheets closer, wrapping myself in that comforting scent as I drift off into a restless sleep.

The alarm clock screeches, and with every blaring beep, the throbbing in my head deepens. My arm flails out wildly, slapping against my nightstand in an attempt to crush the source of the sound. I smash my hand into the button on the clock until it stops. My half-lidded, bleary eyes catch a glimpse of something small and white. I blink away the blurriness to find a bottle of acetaminophen and a half-filled glass of water on the nightstand.

Recalling the events of last night, I don't remember thinking clearly enough to be so well-prepared for my impending hangover, but I'm not about to look a gift horse in the mouth. I pop the cap and swallow three of the bitter tablets before guzzling down all the water, the lukewarm liquid lessening the dryness in my mouth. I press my hands into the mattress, pushing myself up to sit on the bed. My stomach lurches in response, inducing an instant feeling of regret for how much wine I drank.

Shit, why is it so bright in here? Wait, actually, *how* is it so bright in here? My eyes widen with sudden, sobering clarity. I jump out of bed with such force that the mattress squeals. The sheet wrapped around my midsection ripples and dances to the floor.

"No, no, no, no, no," I chant my panicked mantra as I pull on the dirty jeans left in a pile beside the bed. My bare feet patter against the floor as I race through the house, poking my head into the doorway of each room. By the time I reach the kitchen, my anxiety has peaked, morphing into a cold blob of terror that lines my now queasy stomach.

I closed every curtain in every window, but now, they're all open.

A cold shiver runs through me. I wrap my arms around myself to stop the shaking in my limbs. The pounding in my head gives way to dizziness as chaotic and muddled thoughts bounce between my ears.

He's been in my house. Again. But worse than that, he's been in every room. He was in my bedroom while I slept. Did he...did he touch me?

I have no control over my mind as images flood in, as if displayed on an enormous movie screen. I watch in horror, unable to look away. A man dressed in black and wrapped in shadows stands beside my bed. His fingers dance along my skin, toying with my scantily clad body. He grips my nipple between his thumb and forefinger, pulling and pinching.

I shake my head, trying to dislodge the thoughts, but my body has already taken hold of them. My stomach tightens as liquid heat pools in my core. I press my thighs together to quell the ache developing between them. I scowl, looking down at my body. "Are you freaking kidding me? I know it's been a while. Okay. *A long time.* But that's just sick!" I yell at the traitorous, horny thing between my legs.

I rummage through the kitchen junk drawer, throwing aside screwdrivers and rubber bands until I find the scrap of paper hidden beneath the random sea of stuff. Scribbled on it is the number for the sheriff's office. The line rings twice before someone picks up.

A soft, feminine voice answers, "Page County Sheriff's Department. How may I direct your call?"

"Sheriff Lynnfield, please. It's important. This is Ava Moore." My speech is quiet and unsteady.

The line clicks and rustles with static. A man clears his throat. "Ava," Lynnfield grumbles, "what seems to be the problem?"

"My stalker. He's back. He's been in my house this time. He's been—"

"Alright, alright, calm down," he responds in a condescending tone that you'd reserved for children and crazy people. "Look, it's probably just an ex-boyfriend trying to mess with you. I'll send someone by this afternoon to talk to you."

"O-okay," I manage to croak out before the line goes dead. My heart sinks in my chest and deflates like an old balloon. There's a calmness that sweeps over the panicked screaming of my nerves, a recognizable sense of hopelessness. I've felt it before and I know it all too well.

Raking my fingers through my tangled hair, I try to channel my yoga teacher. What does she always say? Breathe in the calm and breathe out the relaxation? By the time I realize it isn't working, I've practically hyperventilated myself. I let out a forceful grunt through my gritted teeth.

My stomach grumbles, reminding me that I haven't eaten yet. Food and coffee will soften the blow of the worst morning ever, right? Or at least make me full and jittery. I toss a couple more spoonfuls of ground coffee than usual into the coffee maker, and press the brew button before turning my attention to the refrigerator. When I pull it open, what I see makes my blood boil. My chicken salad sandwich sits wrapped in its clear, plastic film half-eaten, huge bite marks marring the edges of the sourdough. He ate my lunch. He came into my home, threatened me, scared me, and ate my *goddamn lunch*.

After chugging down a larger than normal mug of coffee and wolfing down a bowl of cereal, I drive to the local hardware store for new locks. I feel like an idiot having drawn the line at a sandwich, but I'll be damned if this nutcase is going to make himself at home in my house.

In the early evening, just as the sun is beginning to set behind the tree line, Deputy James Becker knocks on my door. My eyes go wide at the sight of him. In high school, James was tall, lanky, and unimposing in every manner. He was smart and kind, but his Saturday nights weren't spent on dates with cheerleaders. He didn't have time for that; he was always either studying or working on his parents' small farm. We were friends in that distant way that high schoolers were, tossed together into a sea of hormones, petty gossip, and homework, only to part ways soon after with few words spoken.

The man standing on my front porch would have no trouble getting a date now. His uniform stretches tightly over his broad chest and shoulders. The last bits of sunlight illuminate his brown eyes, warming them into reflective pools of honey. His blond eyelashes stand out against his tanned skin. A light stubble covers his square jaw, adding a ruggedness to his handsome face.

He takes off his hat and rakes his hand through his sandy-blonde hair. My eyes settle on his large, calloused hands, wondering what they would feel like against my skin. I look up just as he raises an eyebrow at me questioningly. I realize that I've been staring, drinking in the sight of him like a cool glass of water on a hot day. My cheeks warm in embarrassment as I step out onto the porch. I walk past him to place my hands on the railing and turn my face toward the woods, willing my cheeks to turn back to their normal color.

Something inside me purrs when his husky voice cuts through the silence. "Ava, it's so good to see you." I turn back to him, and my face heats as he looks me up and down with a boyish grin that demonstrates his appreciation for what he sees. He clears his throat and his lips turn down. "I'm sorry it's not under better circumstances."

"Yeah, you too."

The sun glints off of his gold class ring when his hand touches mine. "Tell me about what's been going on," he says with his eyebrows pinched together in concern.

I stare at our hands, my eyes tracing the initials carved on his ring. I blow out a heavy sigh. I can't tell him everything. I can't stand the thought of it all being in a police report. My eyes cast upward, meeting his gaze. To my surprise, his eyes aren't filled with suspicion, but compassion and worry. My eyes blur as the tears begin to fall, running down my cheeks. When I open my mouth, a dam opens and the words spill freely. I tell him everything. With every word, I feel the weight of my problems falling away.

James steps closer, his arm wrapping around me while his hand rubs gentle circles over my upper back. I lean into him, pressing my head to his shoulder, breathing him in. He smells like citrus and sandalwood. Warmth fans out from his hand, branching out and reaching through me until my entire body feels relaxed. Is this what it feels like to be safe? Does protection feel like a warm blanket and strong arms? It's so foreign to me that I'm not really sure.

"It's going to be okay, Ava," he whispers against the crown of my head. "I'm going to find this guy. I won't let anything happen to you."

I nod, feeling entirely certain that he means that.

"I'm going to drive by your house tonight and stay close by. Have you replaced the locks?"

"I, uh, haven't yet, no," I stumble around my words, embarrassed that I have yet to install the new locks I bought.

He pulls his hand away from my back and smiles down at me. "It's okay. I can help you install them if you need it." He reaches into his pocket and hands me a business card. "My cell number is on the back. I want you to call me if anything happens…or if you're afraid."

"Thank you," I say quietly as I give his hand a little squeeze. "Do you…maybe…want to come in for a cup of coffee?"

His mouth turns up into a wide smile. "I wish I could, but I have a couple more stops to make tonight. I'd really love a rain check, though."

I press my lips together, trying to avoid the frown they're trying to pull into. I can feel the warmth rushing to my cheeks which are surely turning a vibrant shade of pink. What am I doing? I get hot over thoughts about my stalker and now I'm trying to ask a deputy on a date?

His finger presses gently under my chin, lifting my gaze to his eyes. "I'm serious about that rain check, Ava," he says confidently.

At his insistence, I go back inside and lock the door before watching him leave from my window. I feel a lightness that I didn't expect. He believes me, and everything's going to be okay.

Chapter Eleven

I press my back against an oak tree, trying to ignore the aching in my bones. My knees are beginning to protest against my crouched position. My toes are starting to go numb from the damp ground that's leaking through the soles of my boots. I pull up my hood and wrap my jacket closer around me as the cop knocks on Ava's door.

I click my tongue. "Tsk, tsk. Disobeying already, my rebellious little bird?"

When Ava steps out onto the porch, she's a beautiful mess. Her eyes are swollen and pink. Her hair is tangled and tossed up into a messy bun. My chest swells with the knowledge that I've affected her so much. That her thoughts have been focused on me, as mine have been on her.

While I watch them talk, that prideful feeling evaporates into a haze of irritation. It boils and floats up my throat like hot steam. I can feel it ripping at my skin and bursting from my pores.

My formerly petrified girl stands there at the door, pink-faced and ogling at the fucking cop. My fists ball at my sides, rage uncoiling inside me. Her eyes wander over him, hungrily. She looks like she's ready to tackle him. My foolish girl is ready to throw herself at the first man she thinks can protect her from me. He could never give her what she needs, what I know she needs.

The squeezing ache in my chest lessens as she steps away from him, looking out into the trees, looking toward me.

"That's right, baby," I mumble, "look at me. Don't look at him."

That crushing feeling around my heart comes back with a vengeance when he stands beside her, close enough to touch her. Pretty tears trail down her cheeks as she talks, reflecting the dimming sunlight.

His hand snakes up behind her, his dirty fingers rubbing circles on her back. I grit my teeth so hard I can hear them scraping together. They vibrate in my mouth, shooting tendrils of pain toward my temples. To force down the ball of anger that's lodged in my throat, I swallow hard. The longer that motherfucker touches her, the more it chokes me.

Fighting the urge to shoot him where he stands, I raise my clenched fist to my mouth and bite down. When she lays her head on his shoulder, the taste of copper fills my mouth. The sight of her chocolate hair pressed against his arm seals his fate. The final nail in the coffin is him tilting her chin up with a finger to meet her gaze. No one gets to peer into her gaze but *me*. I pull my bleeding knuckles from my mouth as my fury softens into selfish resolve.

At the cop's command, she goes inside the house and locks the doors. A clenching tightness strangles my stomach as her wide, puppy-dog eyes track him from the window.

"So obedient for the right master, aren't you?" I huff out through clenched teeth. "I'll teach you who you belong to."

I spin on my heels, causing a flurry of mud to spit up from the ground, caking my jeans with speckles of wet dirt. Dark trees loom around me, forcing me to weave and bob my way back to my car. Graceless in my anger-fueled haste, branches whip at my body, depositing scratches on my hands and twigs in my hair.

Just after sunset, I pull into the nearly empty parking lot at Quick Stop Gas. My car crawls to a stop on the side of the building. I pull the brake, nestling myself between a grimy public bathroom and a line of air pumps. A broken flood light dangles from twisted wires above me, blanketing the area in darkness.

Parked not ten feet away, Deputy Dipshit is sitting in his car, stuffing his face with a greasy, fast food burger. My mouth curls into a disgusted scowl as I watch him shovel it into his mouth. A shower of crumbs falls onto his shirt, which he wipes away carelessly onto the floor of his car. The leather of the steering wheel whispers and crackles beneath my steel grip.

I shake my head and force out a long sigh. I reach into myself, into the depths of my mind. Envisioning a black lake where my emotions ripple against the surface. I push them back further and further until the water is still and calm. Only when my grip loosens and the rise and fall of my chest is steady, do I get out of the car.

I slump my shoulders forward slightly and pull my mouth into a wide smile before rapping my fist gently against his window. He looks up, eyes widened by surprise as the window rolls down. His eyes roam over me suspiciously. I raise my voice an octave, putting on my best local accent.

"Hi, Deputy…uh," I glance at his nametag, "Becker." I clasp my hands in front of me, twirling my fingers in mock shyness. "I'm real sorry to bother you, but I was hoping you could help me out."

His face softens. He nods and cocks an eyebrow questioningly.

I point back to my car. "You see, my car's got a flat and I don't know if I can put on the spare on my own."

His chest puffs up as he swings the door open. "Of course! I'm happy to help. Let's get you situated and on your way."

My smile widens as I walk back to my car with the deputy following closely behind. I pop the trunk and grab the tire iron, holding it against my leg. The deputy stands at my side, his face alight with that good, hometown boy charm.

He runs his palms down the front of his polyester pants and reaches toward the car. "Let's get that spare out and get you going."

Just as his hand makes contact with the handle above the spare tire well, the tire iron makes contact with his head. He groans and his eyes shudder closed as his limp torso flops over the trunk with a thud.

"Too fucking easy." I chuckle, shoving his legs in behind him. I wipe the metal bar against my jeans before tossing it in beside his head and slamming the trunk. I shoot off a quick text to Ricky with the location of the cop car and its keys, which are conveniently still in the ignition. Ricky's a mechanic, as well as the owner of a local chop shop. Our arrangement is simple: he doesn't ask questions, and in return, he gets the cars and whatever profit he can make from them.

The moon is high when I pull my car into the familiar clearing near my graveyard. The scent of pine floats along the cool wind that whistles through the trees. A symphony of crickets welcome me back to my quiet place in the woods. Looking out into the vast forest, I find myself wondering if Ava would like it here. The view isn't too different from the one outside of her windows. We could have a picnic over the graves of her would-be lovers.

When I pop open the trunk, Becker is still unconscious. I yank at his torso until he tumbles onto the ground, vibrating the dirt beneath him. With several layers of folded rope, I create a make-shift gag which I slip into his mouth and tie behind his head. Another rope binds his ankles, and a third binds his wrists. One final piece wraps around his stomach, it's outstretched length giving me a line by which to drag his limp body.

I hoist the rope against my shoulder, pulling him behind me as I hike through the woods. The leaves beneath him rustle and crumble, leaving a trail of trampled foliage in our wake. He moans and whimpers as branches snap against him. When we arrive, his hair and clothing are embedded with leaves and sticks while his face is scratched and bleeding.

I leave him on the damp ground in the center of the clearing.

His panicked eyes dart back and forth, searching. Searching for help, for a way out, for rescue. He'll find none of those here. The moonlight glints off my shovel as I pull it out from behind a tree. The reflection bounces through the air, flitting over his face. A gasp wheezes out from around his gag as it catches his attention. I throw him a wink before I begin to dig into the packed soil. His dull whimpers turn to muffled screams as he watches me dig his grave.

By the time the hole is sufficiently deep and wide, I'm covered in dirt. A thin sheen of perspiration coats my skin. Wiping my stained hands down my thighs, I look over my girl's aspiring savior. Sweat beads down his forehead, dripping between his wide, frightened eyes. His hair is matted with mud and debris clings to his damp forehead. His body lies crumpled on the dirt, quivering and whining like a cornered rodent. Some hero he turned out to be. My little bird deserves better.

His legs thrash against his binds as I pull him upright. Gouged lines appear in the earth as I drag him to the grave. My leg connects with the back of his knees, sending him toppling to the ground. The crack of his knees connecting with the dirt echoes in the quiet clearing. I look down at him, my mouth pulling into a smug grin.

"I was planning to kill you quickly, Deputy," I say, loosening the rope from his mouth. "I was going to make this very easy for you… until you touched my girl."

He coughs and gasps. Dirt and saliva dribbles down his chin as the rope falls away.

He shoots me a quizzical look. "Y-your girl?"

I widen my stance, arms crossing in front of my chest. My eyebrows raise as if to say *think.*

His eyes widen in sudden recognition. "Jesus, you mean Ava?!"

His head rocks to the side as my fist collides with his nose. The crunch and squelch reverberate against my hand as the bone fragments beneath his skin. He yells in pain, the sound loud enough to shake a few birds from the branches above us. Fluttering black shapes soar across the moonlight.

Sputtering against the blood running from his nose, his howls turn into pleas, "Someone help! I need help!"

"Don't waste your breath," I chuckle as my fist rams into his gut, "no one can hear you out here."

He groans, folding in on his stomach. His throat bobs as he swallows hard, gagging.

Between ragged breaths, he pleads, "D-don't do this. I'm…I'm a cop. They'll come. They'll come looking for me."

I throw my head back and bark a laugh. "Oh, I very much doubt that. Not after they read the suicide note you left on your laptop." I crouch down to meet him at eye level, my voice soft with mock sadness. "It's too bad you were struggling with so many demons that you couldn't talk about."

Despite balking at me over the phone for several irritating minutes, Shawn did as I asked and hacked into the deputy's personal computer. A clever trick to ease the suspicion of him going missing. Along with disabling his cell phone, there won't be a way to find him.

For a kid who's lived around criminals for most of his life, Shawn still gets testy about *"killing the good guys without reason"*. In this case, I'd say I have a very good reason. Whether or not he believes that is another matter entirely.

The deputy's face shatters in shock and his eyes turn glassy with unshed tears. I swear I saw a flash of acceptance in those eyes as he blinked away the tears.

"Now, tell me," I continue, "which hand?"

"W-what?"

"Which hand did you touch her with?" I snap.

"Oh, God. Oh, God, please," he chants. His eyes are wide, laser focused on the serrated knife I pull from the back of my jeans.

A pointless question, really, given that I already know the answer.

The putrid stench of urine wafts into my nose as I slice the rope at his wrists. The moment his hands are free, he lashes out, trying to push me away. I grab his hands, shoving them to the ground. The fingers of his left hand crunch under my boot as I pin the other to the dirt with my own hand. At the ragged kiss of the blade against his wrist, his pained screams flow through the forest.

The skin gives easily as I saw, quickly giving way to the dense muscle tissue beneath. The coppery tang of his blood fills the air, masking the scent of his cowardice. My grip tightens against the handle of the slick knife as I tear through tissue and bone. Amidst the song of his agonized wails, plays an orchestra of squelching and spattering. His screams quiet into hoarse whispers.

For several moments, he stares at the severed hand on the ground—his hand. His mouth opens and closes as the shock sets in.

"Please…please…don't kill me," he begs. "I-I won't tell a-anyone."

Grasping his severed hand and pulling it from the puddle of mud and gore, I smack it against his cheek. "You can't bargain with monsters, Deputy. Not after you touch what belongs to them."

He turns his eyes to me and I watch them change. They harden with pride and defiance. "Ava deserves better than you," he declares.

I chuckle lightly. "Well, on that, we agree."

My knife slides into the corded muscles of his neck. As I pull the knife out, he gurgles and gasps. Blood erupts from him, soaking his clothes and the ground beneath. I shove my boot against his back, shoving his body into the grave.

Now, it's time to teach my little bird a lesson.

Chapter Twelve

James believed everything I told him. The sincerity of his concern was evident on his face as I recounted what's happened over the last several days. When I fell into bed last night, I wrapped myself in his pledge to protect me. I felt at ease, calm, and maybe even a little excited. He had given me a rain check for coffee and I plan to take him up on it.

I woke this morning with a lightness, a sense that everything will be alright. It propelled me forward, launching me into my work where I found myself once again lost in a story. Inside the fantastical world of the book, I became someone else. My hands shook as I held a blade to the throat of my enemy, only to find that they were my ally all along. My legs trembled as we sprinted through a city of brightly colored shops and sparkling, silver bridges, racing against the clock to save my lover from a horrible fate. My eyes glazed with tears when we discovered it was too late.

A dull vibration startles me. Pushing my glasses up onto my head, I pull my tired eyes away from the pages. I press my palms against them, rubbing away the haziness that comes from too many hours of reading. My phone lies blinking and buzzing on the desk. I roll my eyes at what's surely a text from Emily, describing her most recent date in more detail than I need. My gaze shifts to the window, where the sun is making a lazy descent toward the horizon, washing the trees in an orange glow.

Another buzz has me snatching my phone from the desk and mumbling, "Alright. Alright, you impatient woman."

When I unlock it, it's not Emily's name I see, but an unknown number.

> Hello, little bird. I left a gift for you by your kitchen door. Why don't you go check?

Panic rushes into me. My lungs seize, like the first breath on a cold, winter day. The room swirls around me, suddenly brighter and smaller than it was before. No, no, no, no. This isn't happening. I force out a shuddering sigh and type out a reply.

> Who is this?

Nausea curls in my stomach as I watch the three bubbles on my screen, blinking, blinking, blinking. Why did I text back? Somewhere in my head I didn't expect a reply. But my phone buzzes again.

> You know who this is.

My breaths come hard and fast as I drop back into my chair. Navigating away from the text, I pull up James' number and crash my finger into the call button. His voicemail picks up immediately. I try three more times. His phone is off.

Crap, crap, crap. This is not good. I need to consider my options here. My stalker left a *gift* at my door, which means it's outside… where he's probably waiting for me. I can't go outside. I'm safer in here…aren't I? I haven't replaced the locks, so maybe not. He got in here before.

A choked sob catches in my throat. Even as my eyes fill with tears, I don't let them fall. Not now. I can't fall apart now. Not when I need to figure out what to do.

I yelp at the sudden vibration of my phone. Another text comes through.

> I won't touch you tonight. It's safe for you to come out.

I suck in a deep breath until my lungs ache from the pressure. My feet shift anxiously inside of my slippers, a cool coating of sweat forming between my toes.

As I pull myself away from my desk, a mumbled mantra falls from my quivering lips, "This is a bad idea. A very, very bad idea."

Back hunched just below the level of the windows, I creep into the kitchen. The *swish, swish* of my slippers against the hardwood floor follows behind me. I peek around the corner into the kitchen, where early evening shadows slither from edges and crevices. Their silhouettes warning me away, begging me not to venture here.

No, it's no different than it was before. This room is the same. It's all the same. It's just panic.

Slowly, I rake my fingers through my hair, pressing my nails into my scalp to soothe the tension building in my head. My gaze shifts to the door. It's nearly dark now.

A tiny, scared voice yells inside my rattled brain, *You can't go out there in the dark. Now is your only chance to grab whatever it is. He can get to you in the dark and you won't see him coming.*

My legs twitch with sudden determination. Like a runner bracing for a sprint, I press my head forward, arms slightly raised at my back. I dash toward the door, yanking the deadbolt open and ripping the door open. My breath leaves me in a gasp when I find a black box only inches in front of the entrance.

My hands wrap around it before I slam the door again. My quivering thighs give out under me. The door scrapes against my back as I slide down to the floor.

Despite the fraying of my nerves and unsteadiness of my hands, I gently place the box on the floor beside me. My *gift* sits in a black, cardboard box about the size of a toaster. A matching, fitted lid placed on top. Four strips of silky, red ribbon wrap neatly around it, meeting in a large bow at the top.

Staring at the elegantly wrapped package, the room seems to close in around me. The walls push in on me, closer and closer. My vision tunnels, focusing solely on that damn box.

When the phone I'd forgotten was in my pocket buzzes, a shriek barrels out of my mouth. My fingers stumble against the touchscreen as I pull up the text message.

> Open the box, little bird. It won't hurt you.

I pull up my recent call list and dial James again, only to still reach his voicemail. It looks like I'm going to have to do this on my own. Resigning myself to that fact, my jittery digits reach for the box. I lift the lid gingerly and look inside.

The cardboard lid slips from my fingers, falling to the floor with a dull thud. My throat tightens at the metallic tang of rust that rushes into my nostrils. My eyes go wide at the sight of the horrific souvenir. A man's severed hand. Raw, mangled, and gruesome. On his finger, a gold ring is embossed with the initials *JB*.

James' hand.

A feeling of helplessness crashes over me like a wave in a frigid ocean. It breaks, colliding with me and sending cold nausea into the pit of my stomach. The frozen knot in my gut surges upward. I lean away and vomit on the floor. My stomach heaves until there's nothing left to expel but painful, dry gags and sputtering breaths.

Snatching my phone from the floor, I do what any totally out of their mind person would do—I text my stalker.

> What did you do?!

Blinking back the tears that blur my vision, I keep my eyes fixed on the screen, those taunting dots winking at me as he types.

I told you what the consequences would be if you called the police again. You chose to disobey me. And as promised, someone died.

Realization hits me like a slap to the face. Cold, bitter reality. I brought James into this. I brought him into this, and now he's dead. The words on the screen blur. The room begins to shake and tilt. It takes a moment for me to realize why. With my arm wrapped around my knees, I rock back and forth. The hard floor pressing painfully against my hips as my weight shifts forward and back.

A thought nags in the back of my mind. It scrapes and scratches against my skull. I shake my head, as if I could dislodge it. Why his *hand?* Why did he cut off his hand?

There's only one way for me to find out. With fumbling fingers, I ask the only person who has the answer.

Why his hand?

His reply is quick, making me wonder if he's staring at his phone, awaiting my responses, too.

That hand touched you. No one touches what's mine.

My mind fogs, my thoughts becoming muddied with confusion and conflict. My fingers rush to type a reply, but it comes out wrong. I type and delete, type and delete, until my question forms.

What does that mean? What's yours?

His reply comes though so quickly that he must have needed no time to think about it.

You, little bird. You're mine.

I read it again and again until my eyes glaze and my focus wavers. The words linger in my head, replaying on loop. *You're mine.* The confusion in my mind dissolves, melting into a puddle of hot anger.

My grip on my phone hardens until the plastic groans, threatening to crumble in my fist. Just as I ready my arm to huck it across the room, it vibrates against my skin.

> Leave the box. I'll clean up the mess. I wouldn't want my sweet little bird to get her pretty hands dirty.

My fury at his declaration of perceived ownership eclipses any sense of caution left in me. As I stand, my legs no longer quiver in fear. My muscles are taught and aching with rage. I rip the door open and kick the box outside. The wood groans and cracks when I slam the door shut again. He'll clean up the mess? What kind of psycho leaves a severed hand and then expects that I'd let him come inside and clean up for me?

The sob that's been stuck in the back of my throat dislodges. I break under the pressure of my anger, fear, and sorrow. My tears fall as weeping, whimpering sounds escape my mouth. The waterfall continues, blurring my eyes and staining my cheeks.

My body works on autopilot, as if something else takes control of my limbs while my own mind hides somewhere deep inside of me. The entity moving my body scrubs the droplets of blood that seeped through the thin, cardboard box and wipes my vomit from the floor. I rid my kitchen of the evidence of this night. Of James' death. Of the contents of my stomach. Of my tears. Of my pain.

Chapter Thirteen

Watching Ava open her *gift* was thrilling. True to her name, she scurried around the house like a frightened little bird. She flitted between rooms, crouching under the windows to hide from me. But I saw her.

And fuck, was she perfect. Her eyes were wide with fear, the tears streamed down her face leaving pink streaks in their wake. The innocent soul inside of her cracked and crumbled at the first sight of gore.

With a little incentive, a little fear, she obeyed almost all of my commands. I'm not surprised that she didn't want me to come inside and clean up for her, so I let her have that little bit of rebellion. Even her partial obedience had my cock straining against my pants. The urge to stroke myself was nearly unbearable when I received her panicked texts, when I heard her little gasps and sobs through the thin windows.

Unsurprisingly, she threw up soon after she saw the deputy's mangled hand. I'm not unfamiliar with the experience. Even I threw up my first time seeing true horror. Of course, that was a long time ago, but I'll never forget it: the heavy smell of copper that burned in my nostrils and traveled down my throat; the way the room spun and my stomach churned as I stared down at the corpse that used to be my mother. I'll never forget the day that turned me into a monster.

I rattle my head from side to side, as if the memories will fall away like raindrops on a shaking dog. Some things are better left in the past, existing but not thought of.

Some part of me hates to watch her clean up a mess I caused, but I let her. I suspect she's had enough for tonight. My presence in her kitchen might break her. I won't let her break, though; not until she's ready for me to put all of her pieces back together. When she breaks, the shards of her former self will fit snuggly next to the broken bits of mine. Our damaged pieces will fit together to form a whole—a twisted puzzle that only we understand.

Watching her through her kitchen window, my fingers twitch. They ache to reach out and touch her. My fingertips tingle with the memory of her warm, soft skin. I find myself wanting to comfort her. It's a foreign feeling, wanting to hold someone. A dull pain that presses and pulls inside of me, like a string being pulled taut, only loosening when I'm close to her.

A few yards away, I watch as my little bird panics. On her knees, she cleans the remains of our interaction. Her delicate hands scrub furiously against the hardwood. Every so often, she pauses, her body head falling onto her thighs as the sobs shake through her core. When the floor is shimmering and streaky with disinfectant, she stands. Her head turns back and forth, examining the room, as if she expects it to tell her what to do next.

Pulling the hood of my sweatshirt over my head, I approach the door. I press the discarded lid back on the box and pull it under my arm. My lips curl into a proud grin as I wipe the speckles of blood off of her doorstep with my sleeve. A gentleman always cleans up after himself. I may have frightened her tonight. I may have made her sick, and sad, and afraid. But I would never make my woman clean up after me.

And of course, I didn't do any of this without reason. She needs to understand that she's mine.

And no one touches what's mine.

Just as I move to step away, she looks up. When she sees me, her eyes widen in shock and she lets out a shriek. The shrill squeak that bubbles out of her mouth echoes through the kitchen before she throws her hand over her mouth to stifle it. If it wasn't dark outside and my face wasn't hidden by the shadow of my hood, she'd be staring at me right in the face.

She throws her body to the floor, landing with a loud thunk that vibrates through the wooden door. I press my lips together, suffocating a laugh against my teeth. While I do love the idea of my little bird shivering on the floor, I'm less than thrilled about it happening when I'm not there. I send her a text, coaxing her out.

> You can stop hiding now. I'm leaving.

I step away, walking back to the woods where my car is tucked away behind rows of trees. Standing in front of the tree line, I glance back just in time to see wisps of brown hair pop up above the windowsill.

I ball my hands at my sides, forcing myself to keep moving into the woods. Her sudden obedience makes this very difficult. The desire to see her submit to me fully claws at my mind, scraping and scratching. In spite of my need, I keep walking.

Standing in front of the metal security door behind Club Gara, the wind whips its icy tendrils against my cheek. I pull my jacket tighter around me to stave off the chill. The building's crumbling brick exterior leaves it indistinguishable from the rest of the block.

The chatter and giggles of patrons at the front entrance echoes from around the corner, spilling into the alley. The club's location and modest external appearance gives the tourists a feeling of exclusivity, like they've been welcomed into some underground secret. If only they knew what went on in the hidden rooms that sit adjacent to the bar.

I turn my body to face the security camera mounted above the back door. My jacket falls open, flashing the butt of the gun in my waistband, and I raise my eyebrows in question. A loud buzz vibrates through the door before the clink of metal hitting metal sounds as it unlocks.

Pushing the heavy door open, I'm met with a rush of warm air. The scent of alcohol and sweat wafts around me, escaping into the alley as I step inside. A tall man steps in front of me, the colored lights around us washing his golden brown skin in shades of red and purple. Militant in appearance, his hair is cropped short and his face is clean shaven. His broad chest and muscular arms are on display in a t-shirt that's two sizes too small. Whether he wears it for intimidation or attention, I couldn't say.

His brown eyes scan me, roaming from my feet up to my face, as if he's assessing what kind of threat I may be. Seemingly satisfied in his assessment, his head bobs up and down in a short nod. His beefy hand stretches out, pointing toward a black, metal door across the club.

The violent hum and thump of electronic bass reverberates through my core as I maneuver around scantily clad, sweaty people. Pushing through the wall of gyrating, grinding bodies that spread across the dance floor, I ignore the eyes that fall on me. I ignore the frustrated grunts and snarky quips of drunk partiers as our elbows bump.

When I reach the door, I straighten my jacket. My palms rub down the sleeves as if it could remove the scent of everyone in this place. The only scent I want on me is Ava's. Smelling her on me all day would drive me mad, making me feral with lust and pining for her. I can't think of anything I would enjoy more.

Another security camera whirs, rotating in my direction. With a metallic clunk, the lock disengages and the door opens. I step inside, allowing the door to close behind me with a loud bang.

The club music cuts with the close of the door, replaced by the delicate plucking of string instruments and light taps of drums. The nasally buzz of a wind instrument hums in my ears, evoking images of undulating belly dancers. I chuckle under my breath. Given the owner's predilection for peacocking, I wouldn't be surprised to see a few.

For a moment, I'm stuck between the door and a row of purple, velvet curtains that dangle from ceiling to floor, blocking my view inside the room. Particles of dust float around me, shimmering in the glow of an overhead lamp as I press myself between them into the room beyond.

My lips press together in a thin line as I examine the gaudy, overstated decor. Deep purple walls loom upward and press together into a domed ceiling where lines of gold sweep inward, meeting around a crystal chandelier. On the floor, royal blue shag rugs sit beneath short, mahogany tables. In lieu of seating, large square pillows litter the floor. Their colorful patterns are inlaid with sparkling gold threads.

The room would look like some luxury lounge venue—if it weren't for the rows of weapons that line the walls. Heavy metal racks in various shades of shining purple metal are fitted with guns, knives, swords, and explosives. All untraceable and all for sale at a hefty price tag.

A booming laugh echoes around me, drawing my attention to a man standing just beyond a large archway at the far corner of the room. His stature, at well over six feet tall, forces him to duck his head to step through. His dark chestnut eyes meet mine with a warmth that can only be interpreted as friendship.

His long legs make short work eliminating the distance between us, and I soon find myself in the uncomfortable embrace of his muscular arms. His chest rises against mine as his heavily accented voice booms in my ear.

"*Habibi*, my friend, how good it is to see you!"

My eyes roll as I step away from him, putting myself at a comfortable distance.

"You've redecorated," I deadpan.

"My buyers eat this shit up," he says with a laugh. "Come, we'll have a drink."

He steps away, gesturing to a table in the corner of the room. I follow, knowing well enough that Malik won't do business until we've finished with the pleasantries of small talk and mint tea. Friendships are mostly unfamiliar to me, but I've come to accept his in recent years. Not with the openness that he shows, but with the small amount I can give.

I drop myself down to a large green pillow, partially tucked beneath the table. Patterns of leafy vines and gold flowers stretch out beyond my thighs. I feel utterly ridiculous. A black cloud pressed against a rainbow or color. Malik, on the other hand, fits perfectly in the space. He wears a bright emerald blazer over his broad shoulders. Matching emerald dress pants fit tightly on his large legs.

His face is plainer than he is. His skin, the color of damp sand, is beginning to show the lines of his age. Wrinkles spread out from his eyes, as you'd expect from a man who laughs often. His short-cropped, black hair is accented by the small gold hoops dangling from his ears.

A young woman approaches, her silky, blue dress swirling around her feet. The chandelier above dances over her light brown skin, making her glow. She pays me no attention, her eyes set solely on Malik. His lips turn up in a wide smile, causing a rush of pink to flow into her cheeks. As she stares at him, wide eyed with awe and not just a small amount of desire, that spark of jealousy inside me zaps at my lungs. My little bird will look at me like that someday, but for now, that ache strikes me like I've stuck my finger in an electrical socket.

The woman bends at the waist, her long dress pulling tight over her curves as she places a tray of tea and small cakes on the table. Malik watches her with a hunger in his eyes that only dissipates when I clear my throat loudly. The woman smiles warmly, a soft giggle bubbling past her lips before she walks away.

Malik's eyes turn to me, the wolfish grin on his face telling me he's enjoying showing off. He waves his hand over the tray, gesturing for me to accept the offer of food and drink before he speaks.

"Tell me, friend," he asks, "are you still working for *elmar'a elshiriyra?*"

My eyebrow quirks up in question.

"You know," he continues, "the evil woman, Bianca."

I roll my eyes, unsurprised by the question. The bad blood between the arms dealer and the Rossi family is long-standing. Years ago, after a deal went bad between them, Bianca took his younger sister, Rana. A fiercely loyal man, Malik searched for Rana, but with resources that barely compare to the ruling families in this city, he's fallen short.

Even my heart, as cold and shriveled as it may be, clenches to think of Rana's fate. She was young, barely seventeen when she was taken. The rare beauty would have caught Bianca's eye right away, even before she realized her age.

At best, she's been sold off to the highest bidder to live out her days in a gilded cage. At worst, she lives in a far worse cage, body ravaged by drugs and the most horrific desires of bad men. A shudder runs through me, making my shoulders shake. If Malik notices, he doesn't say so.

Last year, Malik tried to broker a deal with the head of the Volkov family, whose resources are far greater than his, in an attempt to get Rana back. But the promise of weapons and Malik's small crew for support wasn't enough to entice them into starting a war. Not when their own resources only barely rival those of the Rossi family.

"You know I don't work for her," I state dryly, "I take jobs from whoever can pay."

Malik chuckles softly. *"Mafeesh fur'a,* my friend. There's no difference."

His face softens in understanding, maybe even forgiveness, as his lips curl into a smile.

"What can I do for you today?" he asks before wagging his eyebrows. "Or have you finally visited me on a purely social call?"

I scoff out a small laugh from my nose. "I have a weapon to dispose of that you might have interest in, police-issued."

Malik's eyes sparkle as I withdraw Deputy Douchebag's handgun from my waistband, and place it on the table. He reaches for it, turning it about in his hand.

Nodding his head, he says, "This could be of use to me." His eyes meet mine as a dark smirk pulls across his mouth. "I'm awfully curious as to how you ended up with this, my friend."

I stand, stepping away from the table back toward the door. Looking back over my shoulder, I only say, "It's about a girl."

I exit the room, followed by his booming laughter and the clattering clink of teacups being knocked over.

Chapter Fourteen

With the events of tonight, sleep will never find me. I envision myself spending the night awake and alert, hiding from the monsters that I now know really do go bump in the night. Surely, I'll spend every minute scouring the dark corners of my home for creeping shadows until the sun banishes them away.

Shit. My home. My former sanctuary. It feels tainted now, like it's filled with ghosts. I've never been one to believe in the restless spirits of the dead, but tonight, my mind reels and spirals away from me. Will James haunt me? Will he blame me for his death? Will his soul hunt for me from beyond the grave?

Oh, God. Does he even have a grave? Will his family have a body to grieve over?

The tangled web of my thoughts winds and curls against my skull. The throbbing headache they leave in their wake threatens to burst through my eye sockets. As my thoughts rage out of control, my stomach clenches, promising a renewed bout of dry heaving.

Breathe. Breathe. Breathe, some small voice in the back of my head chants. On a shaky inhale, I try to dispel the dread that's pooled in my stomach. Ignoring the bile that's creeping up my throat, I turn on the shower.

My clothes are soaked with disinfectant and vomit when I finally strip them off. Being entirely unable to see myself ever wearing them again, I toss them into the trash bin instead of the laundry basket. Like my home, they too, feel tainted.

Stepping into the shower, I revel in the burn of the scalding water against my skin. I scrub every inch of it until it's irritated, pink, and blotchy. With a hard-bristled brush, I scour my fingernails, refusing to allow a single speck of grime underneath them. In my determination to wash away this day, I barely notice as the water begins to cool.

It isn't until I'm hit with the frigid spray of late autumn well water that I register how long I've been washing. Cursing that stupid, old water heater, I step out and dress myself in my warmest pajamas. I shiver against the fleece-lined lounge set and wrap my arms around myself. It's more in an effort to keep myself together than to combat the chill in the air. I suspect that if I were to let go, my body might simply fall to pieces. They'd tumble to the floor, pieces rolling under the bathroom vanity to hide with the dust bunnies.

With nothing left to clean, I crawl into bed and tuck the blankets under my chin. Despite, or maybe because of, my frayed nerves and consistently fluttery heartbeat, exhaustion hits me the moment my head finds my pillows.

The moment that sleep pulls me under, the monsters I'm hiding from, or should I say, *the monster,* finds me.

A nameless, faceless being cloaked in darkness towers over my bed. Shadows seem to grow from behind his massive frame, blanketing the walls and stretching across the ceiling. Like smoke, they whirl and dance.

Long fingertips that end in pointed claws grab my ankle. I wince, anticipating a biting pain that never comes. Instead I only feel the warmth that radiates off of his soft fingertips. They lazily stroke my skin, caressing my legs. His fingers move higher and higher, grazing my knees, crawling up my thighs.

There's no pain in his touch, only heat. Each brush of his skin against mine is an ember, burning hotter as they move until my skin is on fire. Liquid heat pools between my thighs. My body writhes under his touch, seeking more.

I gasp when his palm brushes over my bare waist. My back arches, pushing myself into his touch. His large hand travels up between my breasts, his pinky grazing over my nipple. My breath leaves me in a whispered moan. That whisper morphs into a yelp when he pinches my nipple between his thumb and forefinger.

My body lurches up so suddenly that my head knocks against the headboard. I stumble to catch my breath as my head swivels around the room. My breathing calms as I realize that I'm in my bed, alone. I press my thighs together, trying to calm the ache in my core. At the feel of the slick warmth between my legs, my face pulls into a scowl.

What the Hell is wrong with me? I should be traumatized. *I am* traumatized. So why am I having hot and heavy dreams? And why is *he* the star in them?

I mean, I can't pretend that I've never had dark desires. What woman hasn't thought about being taken roughly, being entirely dominated? I'm not a prude; I've read the books. You know, the spicy ones about bad men sweeping women off their feet. But this is different. This is definitely different. This is the real world where bad men are, well, just bad. Aren't they?

A knot forms in my stomach, the result of the war forming between my head and my pussy. Shaking my head, I shove the thoughts down deep inside of myself. I'll leave them there to be dealt with another day.

An aggravated grunt falls from my mouth as I slide out of bed and stuff my feet into my slippers. A single thought has me shuffling toward the closet:

I have got to get out of this house.

With unshaking determination, I grab an old, beat up duffel bag from the floor of the closet and stuff it with a heap of clothing. Tossing the bag on my bed, I fire off a quick text to Emily.

> Can I come stay with you for a few days?

Immediately realizing the alarm that text will cause her, I send another.

> I just really miss my bestie. I could come over after work tonight?

I dress quickly, throwing on a pair of blue jeans and a thick sweater before making my way to the kitchen for a much needed cup of coffee. My feet halt at the edge of the kitchen. Surveying the room, nothing seems amiss. There's no indication of what happened the night before, save for the lemony tang of disinfectant lingering in the air.

Forcing my feet to take small steps, I push forward. Every time I hesitate, I remind myself that this is a morning like any other; I just make my coffee and get to work. I keep reminding myself of this as I go through the motions of my usual morning routine.

My feet end up a nearly a foot in the air when my cell phone buzzes in my pocket. My jumpiness causes my coffee to slosh out of the cup and onto the counter. I shake my head, internally chastising my fretfulness. At another buzz, I pull my phone out to find two texts from Emily.

> I miss you too! Be here around 6? I'll get the drinks, you buy the pizza!

I type out a quick confirmation before refilling my half-empty coffee mug and wiping up the remnants of the previous cup with a dish towel. Knowing I'll get through the day by the power of caffeine and will alone, I gulp down the contents of the mug in a hurried swig.

Pouring another, I stare at the kitchen. How can a room look the same, but feel so different in the span of a day? No longer willing to think about it, I rush out of the room and into my office.

The day passes in a blur, despite my nerves causing me to jump at every sound. Living in an older house that's in serious need of maintenance work, sounds are plentiful. When five o'clock rolls around, I practically dive out of my chair.

The tension in my shoulders uncoils when I approach the front door of Emily's apartment building. The six story building at 281 Field Street is situated at the center of the block just a few miles from the heart of the city. Its brick exterior is almost identical to the row of buildings surrounding it.

When she first moved here after college, Emily had said she chose the location for two reasons: one being its close proximity to the best restaurants and bars in the city, and the second being its nearness to the Metro Station on Brown Street. That particular station connects to one directly in front of the biggest newspaper in the city.

Even before we left college, she was determined to work at the City Herald. In the years since, she's worked her way up from mailroom worker, to newsroom assistant, to journalist. But in true Emily fashion, she isn't done yet. She won't be satisfied until she's the lead investigative journalist for the entire paper.

Thinking about how far she's come, my lips pull into a smile that crinkles my eyes. I fidget with my bags, hiking the straps of my duffel and purse up onto my shoulder to free my arms before pressing my finger to the buzzer for apartment 306. I pull my scarf up over my chin to fight off the cold breeze that tumbles through the narrow street.

A loud buzz and clank sounds when the door unlocks. As I rush into the lobby, I let out a satisfied sigh at the welcomed surge of warm air that envelops my body. My body warms as I trek up the three flights of stairs to Emily's door. I pause at the top of the second staircase, my thighs aching, reminding me of how many yoga classes I've skipped recently. I'd like to think that having a crazy, murderous stalker is a good excuse to skip a workout, but my body clearly disagrees.

By the time I reach Emily's door, I'm huffing out breaths like I've just sprinted a quarter mile. I smack the heel of my palm against the door while reminding myself to do more cardio. My frustrated thoughts fall away when the door swings open to reveal the beaming smile on my best friend's face.

"Bestie," Emily sings out, her high pitched voice echoing through the narrow hallway.

Despite everything that's happened recently, and even with the lingering fear clawing inside me, I grin. Shuffling inside, I push the door closed behind me. It feels like an ironclad barrier separating me from the worst of the world—from him. My bags fall to the floor with a thunk as Emily pulls me into a tight hug. Her body presses against me, her warmth settling straight into my bones.

She releases me from her arms and stares at me, her forehead creased with worry. Hoping to avoid the questions swimming in her eyes, I scurry away and drop myself onto the couch with a heavy sigh. Her eyes are glued to my face as I sink into the soft fabric.

My eyes wander, roaming over Emily's apartment. It's small, as most are in this city, but lovingly maintained and impeccably decorated. Abstract paintings in tan, blue, and gold accent the white walls of the main room. A round, glass-topped coffee table with gold legs sits at its center, surrounded by the cream-colored couch and matching chair.

Off of the main room are two doors that lead to the bedroom and bathroom. Each room is outfitted with its own color scheme. Deep blue and aqua in the bathroom, and yellow and orange in the bedroom. Nestled in a corner by the front door is a narrow kitchen. Its stark white tiles are offset by red dishes and appliances displayed on open wood shelving.

When my life calms down, I should ask Emily to help redecorate my house. Can new decor make my home feel safe again? Can it push away bad memories? Is a girl with a chic home less likely to be followed by nightmares?

"So," Emily's voice pulls me out of my thoughts, "are you going to tell me why you look like death warmed over, or do I need to pry it out of you?"

The sound that escapes me is something between a heavy sigh and a groan. Hoping it will buy me some time to think of an answer that will satisfy a budding investigative journalist without totally freaking her out, I respond, "Pizza first, questions after."

She rolls her eyes as I pull out my phone to place our usual order of ham and pineapple pizza. At the sound of clinking glasses, my eyes shift upward to find Emily making cocktails in the kitchen. Knowing that there's no way she's going to wait until the pizza arrives, I have until the drinks are ready to get my story straight.

My teeth dig into my bottom lip as I try to organize the jumble of thoughts in my head. I want to tell her everything, to drop the crushing weight of this burden. She would help me carry it if I let her.

The sense of relief I felt when I told James was palpable. Oh, God. *James.* My stomach clenches. Bile rises in my throat as my mind replays the images of his severed hand, his blood on my kitchen floor. When I look at Emily in her own kitchen, I blink back tears. My fingers dig into the arm of the couch as visions of her mangled body flash behind my eyes.

Just as the thoughts come to me, I know instantly that I can't tell her. I may be responsible for James' death, but I won't be responsible for hers. I press my hand to my mouth to block a sob that threatens to let loose. She can't get hurt because of this.

"Ava," Emily says as she places two cocktails down on the coffee table, "what's going on?"

My heart is weighted with guilt at the idea of lying to my best friend, but there's no other way to keep her safe. What's that thing people say about lies? The most believable lies are based in truth?

"There was this really nice guy in my high school, James," I explain. "I saw him recently and we were going to have a coffee date."

Emily's face contorts in confusion. "This doesn't sound like a bad thing, but your face says otherwise."

I release a long breath before continuing, "He died yesterday."

Emily's eyes widen in understanding. The couch cushions shift as she sits beside me. Her hand grasps mine and squeezes gently.

"What happened?" she asks quietly.

"He was a deputy with the local sheriff's department. He died… well, just doing his job."

My mouth dries as the partial truth rolls off my tongue. I grab one of the fruity cocktails from the table and take a long sip.

"I just need a distraction. Tell me about your most recent date," I plead, hoping to redirect the conversation.

Emily's head bobs up and down as her eyes soften.

A sultry smile slides across her face. "Girl, prepare yourself. I've got some salacious details for you!"

I breathe a sigh of relief as she launches into a story about Matt, the handsy attorney. No matter how many lies I have to tell, I'll keep her safe from this.

I peel my eyes open, blinking against the sunlight that streams through the window in Emily's living room. The dull roar of a hangover burns inside my skull, reminding me how many cocktails I drank last night. I chuckle, recalling Emily's animated retelling of terrible dates and lusty encounters.

The warm, earthy aroma of coffee wafts through the room, beckoning me towards the kitchen. Despite my lower back protesting as I pull myself from the soft couch cushions, I feel lighter. My bare feet tap against the tile floor while I follow my nose to the freshly brewed coffee.

A yellow sticky note is stuck to the coffee maker, sporting Emily's neat, curly handwriting.

Went to work. Make yourself at home!
XOXO, Em

I pour myself coffee into the largest mug I can find before retreating to the couch and pulling my laptop from my bag. Feeling safer than I have since this all began, I dive into my work, keeping my mind firmly planted there instead of in the craziness that is my life.

Any thoughts that pop up about *him* are pushed into the back of my mind, locked behind a concrete wall of my will. Mastering the art of compartmentalization in the face of horrible circumstances isn't easy. Though it's been years since I've had to use this particular skill, those blocked off areas of my mind snap back into place with little effort.

When you're the child of an angry alcoholic, you learn quickly to erect mental barriers to keep yourself sane. Maybe sane isn't the right word—alive, is more accurate. My father ensured that my barriers were ironclad.

The day rushes by in a blur of emails and editing notes. Before I know it, evening has rolled around. The sky begins to darken and little lights begin to twinkle around the city, popping up outside the windows like low-hanging stars.

As I stare out of the window, watching those lights glitter, a knock at the door startles me. My anxiety instantly renews, bubbling up in my chest and squeezing my lungs. Who could be here? Emily didn't mention anything about a visitor or package being delivered, and she isn't due home from work for at least another hour.

I keep my footsteps small and light as I creep toward the door. My shoulders sag in relief when I look through the peephole. A short, middle-aged man stands outside the door, a cardboard drink tray and a small brown, paper bag balanced in the crook of his elbow. He pushes his graying hair away from his face, revealing gentle eyes that crease at the edges from his smile.

"Uber Eats delivery," he calls out.

He must have the wrong door. Feeling it would be rude to ignore him, I open the door and smile at him.

"I'm sorry, but I think you might have the wrong apartment. I didn't order anything," I say.

His lips pinch together, and he makes a thoughtful noise as he looks down at the order receipt. "The order's for Ava Moore. It's all paid for, tip and all. Are you Ava?"

My mouth rounds in surprise, while my heart clenches. Did Emily order me a treat?

I answer excitedly, "Yes, that's me."

"Enjoy!" he says as he presses the drink tray and bag into my hands.

I barely have time to utter a thank you before he turns on his heels and walks away. I hurry back into the apartment and put my goodies down on the kitchen counter. I rip open the brown, paper bag with delight. I've never been one to turn down a good snack, and I've got the hips to show for it.

The scent of cinnamon and pumpkin waft up from the bag, making my mouth water. I've barely laid my eyes on the plump, sugar-coated pumpkin muffin before a chunk of it is in my mouth. I hum, enjoying the moist sweetness of the baked good.

Grabbing the coffee cup from the tray, I take a long sip. I mentally tell Emily how much I love her when the pumpkin latte hits my tongue. Looking at the cup, I notice there's something written on the side in black marker. While popping another piece of muffin into my mouth, I pull my reading glasses down off of my head so I can see it better.

As I read the lettering, the muffin turns to ash in my mouth. Scrawled on the side of the cup are the words:

LITTLE BIRD

My heart rate skyrockets, thumping inside my chest like it's trying to break free from my ribcage. I drop the cup like it's on fire. It crashes into the counter, spilling its contents in a dribbling, syrupy mess.

"Shit!" I yell as I grab a roll of paper towels. I can't mess up Emily's apartment. Awareness crashes into me, forcing me to suck in a hard breath. Emily. He found me at Emily's. He knows where she lives. He even knows her apartment number. She's in danger.

I jolt in surprise when my phone buzzes in my back pocket, pulling me from my spiraling thoughts. When I take my phone out, it blinks to life, displaying a new text message from an unknown number.

You look tired, baby. Go home and rest.

My eyes widen at the message. Would he hurt me if I don't leave? Would he hurt Emily? Would he kill us? He hasn't done anything to harm me physically. Maybe he doesn't want to.

I shake my head furiously at my own ridiculous thoughts. It's insane to think he wouldn't want to hurt me. He's crazy, and violent, and he's *stalking me*. Why would I even consider that he wouldn't want to hurt me? Either way, I have to leave.

"Shit, shit, shit," I chant while stuffing my laptop and clothes back into my duffel bag. I have to get out of here. I can't put Emily in any more danger than I already have. I throw the remnants of the latte and muffin in the garbage before pulling on my coat and heading for the door.

Guilt squeezes at my heart as I send Emily a text about a forgotten doctor's appointment early tomorrow morning that I can't reschedule. A blatant lie, but a necessary one. I have to keep her far away from this mess I'm in.

Chapter Fifteen

I step out onto the sidewalk and am immediately blasted by a cold wind that demands that I pull my coat tighter around my chest. My whole body feels cold. The temperature outside is nearing freezing conditions, but it's not only that that has me shivering. The reality of my situation is wrapping its icy fingers around my throat, forcing my breaths out in small huffs.

I stare down the city street in the direction I need to go. The wind whips between the buildings, throwing crumpled papers and old napkins into the air. They dance in the wind like some kind of garbage ballet. I suck in a deep breath through my nose. At least the cold air hides the smells of the city. With an exacerbated grunt, I force my feet to move.

The walk from Emily's apartment building to the parking garage is nearly half a mile. The lump of anxiety that's been curling in my stomach begins to warm into a heated ball of anger. Had I known I'd be leaving Emily's today, had that asshole given me a choice, I would have done it when the sun was out. *But no*. I couldn't possibly have a reasonable stalker, one with some sense of compassion. So here I am, freezing my ass off, walking to my car in the dark.

My grip tightens on the straps of my bags until I hear the

pleather crunching in my fist. That asshole knows where I live. He knows how to get into my house. He can find me anywhere I go. There's nowhere I can hide that he won't find me. How can I run from this?

Maybe I shouldn't run at all. Maybe I should just wait for him and punch him in his stupid face. A very undignified snort leaves my mouth as I recognize how terrible that idea is. I've only seen him briefly through a window, but he looked huge. I'm not a petite woman, but I'm certainly not a strong one, either. He'd probably kill me if I tried.

My train of thought is derailed suddenly when I catch movement out of the corner of my eye. Across the street, three men are walking in the opposite direction as me. A tall man with wispy, blonde hair walks in the center of the two other men. His hair falls over his face just above his eyes. The arm draped over his shoulder belongs to the portly man next to him. The hood of his dark jacket covers most of his face. The third guy is short in comparison to the others, with long, black hair pulled back into a ponytail that reaches his lower back.

Blondie swivels his head in my direction and lets out a sharp whistle that stops his buddies in their tracks. I quickly cast my eyes downward. My legs cramp, trying to halt my movement. They want me to freeze like a deer in headlights. A little voice in my mind cries, *If I'm frozen in place, I'm safe. If I lock my mind away, I'm safe.*

I shake my head, dispelling the voice and force my legs to keep walking. My shoes thunk against the pavement as my pace quickens. The men all turn toward me and my stomach clenches.

"Aw, don't be like that, baby!" Long Hair yells.

"Yeah, we're nice guys," Beanie adds with a chortle.

I pull my phone from my back pocket and hold it out in front of me, pretending to be engrossed in something. Anything, really. I'm startled when it buzzes in my hand. Though this time, I'm not surprised when I see a text from an unknown number.

> Just keep walking, little bird. I'm here. I won't let anything happen to you.

He's protecting me? My stomach flutters in a way that I refuse to acknowledge. Betting on the knowledge that maybe he doesn't want to hurt me and with my anger still simmering, I text back with a little more cheek than I have before.

> Are you trying to tell me I have scary dog privileges? That you're my scary dog?

The reply that pops up on my screen nearly stops me in my tracks.

> Woof.

Momentarily forgetting my anxiety, I burst into laughter. Did he just make a joke? Does he actually have a sense of humor?

My fingers twitch, wanting to reply. Despite my better judgment, which seems to be failing me, I give into the urge.

> I've always wanted a dog.

The moment I hit send, I regret it. Does he think I'm flirting with him? Am I? I will not let myself humanize him. I will not think of him as a man. He's a stalker and a murderer. He has no redeeming qualities.

I huff out a frustrated breath as I try to bring myself back to reality. He's watching me. That in and of itself is terrifying. So why do I feel heat beneath my skin? Why is my stomach doing that fluttering thing? Why is a blush surely creeping up my neck and turning my face pink?

Clutching my phone to my chest, I begin to move at a hurried pace to avoid the leering men on the other side of the street. I yank my coat tighter around me and pull the collar over my ears as a cold wind dances through the street. It whips against buildings and whistles through alleys, drowning out the sound of…actually, the catcalling stopped. Too afraid to turn around and see why, my feet move beneath me and my walk morphs into a jog. By the time I reach the parking garage, my legs and lungs ache, but I send out a little thank you to the universe for getting me here safely.

Chapter Sixteen

I watch my little bird from the shadows when she leaves her friend's apartment. I know why she decided to stay there. I know she's upset and seeking comfort, but I can't let her. I need her isolated and afraid. I want her to find the comfort she needs, but I need her to find it with *me*.

Someday, she will. She'll come to understand that I can protect her entirely, her body and her heart. Could she stomach giving her heart to a monster like me?

When she steps out of the building, the wind whips her hair around, throwing the earthly locks into her face. She grips her coat tightly around her arms and huffs out little frustrated grunts. She smacks her feet down onto the sidewalk like a child who didn't get her way.

I chuckle as her face scrunches up into an angry scowl. A little voice in the back of my mind whines at me. In the quiet voice of my late mother, it tells me I should be more sympathetic. It's probably true. I'm not the man she would have wanted me to be; I'm not good or kind like she was.

Still, I can't wipe the grin from my face. Ava's angry with me, but she's obeying. I follow along from across the street, hiding in amongst the dark corners and shadows of building overhangs.

When three horndogs start barking at her, her shoulders grow stiff. They stand across the street, leering at my woman.

Ava's fist clenches tightly around the straps of her bags until her knuckles blanche. She's afraid, but this time, it's not of me. My fists clench at my sides as I try to rein in my rage.

She pulls her phone out of her pocket, trying to ignore the men. An idea hits me. Maybe I can be her comfort now, if just a little bit.

She jumps when the phone goes off in her hand. When she reads my text, she freezes and her eyes widen. I expect this reaction from her. What shocks me is the little grin that her mouth pulls into. She worries her bottom lip into her mouth and texts me back.

Her response makes my breath catch in my throat. Is she flirting with me? Teasing me? Holy fuck, does she want to talk to me? A wide smirk pulls across my face and I tease back.

When the sweet sound of her laughter echoes through the night air, my heart stops. If my obsession wasn't entirely solidified before, that sound would have done it. I can't recall a time that I've ever been invested in making a woman laugh, but suddenly my mind races, fumbling through a million ideas about how to make *her* laugh.

Her beautiful laughter catches the attention of her wanna-be suitors. Their eyes snap to her face. My chest feels compressed, squeezed by anger. My thoughts scream, *mine, only mine.* I hunch my back slightly and pull my hood over my head as I approach the fuckers that think they have the right to look at what's mine.

"Hey, man," I drawl with feigned drunkenness, "you got a light?"

The short guy with a greasy ponytail trailing down his back mumbles something and reaches into his pocket. While his face is downturned, I jam my switchblade into his neck. Thick, dark blood spurts from his wound when I yank my hand back. His lips part on a silent scream.

His buddy turns his head with a confused sound as blood splatters into his cheek. My feet swivel, placing me directly in front of him before swiping the blade across his throat. He gurgles a pathetic cry as he falls to his knees.

The short, fat one looks down. When he sees his friends on the ground, he whimpers and pivots his body, preparing to run. When he lifts his leg to flee, I crash my boot into the back of his knee. He topples to the concrete, landing on his stomach with wheeze. I press my boot into his back and crouch down until my eyes meet his wet, teary ones.

"She's mine," I growl into his ear as I stab my knife into the back of his pudgy neck. His body twitches as his spinal cord severs.

When I look back across the street, my little bird is gone.

Wiping the blood off my blade onto the hoodie of the man lying beneath my foot, I step over his crumpled body, narrowly missing the puddle of urine that's pooled between his legs. Inhaling deeply through my nose, the coppery tang of blood rushes into me. A smile pulls across my face. Some primal caveman instinct inside me puffs with pride. *Keep female safe*, it screams and pounds its chest.

I quickly follow Ava back to her car and press my body against a concrete column in the garage. She sits in her car, her eyes barely leave her phone screen. A warm and unfamiliar feeling ignites in my chest knowing that she's staring at our text message exchange. That she's thinking about me.

Her teeth stink into her bottom lip and her cheeks quiver, suppressing a smile. I imagine running my tongue over her bottom lip, the little gasps she'll make when I bite into it. My cock twitches in response. My fingers ache as I fist the edges of my jacket. They tingle, craving the feeling of her soft skin.

Soon, I remind myself. Soon, I'll have her. Soon, my little songbird will sing for me. But not tonight. Tonight, I'll remain in the shadows.

After watching Ava leave the garage, safely tucked away in her car, I leave Charlton and head home. It doesn't take me long to get there, since I live just twenty minutes outside the city. As my house comes into view, I huff out a sigh. It's quieter here where the sprawling landscape of my extensive property gives me privacy and lets me avoid neighborly conversations.

The moment I open my front door, my bed seems to be calling my name. I shuck off my clothes as I move through the house before dropping my body onto the bed. My body sinks into the mattress. I yield to the comforting embrace of my bed, but sleep doesn't take me. My mind won't quiet. My thoughts whirl and churn like the clouds of an oncoming storm.

Inside my head, a battle rages. A war between who I was, who I am, and who I could be. Not who I could be for myself or for the world, but who I could be to Ava. To myself and the rest of the world, I'm a monster. Could I be something else to her, though?

I may not be entirely capable of love, but perhaps I could learn to be, for her.

There was a time in my life when I was able to love. I close my eyes and see a face I haven't laid eyes on in almost twenty years. The face of the last woman I loved, the face of my mother. Once, she was my world. Now, she's my only regret. Guilt squeezes my heart, bruising and crushing the useless organ in my chest as the memories bleed into my mind.

It feels like a lifetime ago, before I became the creature I am now. I was just a kid who left home for college, to make something of myself. My mother was ecstatic when my acceptance letter came in the mail for a school out of state. She scurried around the house, packing my things like it was the most important thing she'd ever done. She drove me to the station and put me on the train with a packed lunch. She made me more sandwiches and cookies than one kid could possibly eat, but I just assumed it was because she was so proud.

I was so caught up in my own excitement that I didn't see the real reason she wanted me to leave. I should have looked harder at the man she'd be left alone with in my absence. He was always cruel, but I should have seen how much worse he had become. But I was naïve, too young and consumed by my own future plans to see what was really happening. I was blind to the worst parts of my father, to all the things my mother kept hidden from me in the name of protecting me.

At the start of winter break, I sat on the train with my mind buzzing excitedly. I thought of all the stories I'd tell her about my courses and my friends. I was so excited that I didn't think twice when she didn't meet me at the train station. I was sure she must have gotten caught up, making some extravagant welcome home dinner.

But that wasn't what happened at all. I walked in the house to find her lying on the kitchen floor, bloodied and bruised. Her face was pale, too pale. She stared up at the ceiling, her eyes clouded. My father stood over her, his face spattered in her blood and brain matter. When the hammer fell from his hand, I picked it up.

In that moment, my childhood, something I didn't realize was so fragile, shattered like glass. The pieces crumbled around me, skittering to the floor. When I reared back and sent that same hammer into his head, I became something worse than he ever could have been. I became what he made me, a cold and unfeeling thing.

I wave my hand in front of my eyes, as if I could force the memories to dissipate like smoke in the air. I steer my mind back to my little bird.

I'll never be a good man. I know that. I'll always be a monster. But I'll be her monster, her watchful shadow. I may be her ruin, but she'll be mine, too. When we're destroyed and broken, I'll shove our pieces back together until we're whole.

Chapter Seventeen

It's been a week since I came home from Emily's apartment. A week of anxiety gnawing at my insides. A week of being jolted awake by dreams of a shadowy figure touching my body. A week with no sign of him.

I toss my reading glasses onto my desk and rub my palms over my face. With a heavy sigh, I turn my gaze to the window where the sun dropping low sets the horizon ablaze in orange light. Staring out into the sunset, I let my mind wander.

I should feel relieved that my stalker hasn't made an appearance. The knots of unease in my gut should be unraveling. And yet, I somehow feel less at ease than I did the night he watched me leave Emily's.

What's the matter with me? Why do I feel like this? How can I possibly feel the familiar ache of rejection squeezing my chest based on the actions of someone I don't even want? Someone I definitely shouldn't want.

And yet, whenever I think about this man that I definitely don't want, my body reacts. A flood of warmth pools low in my belly, sending the butterflies I try desperately to ignore fluttering. My nipples harden, brushing uncomfortably against my sweater.

My phone vibrates against the desk, pulling me out of my thoughts. My stomach clenches in anticipation, but immediately releases when Emily's name pops up on the screen. I open the text message to find a photo of a man I've never seen before.

A man, who's maybe forty-years-old with wavy, brown hair swept back from his face to reveal his warm brown eyes. He has a distinctly masculine face with a straight nose and strong jaw. A speckling of dark stubble lines his cushiony lips. His olive skin looks soft and warm next to his hunter-green sport coat.

When my phone starts to ring, the image disappears, replaced by Emily's smiling face surrounded by hearts. I wait a few seconds before picking it up, shifting my hips to the 90s jam I chose as Emily's ringtone.

"Why are you sending me photos of Italian cologne models?" I ask, hoping my tone conveys how far my eyes are rolling back in my head.

Emily scoffs. "He's not a model. He's your date for tomorrow night."

"I'm sorry. My what?"

"Just hear me out. His name is Max and he's a financial advisor who I recently worked with to get some finance information for a news story. He's really sweet and single. He thinks you're gorgeous and he'll meet you at Deluca's Bar tomorrow night at seven."

My face pulls into a scowl and I huff out a sound that's something between a sigh and a growl. "Nope, definitely not happening," I confidently proclaim.

Emily counters, "You have two choices. Either you go on the date or I'm coming over for a girls' night."

"Umm, well…" I stumble over words and noncommittal sounds as I try to navigate the muddy mess in my brain.

I haven't seen or heard anything from my stalker in a week, so there's a chance that he's simply given up and moved on. If not, Emily coming here could put her at risk. My heart clenches at the thought of putting her in danger. I can't take that chance.

Plus, if I go on a date with someone else, the shadowy creep will probably lose interest and be done with me entirely. Surely, I'm not worth the trouble. I know that I'm not.

My father's booming voice resonates inside my mind. It screams, *You're nothing, Ava. I never wanted you. No one will ever want you.*

I nod my head with a sudden confidence that this will go exactly as I expect. Exactly as my father would have expected. My date will be unimpressed and my stalker will disappear. My life will go back to normal. I'll be alone again. My mouth goes dry and my heart threatens to jump out of my chest. But this is what needs to happen, isn't it?

"Okay," I declare in a voice that I hope doesn't shake with the well of emotions threatening to overflow from my eyes. "Tell Max I'll meet him at seven."

Cold air whips my hair around my face as I step out of the parking garage next to Deluca's Bar. I suck in a deep breath, trying to calm the nerves that are fluttering in my belly.

I've never liked first dates, but this one feels different. This one feels worse. A feeling of foreboding lingers in the back of my mind. I shake my head and scoff. I'm being crazy. I've been stressed and overwhelmed. That's all this is.

A warm glow seeps out from the large windows of the bar washing the street in soft, orange light. Pausing in front of the door, I wipe my sweaty palms against my dress and try to push the sense of dread out of my mind.

When I push the door open, the sounds of the busy venue swirl around me. Conversations hum, laughter bubbles, glasses clink. My eyes roam around the room, lingering at booths and bar tops until they meet a pair of eyes at the end of the bar.

Max's chocolate eyes crinkle into small almonds as he smiles. He sweeps his hand over his brow, pushing his wavy hair behind his ear. When he stands, my breath catches in my throat. His perfectly tailored jacket hugs his broad chest and slim waist. Dark jeans cling to his muscular legs. Damn, he looks good.

His eyes widen as I pull my coat off of my shoulders. I can feel those eyes roaming up and down my body. My cheeks warm and I'm suddenly thankful for the short walk it takes me to reach him. I stare at my shoes, avoiding his heated gaze until he's right in front of me.

He greets me with a warm smile. When he wraps his arms around me, pulling me into a hug, I tense. I wait for the hands on my back to lower and grope, but they don't. I loosen my arms and reach them around his back. A chuckle rumbles through his chest when I press my head against him.

He releases me and pulls out a bar stool, motioning me toward it with the wave of his hand. I smile, surprised by the kind gesture. Maybe this date wasn't such a bad idea.

Max sips on a gin and tonic while I order a glass of wine. I turn toward him, expecting him to tell me about his life, his job, his general male prowess. He doesn't.

"Please," he says in a voice as smooth as silk, "tell me about yourself."

I hesitate, taken aback by the genuine look in his eyes. A look that says he truly wants to know about me. Nodding with a new sort of confidence, I do something I'm not very used to doing—I talk about myself.

Before I know it, almost two hours have passed along with two more glasses of wine. Unlike many first dates I've had, I haven't found myself itching to get away or making excuses to leave early. We've talked about work, family, friends, and of course, our persistent matchmaker, Emily.

I think I could see myself with someone like Max. He's warm, kind, and frankly, normal. My mind wanders, picturing what my life could look like with someone normal, someone without baggage. Could it last once he found out about mine, though? Will he throw me away when he discovers how broken I am? Could I be content to be just a normal woman with a normal man?

I spend my days with my brain and heart thoroughly rooted in books. On every page, romance, suspense, and danger blend together into something breathtaking. But that's not real life. Real life is working, cooking dinner, going to the movies, and cleaning the damn bathroom. It's not some romantic adventure. There's no princes or villains. There's just this.

I take a large gulp of my wine, hoping that the alcohol will calm my busy mind. I have to move forward with normal. Normal is what every woman should want. It's what I should want.

If I decide to be normal, will my stalker let me go?

Chapter Eighteen

A little red dot speeds across my phone screen. I've watched it move from the scarcely populated area by Ava's home, down winding roads, and onto the highway leading directly into the city. The app I installed on both of our phones alerted me the moment hers left her house.

"Where are you going, little bird?" I mumble at the moving dot.

I clench my fists at my sides, frustration crawling through my muscles. The damn tracker can only tell me her location, but doesn't give me access to anything else. I should have made Shawn hack her phone entirely so I could have figured out what she's up to.

A loud groan from behind me makes my head turn. A few feet away from me sits a man named John Merrick, strapped to a metal lawn chair. His head lolls back and forth with his chin pressed against his chest. A dim overhead lamp glints against the sweat and blood matting his patchy, brown hair.

My eyes roam around the unfortunate space in which John is going to die. A monochromatic basement where cracked concrete walls are stacked over a cracked concrete floor. A thick coating of dust covers the only items in here, a small hoard of soggy cardboard boxes. The musty scene of stagnant water clings to their exterior, polluting everything inside and making their marker-written labels droop. He'll die surrounded by old, forgotten holiday decorations and broken lamps. How festive!

I approach John and grab a chunk of his dirty hair to lift his head. When our eyes lock, he screams under the duct tape covering his mouth.

Tilting my head toward him, I ask, "You have a woman, Johnny?"

His head bobs up and down as a new stream of tears dribbles from his sunken eyes.

"Mmm," I hum, "so then you must know how infuriating they are."

He nods rapidly in response and grumbles some incoherent noises. I hold my phone screen up to his face before continuing, "This woman, *my* woman, is apparently on her way into the city tonight. I don't know where she's going, but I'm going to find out. Unfortunately, that means we're going to have to cut this little chat short."

His eyes widen and a fresh wave of muffled grunts get stuck between his mouth and the tape. A crackling hiss resonates against the concrete when I rip it from his chapped lips.

"P-please," he cries, "d-don't kill me, man."

Looking down at his battered, swollen face, I scoff. "You should be grateful, Johnny. Since my girl is off doing, well, whatever the Hell she's doing, I'm going to make this quick." I gesture toward my clothing soiled with his blood and spit. "Obviously, I can't go out looking like this, so I need time to get ready."

Honestly, the guy is getting off much easier than I had originally planned. He's taken a beating, but his fingers and toes are still attached. Luckily for me, I wasn't paid to get information out of him, an act which I obviously no longer have time for, anyway. I was just paid to make it hurt before I end it.

I was a bit surprised when I got a call from Bianca asking me to take care of Johnny, given how much she enjoys this kind of work. Despite the fact that I'm certain she's throwing more jobs my way in an attempt to get me to work for her exclusively, I'm not in the business of turning down good pay.

I pull a knife out from behind my back, and watch the blade's reflection in his glassy eyes. His lower lip quivers. He sniffles, but it doesn't stop the trail snot and tears from dripping onto it. His eyes close, a small gesture signaling that he's accepted his fate. There's no way out for him, and we both know it.

I don't feel guilt. Not when a sob breaks through his lips. Not when I drag the blade across his throat. Not when he opens his mouth in a desperate attempt to take a breath. His actions led to his death; I'm just the tool by which he met it.

The little red dot on my phone led me to a bar on Milton Ave, a bustling restaurant district near the center of the city. Once inside, I weave through the small crowd at the bar until I find an empty booth in the back corner. The worn, faux leather seat crinkles and whines when I drag myself onto it. My knees bump the bottom of the table, but I force myself to look comfortable when the middle-aged waitress takes my drink order.

My eyes move around the room, scrutinizing every detail of the place my little bird chose to visit this evening. Square, glass lamps dangle from heavy cords above the tables and bar, drenching the area in yellowed light. The dim lighting almost hides the bar's need for refurbishment. The dark varnish on the heavy wood tables is scratched. Its edges curl upward like it's trying to escape this early 1990s hellscape. The floor tiles, that I suspect used to be beige, have browned with age. Brown and biscuit-colored patterns crawl up the dried wallpaper until they meet with cracks and cobwebs at the edges.

Ice cubes clink together as the waitress' shaky fingers place a glass down on the table. I smile at her briefly before she schlepps away, her shoulder hunched under a heavy tray of filled pint glasses. Looking down at the sweating glass in front of me, I rake my fingers through my hair, taming the messy strands that haven't had a chance to dry after the shower I took at warp speed to remove Johnny's blood from my body.

Amidst the chaotic hum of conversations, my ears prick up, seeking out one familiar, feathery voice. My eyes rocket upward at the sound of her laugh, floating over the dull notes of everyone else in the room. At the sight of her, my fingers clench against the whiskey glass, threatening to crack it.

She's not with her blonde friend, like I expected her to be. She's sitting with a guy. The way he's looking at her tells me that they aren't friends. His beady eyes roam up and down her body, lingering on her hips and breasts.

She's not dressed for drinks with a friend, either. She's dressed for a date. A lilac dress held up by skinny straps encases her curves. It scoops down below her clavicles, leaving her neck and shoulders bare. It falls just below her knees, but the silky material clings to her, showing off her figure.

She's even switched out her purse to a small black one that matches her high heels. She dressed to impress, and it's working. My fingers clench as I imagine ripping out the eyes of every man who's looked at her tonight.

When she tilts her head and twirls her finger around her hair, my teeth grit. She's fucking flirting with him. I force myself to let go of my glass before it shatters in my hand.

Clearly, my little bird still doesn't understand who she belongs to. I gave her a week's reprieve, thinking she'd be lonely without my presence. No, not thinking, knowing. I watched her from corners and shadows, keeping quiet and hidden. She didn't know I was there, but I'm certain she wanted me to be.

No matter how hard she tries to deny it, I see her desire. I watched it pull at her, twisting up her insides. Every night, that desire flooded her mind, creating an opening for me to haunt her dreams. Every morning, she startled awake, panting and sweating.

The first time, I thought she'd had a nightmare. But when she opened the drawer of her bedside table and brushed her fingers along the notes I left for her, I knew what she had really dreamt about. She pushed her t-shirt up to her breasts, trailing her fingers over her stomach. They caressed and teased until lines of goosebumps formed on her soft skin. I watched with rapt attention as her hand snaked downward, slipping into her panties. She moved her fingertips in small circles around her clit until she cried her release into her pillow.

I stare holes in Ava's date, as if I could kill him with will alone. Why the fuck is she hanging around with this loser? Does she really think that a wimp in a tailored jacket can satisfy her needs? She doesn't need this cookie-cutter Stepford husband. She doesn't need his white-picket fence promises. She needs *me*. She needs what *I* can give her, a darkness that matches the one that's buried so deep inside of her, that she isn't even aware of it.

He pushes his barstool back and stands up before bending at the waist to whisper something to her. His mouth is inches away when he reaches for her, brushing a lock of her hair away from her face. Her answering smile makes my blood boil. The sagging booth beneath me whispers an airy protest as I vault off of it, readying myself to rip him away from her.

Before I have a chance, he turns on his heels and walks into an alcove below a chipped wooden sign that reads *Restrooms* in dingy, yellow lettering. Two options immediately present themselves to me. I can follow him into the men's room and end his miserable existence, or stay and take what's mine. My eyes dart toward the bathroom and quickly back to Ava. A flirtatious smile lingers on her face, pulling the edges of her plump lips upward. Her pale, mossy eyes stare longingly at the entrance to the alcove.

My legs move without direction from my brain. The electrical impulses in my muscles yank me toward her until my chest is inches from her back. The sweet scent of her hair fills my nostrils, tempting me to press myself closer to her. She gasps as I wrap my arm around her torso and press my chin against her ear. She jerks her head to the side, but I force her still with my own. Her pulse quickens, pumping wildly in her throat.

"Did you really think this was a good idea, little bird?" I whisper against the shell of her ear. "Did you think I wouldn't follow you here? That I wouldn't come to claim what's mine?"

Her body tenses, her shoulders pulling inward, toward her chest. The muscles in her arms seize, trembling in my hold. A shocked inhale pushes her back against me before her breathing halts. Her neck bobs against a hard swallow and her cheeks begin to pinken.

"Breathe," I command softly, brushing my hand over the small of her back.

A soft whimper escapes her lips as she forces the air from her lungs. The sound catches the attention of the bartender, who looks up with narrowed eyes. His gaze travels from her face, to mine, then to my arm that remains encased around her. His head tilts, causing a ringlet of dishwater blonde hair to fall into his face. He rakes his hand through his curls, pushing it back as our eyes connect. His spine straightens, his chest puffing outward as his eyes glint with steely resolve.

His hardened stare locks with Ava's wide eyes. "Is this guy bothering you?"

I lift my head away from hers, standing upright. My arm tightens around her, gently squeezing against her stomach. Her lips pull tightly upward, the forced smile wrinkling the corner of her eyes.

"What?" She blinks and shakes her head. "Oh, uh, no, we're fine." She waves her hand in front of her in a confirming gesture.

I lean my head toward her until my lips brush the back of her neck. "That's my good girl."

Her upper teeth dig into her bottom lip, stifling a soft cry. She leans back, ever so slightly, pushing the delicate skin of her neck toward my mouth. I chuckle as a rosy blush spreads from her chest up to her hairline.

Some part of her, somewhere deep inside, knows that she's mine. It knows that we are inevitable. She only needs to give in to me. Tonight, she'll get a taste of what submission feels like. Tonight, I'll introduce her to a freedom she'll only find within a gilded cage.

Chapter Nineteen

The corners of my mouth uplift in a small smile as I peer down the corridor, watching the way Max's thighs move against his tight jeans. Perhaps normal wouldn't be so bad; the view certainly isn't. Running my finger along the edge of my wineglass, I turn my eyes back to the bar. Ripples of yellow light from the dim, overhead lamps twinkle against a line of half-filled liquor bottles behind the bar. The amber liquids inside cast tiny reflections against the glass shelves on which they sit.

My body jolts in alarm when a thick, muscled arm wraps around my waist. For a second, I think Max must have snuck up on me, until I look down. Draped over my stomach is an arm clad in a black dress shirt, rolled up to the elbows. Intricate black and gray tattoos swirl down the corded muscles of the forearm. Like swirling shadows, they spin and curl, spreading down the wrist, and wrapping around the strong fingers of an enormous hand.

As the heat of a large chest presses against my back, my mind nearly short-circuits trying to identify the familiar scent surrounding me. A memory lashes against the inside of my skull, making my breath catch in my throat. *Curling up in my bed, nestled in blankets that smell of warm, syrupy vanilla and rich leather.*

My head swivels to the right, desperately trying to see the person holding onto me, but a stubbled chin pressed against my ear halts the movement. Searing, hot panic engulfs my chest, making my heart feel like it's encased in flames as it hammers inside me.

Warm breath dances along the shell of my ear, sending shivers skittering down my arms. A deep, baritone voice whispers, "Did you really think this was a good idea, little bird?"

My legs begin to shake at the sound of that nickname, *his* name for me. My ankles quake nervously, making my high heels clink against the legs of the barstool.

"Did you really think I wouldn't follow you here?" he continues. "That I wouldn't come to claim what's mine?"

My vision begins to swim. The twinkling bottles behind the bar ripple in and out of focus. The flames licking at my heart have crawled up my throat, heating my face.

"Breathe," the voice commands. A hand presses against my lower back. The warmth of his hand seeps through the thin fabric of my dress, nestling into my bones. All of the air heaves out of my lungs with a sound somewhere between a sob and a squeal.

When my eyes refocus, they connect with those of the man behind the bar. His brows crease as his eyes narrow. "Is this guy bothering you?" he asks in a voice thick with concern.

The arm snaked around my waist squeezes and my stomach tightens in response. My mind falters, fumbling through warring thoughts. I could scream. I could beg for help. But at what cost? An image flashes in front of my eyes. The memory of James' mangled, bloody hand in a box on my kitchen floor. I can't be the cause of another death. If I try to get away, he could kill the bartender for trying to help. No, not could. He *will* kill him.

Shaking my head to ground myself, I ask, "What?" I force my cheeks to rise into a smile that feels too tight for my face. "Oh, uh, no, we're fine," I state in a voice that I hope conveys some level of normalcy.

When I feel his mouth against the most sensitive part of my neck, I bite down on my lower lip to hold back the desperate sound that rises from my throat.

"That's my good girl," he whispers against my neck.

A throbbing ache awakens in my core at the sound of his praise. Before I have a chance to think about my actions, my head presses back into him, seeking out the warmth of his lips. When I realize what I've done, my cheeks heat. I wiggle in my seat, trying to pull away, but his arm around me is like steel holding me in place.

He clicks his tongue in disapproval before I feel his lips against my ear. The sound of his deep voice vibrates through me, sending a pulse of warmth through my belly.

"We're leaving now," he demands.

Attempting to wet my tongue, which suddenly feels like sandpaper, I swallow hard. When my lips part to protest, no sound emerges. My mouth opens and closes like a fish struggling to breathe on land. Not trusting my voice to convey anything besides the scream that feels like it's permanently lodged in my throat, I shake my head.

"Mmm," he hums against the side of my head. "I'll put it to you this way: if you don't leave with me now, I'll kill your date and anyone else who tries to stop me from taking you out of this bar."

My eyes dart left and right. There are at least twenty people at the bar alone. There could be dozens more in other parts of the building. I don't doubt that he would kill any one of them, perhaps a lot of them before someone could stop him. They'd die and I'd live to see the horrific event. Bile rises in my throat as I envision their bloodied bodies draped across the bar.

Blinking back the hot sting of tears forming in my eyes, I nod. Slowly, he releases his arm from around my waist, letting his fingers skim gently over my stomach. The heat at my back recedes as he steps back. Closing my eyes, I let out a slow, purposeful exhale before turning around to face him.

Opening my eyes, I take in his broad chest. The muscles strain against the fabric of his shirt. Slowly moving my gaze upward, I note the large, black rose tattooed on his neck. The delicate flower is somehow menacing in its appearance. How many tattoos does he have? What scars do they hide?

Since he stands nearly a foot taller than me, my line of sight stops at his neck. Something inside me demands that I lift my head and look at his face, but I can't. I'm afraid of what I'll see. Does he look like a monster? I pinch my eyes closed, refusing to look.

His hand touches my cheek. I flinch, expecting pain that doesn't come. For a moment he stills, his hand lingering on my face.

"Shh," he whispers, "it's okay."

Then he gently caresses a line from my temple down my jawline. He pinches my chin between his thumb and forefinger, tilting my head toward him.

In a tone that can't be construed as anything but a demand, he says, "Look at me."

There's a screeching voice in the back of my head that begs me to keep my eyes closed, to shut it all out, to go to that place inside my mind where everything is quiet and safe. But there's something else, too. Another voice that tells me to look. Some incessant need that demands that I do so. This broken thing inside of me that isn't afraid of the monster. This nagging desire that wants it to come closer.

My eyelids peel back and my mouth falls open at the sight of the man in front of me. Thick, black hair falls against his forehead, seemingly the only part of him that looks soft. His face is made up of hard lines and sharp features. Dark stubble lines his strong jaw and full lips. Icy blue eyes stare back at me. He leans forward, his eyes never leaving mine. Staring into his eyes feels like falling into a frozen lake. Shards of crystalline ice in shades of lighter and darker blues create a jagged path into his black pupils.

He's both terrifying and astonishingly beautiful at the same time. My lungs tighten, the feeling similar to the first time I saw an enormous bobcat in the wild. I don't want to take my eyes off of him, but it's not just out of fear. There's this odd feeling when you see something breathtaking that could easily kill you. Some unknown part of you eases, like you might accept your end at the hands of something that beautiful.

I'm startled out of my daze when he pulls my coat from the bar and wraps it around my shoulders. He doesn't move away as I shove my arms into the sleeves and pull the warm fabric tight around my chest. No longer trusting my ability to form coherent sentences, I remain quiet, allowing him to grab my arm and lead me toward the door.

Pausing in front of the door, I ask, "Shouldn't I at least tell my date?"

His mouth pulls into a grin. "Don't worry. He already knows." He nods his head toward the bar.

I look up to find Max standing at the end of the bar with his lips downturned and brow furrowed in confusion. My mouth opens, an apology on the tip of my tongue, but before I can voice it, my chin is jerked forward by a strong hand. I look up into those stormy, blue eyes a second before his lips crash into mine.

He kisses my closed lips with an unexpected softness, pressing his pillowy lips against mine. His arm wraps around my lower back, pulling me into him. I gasp as my breasts press against the hard planes of his chest. He uses that to his advantage, pushing his tongue past the open seam of my lips.

His tongue skims over mine. The sweet and spicy taste of peppermint and whiskey tangle in my tastebuds, the heady mixture shocking my senses. My nose bumps his as I press myself closer to him, tangling my tongue with his.

The second that my brain registers that I'm kissing him back, I pull away. What am I doing? This guy is a psycho but the flood of liquid heat between my legs tells me that my body doesn't care.

Squeezing my thighs together, I shift my stance, desperately trying to release the building pressure in my core with friction. His lips pull into a devilish smirk that makes my cheeks heat and my gaze drop to the floor.

I don't dare look back at Max while the arm around my back pulls me outside. The monster at my side presses himself close to me and begins leading me down the sidewalk. A gust of cold air whips at my face, pulling me out of my lust-induced stupor. My feet stop moving, my heels driving downward into the concrete to stop us. I shove my arms against his torso, but it's like trying to shove a brick wall.

"You're coming with me whether you walk or I carry you," he states plainly.

My body trembles. Alone with him against the backdrop of a dark city night, a new fear arises inside me. One that causes burning tears to well up in my eyes. I'm trapped.

Chapter Twenty

"I-I'll scream," I threaten, trying to keep my voice from shaking. I fail, my voice holding all the confidence of a cornered church mouse.

His eyebrows raise and his mouth tilts up into a smirk. "Go ahead."

I suck in a breath, forcing my lungs to expand beyond their capacity as I prepare to release the most blood-curdling screech I can muster. My mouth opens, but his open palm quickly covers it.

He leans in close, his breath dancing along my jaw. "But know that everyone who hears you, dies tonight."

The statement makes my jaw drop, but the only sound that escapes is the soft whoosh of my breath. It wheezes from between my lips like a deflating balloon. My heart feels like it's doing the same thing, shrinking and deflating under the crushing weight of my fear.

"Your screams," he says, his thumb caressing my bottom lip, "are for my ears alone, little bird."

His arm drops away from my back, leaving only the chill of the night air in its place. He steps back, putting space between us. Looking at his long arms and the span of their reach, the few feet between us feel like only inches. My knees quake, unable to remain still while the anxious energy zaps through my nerve endings like little sparks of lightning.

His arms cross over his chest and he waits, eyebrows raise in question. He's testing me, daring me to defy him. Finding myself suddenly unable to meet his steely gaze, I look anywhere but at him.

My eyes dart back and forth, seeking out the lives that would be snuffed out if I cried for help. Across the street, a group of college boys nearly tumble out of a bar with their arms linked to hold each other up. Their laughter echoes on the breeze. It bounces down the busy street, passing a middle-aged couple leaving a restaurant holding hands. It ripples through an alleyway where two young men kiss, their bodies molded together as they tease and giggle.

My heart seizes in my chest. I press my lips together tightly, forcing back the cry that begs to jump from my throat. My life isn't worth all of theirs, but I don't doubt his words. Not after what he's done already.

My eyes travel back to the monster in front of me who has a cruel grin plastered on his face. Panic squeezes its icy fingers around my lungs. Chills skitter down my limbs, raising goosebumps on my skin. My eyes connect with his for a moment and his lips tip up. I don't give myself a moment to think before I spin on my heels and run.

My heels clatter against the concrete as my legs pump wildly, desperate to put distance between us. I sprint down the sidewalk, flying past busy shops and restaurants. My body weaves, narrowly avoiding a collision with a man strolling leisurely.

He yells out, "Watch it, lady!"

I can only hope my panicked eyes convey my apology because I don't stop. I cannot stop.

At the nearest intersection, I pivot my body hastily. I wobble on my feet, nearly pitching forward as I make the rapid turn.

The deep bass of his voice booms behind me, "Run as fast as you can, baby. You'll regret it when I catch you."

His laughter ricochets against the concrete and bricks around me, making it sound like he's everywhere all at once. A sob rips from my throat and I push my legs faster, faster, faster.

Using what I hope is accurate information from every action movie I've ever seen, I careen down the streets, turning as often as I can. Streetlights whiz past, becoming a hazy blur against the tears in my eyes. I try to track my movements in my head. *Left, right, left, left, right.*

I sneak a glance at the nearest street sign, Layton Avenue. I don't even know where that is. I have no idea where I am. Looking around, I realize that the bustling shops and businesses have thinned out, leaving me surrounded by only empty warehouses and construction sites.

The sounds of the city have faded, too. I can scarcely make out the sound of distant car horns over the rapid pounding of my heart. Tears stream from my eyes, dribbling down my cheeks and neck. My feet, having gone numb at least a quarter of a mile ago, quake beneath me, causing me to lose my footing and tumble forward.

My knees crash into the uneven concrete, sending a sharp pain vibrating up my leg. Fire erupts in my palms as my hands slide against the ground. Pressing my elbows into the road, I push myself back up just enough to stumble into the nearest alley before falling to the ground beside a rusted, metal dumpster.

Crouched down with my heels teetering beneath me, I fall apart. I press my aching palm to my mouth to stifle the sob that rips through my body.

How did this happen to me? How did I end up here? I should never have agreed to go on this stupid date. I should have hidden in my house with the doors and windows locked, praying he wouldn't come back. But now, he's here.

And he's pissed.

I squint, trying to adjust my eyes to the darkness around me. Slivers of light fall from distant windows and sporadically places streetlights, illuminating just enough for me to see the place I may likely die in when he finds me. Used tissues and empty candy bar wrappers skitter across the ground, pushed by a cold wind. A wind that bites at my bruised knees and nips at my ankles.

I didn't think he'd kill me before, but now I'm not so sure. Is this really where I'm meant to die? Alone, cowering behind a damned dumpster?

My father's voice echoes in my mind. *You're not strong. There's no fight in you, girl. You're nothing but a scared, little rabbit.* I shake my head, forcing the thoughts to dissipate.

I can't die tonight. I won't. I just need to stay hidden. I just need to hide long enough that he gives up his search. I'm not worth the trouble of searching in the cold. Surely, he'll see that.

Chapter Twenty-One

The words tumble out of me, springing straight from the heart that seems to only warm in her presence, "Your screams are for my ears alone, little bird."

I let my arm fall away from her and step back, giving her space to decide her next move in our little game. A game that perhaps she hasn't figured out, that I will win at any cost. She wraps her arms around herself, rubbing her arms in a soothing motion. Her body trembles, from her shaking legs to her quivering, pink lips.

Her wide doe eyes scan the streets, pausing at each small grouping of people that line the sidewalks. Those eyes glisten beautifully, sparkling with unshed tears. Her plump lips press together into a thin line, but it doesn't stop the tiny whine that squeaks through them. Hearing the sweet sound of her fear, I suppress a groan.

A small smile creeps across my mouth when her eyes sweep back, catching mine. It widens when she turns and runs down the street. I bounce impatiently on the balls of my feet, aching to chase her. My fingers clench, balling my hands into fists which I tap against my thighs. I won't let myself run after her just yet. She needs to understand the lengths I'll go to catch her. She needs to run as far and as fast as she can so that she can see that there's no escaping me.

I allow her to put a few city blocks of space between us before I follow the sound of her rapidly clicking heels. A chuckle rumbles in my chest when she pivots clumsily onto the next street, nearly toppling over in the process. The wind whips at her dress, pushing it higher up her thighs as her legs pump beneath her.

My clumsy, careless woman. She careens down Rayton Avenue, pushing herself further away from help and closer to the warehouse district. Pausing at the corner, I call after her, "Run as fast as you can, baby. You'll regret it when I catch you."

I slow my pace to a light jog, following the echoes of her heels crashing against the concrete. She zigs and zags through the streets, further and further from the heart of the city. Further into the darkness where I'll trap her alone. My fingers itch at my side, desperate to feel her soft skin against them.

My neck cranes, my ear lifting toward an alley where I hear the clacking of her footfalls begin to slow. I quiet my own steps, tiptoeing toward the sounds of her ragged breaths and muted sobs. Resting my palms against the chilled brick of an empty building, I peer around the corner.

A cold wind whips through the alley, pulling with it the sweet scent of her skin. From behind a dumpster, locks of earthy brown hair flutter. Her soft whimpers and sniffles bounce off of the metal she hides behind, making the sound louder despite her attempts to quiet herself.

I step closer. Close enough to see her head ducked down, pressed against her bleeding knees. Her hair falls in tangles around her head. It's damp with sweat. Her body shudders, her muscles twitching against the cold. She whispers quietly against her legs. A mantra repeating softly, "Just stay hidden. Just stay hidden."

Something inside my chest thrashes at the sight of her. It scratches and claws inside me, screaming for me to take her away from here. It gnaws on the edges of my heart, shrieking for me to soothe her, to protect her. *Soon,* I tell it. *This is all for her. She will break, and then I'll make her whole again. Soon, she'll know that she's mine.*

"You can't hide from me, little bird," I say softly in the kind of gentle tone one uses to soothe a feral animal. "I'll always find you."

With a yelp, her head rockets upward. Her eyes connect with mine and widen. Panic ripples across her face, tightening her features. Her breath comes in short, strained pants. I reach for her, causing her to flinch and recoil. Inwardly, I wince as she presses her back against the dumpster. That nagging thing inside of me hates to see her dirty and cold. I immediately push it down, forcing it to recede back into my chest.

My fingers wrap around her arm and I yank her to her feet. She wobbles on unsteady legs before falling into me, her chest pressed against mine. I close my eyes, reveling in the rightness of her warm body against me. Her body tightens when my hands grip her waist.

With her in my arms, I step forward to press her against the wall behind her. She hisses when her back hits the rough bricks. She winces as I lean into her, sandwiching her between me and the wall. Her wide, glistening eyes meet mine as a tear rolls down her cheek.

I rub my thumb against her heated skin, catching the droplet before it falls. Placing my finger in my mouth, I lick her salty sweetness away. The look of fear in her eyes seems to flare when I hum contentedly.

The muscles in her face scrunch up and she clamps her eyelids shut tightly. She tilts her chin down toward her neck, trying to make herself small. Her voice comes out in a whisper as she begs, "P-please don't kill m-me."

I chuckle. Not only at the absurdity of the concept of me killing her, but also because that dark, monstrous part of me delights in her fear. Her desperate plea settles in my blood and rushes straight to my cock.

"I have no intention of killing you," I state, expecting some of the tension in her muscles to ease.

It doesn't. Her body stands rigid and still. Her chin remains down and her eyes firmly closed. That won't do. I press my thumb under her chin and lift it up.

"Eyes on me, precious."

The term of endearment feels strange in my mouth. Probably because I can't recall ever using one before. But her response makes me want to say it again. She shakes in my arms as a shudder runs through her. Hesitantly, her eyelids peel open and her mossy-green eyes meet mine. A rosy-pink flush spreads through her cheeks.

I press my lips against her forehead. "That's a good girl."

My hand drops away from her waist, my palm running down from her hip to her knee. She tenses as my fingers creep under the hem of her dress. I brush them over her skin, tracing a line up her thigh. I groan at the feeling of her soft, buttery skin.

Her skin is perfect, soft, and smooth. I trail my hands over the tops of her legs, my fingers tracing the creases at the tops of her thighs. As I feel that delicate skin beneath my fingertips, realization crashes into me. My hand stills on her thigh for a moment before my fingers squeeze. She yelps as I grip her upper thigh.

"You're not wearing any panties," I state. My voice lowers, bordering on a growl. "You were going to let him touch you?"

Ava's eyes widen. She opens and closes her mouth, but only a few small, incoherent syllables tumble out.

"Answer me," I demand.

Her response is whispered and breathless, "I don't know."

My eyebrows skyrocket to the top of my head. "You don't know?"

"Maybe," she whispers.

My pulse quickens, stuttering in my veins. Hot, festering rage curls in my gut. My fingers flex against the sudden feeling of bugs twitching under my skin. I slam my palm against the wall beside Ava's head, forcing bits of brick to crumble onto her shoulder, making her flinch again.

Maybe? Maybe she would have let him put his hands on what's mine? Fucking *maybe*? I press my palm into the wall until pain radiates through my fingers. I should have ended her pathetic excuse for a date back at the bar. I should have broken every one of his fingers. She wouldn't want his mangled hands touching her after that.

Even as she shrinks back against the wall, Ava's eyes harden, glinting with fiery resolve. Her jaw ticks before she opens her mouth.

"What do you care?" she rasps. Her voice is coated with anger, but she can't hide the slight quiver of fear that shakes it. "I'm not yours. You don't own me!"

I cock my head to the side, stunned by my shy bird showing me her claws; small and blunt, though they may be. In my time watching her, she hasn't shown them to anyone else. Her eyes are bright and angry, still containing some tiny smoldering embers of her fire; the one that was stomped out by whatever life has put her through. Something perhaps I haven't discovered about my little bird yet.

I peel my hand back from the wall to place it on her throat. My fingers wrap loosely around her neck as my thumb draws slow lines up and down her jugular.

"Yes, you are. And yes, I fucking do," I growl. "I think you'll find that I'm very possessive of what's mine." Her face scrunches up as a fresh wave of tears slips down her cheeks, but I don't stop. I can't—not until she understands. "I *want* to kill every man that looks at you, but I *will* kill any man that touches you."

"What do you want from me?" she asks, her voice hitching with something between a sob and a hiccup.

I lean in, my lips only millimeters from hers as I breathe the word, "Everything."

She leans forward, pushing her lips closer to mine. A tiny whimper escapes from between them. Her eyes are rounded in fear as they flick between my eyes and my mouth. Her pupils expand under my gaze. My own eyes widen in surprise and a smile twitches at the corners of my mouth. She wants me. At the thought, my cock hardens, pressing painfully against my jeans.

Fuck, I want her in a way I've never wanted any woman before. She's a spring of fresh water in the desert, and I'm a man who's been dying of thirst for years. I force out a heavy breath, trying to calm myself. I remind that thrashing, desperate thing in my chest,

I'm not doing this for me; this is for her. She needs to feel the safety of her cage. She needs to know the freedom she'll find in her submission.

In one swift motion, I reach beneath her dress. Her wetness spreads over my fingertips. She watches me, a scarlet blush blooming in her cheeks. The color deepens as I lift my hand toward my mouth and suck her arousal from my fingers. She presses her hands against my chest. The muscles in her legs clench as if she's preparing to run, but I don't give her a chance.

My hands snake around her wrists and I wrench them behind her. I wrap one hand around them and press her hands into the bricks. She cries out when the jagged wall bites against her soft skin.

"You remember what I said about people hearing you scream?" I ask. "Same rule applies now."

She gasps when I press my knee between her thighs, forcing them apart. Sparks erupt at my fingertips, as I caress a lazy line from her knee to her center. I cup her sex. I nearly moan at the feel of the wet heat spreading across my palm.

"Mmm," the sound rumbles from my chest, "you're so wet for me."

I skim my thumb gently over her folds until it reaches her clit. Her thighs quiver. She presses her lips together, but it doesn't stop the needy whine that sounds in her throat.

I lean in close, my mouth grazing her ear. "And so responsive to my touch."

Slowly, I circle the bundle of nerves with the pad of my finger. She bites into her lower lip and sucks in a deep breath through her nose. Her exhale tickles against the side of my face. I continue my unhurried exploration until she whines again. I know exactly what she wants, but I won't give it to her; not until she gives in.

It doesn't take long before she rocks her hips back and forth, begging for friction. I press harder, letting her angle herself to have me rub exactly where she wants it. I feel her breath quicken. Her legs wobble beneath her, tipping her body away from the wall. I wrap an arm around her back to hold her up. She pants, but stays quiet. I pinch her clit until she moans a desperate, filthy sound.

I release her wrists from behind her back and press her head to my shoulder. "Shh, precious," I whisper against her ear. "I need you to be quiet for me."

When she presses her face into the crook of my neck, I reward her by pushing a finger into her. Her breath fans across my neck as a strangled noise falls from her lips. She rocks her hips into me, forcing me to sink deeper into her wet heat.

I'm so shocked when her arms suddenly wrap around my neck, that my arm loosens from around her and I almost drop her. Her hands paw at my upper back, her fingers digging into my jacket. I groan at the feeling of her body pressed against mine. Everything in me is desperate for her. My cock twitches, aching to be inside her.

I push a second finger into her. She gasps as her pussy stretches to accommodate my large digits. I hook my fingers inside her until I find the spot that makes her writhe in my arms. She tightens around me, her warm sheath pulling my fingers in. She pleads for her release in tangled, intelligible syllables. As her pussy begins to clamp down, signaling her impending orgasm, I pull out.

"No," she rasps, wrapping her arms tighter around my neck.

She lifts her head back from my shoulder. Her hair is a tangled mess, hiding her face. I brush an errant strand away from her eyes and press a kiss to her forehead. Knowing that the haze of her arousal is lifting, I keep my voice soft.

"Only good girls get to come…and only when I say so."

She blinks several times. Her eyes crinkle in confusion. Her mouth opens, but only a tiny panicked sound escapes.

"Have you been a good girl tonight?" I ask.

"Um, I-I…"

"No," I interrupt, "you most certainly have not."

My chest tightens painfully when she drops her arms. My body rebels, immediately missing the weight of her against me. The night air feels colder than ever as it brushes against my neck. I force out a heavy exhale, willing the ice inside that's suddenly formed in my lungs to dissipate.

My disheveled little pet stands in front of me with wide, fearful eyes. Like a small animal preparing to run, she bounces on her heels. Her eyes dart around the alley.

I shake my head to clear the jumble of thoughts bombarding me all at once. I find myself suddenly unable to tolerate the idea of her running in the cold, nor the concept of her not being in my arms. I don't give her a chance to run this time. I can't. Instead, I bend low, banding my arms around her thighs, and toss her over my shoulder.

Chapter Twenty-Two

The thumping of his footsteps resonates through my stomach. Each step jostles my body, which is draped over his shoulder. I close my eyes, hoping to ease the dizziness caused by the blood rushing to my head. My fingers are curled in a death grip on either side of his waist.

A frigid wind whips by, crashing into me and causing a ripple of shivers to cascade through my body. Attempting to use his warmth to soothe my chilled limbs, my grip becomes an awkward, upside down hug. I pull myself closer to his back, pressing my chest into him. A deep hum vibrates in his chest. I immediately release my arms, letting them dangle over my head.

Is...is he enjoying this? The warm, bubbling feeling of rising anger churns in my gut. Combined with the frozen fear in my lungs, I can scarcely breathe.

My hands clench into fists before I crash them against his back. Over and over, I slam them against him. My mind somersaults over everything—what's happened, what's to come, and why.

Alarm bells blare inside my head. This isn't right. None of this is right. Where is he taking me? And what will he do to me when we get there? This can't be freaking happening to me. Why did he choose me? No one chooses me.

I pummel his stupid, hard back until the slight ache in my hands becomes a dull roar. No matter how hard I hit, he doesn't make any attempt to stop me. He doesn't even make a sound. I feel like a flea punching an elephant; it's useless.

I drop my hands, feeling utterly defeated. Tears stream from my eyes, drenching my face and dribbling down the back of his jacket. A sob rips from my chest. It's followed by another and another until I'm bawling against his back.

The arm banded around my thighs tightens. I flinch when his hand lands on my back. My muscles tense, anticipating pain. But the pain doesn't come. Instead, his hand moves, rubbing in slow circles.

"Shh," he murmurs softly, "you're okay."

I will my body to remain tense, desperately holding on to the knowledge that I'm not okay at all. I beg my muscles to stay locked up, ready to leap from his arms and away from danger. Despite how hard my mind fights, as the minutes wear on, my body begins to relax.

"That's it, precious," he coos. "Calm yourself."

I crinkle my nose, hating the effect his soft praise has on me. Hating how he can feel my limbs loosening in his hold. Hating how warm his body is against mine. Hating the closeness of him. Hating that my skin still tingles from his touch. But more than anything: hating that I wanted him to keep touching me.

My body rocks forward suddenly. I wrap my arms around his waist, afraid I'll go tumbling off his back. I look up, suddenly panicked, only to find that he's just stepped us over a curb. I could let go of him. I should let go of him. But I don't. My hands remain firmly planted on his sides.

My mind wanders to the hard surface under my palms; to the feel of his muscles moving beneath them. He's strong. I've never had a man carry me before, but it seems effortless for him. Is he this hard everywhere?

No, I inwardly chastise myself, *do not think about this. Do not think about his body. He's a freaking psycho who cornered you in an alley and is carrying you to…well, who knows where. He could be dragging you to your death!*

But the thoughts don't stop. If anything, they spiral further in the exact wrong direction. My mind replays the entire encounter on loop. Remembering the feel of his hand on me, I press my thighs together. I'm not sure if it's to hide my reaction to him or to seek out more friction, but I can't stop. His dark chuckle drifts to my ears, making my face heat with embarrassment.

We turn into another street and the sounds of the city become louder. My ears perk up at the whooshing of passing cars and the chatter of people. People who can now see me being carried down the sidewalk like an ill-behaved child. With my private embarrassment suddenly becoming public, I begin my struggle anew. Shoving my hands against his back, I push hard in an attempt to pull my head up.

"Stop," he commands in a voice darker and deeper than before. His tone leaves no room for argument. The demand skitters down my spine like a chilled wind, halting my movement.

When he begins to lower me to the ground, my heart thunders in my chest. My brain backflips with a rush of fear so strong it makes my head spin. I wrap my arms around his neck, suddenly terrified of what will happen when my feet hit the ground. To my dismay, it doesn't stop my slow descent to the sidewalk below. My grip on his neck has only served to anchor my body to his. In a painfully sluggish movement, he pulls my body down. My nipples ache and harden as they rub against his jacket. His lips trail slowly down the side of my face.

When my feet hit the pavement, my knees shake, threatening to refuse to hold my own weight. I tilt my chin back, finding him smirking down at me. I rip my arms away from him so suddenly that I almost fall over. He steps back, putting precious distance between us. I pivot on my feet, preparing to run, but his hand is on my arm before I have a chance to take a step.

He pulls me toward a black SUV that I hadn't even noticed we were standing in front of, and opens the door. His hand sweeps out, gesturing for me to get into the passenger seat. My mouth drops open, but nothing comes out. Is he insane? Does he really think I'm going to get into a car with him?

His lips curl up into a knowing smile. "You can get in the car on your own," he gestures again to the open door, "or I can tie you up and put you in the trunk. Your choice, little bird."

If it were anyone else telling me this, I wouldn't have believed them. Surely, no sane person would throw someone into their trunk in the middle of a crowded, city street. But the man in front of me is clearly not a sane person. A shudder runs through me as my mind flits to the potential collateral damage he might cause if I don't do as he asks. With a defeated sigh, I get into the car.

My eyes go in and out of focus as I watch the city lights race by. They twinkle and elongate as we rush past until they slowly begin to blink away, lost to the distance. The further we get from the populated metropolis, the darker the night becomes. When there's nothing left to see from the window but my own haggard reflection, I turn to look at my captor.

"Where are you taking me?"

He glances at me quickly before returning his eyes to the road. "Home."

"Your home!?" I wince hearing my own screeching voice.

He snorts a short laugh through his nose. "No, precious, not tonight. I'm taking you to your home."

My stomach flips at the implication in his response. He's not taking me to his home *tonight*? Does he plan on taking me to his creepy stalker lair some other night?

I cross my ankles and pull my shoulders in, suddenly feeling the need to make myself small. My hands latch on to the edge of my dress. I rub the fabric between my fingers, which seems like a better option than watching them shake in my lap. My breathing becomes heavy, or at least it seems heavy in the quiet space.

I glance toward him. If he notices my anxiety, he doesn't show it. His proud nose remains forward, eyes firmly planted on the road ahead. Slivers of moonlight seep in through the windshield, highlighting the strong features of his face and reflecting off of the black locks that surround it. Even in the dim light, he's devastatingly gorgeous.

His full lips curl into a wolfish grin. "See something you like?" he asks.

I blush, realizing I'm no longer glancing at him from the corner of my eye. My entire head has turned toward him as I stare. I whip my head forward before replying in the snarkiest tone I can manage, "There's nothing I like about you."

His smile widens, clearly indicating that he doesn't believe that. I'm not even sure that I believe that, but I'm entirely unwilling to explore that particular issue right now. I press my cheek against the window, hoping the cold glass will cool my heated face.

We sit in deafening silence for what could only be minutes, but feels like hours. Nervous energy twitches in my veins, demanding that I verbalize something…anything.

"What's your name?" The question pops out of my mouth before I can think better of it.

"Grayson," he says, "but you can call me Gray."

"Gray?"

His voice is light, reflecting the smirk on his lips. "Or you can call me master."

My lips turn down into a grimace that I hope he can hear. "That's never going to happen."

The car slows as the road morphs from an arterial thoroughfare into a winding, rural road. Towering forests surround us, making the tree line more dense. The sign for Windon Farms zips by my window, telling me exactly where we are. There's a bend in the road about two miles ahead of us. In order to stay on the road, we'll be forced to slow down significantly. It may be my only chance.

With the ghost of a plan scarcely formed in my head, I quietly unbuckle my seatbelt. Then, I steel my nerves and wait.

The car slows, lurching forward just slightly as we edge around the angle in the road. I flick my eyes toward the man I now know as Gray. He's staring at me intently, his eyes sparking with something dangerous.

"Don't even think about it," he demands through his clenched teeth.

But I've thought about it and there's no going back. I feel my lips peel up into a smile, though I don't have time to think about why the Hell I would be smiling at a time like this. My fingers are already gripped tightly on the door handle. I shove my shoulder against the door, forcing it open and let myself tumble from the car.

Covering my head with my arms, I let the momentum take me. My body bounces and rolls, careening straight down a hill and into the woods below. The frigid night air stings against my heated skin. Branches nip at my arms and legs, scratching my skin as I plummet downward. My stomach crashes into the trunk of a heavy oak tree, stopping my movement and forcing my breath out in a gasp.

The sound of screeching tires echoes through the woods, reminding me that I can't stop. The bark of the tree scratches my palms as I hoist my aching body up. Fallen leaves tickle my ankles as my heels sink into the moist dirt below. Knowing that I won't get far with the inconvenient shoes, I rip them off and toss them behind me.

My eyes dart around, scanning the trees for a path. A round, autumn moon hangs high overhead, bathing the area in a faint, silver light. With no straightforward path ahead, I rush forward, darting around stumps and trees. For the second time tonight, I run as fast as my legs will carry me. Ignoring the biting pain in my feet, I dash over sharp rocks and upturned sticks.

My heart thunders in my chest. I suck in deep breaths, my lungs burning against the cold air. I pump my legs desperately. Branches whip by, slashing my legs and ankles as I sprint. I refuse to look down at the damage they've caused. I refuse to acknowledge the pain radiating up my legs.

When it feels like I've run for miles, the pain has become dull. My legs are shaking and numb from the cold. I press my hands into the bark of a huge tree, using it to keep myself upright as I circle around it. Behind the shade of the looming tree, where all the moonlight is blocked, I let myself fall to the ground. I press my hands to my mouth to quiet my breathing.

As my body calms, I realize how cold I am. If I don't get out of here, I'll freeze to death. I pull my knees up to my chest and wrap my arms around myself. I reach around myself, feeling under my arm for my purse, only to realize that it isn't there. Did I leave it in his car? Did I even have it when I got into the car? Realizing that there's no way for me to get help without my phone, my eyes fill with tears. They stream down my cheeks, leaving cold trails behind.

"It's okay," I whisper. "It's going to be okay. You just have to wait him out. He'll leave. You're not worth the trouble. He'll see that. Then when he's gone, you can find a way out of here and get help."

Hours, or maybe only minutes, pass while I sit with my back against the hard tree bark and listen. The muted sounds of the forest float around me. A soft wind howls, rustling the branches of nearby trees. Crispy leaves clatter against each other as the wind carries them. Somewhere in the distance, an animal chitters. I close my eyes and listen to the symphony of the forest.

A sharp crack sounds behind me as a branch snaps. My eyes rocket open. A startled scream climbs up my throat. It barely passes my lips before it's smothered by a hand clamping down over my mouth. My body is yanked up and pulled against a hard chest.

The scent of vanilla and leather surrounds me, invading my senses. Gray's hands grip my upper arms, pinning my back to his chest. Without my permission, my body sinks back into the delicious warmth of his body.

His arm wraps around my stomach, tightly securing our bodies together. He leans down until I feel his hot breath against my neck. Goosebumps prickle over my skin and I shiver. I try to tell myself that it's a reaction from the cold and not his nearness.

His voice rumbles in my ear. "Hasn't anyone ever told you, you can't run from monsters?"

I lift my foot and jab it out behind me. It meets its target, connecting with his shin. Unfortunately, with my near-frozen bare feet, my hit has all the power of a rabbit hitting a black bear. Realizing how epically my attack has failed, I lace my voice with as much venom as I can before I spit at him, "Fuck you."

His hand wraps around my throat. His thumb presses into my chin, forcing my gaze upward. He stares down at me, his blue eyes sparkling with humor. The edges wrinkle as he laughs.

"Oh, little bird," he says, "I'll fuck you." He leans down, letting his lips brush against my forehead. He whispers against my hairline, "But only when you beg me for it."

The hand at my throat tightens just enough to make me gasp. His palm presses down against my sternum until my knees buckle. I expect the ground to rise up and crash into my already aching knees, but it doesn't. With his arm banded tightly around my waist, he lowers me slowly.

My face crinkles in confusion. My mind flounders, flopping between being utterly petrified and slightly swoony from his gentle touch and the warmth of his body against mine. I mentally slap myself and try to push the idea of *swooning for my stalker* very far from my mind.

As my knees make contact with the ground, fallen leaves crackle and crunch. Twigs and plant litter scrape against my bare legs. The earthy smell of soil and decay wafts up from beneath me.

He kneels down at my side, never taking his hands off me. The leaves shift under me, sending prickles and itches skittering across my skin. The hand at my throat falls away. I shift my knees, trying to pivot my body to put space between us. The arm around my waist tightens almost to the point of pain. The other lands between my shoulder blades.

With one quick shove, my chest collides with the ground. I turn my head sharply just before, making my cheek scrape against the dirt. I sputter and spit against a leaf that's slipped between my lips.

I'm trapped, unmoving with his body pressed tightly against my side and my face in the dirt. Humiliation becomes a hot, acidic feeling bubbling in my stomach.

A cold breeze whips by, lashing against my skin. I shudder, suddenly keenly aware that I'm entirely on display, my rear up in the air and panties missing. Tears burn in my eyes, some sliding down my cheeks and creating tiny mud puddles on the ground. The sound that escapes my lips can't be described as anything other than a pathetic whine.

"Do not fucking run from me again," he growls against my neck. "My patience isn't limitless, and tonight, it's run out."

I squeak in surprise when he grips my hip and yanks my body into his lap, my stomach landing over his thighs. His fingers dig into my skin, surely bruising. I can feel his hard length pressed against my waist. My stomach flips as I try desperately not to think about his cock.

His other hand trails up my leg until it's resting on my ass. His palm rubs a slow circle against my cheek. He repeats the action on the other side. My skin tingles under his touch. When he pulls away, I feel the loss immediately. My skin feels too tight, too cold, too desperate for his warmth.

The air whistles behind me before lightning strikes my ass. A horrible sting lights my nerve endings on fire. I'm not sure the pain registers before or after I hear the slap of his open palm against my skin for a second time. I don't know when the screeching howl explodes from my lips. Is it an echo I hear bouncing between the trees, or am I screaming again?

Rapid slaps thunder against my aching backside. I wiggle and shift in his grasp, trying to get away from the burning ache that rains down on my sensitive globes. "Stop, stop," I sob.

His breath is hot against my neck when he speaks. "You need to understand who's in charge here, precious. You. Belong. To. Me," he growls, punctuating each word with a painful smack.

I listen to the sound of his hand connecting with my ass and the symphony of my pitiful cries. My body feels like it's covered in molten lava. The tiny reprieve between hits seems shorter and shorter. The cold night air scarcely touches me. Each time he spanks me, the burning embers light anew, igniting my skin.

"Will you run from me again?" His chest rumbles with his demand. The deep bass of his voice booms against my ear, sending shivers down my spine.

Will I? Wouldn't I be crazy not to? Wouldn't it be the definition of insanity not to run from a man who hurts me like this? Who humiliates me like this? It's true; it must be. And yet somehow, underneath the fiery pain, something else is blossoming inside me. Something that makes my core clench. This demanding thing inside me that wants to give in to him.

"No," I whisper into the dirt.

"Apologize," he commands. "Apologize to your master."

I hate that word. Master. I hate how it sounds in his grumbling voice. I hate how it calls to that awful, needy thing inside me. I hate how it makes me shift my hips, pressing my thighs together. I hate that I can feel the wetness dripping between them.

"I-I'm sorry," I whine.

His hand slams down on me again, this time harder. My jaw clenches so hard that I can feel my teeth scraping together. My mind staggers, cluttered and confused. The tiny, frightened voice inside my head begins screaming, *I said what he wanted! I said I was sorry. Why hasn't he stopped?*

The thunderous strikes continue, quick and constant. I squirm against his grasp. The soil is cold against my hands as I dig my fingers into the ground. My arms tremble, scarcely able to hold up my own weight as I try to pull away from his body. Chunks of dirt and leaves fly into the air as I try to heave myself forward. I claw and dig, but I can't get away.

The tension in my muscles makes my entire body shake. I'm certain my knees would have given out long ago if he weren't holding me against him. Another stinging lash whips against my skin and I can't take it anymore.

Suddenly, words tumble from my lips, but they aren't mine. They can't be mine because I wouldn't say those words. They can't be mine because I wouldn't give in. The heated, throaty voice isn't mine when it croaks, "I'm sorry, master."

I close my eyes and bury my head in my hands, waiting for his next strike. It takes a moment for me to realize that the sound of his palm connecting with my ass has ceased to echo through the forest. The next touch I feel is gentle; his hand rubs soft circles over my cheeks until the molten burn dulls into a heated ache.

"That's my good girl," he coos against the shell of my ear.

The hand that's been holding me up slithers up my stomach. The threads of my dress scream in protest as he tears it open down my sternum. I shiver when the cold air hits my chest, but the sudden heat of his palm against my breast makes my breath catch. His thumb traces slowly around my nipple, and I tell myself that it's just the cold making it stiffen into a hard bud. I struggle to keep my back straight as he rolls it between his fingers. When he pinches my nipples, I fail, arching my back and forcing my breast further into his hand.

He continues his teasing exploration of my breasts, rubbing and pinching until I'm writhing in his lap, unsure if I'm trying to pull away from him or get closer. When I feel the finger of his other hand trace a line up my slit, my eyes rocket open. Like a bucket of cold water has been dumped on me, my mind sharpens with a sudden sense of clarity.

This is insane. *He* is insane. And if I let him touch me, if I enjoy it, then I'm insane, too. I push my hands out to the side and shove at him. This time, I know for sure that I'm trying to push him away. My hands meet the hard muscle of his stomach. I press my fists into him, but I may as well be pushing a boulder because he doesn't move an inch. He holds my body tightly and runs his finger up and down my slit slowly.

My face heats in embarrassment when I feel the wetness spreading down my thighs. Without my permission, my body responds to his touch. I bite back a moan when his finger brushes against my clit. He circles it with his finger and flicks the sensitive bud until I cry out.

"That's it, precious," he purrs, "I want to hear my little bird sing."

I choke out a needy groan as two fingers enter me. He scissors them inside me, stretching me. His hands are already huge, but when he opens his fingers inside me, the feeling of fullness makes me gasp. My hips begin to move of their own accord, grinding into his hand. My pussy clenches around his fingers, wordlessly begging him for more. He hooks his fingers inside me, rubbing them against the spot that makes my eyes roll back. I rock my hips forward until his palm is pressed against my clit. Grinding into him, I chase my release.

My core tightens. Hot lava boils in my stomach as the pressure inside me builds. It threatens to boil over, to consume me entirely, and I'll let it. My inner walls clamp down as the first ripple of my orgasm begins to tear through me. Without warning, he yanks his fingers out of me and lays a stinging slap on my pussy. I scream in pain and frustration.

"Did you think I was going to let you come without my permission?" He clicks his tongue like he's scolding a child. "And after you've been so disobedient?"

The world tips as I'm swiftly pulled to my feet. When my legs refuse to hold me, I crash into his chest. My body sinks into him, seeking warmth and steadiness. I tell my arms to push him away, my legs to step back, but they don't move and he doesn't shove me away.

He must be angry, though. And if he's angry, I need to make myself move away from him. Hesitantly, I lift my chin. I tilt my head upward until I see his face. I tense immediately, expecting to find him glowering down at me. Only he isn't. In fact, he doesn't look angry at all. He's smiling.

For a moment, I can't seem to do anything other than stare at him and wonder if his smile is real. His eyes seem brighter, as if the ice in his irises has thawed into a sparkling, blue lake. Did I notice that little dimple in his cheek before? I'm sure I would have remembered that.

In the dim light of the forest, his face is more alluring than it should be. The shadows that spread across his face seem to make its hard planes deeper and yet somehow softer. It's as if the night knows him, like it belongs to him.

The sound of masculine approval that resonates in his throat jolts me out of my stupor. How long have I been staring?

Eager to fill the tense silence, my mouth moves, forming blundered words and syllables. "I-I…uh…"

Before I can make a coherent sentence, his mouth crashes into mine. His kiss is hard and unforgiving. It's desperate and demanding. His lips move against mine. His teeth nip at my lower lip until I moan into his mouth. His tongue parts my lips and he tastes me. I grip his shirt in my fingers to steady myself, but I can't seem to force my body to step away. I'm not sure if I even want to. He kisses me like no man ever has before. He kisses me like he needs me.

When he pulls his mouth away from mine, I'm breathless. My lip quivers and a shiver runs through my body. I open my mouth to speak, but before any sound can escape, his hand is over my mouth. A sticky sweet smell fills my nose. It envelopes my nose until I can taste it on my tongue. The trees around me begin to sway, their images warping into a hazy puddle. My vision tunnels. The edges of my view become fuzzy and dark.

Gray speaks to me as the world around me slowly melts into darkness. His voice becomes softer, further away with each word.

"I've got you, little bird. It's okay…."

Chapter Twenty-Three

The yellow-tinted glass surrounding the light over Shawn's kitchen table casts the room in a muted, amber glow. It morphs the deep blue tiles and countertops into a dull aqua. Blue cabinets stand out against foggy gray walls like storm clouds shadowed over a blue lagoon.

Shawn slouches in his chair, his willowy frame hunched over the table. He shoves a hand into his dishwater blonde hair, yanking it away from his eyes. As he looks up at me, his lazy grin flattens into a thin-lipped frown.

"What do you have for me?" I ask.

He stares mutely across the table, his gaze unsteady, flitting between my face and hands. He narrows his eyes, wrinkling his forehead with concern. His fingers twitch around an energy drink can, tapping out an anxious rhythm against the metal.

"You have dirt under your fingernails." The words rush out of him so quickly that I'm not sure he meant to say it aloud. He pushes a heavy breath out from between his pursed lips. "You have dirt under your fingernails like you just dug a grave, but I *know* you didn't have a job planned for tonight."

I lift my hand above my face, letting the lamp light highlight the grit and mud caked around my cuticles. "So it would seem," I state dryly.

He's seen me in plenty worse states, but normally, I would have showered before knocking on his door. Tonight, I couldn't bring myself to wash off the smell of her that clings to my clothes. A grin teases at the corners of my mouth as I breathe in her scent. I might consider never washing them again.

"Shit," Shawn exclaims. "This is about that woman, isn't it? The one you had me make a file on. What was her name? Ava Moore?"

I glower at him, hating the sound of her name in his mouth.

His eyes go round and his pupils expand into black marbles floating in his eyes. "Shit, man. Did you kill her? Oh, God, this is so fucked up! Did she even do anything to you? Did you just murder an innocent woman?!"

Shawn rubs his palms against his eyes before dragging them down his face. Panic grips him, making his rapid breaths wheeze out of him like a leaking balloon.

I roll my eyes. For someone in this line of work, Shawn has surprisingly not let go of his morals. In his mind, I should be some kind of Robinhood, only doling out punishment to the wicked. But I'm not a hero, nor will I ever be one.

"She's alive," I say.

He looses a heavy sigh. "Okay, good. She's alive." He sucks in a sharp breath before continuing, "Uhh…where is she? Oh, Christ, is she tied up in your basement or something? Did you kidnap her?!"

"She's alive and well right where I left her, sleeping in her own bed."

Shawn's head tilts until his ear is practically resting on his shoulder. "Where you *left her*?"

A smile creeps across my face and I nod. Like the remnants of an electric shock, my hands still tingle from being against her skin. The warmth of her lingers on my fingertips. I hated to leave her, but I can't ignore my work, at least not yet.

I've never considered retirement before, but now I wonder. Perhaps when she gives herself to me completely, we'll leave the city and find a quiet place just for the two of us. Money is no obstacle; I have more than we'll ever need. I'll take her anywhere she wants to go.

"Wait a second," Shawn screeches, his voice jumping two octaves. "Are you saying that you're like…*together*? Meaning she actually *likes you*?"

I chuckle. "Not yet, but she will."

Someday she'll realize that everything I do is for her. She'll see that everything about me that scares her is nothing more than exactly what she desires, but won't admit to. On that day, she won't just like me, she'll love me. Her heart and soul will be mine.

I close my eyes, remembering the relief I saw in her when she finally relinquished control to me. When she acknowledged me as her master, I watched some of the tension ease out of her shoulders. Her fingers loosened their death grip on the dirt and her breathing quieted. She doesn't recognize the significance of it all yet, but she will.

She's been taking care of herself for a long time, relying only on herself for all of her needs. I won't let that continue. I'll give her everything she needs and more. I'd burn the world for her if she asked me to.

My eyelids drift open to find Shawn staring at me with his mouth agape and concern written across his face.

"She will?" he questions. "As in you're going to…what? Force her to like you?" As if his brain is working faster than his mouth, he grumbles out a string of half-formed words before he shoves out a long sigh. "It doesn't work that way, dude."

"You're wearing on my patience," I bark. "Tell me about the job."

He straightens in his chair, schooling his features into a mask of relative calm, which for Shawn, means he still looks a bit like a deer in headlights. He wrenches open his laptop with shaking fingers.

"Right, of course," he says while rapidly tapping against the keyboard. "The wicked witch of the West has a job for you."

"Bianca?"

Shawn makes an affirming grunt and bobs his head.

I pull my head back in surprise. For months, Bianca has been insistent about contacting me directly. Often demanding in person meetings so she can proposition me, convinced that I'd willingly become her personal assassin and plaything. I shake my head, dispelling the disgusting thought of her hands on me. I'd rather walk over hot coals than let another woman touch me. I'm Ava's—I have been since the moment I saw her. And no matter how much she tries to deny it, she's mine.

He spins the laptop around to face me. On the screen is a photo of a middle aged man unloading groceries from the trunk of a mid-sized, blue sedan. He stands in front of a small but well-maintained yellow house holding a paper bag labeled *Munson's Grocery*. His light but slightly yellowed skin glistens with a thin layer of sweat. It coats his brow beneath short-cropped, salt and pepper hair.

The picture looks like it was taken from across the street, likely from a car or surveillance van.

"Who's that?" I ask.

"Michael Crawford. He was a pretty low-level guy in Bianca's organization before he stashed some of her money and high-tailed it out of the city. Her people found him a few months later. He's staying in a house about two hours north of here in Wilmington."

"He must have stolen a lot for her to devote the resources to finding him for months," I surmise. "You dug into the information you got to confirm everything?"

Shawn nods. "Yeah, everything checks out."

"Send me the file. I'll take care of it tomorrow."

As I walk toward the door, Shawn mutters softly to himself, "And don't hurt that girl."

An annoyed sound snorts out of my nose and I close the door with enough force to make something rattle on the other side. I would never hurt her. I shake off my irritation and step out onto the street. The wind whips around me, blasting frigid air into my face.

I pull my jacket up to my chin, releasing some of the sweet scent of Ava's hair that clings to it. As I walk back to my car, my mind wanders. It tumbles over thoughts I've never had about any woman before her.

Is she warm enough in her bed? Is she safe? Is she dreaming about me?

Chapter Twenty-Four

I've barely peeled my eyes open before the throbbing pain in my temples forces them closed again. I groan and throw my hand over my eyes, trying to block out the morning light that streams through my bedroom window. I feel like my head has been clamped in a vise, crushed into some awful, tiny shape that no longer resembles a human skull.

My yawn turns into a grimace when I taste the chemical tang in my parched mouth. My throat feels constricted and dry, like it's full of sand. I shake my head, attempting to clear the fog that's permeated through my brain.

What the hell happened last night? I went on a date, didn't I? I can't remember what happened. I can't even remember how I got home. Did I get so drunk that I can't recall the details? Was I roofied or something?

Panic begins to tickle at my nerve endings, making the hairs on the back of my neck stand on end. My breathing becomes ragged, sawing in and out of me. It feels like an unnatural action that I need to think about in order to perform. I gulp down air, desperate to clear the fog in my mind.

It hits me all of a sudden. It hits me like a ton of bricks crashing through a window. The glass crackles and breaks so quickly that I barely notice the change before it shatters. And when it shatters, the memories flood in.

I remember it all. His presence, large and ominous, looming over me. The despondent, rejected look on my date's face. Strong arms around me. Running through streets and alleys and forest. The cold air whipping at my face and freezing my lungs. Hiding in the darkness. His body pressed against me. The scent of him, like syrupy vanilla and leather wrapped around my body. His lips pressed against mine. His hands expertly winding me up into a tightly coiled, desperate mess. The way I crumbled in the face of his commands.

"Nope, nope, nope," I chant. "Not thinking about this, definitely not thinking about this."

I feel the heat spreading across my face while I try desperately to think of anything else. My fingers clench around my bed sheets until my knuckles turn pasty and my breathing slows. As I drag the blankets down my legs, my muscles practically scream in protest. Everything feels too tight, too constricting, like I'm covered in layers of thick cotton. It isn't until I look down at my legs that I realize why.

Practically every inch of my skin, from the tips of my toes to my knees, is covered in gauzy cotton bandages. I shove my fingernail under a piece of medical tape affixed to my knee and peel away the dressings. My legs, which I would have expected to be caked in a layer of mud, are clean, save for the cuts and scrapes spreading across my skin. Even those are clean and covered with a glossy layer of what smells like antiseptic ointment.

I run my fingers through my hair, which, while slightly damp, is similarly free from leaves and dirt. I ignore the way my stomach somersaults. I also ignore the warm feeling in my chest when I notice that I'm no longer wearing a dirty dress, but a clean t-shirt.

My stalker, *Gray*, as I now know his name is, took care of me. After everything, he took care of me like I'm something that matters. Like I'm something precious. My thighs clench at the memory of his deep, baritone voice whispering *precious*.

My feet land clumsily beside my bed as I scramble out of it. I will the butterflies in my belly to stay behind, wrapped up tightly in a cocoon of sheets and comforters, never to be seen or heard from again.

Desperate for the kind of clarity that can only be achieved with coffee, I fumble my way to the kitchen on aching legs and sore feet. The bubbling of my coffee maker hits my ears and I send up a small thanks to the universe for the miracle that is timed appliances.

A small sense of relief settles in my chest at the normalcy of the moment. The coffee drip, drip, drips into the pot. The warm, earthy scent wafts through the room. The refrigerator hums softly, keeping my creamer chilled and ready. When I pull open the refrigerator door, my heart drops to my feet.

My normally sparse fridge is packed, practically bursting, with food. Food that I definitely didn't buy. Stuffed in behind my coffee creamer are half a dozen bottles of different fruit juices. My usually empty produce drawer is packed with a colorful nest of oranges, apples, and pears. A full sized casserole dish takes up most of the top shelf, leaving my nearly week old chicken salad fighting for room in the back. I shove the tin foil top aside and stare down at a full sized lasagna, my favorite meal.

"Coincidence," I mutter, "everyone likes lasagna." The lackluster justification tastes bitter on my tongue, as if even it doesn't believe that this is really a coincidence.

Angry, frustrated sounds sputter out of me as I dump an obscene amount of creamer into my coffee.

Sitting at the kitchen table, I stare at the steaming caffeine in my hands. The brown liquid and cream whirl around each other until they look like the mud that cakes the underside of my car in springtime. My stomach roils. *Holy crap, my car! I drove it into the city last night. I have to get it. Can I even get it? Did I even bring my purse home? My car keys?*

Coffee sloshes across the floor as I scramble for the door. My hand lands on the knob with enough force to send a zing of pain up my arm. I wrench the door open and fly into the porch. My car sits in the driveway, parked in its usual spot, as if nothing ever happened. My head swivels, searching for something, anything out of place. But there's nothing. Even as I step back inside, there's nothing. My keys and purse are laid out on the little table by the door, sitting atop a small heap of junk mail.

A mixture of emotions churns in my belly, turning my coffee into a lead weight that moves and sloshes inside me. I breathe through the feeling, wondering if it's nausea or those incessant butterflies that don't belong anywhere near me.

As I thumb through the memories of every man I've ever known, I realize that no man has ever truly done anything kind for me. I've had dates and even a few boyfriends over the years, but none who would have lowered themselves to take care of me—to wash me, dress my wounds, and feed me. Granted, none of them have stalked me, drugged me, or killed for me, but that's something else entirely.

Could this all be part of some twisted show of devotion? Some kind of psychotic love? The thought makes my heart skip. It thumps erratically in my chest.

My bare feet smack against the linoleum as I pace the length of the kitchen, inwardly chastising myself for even considering something so crazy. *It's not love,* the logical part of my brain screams. *He doesn't love you. He can't love you. No one loves you, not like that, at least. He's insane, he's dangerous, and you cannot develop feelings for him. You can't justify his insanity just because he leaves food for you.*

As if summoned by the thought, that stupid, needy part of my brain cries, *but he isn't dangerous to you. He wants to take care of you. It feels so good for someone to take care of you.*

After guzzling several mugs of coffee, I do the only thing that I can think of to keep my mind off of him—I throw myself head first into my work. I escape into mystical worlds where nothing is as complicated as my life has become.

A thumping beat blares from my phone, suddenly ripping me out of a fairytale romance and dropping me unceremoniously back into my office chair. When I lift my eyes away from the pages of the beautiful story, my office is glowing orange with the dim light of the evening. I slurp a mouthful of coffee, which went cold hours ago, before picking up the phone.

"Oh my God, Ava!" Emily shouts before I've even opened my mouth.

I cough, expelling the sudden tightness in my throat. "Uhh, hi, Em."

"Girl, do not just '*hi, Em*' me! You have secrets you need to spill right away."

"Oh, I…umm…well," I stutter through single-syllable words and sounds as my brain desperately tries to figure out some kind of response.

Emily's sigh drifts through the speaker. "Look, I'm not mad at you, honey…but Max told me about your *interrupted* date."

My heart practically falls out of my chest and lands on the floor. "Oh. He told you about that, did he?"

She huffs out an exasperated sigh. "Ava, why didn't you just tell me you were seeing someone?"

"Well, I'm not. Not really. We're not together or anything. It's not a thing," I sputter, simultaneously explaining and avoiding the truth of the situation.

"Look, I know that you're private about that kind of stuff, and with everything you've been through, I get it. But from the way Max described it, it sounds like you're hot and heavy with a badass super hottie."

"We're not hot…or heavy," I deny. "We're just—"

"Don't try to deny it," she interrupts. "He said you *swooned*." She drags the word out like she's singing a song.

My face heats. No matter how much I want to voice them, I smash my lips together to prevent any further denials from spewing from my lips. I want to pretend that Gray's dominating presence doesn't make me melt. I want to pretend that his touch doesn't set my nerves on fire, but I can't.

When I don't respond, she continues. "This is a good thing, Ava! I'm happy for you. I just wish you would have told me."

"Oh, well, thanks for that," I say, trying to imitate the happiness in her voice. "And I'm sorry I didn't tell you. I just…didn't know what to say. It's new and we aren't official or anything."

A muffled voice yells something I can't understand before Emily continues, "Look, I have to get back to work, but I just want you to know that I'm really glad you're seeing someone. Truly, I'm happy that you've found something other than your dull routine of books and work. Please, give this one a chance, babe."

"Thanks, Em. I'll…uhh…try, okay?"

"That's the spirit! I've got to run. Love you lots!"

My phone drops to the desk with a clunk. Letting my arms drop by my sides, I sink down into my chair. I stare holes into the ceiling while Emily's words replay in my mind.

Something other than my dull routine? What's wrong with my dull routine? I know my life isn't exciting, but it's average. It's safe. At least it *was* safe before he made an appearance. He stomped through my quiet life and crushed every semblance of control I had over it.

Control. That's what he wants me to give him. Haven't I had enough men try to control my life?

My father's face flashes through my mind, drunk and angry. He controlled me through pain and fear. Maybe he still does. Who would I have become without him? Would I have been like Emily— fearless and adventurous? What could I have been if I wasn't broken?

I scrub my hands over my face and shove the images of my father aside. I let go of a shaky breath and remind myself that he hasn't spoken to me in years.

"You're safe," I breathe.

That nagging, horny creature that lives somewhere behind my eyeballs perks up and murmurs, *Gray will keep you safe.*

A laugh snorts out through my nose. Would shacking up with the big, bad wolf make Red Riding Hood safe? That's what Gray is; he's the wolf. He's the bad guy.

What the Hell does it make me if some part of me wants him?

Chapter Twenty-Five

The moon's reflection glimmers in the dark water of shallow puddles along the suburban streets of Wilmington. Neatly trimmed shrubs outline tidy square lots with short-cropped lawns and tidy, square houses all painted the same color. Beige. It's all so fucking beige.

Lawns glisten in the aftermath of an autumn rain. I roll my window down, seeking the calming scent of damp foliage. The air that floats into my car is stale and cool. Here, even the earthy petrichor is subdued. Just as they fall, leaves are raked, neatly packed into paper bags, and hauled away. The beige zombies are so offended by nature that they remove it, hiding it from view.

As unbidden images of my own childhood flood my mind, my fingers clench against the steering wheel until my knuckles burn. I recall the quiet calmness of wealthy neighborhoods and polite block parties. It was too late before I realized that behind the closed doors, beige lives often turn black and blue. Though I suppose in my father's case, he turned our lives red.

I slam my hands against the steering wheel, wishing I could crush the images of him out of my head. When a man buys property in the beige jungle, do his balls just wither and fall off? Do they look out around him at the nude-toned nothingness, shrink up into his body, and shrivel up? Or does he need to take a few tennis lessons first?

I switch off my headlights just as my car crawls past the tidy, yellow box at the corner of Maple Road. Dim, amber light falls from the first floor windows, obscured by orange, floral curtains. It paints the edges of the orderly shrubs and nondescript front steps in a faded, amber light. In the quiet dark, the only sound is the mechanical hum of my tires gliding over the pavement. No birds sing. No squirrels skitter. No bats squeak. Even the bugs seem to have abandoned the treeless, beige landscape.

A town like this has its benefits to a man like me. There are no streetlights, no one out late on the streets, and almost no security. I relish in the ease of a job like this as I shift my car into park on the street behind the house. I should think about taking more quick and dirty jobs like this. I could get in, get it done, and be home before Ava slides into her bed. Soon enough, it'll be my bed she crawls into every night.

When my sweet little bird accepts that she belongs to me, when she chirps happily from her golden cage, I'll find a new place for us. I scoff as my eyes pan around the Homeowners Association's wet dream of identical homes. It won't be a place like this. It'll be a quiet place just for us. I'll build her a swing on our porch so I can watch her eyes sparkle as she sips her morning coffee and looks out at the forest. As I picture her wrapped up in her bathrobe, her hair catching in the wind, the tension begins to bleed out of my muscles. A sense of calm washes over me. My mouth pulls into a smile as I pick the lock on the kitchen door.

The door clicks open and I step into a dark kitchen. Pausing just inside the room, I scan my surroundings. No movement catches my eye, and the only sound is the mumbling of a nearby TV. Light from the living room spills across the tile floor, leaving me a few feet of lingering darkness before I meet my target.

Stifling a chuckle, I step forward and pull the serrated hunting knife from its holster at my side. The poor fucker is so woefully unprepared for my arrival, it's laughable. You'd think someone who's on the run from the worst kind of people would have planned it a little better. Surely as someone formerly within her organization would know the resources Bianca has at her fingertips. But that's not my problem.

"Mikey," I announce joyfully, "I'm here to send you to meet your maker. Are you ready for…"

As my boot meets the carpeted floor of the living room, the words turn to ash on my tongue. The knife in my hand suddenly has all the showmanship of a limp dick.

Nestled into the couch, snug as a bug in a fucking rug, is Micheal, the thief. His mouth opens into a surprised 'O', releasing a piece of popcorn that drops down into the bowl resting on this pot belly. He lets out a shriek and tosses the bowl to the floor. Fluffy bits of popcorn shuffle and skitter along the floor. A few pieces tumble under the brown, leather couch, which I now realize is sagging… under the weight of the four huge bodyguards sitting around my target.

"Fuck," the word flops out of me, sounding like defeat and deflation, just before a hard body collides with me, sending us both crashing to the floor. The coarse fabric of his jacket scratches against my chin, swiftly followed by his shoulder cracking against my jaw. Pain zings up my face and explodes like a firework behind my temple.

I tuck my knees up against my stomach and push. The goon above me grunts as they collide with his gut. His face scrunches up in pain, but his eyes glint with determination. With just enough space between us to make things interesting, I make my move. I reach one arm behind my back for the knife while sending the other careening into his face.

I hear the wet crack of his nose shattering as my fist makes impact. The broken shards slide and squelch beneath his skin like a horrific Jell-O salad. He leans back, grabbing his face, and lets out a howl of pain. I whip the knife out from behind me and jam it into his neck. He gurgles and sputters when I pull it out. I try to lean away from the stream of blood that dribbles from his mouth, but it soaks through my shirt, painting me red and sticky.

My eyes catch movement from behind Thing One's ear. Thing Two is headed directly toward me in a blur of brown hair and dark clothing. He belts out a grunting war cry as he barrels toward me. My muscles twitch, desperate to take action. *Hold,* I whisper inside myself, *he's not close enough yet.* When his shins are within arm's reach, I shove my legs outward with all my strength, catapulting Thing One's corpse into his arms. They topple to the floor with an audible thud.

I press my hands into the carpet and shove myself up to stand. As I shake out the residual ache in my jaw, I take in the scene around me. Thing Two is momentarily trapped under the body of his buddy. My target crouches behind another guard. He's smaller and younger than the first. His toned arms are widespread, shielding the thief beneath him. His stance tells me that he won't leave his guardee's side unless absolutely necessary. I'll take him on last.

Across the room, the shadow of an enormous man blocks out the light from the television on the wall. The word *goon* describes him perfectly. Considerable muscles bulge from his arms and legs, threatening to bust through his uniform-like tactical clothing. Even with my substantial height, the gargantuan being has at least four inches and a hundred pounds on me. Even his jaw appears muscled; the hard lines of his face seem to protest as his mouth spreads into a grin. I know that look, the glint in his eyes. He'd enjoy killing me. Unfortunately for him, I feel the same.

I widen my stance, anchoring myself in place. If the toothy smile he flashes me is anything to go by, he must think I'm readying myself to a fight. My own lips pull into a smirk as I loosen my grip on the handle of my knife. My arm whips forward, sending the blade sailing through the air. His eyes go wide as it sinks into the skin just below his Adam's apple. His mouth opens and closes like a fish gasping for air, just before he crashes to his knees in a sputtering, leaking mess.

Thing Two groans behind me as he unceremoniously shoves his counterpart's corpse off of him. It rolls, bumping the edge of a gaudy, golden-edged coffee table. The movement jostles the sculpture atop it, the visage of the virgin Mary who stares at the increasingly morbid scene around her with sad, half-lidded eyes. I grab the heavy bust, knowing that without my knife, she's my best weapon. Pray for us sinners and all that, right?

Thing Two lumbers toward me, his footfalls crashing angrily beneath him. He shoves a bloody hand through his mousey, brown hair, pulling it away from his sweat-drenched face before lunging for me. With the virgin in my hand, I shove the other against his chest to stop his movement. He claws at me, his hands scrambling for purchase against my blood-soaked jacket. Sudden, white-hot pain explodes in my nerve endings as his knee smashes into my thigh. My leg buckles and I stumble back a step, giving him just enough room to send his fist into my cheek.

My vision blurs as the throbbing ache spreads through my face, and I roar in pain. My fingers tighten around the heavy statue in my hand as I hoist it over my head. The crack echoes through the room when it slams into the guard's skull. The weight of it sends him careening into the floor. I smash the virgin against his head until the sound of cracking bone morphs into a wet squelching.

The statue falls from my hand and thumps against the carpet. Slowly, I turn until I face my final foe. As I step toward him, he straightens his back and raises his chin with a confidence that isn't reflected in his eyes. His face is pulled tight like he's sucked his cheeks in. As I look at his face, something akin to sympathy burns in my chest. He's so young, barely into his twenties. His glistening eyes and shaking hands tell me that he's not a killer; not yet, anyway. Maybe it's good that he dies tonight, so that he'll never end up one. Maybe it's a kindness that I spare him from becoming a monster like me.

His spine straightens like a steel rod as I close the distance between us, using his small body like a shield in front of a whimpering, teary-eyed Michael. Though, his build makes him a very ineffective one. His fists ball at his sides, but it doesn't stop them from shaking.

His quivering lips open once, then twice. He swallows hard before speaking, "Who sent you?"

I look down at the pathetic mass huddled by his feet, whose eyes seem to triple in size when they meet mine. "The bitch you stole from."

The two exchange looks with furrowed brows, but neither utter a word. The young guard pinches his eyes shut and sighs before reaching for the gun in the back of his jeans. His hands squeeze around it with a grip that turns his knuckles white. The barrel shakes as he raises it toward me with quivering hands.

At the realization that the kid had a gun the entire time, my eyes roll back into my head so far that I can almost see my own brain. The barrel hovers just inches in front of my forehead. With one twitch, one squeeze of his finger, I'd be dead. Staring into his wide eyes, I raise my eyebrows, daring him to shoot. He squeezes his eyes closed and his face contorts, scrunching up in a pained expression.

"I do not have time for this shit," I mumble on a long breath.

In a swift motion, I snatch the kid's wrist in my hand and jerk it to the side. His grip on the gun slackens and it drops directly into my own hand. In a quiet room full of the dead, his gasp is loud. It bounces off the walls, making it seem like they themselves are breathing one final breath. Once, then twice, the gun goes off with a deafening roar. I pinch my mouth and eyes shut as a hot spray of blood douses my face.

My eyes pan around the room where five bodies now lay sprawled out over the quickly dampening carpet. Limbs are splayed. Heads are caved in and leaking brain matter. It's disgusting, honestly. The shaggy, cream-colored flooring is tie-dyed with various shades of red and brown. My shirt is similarly patterned with warm, soggy, red splatter. I rub my hands over my face, wiping away as much of the blood as I can before transferring it to the thighs of my jeans.

A frustrated sound rumbles in my chest as I stare at the scene around me, realizing that the amount of cleaning I need to do far surpasses what I had expected. The gunshots will likely have alerted the neighbors, so there's no time to take this slow. The only method left is full-scale destruction.

The Songbird's Shadow

My car rumbles. Its body rocks from side to side as the sounds of an explosion ring out through the quiet streets of Wilmington. I watch from my rearview mirror as the little yellow house is engulfed in flames. Maybe a little bit of red will color their beige existence. But how else was I to get rid of the evidence other than a manufactured gas leak? It'll look like an unfortunate accident. The citizens of the single-colored town will cry, impressing each other with their faux grief. Will they give out a prize to those to bawl the hardest? Will they award a metal to those who fall to their knees in anguish? They'll call it a terrible tragedy where a man and his friends perished in a horrible way. But it'll all be bullshit.

The knotted anger squeezing my chest calms at the sight of embers shooting skyward above the house. The ash flutters back down to the ground like snowflakes. Somewhere deep inside of me, the child I used to be smiles. *Let their cream-colored lives burn*, he seems to say, *the way they let us burn.*

"Call Shawn," I yell to the interior of my car.

I suppress a chuckle when my ever-diligent assistance picks up after the first ring.

"Hey, did you—"

I cut him off before he finishes. "Something was off about this one."

His voice lifts an octave. "What do you mean, *'something was off'*?"

"The guy had hired protection; four bodyguards, to be exact. Shit was such a mess that I had to blow the house up."

"Crap," he drags the word out like he's savoring it. "What kind of a low-level thief thinks to hire protection?"

"I don't know, Shawn," I hiss through gritted teeth. "Just figure out what the fuck happened here."

I smash my knuckles into the touchscreen, abruptly ending the call. I've encountered a lot of thieves in my career, but rarely ever smart ones. There's a nagging feeling inside me. It tightens my lungs and wraps my stomach in knots. There's more to this story than we know. We're missing something, and in this line of work, that can be a death sentence.

As I drive, my mind wanders, or maybe it goes nowhere. I'm not really sure. Half-formed inklings seem to materialize in my head and quickly evaporate into nothing. None solid enough to leave an imprint. I just drive. I drive until the rain-soaked pavement of suburban streets evolves into the dark asphalt of busy highways. I drive until the lit roads darken and the asphalt is replaced by gravel paths. I drive until the reflection of my headlights glint off of a familiar metal mailbox on a slanted post. I drive until I find myself parked, staring at patchy wooden siding and a poorly repaired porch.

I press my fingers to the temples, massaging away the dull ache behind them. How did I end up here, in front of her house? Is already she so ingrained in my mind that I would find myself here instead of at my own home? *Home.* The word comes to me unbidden. It screams inside of me. It glides through my veins like water. It douses the flames of violence burning inside them. *She is home.*

Chapter Twenty-Six

The clock in my living room chimes, filling the room with the baritone rumbling of metal keys clashing in a short melody. Years ago, when Mom was still alive, it sounded light and pretty. Age hasn't been kind to the old clock, changing its melodic tune to something clunky like a broken music box. But that seems fitting for the state of my life right now. I glance up at its weathered face. It's after eleven o'clock. I really should get some sleep, but I can't. I'm not ready to dream about the shadow that lingers above my bed when I close my eyes. I'm not ready to dream about *him*.

I pull the blanket tighter around my shoulders and curl my legs up onto the couch before my eyes drift back to the book in my hand. Some of my tension melts away as I run my fingers along its stiff edges. Then, I let it take me away. I let the words drag my consciousness somewhere else. It flits away from my couch, away from my home, away from my world, until it hovers over a vast, dark ocean.

Mary Landry stood on the deck of the most feared vessel in the Pacific, the Ocean's Curse. She wrapped her fingers around the chipped railing, pressing her chest to the wood as she stared down at the blackness of the sea. If she could only reach the pinnace, she could be free.

She pulled a tattered shawl over her shoulders as a cold wind whipped through the night, spraying salty droplets over the bow. Her body trembled when the frigid water began to seep into her nightdress, soaking her bodice. She knew there was no going back now. Even if it meant her death, she had to find a way to escape. A low groan of creaking wood sounded from behind her. She whipped her body around so quickly that she scarcely kept her footing on the slippery flooring. She squinted her eyes against the darkness as a figure stepped closer. She saw his eyes first. They were bright, as if illuminated by firelight. His eyes were as blue as the sea itself, and seemed deep enough to hold all of its secrets.

She held her breath as he approached, a man whose past was so dark that it gave the ship its name. A man who sparked fear into the hearts of all who had the misfortune of meeting him. The captain of the Ocean's Curse, Morgan Blackwater.

He stepped closer, until his chest was mere inches from her own. The scent of the ocean seemed to become stronger in his presence. The soft, gray-light moonlight cast shadows over his face, highlighting the hard line of his stubbled jaw. For a moment, Mary wondered how anything so deadly could be so beautiful.

When he spoke, his voice was deep and raspy. It rumbled like waves crashing to shore. "You're not where I left you."

As he inched closer, Mary pressed her back into the railing until she felt slivers of old wood bite into her skin.

"Locked up in a dark hole?" Despite all the vitriol she pumped into the words, her voice still cracked with fear. "I'm not a woman to be caged, pirate. You cannot keep me prisoner!"

He reached forward, his calloused palm grazing her cheek. His eyes seemed to grow darker, his gaze permeating her very soul. Her legs trembled as a shiver wracked her body.

"Oh, princess," he dragged out the title as if he was tasting it on his tongue. "Do you truly still wish to pretend you're my prisoner?

"I am! You've taken me hostage with the hope that you can trade me for gold and—"

"No!" His hands slammed down on the railing, caging her between his arms. "You are my prize. You are my gold."

I hear his words as if they're being spoken into my own ears. I feel their power, the emotion swimming through them. My stomach tightens and a rush of warmth floods my cheeks.

Mary flinched when his hand found its way to her hip. She could feel his warmth through the thin cotton of her nightdress, reminding her that she was practically naked in front of this man. She looked down at his hand and traced the tattoos on it with her eyes.

My breath quivers as I exhale heavily, letting my hand slip beneath my nightgown. My fingers snake a path from my knee up to my pussy. My skin heats as my fingers dance over my clit. I imagine Morgan Blackwater's hands on me as I stand on the bow of the *Ocean's Curse*. His icy, blue eyes bore into me. His tattooed hands squeeze my waist.

Then, almost as quickly as this flood or arousal began, it cools. I skim back over the pages I've just read before tossing the book to the floor. Morgan Blackwater doesn't have tattoos. His eyes are brown. I wasn't picturing him at all. I was picturing Gray, his eyes, his hands. I was picturing my stalker. What does that say about me?

"Shit," I exclaim, scrubbing my palms over my reddened face. Even in my own fantasies, I can't get away from him. My mind glosses over the details of what's written and replaces it with him. I shake my head, hoping it will dispel the thoughts of him from it.

Click, click, click.

My eyes rocket to the front door where the metallic clinks of lock tumblers moving have morphed into deafening booms. My breath comes out in ragged pants. My limbs stiffen and twitch. My fingers suddenly feel cold.

Click, click, click.

No one else has a key to my house. I try to think about what could be happening, but I can't hear myself over the thundering of my heartbeat. It explodes in my ears. Without permission from my brain, my body tumbles from the couch. My knees crash painfully into the floor, shocking me back to my senses. I crawl behind the arm of the couch. Balancing on the balls of my feet, I keep my legs poised to run.

The door squeaks open and clicks shut. I peek around the corner of the couch and my eyes widen. As if my own thoughts had caused him to appear, Gray stands in my living room. He pushes his leather jacket off of his broad shoulders and hangs it on the coat hook by the door. His hands reach into the pockets of his jeans, pulling out car keys and loose change, which he places on a small side table.

I loosen my jaw to stop the ache that's building in my temples. This asshole is making himself at home. He's making himself at home, in my *goddamned house*. My foot totters beneath me, sending my palms crashing to the floor with a thunk.

I hold my breath as Gray's head swivels in my direction. Leaning down, he tilts his head to the side until our eyes meet. His lips tip up into a grin, but it's not the look on his face that has me suddenly gasping for air. The lamplight glints off of something red along his hairline and on the sides of his neck. Blood. There's blood on him.

My thoughts become staggered, misshapen things. It whips through and tumbles over the possibilities. Is this it? Is this when he hurts me? Is this when he kills me? How can I get away? Where can I go? I dutifully ignore the nagging piece of my brain that says, *stay.* It cries out, *he'll never hurt you.* I know that can't be true. Men always want to hurt me. They always have.

I stand on shaky legs. They quiver and clench, but don't move. I'm firmly rooted in place, pinned to the spot by ice-blue eyes. His eyebrows quirk upward, asking me, questioning me, daring me to do something. So I do something. I spin on my heels and run.

The ends of my nightgown flap behind me, bouncing against my heels as I run through the hallway. The flowered wallpaper blurs as I rush by. I stop fast in front of my office door, causing my bare feet to slide painfully against the wooden floor, but I don't go inside. Instead, I yank the door shut, forcing it to slam so loudly it vibrates against its frame. My feet pad softly down the hall until I reach the cellar door.

The crooked wooden door sits slightly lopsided on the old frame, reminding me of yet another project I've put aside in this house. With my eyes pinched shut, I beg the door to be silent as I pull it open. By some miracle, it obeys. It remains silent even as the latch snicks shut.

Tiptoeing down the stairs, I make a mental note to fix that door out of pure gratitude. I inhale the musty scent of dust and dampness just before my feet land on the frigid, concrete flood. My head bobs up and down, desperate to avoid the network of cobwebs that blanket the ceiling and reach their tendrils toward my hair.

My eyes pan around the dark, musky space. In hindsight, I realize this was an absolutely terrible plan. I've trapped myself in a concrete box with no doors and only tiny windows that I could never fit through. I blink away the tears forming in the corners of my eyes. Crying won't save me.

Thunk, thunk, thunk.

His footsteps beat against the floor. The wood groans overhead. It cries out, screaming the way I wish I could. I feel the scream building in my throat, becoming louder and larger. I'm afraid that soon I won't be able to hold it in any longer. I pinch my lips together, willing my voice to stay silent.

Thunk, thunk, thunk.

The sound is his footsteps inches closer and closer to the basement door. My eyes frantically bounce around the nearly bare room, searching for a place to hide. The plastic bins of Mom's old stuff won't give me enough coverage. Plus, I can't tolerate the thought of dying here with my blood painting the few precious memories I have of her.

As I crouch my body behind the rusted, old water heater, terrible thoughts rush in and threaten to drown me. Will I truly die here? Gray is a monster, a monster who came here with blood on him. Blood that I very much doubt is his own. Has he tired of me? He said his patience wasn't limitless. He told me that he wanted everything from me, but I have nothing to give.

You're nothing, girl, my father's words ghost through my ears. *You're nothing but a waste of space.*

I exhale a shaky breath, feeling the seconds tick by slowly. A soft clicking sound from the top of the stairs has my muscles clenching painfully. The stairs creak under his heavy footfalls. I pinch my eyes shut, too afraid to look up. But even behind my eyelids, I can see his shadow looming over the room. It moves and changes, becoming larger and more monstrous with each step.

His voice floats toward me, soft and cooing. "Come out, little bird. I know you're down here."

Panic rises in my throat like hot bile. I squeeze my knees into my chest, making my body as small as I can. I try to muffle the sound of my panting breath by bowing my head until my kneecaps dig into my forehead. A scream builds inside me like a pressure in my chest.

A hand lands on the back of my neck. The pressure releases, along with my scream.

"You promised you wouldn't run from me again, precious."

Chapter Twenty-Seven

My footsteps are quiet as I step towards Ava. My frightened little bird hides behind a rusted out water heater. Like everything else in this house, I'm shocked it's still functional, given its age and condition. Her shoulders shake as she sucks in frantic breaths.

At the sight of her, something inside my chest tightens. A burning sensation spreads inside my lungs, making every inhale sting. She chose to hide in a damp basement amongst the grime and spiderwebs. She chose this cold, dirty place over my arms.

She isn't ready yet to accept me, but she will be soon. She'll see that the only place she's safe is in my arms.

My fingers reach out, wrapping around the back of her neck. Her shocked scream vibrates against my palm. Some demented part of me twitches and springs to life. The sound of her fear sends my blood rocketing through my veins, pooling in my cock.

"You promised you wouldn't run from me again, precious."

I wrap my arm around her middle and pull her to her feet, pressing her trembling body into mine. Her breath whooshes out of her with a surprised squeak. It's the most adorable fucking sound, and I immediately want her to make it again.

I press my face into her neck, inhaling the sweet strawberry scent of her hair.

"Fuck," I whisper against her soft locks, "I missed you."

Her breath catches and her forehead crinkles. Her mouth opens and closes several times before she pinches her lips together. Her stunned silence has me wondering if she's not used to being told that. I'll tell her every day until she accepts that it's true.

I lay her down on the floor, watching her blue, cotton nightgown slide up her legs. Her hands fumble with the edges of her dress, pulling the fabric down over her creamy thighs. Her wide eyes stare up at me, full of fear and something else. Unspoken emotions swirl in her mossy-green eyes. I suspect they're emotions she recognizes, but refuses to name, at least not yet.

She winces as the cold, concrete floor bites at her legs. My chest clenches painfully and my lungs refuse to expand. That living part of my near-dead heart thrashes around wildly. It seethes inside of me, furious to see her lying in a cold, dirty place. *This is all for her*, I remind it. *She has to feel the sting of the cold before she can admit that she wants the warmth I can provide her.*

I lower to my knees in front of her and reach out until my palms are pressed against her hips. My fingers squeeze her soft body, appreciating the way her supple curves mold around them.

"Why do you keep running from me, little bird?"

Ava doesn't answer. She doesn't shake her head, nor does she open her mouth. She simply stares, eyes locked onto mine.

"Are you afraid of me?" My voice wavers more than I care to admit.

Of course, she's afraid. But how much? Will she be still and recede into herself? Will she be frozen in fear, dragging her conscious-ness into a faraway place to escape me? My heart thumps uncomfort-ably in my chest. I'm certain it'll stop beating altogether if she freezes in front of me. Suddenly, it hurts to breathe. If she's so petrified of the monster before her that she can't move, my lungs will combust.

I stare down at her perfection and wonder, could she be the one person who isn't terrified of me? My throat clogs with an unfamiliar emotion, one that's so far removed from my current self that I can scarcely recognize it for what it is—vulnerability. Its claws tighten around my windpipe, scratching and restricting. Looking down at her, I feel vulnerable. I fucking hate it.

I'm ripped from my thoughts the instant her foot collides with my face. Her heel cracks across my mouth, leaving lightening and fire in its wake. My hand snakes around her ankles, keeping her still beneath me. The ache in my jaw doesn't stop the smile that spreads across my face. The creature living in my heart jumps up and down like a maniac. It tosses confetti in the air, blows trumpets, and screams, *our girl didn't freeze.*

Her eyes widen into large green saucers as she watches me rip an electrical cord from the closest appliance to us. The old lamp had surely seen better days before being trapped in this basement, rusted and forgotten. Now, at least it will serve a purpose. I yank her legs up, forcing the cord beneath her hips before using it to tie her calves to her thighs. She whimpers as her legs are forced open in some kind of inverse frog pose. I loop the remaining cord around her waist, pinning her arms to her sides.

I swipe a hand across my mouth, catching a small trickle of blood from where she kicked me. "I appreciate that you feel safe enough with me to fight, but don't test me, precious."

"What? No, that's…that's not…I don't…" If her words were a staircase, she'd be tumbling down it one stair at a time, clunking her head along the way.

She wriggles her arms and legs, struggling against her binds. The sight calls to the twisted part of me that wants to stalk her, hunt her, take her. My dick hardens painfully, testing the strength of my jeans.

Ava's dress has ridden up to her stomach, revealing her naked core. My lips peel up into a smile. Did my sweet girl decide not to wear panties knowing I'd be coming to see her?

I rub my palms along her inner thighs, tracing slow lines on her skin. A moan rumbles in my chest as I knead my fingers into her soft flesh. My body angles toward her, as if the scent of her sex is a siren's song. The sweet musk wafts into the air and wraps itself around my soul, dragging me closer.

My fingers whisper along the edges of her sex, barely grazing her pink lips. Ava whimpers beneath me. Her legs twitch with a tremor that runs through her body. She sucks her bottom lip into her mouth and jams her teeth into it. My fingers continue their teasing dance, tracing softly around her pussy.

When my finger brushes against her clit, she moans behind her closed lips. That won't do; it's not enough. I need to hear her fall apart at my touch. I need to hear her scream my name. More than anything, I need her to hear her own pleasure. She's hiding from me and she's hiding from herself. I won't let her pretend anymore.

I press my palm against her sex and reach the other up to cup her chin. Her bottom lip is red and puffy from her chewing on it. I press my thumb into it until she releases it from her mouth.

"Your songs are mine, little bird. Let me hear them," I demand.

I rub my palm against her pussy, my hand spreading her arousal. With the pad of my finger, I circle her clit until she cries out and her back arches.

"That's it." I watch her cheeks redden with my praise. "You're being so good, my beautiful girl. You're fucking perfect."

I lean my head downward, closer to her core, and inhale her sweet aroma. My head swims with the intoxicating scent. The need to taste her becomes overwhelming, morphing into a living force that demands it. Her hips buck as I run my tongue up her slit.

I suck her clit into my mouth and she rewards me by moaning deep from her throat. The sounds of her pleasure demolish any remaining restraint I have. I feast on her like a starving man, lapping up her arousal before dipping my tongue inside her.

My eyes drift up to her face. Her eyes are closed, her face contorted with lust.

"Open your eyes, Ava," I growl against her wet folds.

Not only do her eyes remain closed, but she pinches them tighter, little lines forming beside them with the effort.

I slap her inner thigh with my open palm, reveling in the sound of her resulting whimper. "Look at me right now, or I'll stop."

That gets her attention. Her eyes rocket open. As she stares down at me between her thighs, her cheeks take on a redness so deep it's nearly purple.

"That's my good girl," I hum, "you're listening so well."

I reward her by swirling my tongue around her clit while slowly pushing a finger into her perfect little cunt. She wiggles, pushing her body closer to me, silently begging for more. I slide a second finger inside, feeling her stretch around me.

I play with her, watching her reactions and listening to the cues her body gives me. I rock my fingers inside her, pulling them in and out slowly at first before increasing my pace. My fingers curl, stroking a spot that makes her writhe and moan.

She makes a strangled noise in her throat and her pussy tightens around my fingers. She grinds her core against my tongue. A sense of desperation claws inside my chest. I'm desperate to watch her come undone, to know what she tastes like when she cums. But I can't give it to her, not yet.

She whines when I lift my mouth from her, her hips wiggling desperately until I replace it with my thumb. I rub soft circles around her clit. "Be a good girl and tell me what you want."

Her mouth moves, releasing stifled sounds and incoherent syllables.

My fingers still inside of her. "Use your words or you get nothing."

"Please," she begs, "please let me come."

She begs so sweetly that I almost give in. Almost. She needs to learn how to submit to me fully in order to be rewarded. She writhes, desperately struggling against the cord wrapped around her legs, trying to pull my fingers further into her.

"What's my name to you, little bird?" I ask.

She stills, her lips quivering with anxiety. I watch the struggle in her eyes, the flashes of desperation and fear. A tear trickles out of the corner of her eye, dripping down her temple and falling to the floor. She's so beautiful when she cries.

I pinch her clit between my fingers until she cries out. "My name to you, Ava, say it. Say it and I'll let you come."

"P-please," she whispers, her voice shaking with uncertainty, "let me come…master."

"There's my good girl," I praise.

I pump my fingers in and out with vigor, and increase the pressure on her clit. Her legs quake, her fight against her binds renewing as she chases her orgasm. One that I absolutely will not deny her.

I curl my fingers inside of her and pinch her clit, watching her eyes roll back. "Come for me, precious."

"Oh, fuck, fuck, fuck!" she screams, her pussy clenching around my fingers with her release. I press a third finger into her, coaxing her through orgasm. When I pull my fingers out, I watch her arousal drip from her, wishing it was my come. Though if it was, I wouldn't let it leave her body. I'd stuff it back inside of her, keeping her soaked in my scent, marking her as mine.

Soon, I remind the insistent beast raging inside my chest, *very fucking soon*.

Chapter Twenty-Eight

I shove the barbell above me, feeling the burn in my muscles. My pecs and biceps burn with the effort, but I can't stop. Pushing myself harder, I try to burn away the soft feeling of Ava's body against me and replace it with pain. If I don't, there won't be any rest for either of us. I'll break. I'll drive back to her house and drag her, kicking and screaming, back to my home. I'll keep her locked up here until her freedom is nothing more than a fleeting memory. I'll consume her.

My head swims with emotions I didn't think myself capable of. The ironclad barriers and careful concentration I've built up for so many years are crumbling around me. The fence I've erected around the shriveled, beating thing inside my chest is disintegrating. She calls to it, making it beat stronger.

She was so soft, laying in my arms asleep. Her head rested on my bicep, her breath feathering against my neck. Despite some lingering protests and weakly flailing arms, she fell asleep soon after I untied her and pulled her into my arms. I carried her to her bed and laid her down, covering her with blankets. That demanding organ in my chest seemed to settle as I stroked her hair. There was this feeling of rightness in caring for her. It calmed the storm inside me.

It was no small effort to pull myself away from her. It never is. That goddamned organ went from calm to raging, as if it demanded our closeness. As I rose from her bed, her hand wrapped around my wrist, pulling me back to her. I stood, stock-still and dumbfounded, watching her sleeping face. My mind staggered, tripping over the reasons for her hand on me. Was it just a reaction in her sleep? Did she know it was me? Has her soul recognized mine, broken and jagged as it is, before her head has caught up?

Thunk.

The barbell crashes to the ground, toppling a set of heavy weights that scatter across the floor. Clenching my fists at my sides, I ignore the mess now littering the floor of my home gym. I refuse to believe that it's a coincidence or some reaction in her sleep that made her pull me closer. I'm certain that her subconscious is aware that we fit. That our broken pieces can be made whole together.

My phone vibrates, ripping me from my thoughts. I pull it from my pocket, finding Shawn's name flashing on the screen. I press my finger against the screen to accept the call. I scarcely have time to say hello before Shawn's panicked voice screeches through the speaker.

"This was a bad hit, man!"

The words crash into me like an oncoming train. If I wasn't already sitting, I'd be on my ass. I've never been involved in a bad hit before. I've killed more people than I care to count, but it's only ever been my intended targets.

"We got bad information from Bianca," Shawn continues, his voice rising an octave. "She set you up to kill one of Volkov's guys, a turncoat from her own organization."

"What?" I don't know if I say it or scream it, but it's the only word that comes out.

Shawn's lengthy, wheezed breath on the line tells me that I did, in fact, scream it. "I spent hours combing through the data. I pulled every digital thread until I found the real information. It was so well hidden. Michael Crawford's real name was Luca Caruso. He was an accountant who did the books for Bianca before he turned on her and went to the Bratva. He was a fucking mole!"

"Shawn," I breathe, willing patience into my voice. "Are you telling me that we may have just started a mob war? A mob war that we're now at the center of?"

"I…uh…yes, that's a distinct possibility here," he squeaks.

I don't notice how hard my grip on my phone is until the plastic begins to crack in my palm. I slam it against the weight bench. My thoughts darken, reshaping from mere thought to a sharpened weapon. It seems that Bianca has finally tired of the cat and mouse game she's been trying to play with me. She manipulated me into taking a job between the two warring families, something I would never do. And she's set me up to take the fall for it.

The twisted, broken thing that lives inside of me rages. *Make her pay*, it screams.

Despite the cold wind that whips through the city streets, it's busy downtown. Tourists crowd the sidewalks, their teeth chattering and their coats pulled tightly around them. I shove my way past grumbling people, pushing my way into a familiar alley. I need to know how bad this situation is, and there's only one crazy fucker in this city who can tell me.

I slam my palm against the door at Club Gara and flash my gun at the security camera. The door buzzes, allowing me entry. Hot, putrid air hits my face, bringing with it the scent of sweat and booze. A bouncer steps in front of me, all six-foot-something of beefy muscle, blocking me from moving forward. Cautiously, he drags his eyes over me.

"I need to see Malik," I yell over the thumping club music.

He nods and steps aside, leaving me with the unfortunate task of snaking through the grinding, sweat-soaked bodies gyrating on the dance floor. I move through them quickly, making my way to the back of the club where I wait for the large metal security door to open for me. When it does, I breathe a little easier as the sour smell of perspiration and stale beer is displaced by a smokey, floral incense.

"*Habibi.*" A booming voice hits my ears just as a hard body crashes into mine, pulling me into a crushing hug. I release a groan and shrug Malik's arms off.

"I'm here for business," I say, hoping my tone conveys the urgency I feel.

Malik assesses me with narrowed eyes. "Tell me what troubles you, my friend."

"I know you have eyes and ears all over this city. I need to know what they're saying about me."

"Truly?" His eyes widen like I've caught him off guard.

"It's important."

His lips tip up in a smirk and he waves his hand toward a table at the back of the room. I follow him through the jewel-toned lounge, sidestepping low tables and velvet couches. The same young woman I've seen once before lounges on a sofa. She spares a glance in my direction, but her eyes don't linger, not on me, anyway. She watches Malik with hungry eyes and blown pupils. The pang of jealousy that zips through my chest is soft, but present. As much as I love her fear, I long for the day that Ava's eyes follow me out of want rather than just fear.

Dropping down to a large pillow on the floor, my knees scrape uncomfortably against the short table. Malik sits across from me, picking invisible lint off of his canary-yellow blazer.

Impatience pricks at my skin. "I need to know everything you've heard."

"Word on the street is that you're a man being hunted. There are bounties on your head, very high bounties, from the heads of both the Rossi and Volkov families."

"Fuck," I groan, smashing my fist against the table.

"Why does this bother you, Gray? You've had many hits out on you before. This is nothing new...unless..." Malik's small grin morphs into a beaming smile.

"Unless?"

"Unless you've found something worth protecting." His words are like a jab to the gut, souring my stomach. I do have something worth protecting. Someone worth protecting.

"Ah, I knew it!" Malik chirps happily. "The look in your eyes the last time I saw you; it could only be love."

Love? Is that what this is? Is that what drives me to be near her? To protect her? Am I truly capable of it?

A loud crash pulls me from my thoughts. The floor vibrates with the force of it, sending gaudy decorations and trinkets skittering across the carpet. With another thunderous crash, the security door explodes open. Metal scrapes and screams as the door busts off its hinges and slams against the floor.

Dark smoke, reeking of gunpowder and chemicals, billows into the room. Five bodies step through the haze, guns drawn. They step forward in a haphazard line, guns trained on Malik and I. My eyes sweep over them, taking in their appearance. They're definitely low-ranking goons, their clothes are dark but mismatched. Their guns are functional, but not top-grade.

Malik chuckles. "Friends of yours?"

I give him a healthy dose of side-eye before returning my attention to the invaders.

The grunt in the middle smiles. His slightly accented voice is gruff and weathered, sounding like the result of years of heavy smoking. "Mikhail Volkov sends his regards."

Malik's hand wraps around my arm, yanking me toward him. His foot collides with the table, flipping it on its side in front of us like a shield. With a lopsided grin on his face, he unstraps an MP5 submachine gun from the underside of the table. Pulling the handgun from the back of my jeans, I balance on the balls of my feet, readying myself.

The roar of gunfire slices through the room, almost entirely masking the sound of a feminine scream.

"Layla, *yallah!*" Malik yells, a look of fear flitting across his face before it disappears behind a grin.

Malik's girl sprints toward the back door, her dress hiked up to her knees and her body crouched low. She's done this before. I shift my eyes toward the man beside me, my closest ally and realistically the closest thing I have to a friend. The relief is clear on his face as she passes through the back door. Perhaps he understands what I feel for Ava more than I would have guessed.

Glass shatters and couch cushions explode as bullets spray the room, pinging off of metal and crashing through wood. The table we've shielded ourselves behind chips and splinters, shooting shards into my hair.

"Ready, my friend?" Malik shouts.

I hold my hand up, asking him to wait. When the shower of bullets slows to a trickle, I nod. The lights glint off of his polished, leather shoes as Malik's foot collides with the table. It launches forward like a mahogany cannonball and slams into two of the thugs. We jump up as they crash to the ground.

Like the worst kind of synchronized swimming team, we dive sideways, Malik to the left and myself to the right. Blood and brain matter explode before us as we spatter the room with bullets. Pain blasts up my side when I collide with the floor. The stun of the impact only lasts a moment before I scramble, ducking behind what used to be a nice couch.

The ringing in my ears dulls, leaving only the sound of my own labored breathing. I swivel my head around, examining the room. Malik does the same.

"Was that it?" he asks with a shaky laugh.

I make a thoughtful noise in my throat. "I, uh, think so."

Malik's guffaw echoes through the quiet room. "They must think you weak, *habibi*. I hope you'll prove them wrong."

I stand, turning in a circle to take in the chaos around me. Destroyed furniture and bullet casings litter the singed carpet. Stepping lightly, I skirt around toppled tables and chunks of ceramic. The tip of my boot collides with the abdomen of a fallen gunman. He doesn't move. In fact, the only movement from any of our would-be assassins is the slow pooling of their blood on the carpet.

I smile at Malik over my shoulder. "Send me an invoice for the damage."

His laughter follows me as I step into the now empty nightclub, hoping that I've just bought myself some time. Mikhail will need to regroup and find better soldiers to send after me. By then, I plan to have ended this.

"You're certain this is the place?" I ask, my eyes raking over the heavy, concrete building.

Shawn's anxious voice whines through my earpiece. "I've been digging into Bianca's business for three days, man. She seems to pull the bulk of her cash from this place; it's definitely one of hers."

Three days. My fists clench to the point of pain, leaving half-moon impressions under my fingernails. It's been three goddamned days since I've seen my little bird. Three days since I've touched her luscious body.

I've never experienced longing like this, not with any woman before her, nor will I feel it with any other. That, I'm absolutely certain of. There can never be another. That near-useless organ in my chest rattles against its cage, beating restlessly for her. She owns it now. Whether she wants it or not, it's hers.

Staying away from her is more painful than I expected. Need gnaws at my chest, making every inhale feel forced. It hurts, but it's necessary. I can't put Ava at risk. I can't see her until these fuckers recognize that I'm not playing around. Once I've shown Bianca what I'm willing to do to those who betray me, she'll have two choices—run or die.

"There's two guards at the guest entrance in the front and another two at the loading bay in the back. They're armed, Gray. Be careful."

I grunt an agreement before hanging up. I press my back into the side of the building. The rough concrete scrapes across my jacket as I shuffle slowly through the shadows. Nearing the edge of the building, I peak my head around toward the loading bay. Two men dressed in black stand in front of a large roll-up door, automatic weapons grasped tightly in their hands.

I rake my fingers through my hair, forcing it into a disheveled mess, and yank the hood over it. With my head down, I stumble forward, feeling the weight of my knife in my hand. Its comforting heft grounds me as I place my feet at odd angles, taking awkward steps toward the door.

"For fuck's sake," a guard grumbles under his breath, "another fucking drunk." The volume of his voice rises, projecting into the night. "Hey, buddy, you can't be here. This is private property."

"Huh?" I garble a confused sound while continuing to stumble toward the door.

The guards grunt in frustration, but don't stop my approach, not until I'm close enough to smell their aftershave. They march toward me, their angry footfalls crashing on the pavement. Hands grasp my shoulders, boxing me between the two grumbling men.

"Come on, man!" the guy on my left shouts. "Move your—"

My blade slides into his neck and the rest of his sentence comes out as a pained gurgle. His legs buckle, dropping him to his knees. He's become the very distraction I need to put his partner down. I pivot on my heels and drive my arm upward, sinking the knife into the second man's chin. He sputters and groans, falling to the ground in a heap.

I leave their corpses behind, letting their blood paint the pavement. Bianca can clean up my mess tonight, just like she wanted me to clean up hers.

I repeat my charade of feigned drunkenness to take out the guards at the front of the building. They fall easily, their bodies laying in a crumpled pile of blood and army surplus store gear. Shoving them behind an unsightly potted topiary, I stare at the nondescript building that houses so much evil.

It's no different than the suburban home where I was reborn as the monster I've become; plain and monotone. A single-storied Pandora's box, all of the worst of humanity hidden within its gray, concrete walls. My fists clench, rage boiling my blood as I stare at the sin box with no windows. I shove the door open. The stench of cigars and sex crashes into me like a filthy tidal wave.

I step into the wide, windowless room. Dim, amber lights wash its dark pine walls in yellow, making them look aged and dingy. A similar pine bar covers the left wall, bottles of high-end liquor sparkling on the shelves above it. The bartender, a thin, middle-aged man, nods at me before returning his eyes to the bartop. Over and over, he rubs a cloth over the already clean wood. His face is gaunt; dark shadows sit under his sunken eyes. Yellow and purple bruising mars the side of his face. As the seconds tick by, he makes no move to greet me further. Either he assumes I work for Bianca, or he simply doesn't care.

No one acknowledges me as I move through the room, sidestepping around small tables and overpriced armchairs. Even if I stomped through the room with guns drawn, I doubt anyone would notice. My movements are too quiet to be heard over the clinking of glasses and the chatter of men. As I step toward the back of the room, my eyes land on a group of them, some of targets for the evening.

My lip curls in disgust at the sight of them. Half a dozen men ranging from their twenties to their seventies lounge on leather couches with drinks in hand. Their fat stomachs dangle over their dress pants, threatening to pop the buttons off of their suit jackets. Their laughter fills the room, grinding against my eardrums.

A young woman staggers toward them, her steps clumsy and unbalanced. She reaches behind her, yanking her skirt down to cover the frilly bloomers underneath. Her outfit is revealing and clearly not made for her. It sags awkwardly over her skeletal frame. All of the parts of her that should be curved are straight and rigid with bone. The men's eyes dip low as she approaches, their heated gazes raking over her malnourished body.

Bianca may not keep the girls with bruises and track marks at the front of the house, but this one isn't much better off. Her body wobbles with only the effort it takes to stand. Her thin arm shakes under a silver tray, causing the glasses to clink and quiver. She forces out a pained giggle when a man's grimy palm lands on her ass before hastily retreating toward the back of the room where other emaciated women stand uncomfortably, waiting for their turn to be mauled by this establishment's disgusting clientele. My eye catches on something behind them, a door. I know immediately that it leads to the back of the house, the place where the worst depravities take place. And that's exactly where I'm headed.

As I move slowly toward the door, the young hostess turns. Our eyes meet briefly before she lowers her head. With her eyes cast on the floor, she teeters over to me. Her orange hair flops over her shoulder, the dull, lifeless strands swishing with her movements. It brushes her shoulders, sticking into the crevices where her skin pulls taut over her bony limbs.

Her voice is childlike, soft and high-pitched, alluding to her age. She's barely a young woman; she's just a kid. Her syllables shaky with fear. "C-can I g-get anything for you, sir?" she asks.

"Grab the other girls and get out of here, quietly. Run as far away from here as you can."

Her eyes jump to my face, questions swirling in their green depths. They're a soft, mossy-green, like Ava's. My jaw clenches as a sudden wave of fury rockets through my veins. *It's not Ava*, I scream in my head, *she's safe. She's not here.* The girl's lip quivers as she tries to speak. Her mouth opens and closes, but only wheezed huffs escape.

I press my index finger to my lips, asking her to stay quiet. She nods slightly, clearly understanding what I'm asking of her. Brushing my jacket aside, I reveal the handgun in my waistband.

"Go now," I demand.

Her eyes soften, pinkening with tears.

"Th-thank you. Thank you so much," she whispers. Her heels clatter against the floor as she shuffles away.

Discomfort stirs in my gut at her words. I don't deserve her thanks, and I don't want it. I didn't come here to rescue these girls. I'm not some kind of vigilante, fighting for justice. I'm a villain in my own right—just not the kind that traffics women and girls. There's only one woman in this world that matters to me, and she's not here. Knowing that doesn't stop the thoughts that wriggle inside my mind. They nag, curling around my brain, wondering, *would Ava like what I've done here? Would it make her proud to stand by my side?*

I shove the thoughts away, cramming them into a space in my head that I'll never reach for. I'll never tell Ava about the women I saved here tonight. She'll come to love me, knowing only the darkest parts of my soul. I won't lie to her by allowing her to believe that I'm the good guy in her story. I'm not the good guy. I'm the monster under her bed.

When I look back to where the girls were standing, they're gone. At the soft thud that sounds through the room, I know they've left through the front door. I back toward the pigs in suits, watching them quiet. With empty tumblers in hand, their eyes flit around the room, searching for girls to harass. My lips peel up into a grin. The back of the house can wait because these fuckers need to die.

"It's just us now, boys," I announce gleefully.

Their wide eyes lock onto mine, then to the gun in my hand. Their shocked gasps echo through the empty room, but I don't give them time to speak. Men like these don't deserve last words. No, not men. Only cowards prey on the weak. Only wretches lay their hands on children. My father's face flits through my mind. Suddenly, his face is all that I see pasted over their faces. His blue eyes stare back at me through theirs, gleaming with anger. They deserve death.

So I give it to them.

Bullets spray, slashing through their bodies, ripping the blood from their veins. It splatters against the leather couches, dying them red. The few who try to run make it only steps before their skulls explode, spraying brain matter across their friends' faces. Their screams create a symphony that booms through the room, each pained sound a note that I've created. Laughter weaves through each verse, separate but simultaneous. The agonized wails of evil men are my melody, the laughter, my harmony. It isn't until the roar of gunfire ceases that I realize I'm the only one laughing.

My ears ring, a heavy buzzing that crashes inside my skull. When it subsides, the room is still, so silent that I can hear my boots squelching on the blood-soaked Persian rug. Each footstep squishes into the damp fabric as I make my way to the door. Standing in front of the heavy, black door, I suck in a breath, letting it fill my lungs to the point of pain. I erect a mental shield, knowing that the worst of Bianca's business takes place behind this door.

The smell is what hits me first when I shove the door open. The acrid stench of drugs and sweat curdles in the air. It crawls up my nostrils and slithers down my throat. My lips pinch together, suppressing a gag. A long hallway stretches before me, its carpet stained with piss and blood. Soiled wallpaper curls against the walls, its edges peeled and cracked. Stepping into the hallway, I count six doors evenly spaced. Six rooms where the worst of humanity get their kicks from abusing women.

Anger blooms in my chest. *You were never this bothered by Bianca's business before*, a little voice nags in my mind. I wasn't. I always believed she was more monstrous than me, but I never got involved. I never felt rage like I do now. *You never loved a woman before either, not since Mom.* I shake my head, forcing the voice to quiet. This is not the time to analyze the seeming reemergence of feelings in my formerly dead heart.

My fingers twitch as I reload my gun, ready for violence. The first door cracks when the heel of my boot collides with its center. It crashes open, slamming against the wall with a heavy thud. A sweat-covered body kneels on the bed, pumping his shriveled dick in his fat hands. The naked woman before him lays sprawled out across the mattress, waiting. Her dull, brown eyes move slowly, pivoting to meet mine. Tears roll down her sunken cheeks, pooling at her gaunt collarbones.

The pig grunts. He tugs at himself, desperate to force his limp cock into action. Aiming at the back of his head, I don't give him the chance to rise to the occasion. The gunshot screams through the room as his brain explodes against the yellowed wallpaper. His body flops back, rolling off the mattress. His naked corpse drops to the floor with a heavy thud. A soft sound draws my eyes back up to the woman in the bed.

Her chestnut eyes sparkle, as if they suddenly sucked life inside of them. Her palm rests against her lips. A stifled sob tears through her, making her shoulders quake. It isn't until after several soft howls pass her lips that I realize she isn't crying. She's fucking laughing. Her face is splattered with the blood of her would-be rapist. Shards of his skull are lodged in her tangled, black hair. And she's fucking cackling. For a moment, we grin at each other like idiots.

"Get out of here," I say. "Get out of this city and never come back."

Her spindly fingers reach out toward me and I step back to move out of her reach, a scowl pulling at my mouth. Her eyes widen slightly in surprise before she nods once, seeming to understand that I don't want her to touch me. It's not her fault. I just can't stand the thought of a woman's hands on me that aren't Ava's.

She lets her fingers fall, moving away from me to instead grab a dirty robe off of the floor. She wraps it around herself quickly and runs down the hallway and out the backdoor.

I repeat my actions with every door and every sick fucker inside until the stench of the piss-stained hallway is muted by the coppery tang of blood. The floors are littered with corpses that the girls step and crawl over, seeking their escape. The sobs slowly quiet as they leave, until the hallway is silent again.

One last door lies untouched at the end of the hallway, larger and sturdier than the others. The door that leads to the loading bay, the first door that locks the girls in and the last they see when they finally succumb to the effects of the drugs and abuse. The thick wood beats against me as I pound my shoulder into it. By the time it opens, I can feel the bruises forming on my skin.

The door crashes open, revealing an open concrete room. I blink against the harsh, fluorescent lighting, waiting for my eyes to adjust. Once they do, I almost wish they hadn't. There's only one thing in this room, sitting at its center—a fucking cage. Iron bars stretch from floor to ceiling with a single door latched closed with a heavy padlock.

Pressed against the bars are seven women. They stare back at me with tired, glossy eyes. They wrap themselves in dirt-covered arms, hiding their various states of undress. Whatever remains of their clothes are in tatters, crusted with blood and grime. Purple bruises speckle the shaking limbs that barely seem to hold them up.

Their frightened eyes are locked with mine, pleading with me. They search my face, asking for rescue without words.

My jaw locks, slamming my teeth together. As I stare at the injured, crying women, I think I might grind my teeth into dust. A jolt of panic crackles through my veins, lighting my nerve endings on fire. *It's not Ava*, I chant inwardly. *It's not Ava. She's not here.*

The women scatter when I raise my gun, ducking for cover at the back of the cage. They grip each other tightly, their sobs muffled between their bodies. I take aim and pull the trigger. The sound of the blast bounces across the walls, followed by the metallic clang of the padlock hitting the floor.

I pivot on my feet, turning my back on the cage to face the security camera behind me.

"Run," I demand directly into the camera. It's not only an instruction for the women, but also a warning to Bianca. If she's as smart as she thinks she is, she'll get far away from this city and never return. If she doesn't, she'll die.

Chapter Twenty-Nine

Without finesse and with minimal coordination, my fingers crash against the keyboard. The furious *clack, clack, clack* sounds through my office, setting my teeth on edge. Irritation prickles at my skin like the bites of tiny red ants.

Dear uninspired writer,

I stare at the words until my eyes unfocus, blurring the letters. Over and over, I type and delete.

Your manuscript is juvenile and your grammar is abysmal.

"Damnit!" I grunt, jamming my finger into the delete button for the tenth time.

I drop my head, letting my gaze rest on my lap. "This isn't you," I chide myself. "Stop being a jerk and just do what you do. Just edit."

For what feels like the hundredth time today, I yank my eyes away from my unfinished work and refill my coffee mug. Armed with the creamy brew, I feel more settled, more capable. At least, that's what I tell myself.

As the hours tick by, I find myself reading and rereading paragraphs. My normally enthusiastic notes are limited to grammar edits and spelling corrections.

A heavy sigh whistles out through my nose. I've always found solace in stories, a way to escape. Today, every line falls flat. My heart sits lifelessly in my chest, unable to feel the characters.

Four days, the words whisper through my brain like a taunt. It's been four days since Gray showed up here with blood on his face. Four days with no sign of him. Four days since he violated me.

My own voice scoffs inside my head. *Violated? Did you really feel violated?*

I clench my fists in my lap, wrapping my fingers around the hem of my sweater. My body tightens, compressing like a spring. My head drops low, shame washing over me as the admission of my own feelings rings through my head like a blaring alarm. The truth is, I didn't feel violated. I felt afraid, shaken to my core.

"No, I did what he wanted because I was afraid. Only because I was afraid." The lie slides off my tongue like sandpaper.

It wasn't just fear that I felt. When I gave in to him, gave him control over my body, I felt free. I felt a relief I never have before. For a moment, every thought bouncing around in my head had quieted. The scars of my past, the constant presence in my mind that screams my inadequacies, they lifted and I was weightless. I felt wanted. Under his praise, I melted like chocolate in the sun. I became a desperate, wanton thing, aching to please him.

Anger bubbles in my stomach, a queasy, rumbling feeling. He touched me. He made me want him. He made me crave this feeling that no one else has ever given me. And now he's gone. The shadow that's haunted me day and night has dissipated, escaping like smoke through an open window. I'm just the ash left behind by the fire.

He got what he wanted, and it wasn't enough. I wasn't enough.

The ghostly voice of my father whispers in my ear, *You're nothing, girl. No one could love someone like you. You're a broken, useless thing.* I press my palms against my ears, like I can block him out.

My chest compresses, squeezing my heart. I shouldn't have expected him to stay. I shouldn't have deluded myself into thinking he could have been different than every other man in my life. *But he isn't just like every other man, is he?* my own voice whispers through my head. *No,* I respond, *he's worse. He didn't just take control of me. He made me give it to him.*

"How could you be so stupid?!" I scream into the quiet of my office. "He's a goddamned stalker. He's probably moved on to his next victim. You weren't even good enough to keep a psycho around. How could you let yourself think you were special?"

It's just like my father always said, I'm broken. This is just more proof of it. Only a broken thing would be so eager for attention that they would take it from a man like him. He's a murderer, a monster. I should want him gone. I wanted it at first. I did everything in my power to keep him away. I got what I asked for, so why does it make my heart feel like it's being crushed inside my chest?

"Well, fuck him!" My coffee mug jangles, nearly toppling over when I slam my palms against the desk. "I don't need him."

The lit sign above the door to the local bar reads *Jack's Place*. It flickers, letters fading in and out of existence. Its neon lights, much like the rest of the building, have seen better days. There isn't much in this town, but at least we have a bar. For a moment, my courage falters and I wonder what the Hell I'm doing here.

"It's just a bar," I remind myself.

Pushing the door open, the scent of beer and peanuts wafts around me. A bell above the door jingles, drawing the bartender's attention. He's handsome in a small town way. His curly, brown hair is slightly disheveled, as if he'd brushed it with his hands instead of a comb. It frames a kind face, strong but with a hint of softness. He smiles as I approach the bar, his brown eyes warm with welcome.

His cheeks pinken when I push my coat off of my shoulders. Something about the way his eyes flit from my face to my body makes me feel powerful, wanted. His eyes snag on my hips where my sweater dress hugs me, highlighting my curves while still covering me. Something shifts inside me, and for once, I don't hide from the appreciating gaze. I absorb it, twirling my fingers through my hair as I order a drink. I'm not sure where this newfound confidence comes from, this freedom to let him look at me.

You know exactly where and who *it comes from,* the thought slithers through my mind, dragging with it a painful reminder of why I'm here. *Bullshit,* I yell back at the slippery thoughts. I sip my drink, drowning my sorrows in the harsh burn of alcohol.

After three drinks, my blood is alight with a boldness that I've never known. I skim through my phone, through the texts that I should have deleted, but never did. With the kind of conviction that only drunkenness can bring, I text the unknown number that isn't unknown to me anymore.

I hate you.

You're just like everyone else. You used me and left.

Don't ever come near me again.

Asshole!

When he doesn't respond, my heart sinks into my stomach. By my third drink, the fluttery ache in my belly has dulled to a gentle quiver. By the fifth, it's no longer there, replaced with a sloshing warmth. When a man pulls up a barstool next to me and offers me a sixth drink, I barely look at him before agreeing. I lap at my drink like a thirsty dog, not caring that I can't even recognize the flavor.

He sits close, talking next to my ear about something. Sports, maybe? Was it sports? I let him chatter at me, occasionally nodding my head in agreement, or maybe it's just bobbing along to the music. I'm not sure. When a gentle hand lands on my shoulder, I turn my head toward him, actually looking at him for the first time. He's a decent looking man in his forties, not quite as cute as the bartender, but handsome in his own right.

Maybe I should go home with him. The thought flits through my mind and I scoff, maybe inwardly or maybe out loud. The concept makes my lips pucker and my nose scrunch up in disgust. I realize immediately that there'd be no point in going anywhere with him. He's not the man my body is pining after. He won't make me come so hard that I see stars. Only one man has ever done that to me. I pinch the bridge of my nose, willing away the memory of that asshole's hands on me.

It feels like he's everywhere, like I can't shake the thoughts of him out of me. Even now, I can smell the dark aroma of vanilla and leather, a scent that's uniquely him. A pained grunt at my side draws my attention back from my thoughts. The face of the man beside me ripples with pain as his hand falls away from my shoulder. His eyes are wide and frightened, tears dripping from the corners. Wait, something isn't right. There's still a hand on my shoulder.

I whip my head around, the room slightly spinning as my eyes land on the hulking figure beside me. His face is pulled tight and his eyes burn with anger. My body instinctively leans toward him before I right myself, pushing myself back on my barstool until my back bumps into the bar.

"Ma—" I begin and quickly stop myself. I will not call him master. I will absolutely not call him that, no matter how much that nagging, horny part of my brain wants to. "Gray," I utter as dryly as I can.

Unable to shoulder the weight of his gaze, my eyes lower to his chest. "Leave me alone." I hate that my voice wavers.

The guy next to me whisper-screams in my ear, "Shit. Is that your husband? He looks pissed…and I think he broke my fucking hand."

I open my mouth to tell him that he is absolutely not my husband, when Gray cuts me off.

"Yes," he answers, his lips pulling up into a wolfish grin, "and I'm taking my *wife* home. Now."

I open my mouth, an argument on the tip of my tongue, but no words come out. They get strangled in my throat, choking me under the weight of his gaze. His eyes sparkle with unspoken challenge, like he's daring me to fight him. His hand darts out, pinching my chin between his fingers. I whimper when his thumb digs into my skin in a silent warning.

"Let's go, *wife*," he draws the word out like he's tasting it.

He bends forward, pressing his lips against the shell of my ear. His breath whispers across my sensitive skin, goosebumps rising in its wake. "You wanted my attention, precious. Now you have it."

I slurp down a mouthful of my drink, finding my mouth suddenly as dry as the Sahara. Gray drops a wad of cash on the bar that looks like significantly more than what my drinks cost before unceremoniously hauling my body over his shoulder. My head sways back and forth against his back, the alcohol sloshing in my belly with his steps.

Without permission from my brain, my body relaxes into his hold. The warmth of his body tingles through me, warming places I didn't realize were cold. The motion of his steps rocks me as we move. My eyelids begin to droop as we sway. Through the haze of drunkenness, my thoughts tumble through me.

I didn't realize I was tired. I'm so tired. He's so warm, like a big, angry blanket. Why does he smell so good? He smells like sex and sugar cookies. Oh, crap. Did I say that last one out loud?

The chuckle that rumbles through his chest confirms that I might have, in fact, said that last one out loud.

Shit.

Chapter Thirty

When I saw Ava, her perfect ass parked on a barstool in a shitty dive bar, I was simultaneously elated and furious. When she texted me, I ignored every word she said. Soft, gushy emotions that I couldn't identify churned in my chest as I saw them for what they really meant—she missed me. She didn't know where I'd been. She didn't know that I was doing what I had to do to keep her safe, to keep the shitstorm Bianca started from ever touching her. All she knew is that I wasn't there and it was eating her up inside.

Something inside me cracked a little at the fact that she thought I would leave her, throw her away like she was nothing. She doesn't understand that she's everything to me. She doesn't realize the lengths I would go to keep her, the horrible things I would do to ensure she's by my side.

When some fucker put his hand on her shoulder, my blood went cold. It took every ounce of my self-control to keep myself from removing his head from his shoulders. His assumption about me being her husband earned him a small sliver of grace. His fingers may be broken, but he's alive. Though, if I hadn't been so preoccupied with my wayward, drunk pet, he probably wouldn't be.

The way she blushed when I called her my wife made my head swim, likely because all of the blood left it to rush to my dick. I've never considered the possibility of marriage before. I never cared for a woman enough to want it. I'm not even sure I wanted it before it was mentioned tonight. Now that it's in my head, I can't see any other future for me. A ring is just another piece of the beautiful cage I'll craft to keep my little bird.

Ava groans as I place her in my car. She shoves at me. Her heels scrape against my shins as she kicks her feet out awkwardly in an attempt to get out. I press my hand against her sternum and force the seat belt around her. Her fingers fumble to unlock it after it clicks into place.

"Little bird," I warn, letting my voice drop to a threatening tone. Her eyes dart to mine before they settle back into her lap. "You can either sit here in the front like a good girl or you will ride tied up in the trunk."

Her body stills, frozen in the seat. Her shoulders quiver with fear, but the wide eyes that look up with me are filled with heat. Movement in her lap catches my eye and I watch her thighs rub together. Oh, yeah, she definitely missed me.

When I round the car and get into the driver's seat, a memory flashes in my mind. One of Ava diving out of my car and sprinting into the woods. This time, I lock the goddamned doors. Her eyes flash with anger when the locks click into place, but she keeps her mouth shut. Smart girl.

I press a bottle of water into her hands. I know she's thirsty. Her tongue darts out, rolling over her bottom lip, but she pulls her hands back like the bottle is red hot. Rolling my eyes, I open the bottle and take a sip before handing it back to her. She snatches it from me and immediately gulps down half of it.

Ava sits silently beside me, her fingers fidgeting in her lap and her eyes turned away from me, staring out into the dark. Her face is pink and I suspect it's not just the flush of inebriation. Is she still upset that I was away? Does she not realize that I'll never leave her alone again?

She puffs out a loud sigh and mumbles something under her breath.

"I can practically hear the gears turning in your head," I say. "Tell me what's on your mind, little bird."

"I bet," she slurs, her words blending together while still holding an angry bite, "you do this shit with every woman you're stalking. Fucking pervert creep."

I clench my jaw, trying to keep myself from smiling. Is that what she thinks? She's angry with me because she thinks I was with other women instead of her?

"Is my little bird jealous?"

She exaggerates her denial, thrashing her head from side to side, but her eyes betray her. She blinks rapidly, her eyes becoming glossy and wet. My chest tightens at what I see in her face. There's a sadness that pinches her features. Does she really believe I would have any woman that isn't her? What happened to her that would make her think she's anything other than perfect?

"There's only you for me, Ava."

She stills in her seat, her soft gasp audible in the quiet car.

"The truth is, since the day I first saw you, I haven't been able to look at another woman. You can fight this all you want, but you can't escape me. I'll follow you until the day I die, then I'll haunt you in the afterlife. Whether you want it or not, I'm yours, body and black, broken soul. And you are mine."

Ava hiccups a giggle, a fucking adorable giggle. I glance at her, finding her chewing on her bottom lip, smothering a smile. I've never been concerned about showing the full breadth of my obsession to her. There's no purpose in hiding it, given she couldn't get away from me if she tried. I'd hunt her to the ends of the Earth if she ever ran from me. But based on her reaction to my confession, I'm now fully motivated to show her every facet of my need for her.

I open my mouth, ready to tell her more about my demented devotion, until I hear her mumble sleepily. She breathes heavily, her head resting against the window. I glance over at her sleeping form, my lips twitching into a smile. Does she realize that she's so unafraid of me that she's sleeping in my car? When I saw her at the bar, I immediately noticed the dark circles under her eyes, the paleness of her skin. Did she struggle to sleep without me? Did she keep herself up at night, waiting for me?

The thought that pops into my head makes my dick stiffen. My little bird, waiting obediently for her master to come home. I'd open the door to find her on the couch, a silky negligee wrapped around her curves, her creamy thighs outstretched. A delicate leather collar around her neck, a golden o-ring at the center, glinting in the glow of the lamp. She'd look up from her book and smile at me.

Shaking my head, I force my mind back into the car. Why the fuck haven't I moved her into my house yet? My grip on the steering wheel tightens as I try to will patience into my veins. I don't yet know all that she's been through, all that's broken her spirit. I've been trying to move at her pace, to keep her from falling off the edge. Well, significantly faster than her pace, but as slow as I'm capable of taking it with her. I'm not sure how much longer I can wait.

I carry Ava to my bed, her head resting against my chest, her breath gliding over my neck. When I lay her down, she mumbles sleepily, curling herself into my blankets. I peel off her shoes, letting my fingers trace the lines of her delicate feet. My fingers grasp the edge of her dress, pulling it over her head and watching the way it clings to her soft body. I unclasp her bra and groan as her breasts tumble out. They taunt me, their size perfectly fitted for my hands, begging for my touch. I run my finger over her nipple, watching it harden into a tight bud. My hands trail down her waist until they reach the edge of her panties. As I peel them down her legs, her thighs fall open.

Staring down at my little bird, naked on my bed, is testing the strength of my willpower. I imagine shoving my cock inside her, listening to her sleepy moans. Would she be dreaming of me? Would she cry out my name when she falls apart?

I rip my t-shirt off and pull it over her head and arms, trying to rid myself of some of the temptation. It falls to the middle of her thighs, effectively hiding the most tempting part of her. At least it does until she grips the fabric in her fingers and drags it up to her face. She inhales deeply and curls her legs up to her stomach, cuddling into my bed. She's the only woman I've ever allowed into my home, into my bed. She fits perfectly in my space, in my clothes.

I clench my fists at my side to keep myself from ravaging her exhausted body. I remind myself of my promise to her, that I won't fuck her until she begs for it. Seeing her in my bed, I almost regret telling her that. The way I feel about her is consuming, filling every part of me with a sense of possession. *Mine*, the word screams through me.

"Gray." My name whispered under her breath pulls me out of my trance. Ava reaches her arms out to me, her eyes half-lidded and sleepy.

I reach my hand out, placing my palm against her cheek. "I'm here, precious."

"Stay with me," she mumbles. She drags her fingers over my stomach. "Kiss me."

Her unexpected demand crashes into me, nearing knocking the wind out of me. Every cell in my body is yanking me toward her. I press my heels into the floor, keeping myself still. I can't kiss her now. I won't. It's not that she might not remember the kiss that bothers me. I don't give a fuck about that. What bothers me is that she might not remember that she asked for it. I need her to recognize that she wants this. I need her to accept it.

"Shh," I quiet her with a soft sound, "lay down. I'm not leaving you."

She lays back on the bed, her hair fanning out around her face like soft waves of warm earth. Those pale, green eyes, still glazed from the alcohol, remain fixed on me. They drift slowly, perusing my chest and abdomen. My chest involuntarily puffs under her heated gaze.

I unbuckle my belt, pulling it through my belt loops until it's free. The moment my belt is in my hands, something changes in her.

She suddenly jumps up, her eyes exploding open. Her uncoordinated legs scramble underneath her, leaving her tumbling off the bed. She crab walks backward until her back bumps the wall, where she tucks her knees into her chest.

Confused by her reaction, I rush toward her until my shins bump hers. A frightened whimper rattles in her throat as her wide eyes flit from my face to the belt in my hands. Tears stream down her cheeks, painting her face with mascara.

I've seen Ava afraid. I've watched her cower in fear before me, her lips quivering as she waits to see what my sick obsession will make me do to her. But this is different. There's no arousal hiding in the depths of her fear. There's no spark inside her glossy eyes, no fight. She's a cornered animal, frozen in fright.

"Okay, baby," I say softly. "It's okay."

My chest clenches as I watch those terrified eyes hone in on my belt. Keeping my movements slow, I put the belt down on the floor behind me and kick it away. I hold my hands up, showing her that I'm not a threat as I kneel in front of her.

Watching my little bird shy away from me, my mind flashes back to the file Shawn made on her after I first saw her in that coffee shop. The medical records. The visits to the emergency room. The injuries that went uninvestigated. I recall the way she flinched when I first touched her face. What happened to her?

I reach my hand out, running my knuckles along her cheek. Her shoulders shake with soft sobs.

"I-I'm sorry," she whispers, "I'm so broken."

I sit down and pull her into my lap, pressing her head into my chest and running my hand through her hair.

"Why are you afraid of my belt, precious?"

The only sound that escapes her lips is her wheezing breaths and stifled sobs.

"Who hurt you, Ava?"

Her voice is muffled against my chest as she curls her body into me, making herself small. "My father," she says.

I freeze at her admission, at the familiarity. "Tell me what happened."

Through her sobs, she recounts an all too familiar story, one I know well from my own past. She tells me about her alcoholic father, the man who beat her and her mother. She tells me about the death of her mother, the only shining light in the darkness of her childhood. After she was gone, the full weight of her father's anger fell onto Ava's shoulders. For years, he hurt her, whipping her skin with his belt until it was bruised and bleeding.

I try to hide my anger from her, the way my hands shake with rage at how she's suffered. I try to force myself to be calm when I feel anything but. Carrying her shuddering body to my bed, I force my fury into a cage for her, to give her a moment of calm.

"I will never let anyone hurt you ever again," I whisper the promise into her hair.

I've never comforted anyone before. It pulls on feelings that are foreign to me. They crawl and scrape inside my chest, making me ache to smother them with my anger. Anger is all I know; anger, and death, and revenge. She needs my comfort right now, but she deserves my revenge. Her pain belongs to me and me alone. I will make sure everyone who's ever touched her learns this. No one will ever hurt her again, no one but me.

Her tears dry into salty, pink lines and she falls asleep in my arms. When she stirs, the shirt lifts above her hips and I finally see them, the white, streaking scars that blend almost seamlessly into the porcelain skin of her back. At the sight of her scarred skin, my anger becomes a living, breathing creature lurking inside me. It demands to be set free, to seek vengeance for her, to free her from the demons that haunt her.

I punch Shawn's contact on my phone, not letting him utter a word before I bark out an order. "Get me everything you can on Ava Moore's father. Now."

Chapter Thirty-One

I stand by the lake near the cabin registered to Roger Moore, my breath fogging around me. I pull my hood up, shielding myself from the frigid wind that whips at my neck. It's nearing winter and parts of the lake have frozen over, dark sections of crystalized water glitter in the silvery moon. The creaks and groans of the ice whine out into the night.

Light pours from the windows of the cabin, illuminating the decaying wood paneling on its exterior. The old cottage could have been beautiful if anyone had cared for it, but the man hidden away inside isn't capable of that. He's proven as much by his actions towards his wife and daughter, the women he broke.

My stomach twists into knots, unfamiliar emotions churning in my gut. Should some part of me be grateful to him for breaking my little bird? Is he the monster that made her into my perfect, missing piece, my beautifully damaged toy? I shake my head, dispelling the thought.

No, I could never give him credit for who she is. She's so much more than what he made her, so much more than she even realizes. She doesn't understand how strong she is. She thinks her past dampened her fire, but it didn't. It may be hidden deep within her, but the embers still burn brightly. Those little flames that she shows only to me.

Stepping towards the dilapidated cabin, I steel my spine, armoring myself with rage. I'll free my little bird from the shackles of her past. I'll give her the freedom she's never had, freedom from her pain and fear. Then, she'll be ready for a cage she actually wants. I'll build a golden cage around her heart, one that only I have the key to. Then, she'll know she's mine.

The door rattles on its lopsided hinges when I rap my fist against it. Inside, Ava's father groans, mumbling slurred curses. The floorboards creak as he approaches the door. The moment it opens, I step into him. I smell the cheap whiskey on this breath immediately. I whip my arm forward, sending the handle of my knife crashing into his temple. His knees crack when he drops to the floor, the rest of his body following shortly after.

The old man groans, the wrinkles deepening around his cracked lips and sunken eyes. He twitches, his shriveled body jerking against the ropes. His feet totter, their position precarious on the small stool he stands on. I stare at the pathetic creature that haunts Ava, and I imagine what he did to her. The images come to me with barely a thought, given how similar they are to my own memories.

Roger's features are hard, jagged things jutting from his face. His nose is crooked like it's been broken several times and the bones were poorly set. He looks nothing like my little bird.

She's lucky in that fact. Unlike me, she'll never see her nightmare in the mirror. When she looks at herself, she won't see her father's eyes staring back at her. But I wear my father's face like a badge of honor because he's dead and I'm alive, knowing that I'm the one who put him in the ground.

Roger's pained whine fills the room. It's a pitiful sound. He blinks his eyes open slowly before his glazed, brown orbs land on me. I smile, watching his fingers twitch before he realizes that he can't move properly. His eyes dart to the ceiling fan, then to the ropes that tie his neck and hands to it, then to the shaky positioning of his feet on the rickety stool a foot above the floor.

His face contorts. His breathing becomes erratic, panicked. My smile widens into something predatory. Based on the tears that have started to trickle from his eyes, it must be a terrifying sight.

"W-who are you?" he croaks out from between his cracked lips.

I cock my head to the side. "You're a gambling man, aren't you, Roger? A drunk?"

His mouth closes, his lips pressing into a thin line, but his eyes flash with fear.

"Tonight," I say, "you can consider me *the house*. I've come to call in your chit."

He shoots me a quizzical look. "Huh?"

I step closer, running my gloved fingers along the ropes that bind him. "You owe a debt, Roger. You put your hands on something that belongs to me. You damaged it."

"No, no, I-I can pay you back," he pleads. "I can get you cash."

"Oh, Roger," I chuckle, "not this time. Money won't get you out of this."

"W-what," he sputters, "what did I break?"

His throat bobs when I pull the hunting knife from my belt and press the tip beneath his chin. His eyes pinch shut, waiting for the slice of my knife. It doesn't come; I won't let him die that easily. Instead, I lift the knife and cut through the rope that binds his wrists to the ceiling fan.

His eyes spring open as the sound of his choking gurgles fill the room. It takes him a moment to straighten his legs, finally realizing the position he's in. His life now depends on the strength of his wobbling legs. The second he lets them relax, his body will dangle from the rope that anchors his neck to the ceiling.

"Your daughter, Roger. Your daughter is mine and you hurt her."

His eyes widen, the shock evident on his face. His surprise makes my blood boil. He still doesn't see her value. He can't see what I see.

"No, no, p-please! S-she's not worth it." Spittle dribbles from the corners of his mouth as he begs.

"*Not worth it?*" I say in a low voice, daring him to continue.

His face changes, a scowl plastered across his sunken cheeks. His eyes flash with anger. "She's nothing," he seethes, "you'll see. A worthless, broken thing, just like her mother."

My anger cools; icing over, hardening, sharpening. "She's everything. She's fucking perfect, and you are nothing. She's too kind to seek vengeance, but I'm not. I'm going to free her from you."

Stepping toward him, I reach my hands out toward his waist. Roger's wide, glassy eyes trace the movement of my hands, his face pinched with fear. I unbuckle his belt and pull it from the loops at his waist.

"You remember this, don't you, Roger?" I taunt. "Surely, you haven't forgotten how you used your belt on your daughter. Before you die, you deserve to feel what she felt."

"No, no, please!" he whines. "Please d-don't do this!"

I move behind him with the end of my belt clenched in my fist. I let it swing beneath my hand, letting him hear the clink of the metal. The leather whistles through the air as I rear my arm back and then swing it forward. It collides with Roger's side and he belts out a hoarse scream.

Blood begins to seep through his shirt in the place my belt hit, and I grin. "I will match every scar you gave Ava, every way that you marked her perfect skin. You will feel every single one, Roger."

He chokes out a sob as tears stream down his cheeks. "No," he whispers.

"Oh, yes," I chuckle, "this is what you owe her. This is what you deserve."

I swing the belt again and it lets out a satisfying thwack as it collides with his back. The metal buckle tears through his dirty shirt, revealing an angry, red welt on his skin. His balance teeters on the tiny stool beneath him, but I only give him a moment to right himself. I can't have him die yet. Not when he deserves so many more strikes. He deserves to feel the suffering he caused Ava.

"You're the one who's worthless!" I scream. "You're the one who's nothing!"

Forcing all of my rage into my muscles, I swing the belt over and over. His pained wails fill the room as the metal collides with his flesh and rips the skin beneath it. Blood drips from his wounds and the force of the impact sprays it back onto me. Each time the buckle hits his skin, I bark out the words he's used to describe his daughter.

"Worthless!"

Smack.

"Broken!"

Smack.

"Nothing!"

Smack.

I whip him until my breathing is labored and the leather slips from my blood-soaked palms.

When his screams stop and his eyelids begin to flutter, I walk around his pathetic form. His legs quiver, barely holding the weight of his body. His shirt hangs in scraps from his shoulders, their edges dripping with blood. I grab his wrist, my fingers digging into his skin. I wrap the end of the belt around his hand, wiping his own blood into his palm and leaving the belt to dangle from his hand.

"Stay awake, Roger," I demand. His eyes flick to mine and I flash him a toothy smile. "This next part is my favorite."

I slam my foot into the stool under this worthless body, kicking it across the room. He chokes, wheezing and gagging as his body swings from the fan. Bile drips from his mouth. His fingers claw desperately at the rope. Laughter howls out of me, filling the room as I watch him die.

His piss puddles on the floor beneath him, and I step back to keep my boots dry. His pants thicken as he soils himself. I inhale the acrid stench of Roger's death, but all I smell is Ava's freedom.

Chapter Thirty-Two

I squint my eyes open, blinking against the light that streams in from the windows. My head aches with the dull throb of a hangover. I roll over and shove my face into the pillow, hoping for a few more minutes of rest. With my face in the soft fabric, I inhale deeply. My thighs clench at the deliciously masculine scent within its threads. *Sex and sugar cookies*, the words pop into my head. My eyes fly open and I suck in a gasp, because this is not my bedroom.

My eyes pan around the room and I'm surprised by what I find. This isn't the bedroom I expected a psychotic, murdering stalker to have. I expected, well, I don't really know what I expected, but not this. The room is huge and impeccably decorated. The walls and curtains are dark blue. Abstract paintings in blues and yellows are neatly placed around the room along with a few well-placed sculptures. The furniture is modern and black. Everything looks incredibly expensive and it has me wondering what a man like Gray does for a living.

I roll off the bed, keeping my footsteps light as I make my way to the attached bathroom. My fingers fumble around the wall before finding the light switch. When the lights come on, I stifle a gasp.

The tiny, old-fashioned bathroom in my house is no comparison for this room. It's easily five times its size and filled with sleek, black marble. I run my finger along the edge of a stone bathtub that could easily fit three people.

"No, no, no," I whisper to myself, "you cannot be impressed. You absolutely cannot. He's a psycho."

Stepping toward the counter, my head bobbles from side to side, as if I could shake out my admiration. Bad men shouldn't have such nice damn bathrooms.

My reflection blinks back at me from the mirror above the double vanity. My hair is messy and matted, but the dark circles under my eyes seem to have lessened. I comb my fingers through my hair before looking down at my body, which is covered only by a long t-shirt. A t-shirt that doesn't belong to me.

My thoughts become horses. The stable doors burst open, and they sprint away, unable to be caught or brought to heel. *Did he strip me and put me into his clothes? Did he touch me? Grab me, shove me onto his bed, press his fingers against my heated skin? Did he run his tongue along my pussy until I begged? Oh, crap, did we have sex?*

My body pulses with energy that rockets straight to my clit. I clench my legs together as the stupid, horny thing pulses with need. Trying to ignore my body's screaming for his touch, I force my mind back to last night and how the Hell I got here.

Everything is fuzzy at first. I remember the bar, the drinks, the stupid texts I sent him. I remember him carrying me out of there like a damned caveman and putting me in his car. But what else happened?

Suddenly, a memory comes crashing back into my mind and I wish it hadn't. I told him about my father. I told him everything. He knows what he did to me and Mom, how he hurt us. He knows how broken I am. My heart clenches, thumping rapidly in my chest. Anxiety claws at my insides, ripping my stomach into ribbons. He knows how damaged I am now. Why does that scare me so much?

I shove the thoughts away, tucking them into the little box inside of myself that no one can see. As I shove the fear deep into that hidden place where feelings die, my lungs finally pull in enough air.

My heart rate slows to a steady *thump, thump, thump* in my chest. I pull my eyes back to the mirror and focus on the more pressing issue at hand, my teeth. My mouth tastes like sawdust and old alcohol.

There's a single toothbrush sitting in a cup on the counter, his toothbrush. I stare at it for several minutes, its stupid little bristles taunting me with promises of a fresh mouth.

"Screw it," I mumble before loading it up with toothpaste and shoving it in my mouth.

That asshole has invaded my space and privacy a hundred times, so I don't feel bad about invading his. I keep that in mind as I tiptoe out of the bathroom and back into his room, where I rummage through his dresser drawers. I'm a little surprised to find that everything is organized, clothes neatly folded and tucked into their respective places. I always assumed that criminals were less structured than the average person, but that's clearly not the case for Gray.

I mutter curses under my breath when I can't find my own clothes. I do at least find a fresh shirt. It's long, like a dress that reaches almost to my knees. Armed in only a shirt and my bare feet, I stand in front of the bedroom door, staring holes into the wood.

"You can't hide in here forever," I huff. "He'll just barge in, anyway."

My feet don't move. My toes don't wiggle. Absolutely nothing happens.

"Okay, just go. You got this!" My soft encouragement is ridiculously directed at my own feet, but this time, I force them to move.

I push the door open, padding quietly down the hallway. When I reach its end, I find myself standing on a raised balcony, overlooking a posh loft. Smooth, concrete walls scrape upward to a high ceiling, where black light fixtures dangle, looking less light lamps and more like modern art. My eyes lower, taking in the glossy tile floors, fluffy, gray area rugs, and a pair of feet.

Wait, feet?

My gaze jumps up, immediately meeting with Gray's. His mouth tips upward into a devilish grin that has me yanking down the hem of his shirt to cover more of my legs. He stands in the middle of his fancy living room with a phone pressed against his ear. His gray sweatpants hang low on his hips, drawing my eyes to his chiseled abs and that tantalizing line of muscle that dips down below his waistband. He pivots with a smirk, giving me a full and very intentional view of his muscular form. Forcing myself to look absolutely anywhere else, I lock my eyes on his chest and the tattoos that swirl around his upper body.

The black rose at the center of his throat branches off into twisting vines. The thorny black offshoots whirl, morphing into branches that crawl along his collarbones and shoulders. The spindly branches flow like shadows, wrapping around his body. They look like I imagine his soul does: dark, twisted, and hauntingly beautiful.

"A little bird just flew into my living room." His voice hits me, knocking some sense back into me and ending my perusal of his half-naked form.

He chuckles into the phone before his eyes find mine. "No, I'm thinking about getting a bird cage and keeping it as my pet."

I bristle at his words. My anger rises, a little storm inside my belly that has me stomping down the stairs toward him.

"What do you think, little bird?" he asks, dropping his cell phone onto the stupidly pretty, velvet couch.

"I'm not your freaking pet, you freak," I spit, infusing as much anger as I can into the words.

"Hmm," he hums, "we'll see."

I stand several feet away, keeping distance between us. The distance doesn't stop my anger from melting into anxiety. Embarrassment floods through me and I can feel the heat rising in my cheeks.

"Did we…uhh…we didn't…right?" I stammer.

"Didn't what, Ava?"

"I…" the words get stuck in my throat, "you know…"

My face is on fire now and I'm certain my cheeks are beet red. I'm not a prude. Sex isn't new for me. I've been with men before, plenty of times, and never thought anything of it. Talking about it with Gray feels different, more intimate somehow.

A devious smile lights up his obnoxiously handsome face. "Are you asking if I fucked you? You want to know if I shoved my cock into your needy little cunt? Made you scream? Made you beg to come on your master's cock like my good little slut?"

The words dry up in my mouth, so I just nod. My belly spasms at the obscene picture he paints in my head. I've been called a slut before; every woman has and it's terrible every time…except this time. My core floods with arousal. I pinch my legs together, feeling it drip down my thigh.

He steps toward me, his long legs eating up the distance between us. My feet stumble backwards. He moves again, refusing to let me get away from him. I shuffle back until my back bumps into a wall. He doesn't care about my need for space. He steps into me, pressing his hands against the wall to cage my head between them. His head dips, his nose running a line from my shoulder to my ear like, he's scenting me.

I pinch my lips together, blocking the sound that clings up my throat when his breath tickles my ear.

"No, precious, I didn't fuck you," he whispers, "I want you to remember every time I touch you." I shudder as his teeth scrape against my earlobe. "And as I've said before, I'll only fuck you when you beg for it." He lifts his head and grins at me. "But, you did try to kiss me."

I shake my head. "I would never kiss you."

His eyes harden, the sparkle of humor winking out as he presses his face closer to mine. His breath ghosts against my chin, drawing my attention. His lips are inches from mine. I stare at them, remembering the way they crashed against mine after I ran from him in the forest. My mouth dries up, all the moisture in my body seems to have changed course, heading south instead. I swipe my tongue across my bottom lip.

He hums a sound of approval. "That's what I thought. My needy girl."

He pushes off the wall and grabs my hand. "Come here," he says as he leads me into the kitchen.

He motions to the stool at an island in the center of the large kitchen. I raise my eyebrows in question.

"Sit," he says.

Yanking my shirt down over my legs, I pull myself onto the stool. My fingers rub circles on the white marble countertop, grounding myself with the feel of the cool stone. I almost dive out of my seat when the clatter of metal hitting metal rings out, echoing in the minimalist space.

"What are you doing?" I ask, watching Gray drop a frying pan onto the stove.

He pulls eggs and a package of bacon out of the refrigerator. "Making us breakfast."

Making us breakfast? Making us breakfast!? I groan, shoving the heel of my palms into my eyes. My stalker is making us breakfast. The big, raving lunatic is just making us breakfast willy-nilly, like this is no big deal. My murderous shadow stands half-naked, looming over the stove like a muscle-bound Grim Reaper, and he's making scrambled eggs.

"We're not dating!" I bark. "I'm not your girlfriend, so stop acting like it. I don't need to have breakfast with you. Just give me my clothes and call me an Uber so I can go home."

Gray goes still. The muscles in his back twitch as his spine straightens. In the back of my mind, an alarm sounds. The instinctual warning system all humans have that alerts us to the presence of a predator, something higher on the food chain than us. Gray is that kind of predator, a monster inside of an alluring shell.

With painful slowness, he turns to face me, his eyes filled with dark promises. *He didn't like that,* the frightened voice in my head squeaks. *He didn't like that at all.*

My legs quiver, the muscles tightening, preparing to run. They spasm beneath my skin, and yet, I can't move. I'm frozen in place as he steps toward me. He moves slowly. Closer, closer. My heart rate ticks up with each inch until I think it might explode from my chest.

His fingers grip my thighs and my breath catches in my throat. He shoves them apart, pressing his body between my legs. I turn my face downward, staring at my boobs to avoid his gaze. His finger presses beneath my chin, forcing me to face him.

He looks down at me, his mouth quirked into a taunting smile. "Are you sure? It seems an awful lot like you *are* my girlfriend." He holds up his index finger. "You texted me when you were upset, wanting me to bring you home from the bar." His middle finger pops up next to the first. "You woke up in my bed, wearing my clothes." He leans in, his soft lips almost brushing against mine. His nostrils flare and he stretches out a third finger. "And you used my toothbrush."

I shove my fists against his chest. Putting all of my strength into pushing him away, I grunt out a very unladylike sound. He doesn't move back an inch. If anything, he presses himself closer. My nipples pebble beneath the thin cotton shirt as they connect with his stomach. The heat returns to my cheeks, if it even left in the first place. Whenever I'm around him, I feel like my face is on fire.

My face pinches into a scowl. "I didn't ask you to kidnap me, you psycho."

"No?" he asks, his eyes gleaming with humor. "But you knew I would when you texted me. You're a smart woman, Ava." His finger moves from my chin to my throat. His hand wraps around my neck. His grip is soft, a warning, a reminder. His hand doesn't squeeze, and yet, I can't breathe. I won't let myself take a breath, because if I do, I'm not sure I can stop the sound that might come out when I let it go.

The threat of his rough touch does something to me, something it really shouldn't. The heat of his hand on my throat seeps into me. It spreads through me, rushing downward, sending a flood of arousal to my core. *He's a monster*, I force the thought into my head, pounding it against my skull over and over, hoping it will stick. Of course, another traitorous voice inside of me counters, *a monster you want to fuck you, claim you, keep you.*

"You knew I'd come for you," he says, "and we both know that's why you texted me. You wanted to see me. You missed me."

I loose a breath, my lungs unable to hold it any longer. His grip on my neck tightens, a renewed threat, a reminder that I'm playing games with a dangerous animal. My fingers wrap around the edges of the stool beneath me, gripping it until I feel my tendons crackle. The rational part of my mind grapples for control, desperately trying to hold on to my resolve. It screams inside of me to not submit to him. The entirely irrational part of me, however, moans under Gray's powerful grasp.

His fingers dance along my thigh, lifting the hem of my shirt. "Show me how much you missed me, little bird," he growls into the shell of my ear.

Cool air whispers against my folds, reminding me that I'm stark naked under my borrowed shirt. My muscles tense as his fingers press against me. They swipe over my wetness, drawing a line from my center to my clit. When he touches that bundle of nerves, my hips buck, pressing into his hand. I can't stop the husky cry that jumps from my mouth.

He hums approvingly. "That's my good girl. My perfect little slut. So wet, so responsive to my touch."

I pant in little, breathless gasps as he slowly circles my clit. My walls clench around nothing. He's barely touched me, but I can feel the pressure building in my core. My hips press forward, grinding against his hand, searching for release. He pushes me to the edge of orgasm, and just as I'm about to tip and fall off the precipice, he pulls away. I whine at the loss of his hand, a needy, pathetic squawk.

He turns and walks back to the stove, licking my arousal from his fingers. I sit in stunned silence, mortified and fuming. My mind ticks through a list of all of the reasons that I hate him. *Murderer, psycho, stalker, guy who seems to think I can't feed myself, teasing, horrible bastard.*

I try to ignore the savory scents filling the room. I don't want him to cook for me. I don't want him to take care of me. No one has ever tried, not since Mom died. *Don't give in,* the frightened voice inside me whimpers, *he's lying to you. He'll hurt you and leave you, just like everyone else. You're nothing, nothing, nothing.*

My stomach, however, seems to have no such qualms about him feeding me. It releases an embarrassingly loud grumble. He chuckles and it's different. It's a warm, happy sound that bubbles up from his throat. *Nope, nope, nope,* my mind chants, *do not read into that. Monsters are not happy. Monsters are not good. Monsters do not care.*

The piles of eggs, bacon, and toast on my plate taunt me. Steam rises from the plate, along with the smell of something I so rarely get to have—a home cooked meal. It invades my nostrils, beckoning me, demanding that I give in.

"Eat, Ava," Gray demands, his voice soft with an edge of bite that indicates that this is most certainly not a request, but a command.

The fork, clenched tightly between my fingers, doesn't move. Gray's lips tip into a knowing smile before he stabs a piece of the fluffy egg from my plate and pops it into his mouth. His eyebrows quirk up with expectation, only lowering when I snag a piece of bacon and stick it in my mouth. I chomp on it slowly, holding back a pleasured groan as the grease trickles over my tongue.

Gray eats with a cocky grin plastered across his face, his movements significantly more graceful than my own. He moves slowly, small portions of food delicately making their way from his plate to his mouth, while I shovel eggs hurriedly into mine.

"I...I..." I stumble over my words, needing to say something, but entirely unsure of what. "I don't even know anything about you..."

"So ask me, baby." He takes a sip of orange juice, staring at me over the rim of the glass. "I'll tell you anything you want to know."

My eyebrows shoot up into my hairline. "You will?"

"I'd never lie to you."

I shouldn't believe that. I shouldn't even want to believe it, but there's something in his eyes that sparkles with sincerity. Has he ever actually hidden anything from me? He's unabashedly admitted to murder, proclaimed his obsession for me, and said he has no intention of killing me.

My eyes pan around his gorgeous, expensive home, and I ask the first question that pops into my head. "What do you do for work?"

"I'm an assassin."

The fork slips through my grasp, clattering loudly against the ceramic plate. Little chunks of egg pop up, splattering onto the table. I shove my body sideways, my chair screeching across the floor, putting precious inches between me and the murderer sitting beside me. With shaking fingers, I snatch a butter knife from the table. Sunlight from the large dining room windows sparkles off of the metal as I point the dull tip toward Gray.

His eyes dart from mine to the knife. Something that looks oddly like pride glimmers in their blue depths. "I'd never hurt you, little bird," he says with a soft smile. "You're everything to me."

My mind races, thoughts whirling and tumbling like leaves on the wind. *Everything?* The frightened little creature inside of me perks up. *Not nothing?* The knife drops from my fingers, clunking onto the table. Suddenly, the revelation that he's a murderer for hire holds less weight than his admission that to him I'm something more than the nothing I've always been.

"Don't get shy on me now." Gray chuckles, pulling me from my thoughts. "Ask me something else."

"I…uh…how old are you?"

"Thirty-six," he replies, "close to your age."

"What's your favorite food?"

"Pizza."

"Favorite color?"

"Green."

"Favorite movie?"

His lips tip into a smile, not a grin or a smirk, but a panty-dropping smile. "Any you'll watch with me."

I hate that by the time our plates are empty, I can't entirely despise him. The thought sobers me, renewing the war inside of me between what I know and what I feel. I pile our plates in my hand and walk back into the kitchen to put them in the sink.

Turning on the tap, I let the cool water run over my hands, grounding me, giving me anything else to think about but him. After several minutes of scrubbing, I'm surprised I haven't scrubbed the pattern off of the ceramic plates. A surprised squeak pops from my mouth when warm arms wrap around my waist and I'm pulled against a hard chest.

"I like the way you look in our home, little bird," Gray purrs, placing a gentle kiss on the top of my head.

Our home? Did he just say *our* freaking home?! Does he think since I'm here that I'm moving in with him?

"No, no, nope, absolutely not!" The words I intended to shout come out breathy and whispered. My face scrunches up into a scowl and I force my voice to be louder, more forceful. "You are insane. This is insane. Just get me my shit. I'm leaving."

He whips my body around, his arms tightening around me, forcing me to face him. I wince, expecting a sharp slap that never comes. The anger I expect to see in his face when I open my eyes isn't there. His face is a mask of patience, his eyes soft in under-standing.

"I just need to go home, Gray. I really need to go——"

His lips crash into mine in a searing kiss. He claims my mouth with desperate hunger, like nothing has ever been as important. Like he needs this, needs me. Every thought in my head blinks out into nothingness as he devours me. I let myself become lost in his kiss, letting all the world fall away until there's nothing but the two of us.

His tongue parts the seam of my lips and I let him. He swallows my moans as his tongue slides against mine. His hands slide under my thighs, lifting me up like I weigh nothing. My legs wrap around his waist, my arms locked behind his neck, as he carries me to the couch.

Our lips part, both of us breathless and panting. "You're mine, Ava," he growls. "My home, my fucking soul. I've been giving you time to wrap your beautiful mind around it, but you *are* mine. And whether it's here or somewhere else, we will live together. You will never be rid of me."

The sofa groans as we fall onto it, but I can't bring myself to care about the integrity of his fancy furniture when I'm on his lap.

His hand slides up my neck, his fingers gripping my hair. The sharp bite of pain forces me to cry out when he pulls.

"You like that, don't you, precious?" His voice is rasped and full of need. "You like it when I hurt you."

"Yes," I whisper against his lips.

His hand tightens in my hair, drawing my neck to the side and kisses me in the sensitive spot below my ear. His teeth scrape against my neck, pulling a moan from my throat. His cock hardens beneath me, his length pressed against my naked core with only his sweatpants between us. I roll my hips, grinding against him, feeling his impossible size.

His hand slides under my shirt. I gasp as the rough skin of his calloused palms scrapes over my ribcage. His thumb rolls over my nipple and it hardens under his touch. He pinches the sensitive bud between his fingers until I choke out a sound that falls somewhere between a sob and a moan.

His hands move around my body and I feel like they're everywhere all at once. He grabs my hip so hard that I'm certain I'll find bruises there tomorrow. When he wraps his other hand around my throat, my breath catches. My mind races, thoughts bouncing around like ping-pong balls. *I shouldn't want this. This is wrong. This isn't real. It's all lies. He doesn't want me. No one truly wants me. This is a game to him. I'm nothing.*

"Eyes on me," Gray demands. "Get out of that pretty little head. Stay right here with me."

My eyes snap to his and I let myself fall into them. The dark ocean in his eyes sucks me in, drowning me. A wave of calm crashes over me as I focus on him. His words wash over me and my mind quiets. Something inside of me eases, letting go of the pain it's been gripping so tightly, as if I would let him carry it for me.

"There you go," he says softly, "you're doing so well. Keep those eyes on me."

His hips lift, his hard shaft pressing against my core. He rolls his hips and my clit pulses with the delicious friction. He controls me with his hand, pushing and pulling my body, forcing me to grind against him.

Gray purrs in my ear, a dark, raspy sound thick with desire, "That's it, precious. Rub that greedy little cunt on your master."

And goddamnit, I do. I rock my hips back and forth with abandon. With each movement, his cock brushes against my clit and my legs quiver. A filthy sound pours from my mouth as pleasure ripples through my body, which tightens like a spring. Each pass of my hips coils it tighter, tighter, tighter.

"Please," I whimper. I don't even know what I'm asking for. For him to stop? For him to keep going? For more? The heat inside of me is burning and the spring keeps coiling. "Need…"

"I'll give you what you need," Gray promises, his hand sliding up my inner thigh. "Let go for me, little bird. Let me hear you sing."

He pinches my clit between his fingers and the spring inside of me uncoils. I scream out a croaked moan as white-hot pleasure explodes through my body. My pussy spasms, clenching against the emptiness inside me as the orgasm rips me open. I collapse against Gray's chest, panting and riding out the aftershocks.

I let myself enjoy the embrace of his arms, rubbing my cheek against his pec like a cat marking its favorite human. The sweet, masculine scent of him soothes me in a way that it shouldn't. But I let it, basking in the warmth of his body and the way I fit in his arms.

The pleasurable haze begins to lift from my mind and I startle in his embrace. Suddenly needing to be anywhere but on top of him, I wrench myself backward. His arms quickly band around me and I thump back into his chest. He hums approvingly, his hand stroking comforting circles on my back.

"I've got you, precious." *Precious.* A tingling warmth spreads through my chest at the word. "You did so well. You're such a good girl for me."

Like the pathetic creature I am, I melt back into his arms. All the while, that little voice inside of my head chides, *You are so fucked.*

Chapter Thirty-Three

Strawberries and citrus, that'll fix this, right? I huff out a scoff, staring down at the little pink block in my shower. Hot water sprays over it, melting the square into a gooey mess. Scented steam wafts upward, spreading through my bathroom until the whole room smells like summertime.

I roll my eyes, irritated by my own naïveté. "A shower steamer, really? Like this is going to solve anything." It's not as if I've been in this situation before, but thinking it could be made better by bath products seems asinine, even for me. I could dump all the calming toiletries in the world over my body and it wouldn't fix this. I should try anyway, though, shouldn't I?

I crush the loofa to my body, rubbing it so roughly that my skin pinkens. If I can wash the scent of him from my body, scrub away his touch, can I break his hold on me? If only there was a way to reach into my chest and scour him from my heart.

He shouldn't be in there at all, but he is. The walls I've so carefully built around my heart are starting to crack, the stones chipping and crumbling. His constant presence, his words, his caress, they become fissures in the rocks, forcing them apart. *You're everything to me. Precious. I'd never hurt you. Good girl. I'd never lie to you.* His words drift through my mind, waging a war inside of me.

My insides are fragmenting, and it hurts. A sinking feeling churns in my belly as chunks of myself wander and collide. I want to believe what he tells me, to believe that someone wants me. Is it possible that I could become more to someone than what I've always been? A body to use, a soul to break, a speck of nothing in a world of somethings? Can I truly risk letting myself believe? If I allow myself to hope, it could break me. If it's all lies, it'll crack me open like an egg. My soul will spill out into a slimy mess that can't be put back.

My skin heats, not from the spray of the hot water, but from the memory of his hands on me, his rumbling words purred in my ears. There's something heady in the way he blends violence and tenderness that makes my head spin and my core ache. Looking down at the bruises on my hip, purple stains in the shape of his fingertips, I can't help but feel the warmth slithering through my belly. His mark on my skin will fade in a few days, and I can't help but wonder if I'll be sad to see them gone.

My eyelids flutter and close. My hand runs down the length of my stomach, fingers tickling over my damp skin. But it's not my hand I feel; it's his. I imagine the rough texture of his palms skating over my body, igniting a fire within me. It's his hand that inches downward, dancing over my mound. When I open my legs, it's his finger that parts my folds. His skilled touch teases my clit, sending ripples of pleasure zipping through my body. As my fingers swirl around the sensitive nub, I feel his fingers.

The memory of Gray's hands, drawn from my mind, yanks me closer to release until I'm unable to control the way my hips twitch and gyrate. My orgasm looms over me, but without his touch, it feels unattainable, weak and small. It's an ache inside me that can't be sated by my fingers alone, but I don't stop. I don't stop working my clit until my inner walls flutter, however weakly. With a heavy sigh, I pull my hand away, frustrated and aching.

I quickly shampoo my hair before dragging myself out of the shower. My old towel scratches against my skin as I dry myself. *I bet the towels at Gray's are expensive and soft.* I quickly shake the thought away as I shove my legs into a pair of fuzzy sweatpants. The fleecy fabric wraps around me like a warm hug—a very ugly, warm hug. My most comfortable lounge-around-the-house outfit is matching pants and a sweatshirt that are so pink, they look like a unicorn puked them out. Little yellow hearts line the edges, making me look like I'm dressed in the wallpaper from a child's nursery.

"Yup," I drawl with a tone filled with sarcasm, "if the stupid shower steamers can't fix this, surely some hideous, fuzzy lounge wear will." A strange giggle bubbles from my mouth. "Maybe he'll see me in this and never come back."

I try to tell myself that that's what I want, for him to leave and never darken my doorstep again. I told him as much when he brought me home, but I know that it's a lie. When we arrived at my house, my heart did a little backflip because my car was already in my driveway, my keys safely tucked away under my doormat.

I felt like I was watching from afar as he walked me to my door, guiding me with his hand on my lower back. It was so…normal. Like he was just a regular guy dropping me off after a date.

"I have something important I need to do, something I have to do to keep us safe," he had said. "I promise I won't stay away so long this time. I'll never leave you alone again."

Us. He had said it with such casualty, like it was just the way of things. He said it like we're a single entity now, a couple. But what could he have to do to keep us safe?

"You *will* be a good girl for me," he murmured against my lips. It wasn't a question, but a command. And damn, I felt that command rush through me like lightning when his hand wrapped around my throat and his lips crashed into mine. He kissed me like he needed to consume me, to rip out a piece of my soul to take with him. His tongue wrapped around mine, stroking me from the inside until I felt boneless. When he pulled away, the hard lines of his face were drawn down, his lips pressed into a thin line. He looked pained, like it physically hurt him to leave.

"I'll be watching, little bird." He left me with a threat and a promise. I tried not to let hope bloom in my chest. I tried to tamp it down, to shove it back into the box inside me, but the box is cracking under the pressure he's exerting on it.

Thunk, thunk, thunk.

A heavy knock bangs against my front door, startling me. The manuscript in my hands slips between my fingers, pages scattering across the floor. I scowl down at the jumble of papers, wondering why I still print the damn things. *Because paper is better,* the feral book gremlin inside me screeches.

Reluctantly, I leave the scattered mass. Frustration bubbles in my belly. I hate to leave a story mid-chapter to yank myself back into my body, back into the real world.

After my unsatisfying shower, I allowed myself to become someone else, to lose myself in a new manuscript. I became Olivia, a woman trapped by circumstance. I had traveled to a distant world, wrought by an unending war. The sounds of metal rang out as swords clashed on the battlefield. I was a warrior, fighting on the side of humans in the war against the monsters who crawled up from the bowels of the Earth. Their powerful bodies brought soldiers to their knees, their horns and talons gleaming with blood.

I watched the demon hoard advance on us, their ranks marching down the mountain in tight formations. Their leader, a monster far larger than any I'd ever seen, stood at the front of the lines. Shadows writhed along his scaled skin. His eyes never strayed from his path, even as his shadow magic whipped out to suck the life force from our men. His path, as it turned out, led him directly to me, the woman he claimed to be his fated mate.

I shake my head, forcing the compelling story to the back of my mind as I head for the door. A large-brimmed hat peers at me from the small window in my front door. A tan hat, that unfortunately, I recognize.

"Hello, Sheriff Lynnfield," I state through gritted teeth that I hope are hidden by my fake smile.

He tips his hat in greeting. "Ava, I have some bad news."

My heart turns to metal, sinking into my stomach. *James,* my head screams. It must be about the deputy. *Do they know he's dead? Do they know that Gray killed him? Will his actions damn me to a life in prison?* I try not to gasp for air as my breathing becomes shallow.

The sheriff clears his throat in the way that old men seem to do. "It's about your daddy."

My eyes widen, eyebrows shooting up to the sky. "My father?"

"Mhmm," he grumbles an affirmative sound, pulling his hat from his head to rest it against his bulging stomach. Despite the frigid air of late autumn, sweat beads on his bare head. He wipes his hand across his forehead, collecting the beads that have dripped onto his eyebrows. "He was supposed to go on a fishing trip today and…" He lets out a heavy breath. His eyes seem far away for a moment before refocusing on me.

"Well, there's just no easy way to say this," he continues. "He's dead. They found him in his cabin this morning."

I stumble back a step, slapping my palm on the doorframe for balance. "Dead? What?" I stammer. "How?"

"It…uh…well, it looks like a suicide," he says softly as if the news pains him to repeat. Perhaps it does, given how close he once was with my father. "He…he hanged himself."

I shove my tongue between my teeth and bite. I gnaw on my tongue until I taste copper, because I can't say anything. I can't tell him that I'm not sad, that my father was the worst kind of monster. I can't tell him that the bastard deserved a far worse death than one of his own choosing. So, I bite my tongue and let the tears fall from my eyes. He doesn't need to know that they're tears of relief.

"Look," he grumbles, "we don't have all the details. There were some other injuries on him, but we think they were self-inflicted."

Hanged himself? Self-inflicted injuries? A gnawing feeling clenches my stomach because something isn't right about this. My father is, or was, a narcissist. He wouldn't have taken his own life. Somewhere inside of me, I know this, but I won't say it out loud.

The sheriff's eyes don't find mine. He doesn't give me the well wishes and sympathies that he gave when Mom died. He doesn't offer comfort. He simply turns around and walks back to his car.

I listen to the gravel crunching under his tires and my silent sobs shift, their pitch elevating into something else entirely. As I watch him drive away, the sound of my laughter echoes through the woods. Birds scatter from their branches at the hideous cackle that spews from my mouth. I barely register the pain as my knees crack against the wooden porch. Even as I laugh, tears stream down my face, creating sopping wet spots on my thighs.

The frightened little girl that still lives inside me sobs with me. Her tears flow down my cheeks. Her heart beats with my own. *I'm free*, she cries. *I'm finally free.*

When I step back inside, I walk through my home, staring at every aspect like I'm seeing it for the first time. I look at the grooves in the wood of the staircase, no longer seeing my broken, bleeding fingernails dragging my beaten body to safety. Mom's blood no longer oozes through the cracks of the kitchen tiles. The tiny closet in the guest bedroom is just a closet, not a place for a small child to hide.

My home smells of citrus. It no longer holds the pungent stench of bleach that Mom used to scrub the evidence of our pain from the floors.

"We're free, Mom," I whisper the words into every room, hoping that somehow she can hear me.

Emily's eyes are wide as she stares at me from across the table. They're blue, but so different from another set of blue eyes that I think of often. Hers are light and airy like wind blowing over the Caribbean. His are darker, colder, like chips of ice floating through a frigid lake.

"So, he's really gone?" she asks so softly that I can barely make out her words over the noise of the busy restaurant.

"He's really gone. I'm free, Em."

She releases her breath all at once, along with that happy little squeak she makes. The leather of our booth seats groan as we both lean forward, hands reaching for each other. She grasps my fingers in hers and squeezes gently.

"Maybe it's not right to say," she whispers hesitantly, "but I'm so fucking glad your dad is dead."

The laugh that bubbles out of me is loud, the unrestrained sound of pure joy. Our shoulders shake as we chortle.

A server approaches our table and pulls a notepad from the pocket of her apron. "You ladies look like you're celebrating over here!" She shoots us a beaming smile. "How about a drink?"

"Yes, this celebration needs booze!" Emily chirps happily. "I'll have a Manhattan."

The waitress' eyes turn to me. "And for you, honey?"

"A margarita with salt."

"Oh, good choice! I'll be right back with those for you."

My phone squawks out an irritating beep. I shove my hands into my purse, rooting around for all of a minute before I find it hidden amongst tissues and lip glosses. The screen comes alive with a new text from Gray, whose number I finally programmed into my contacts.

> Just one drink, little bird. You're driving home tonight.

My mouth drops open in surprise and I whip my head around the room, searching for him. The restaurant is popular. Even in the early evening, it's filled with diners. Couples hold hands over scratched tables. Groups of friends squeeze into booths, their shoulders pressed together. Singles are perched on barstools, sipping cocktails. I know he won't be in any of those places. My eyes find the dark places, the corners, the edges of the room, the small crevices where the shadows live.

Of course, I'm left wanting. No dark hoods or black leather catches my eye. I type quickly, hoping that Emily won't notice my distraction.

Are you watching me?

He doesn't leave me waiting. His response is almost instantaneous.

Always.

Something unfamiliar sparks inside my chest. Something that feels oddly like bravery, being unafraid of consequences.

And what if I want more than one? You're not the boss of me.

I stare down at my own words, wondering how I can be so brazen. I shake my head as my teeth sink into my lip. Am I channeling Emily's flirtatiousness? Her outgoing nature? I must be, because this isn't me. Or maybe it *wasn't* me.

His reply pops up, pulling me out of my head. I can almost hear his dark chuckle in it.

Oh, little bird, please try me. I'd love to take your bratty ass over my knee again. I'll spank you until you can't sit for a week.

My mouth goes dry as all of the fluids in my body change course, shooting south and dampening my thighs.

"Ava?" Emily's eyes are on my heated cheeks, a smirk pulling at the corners of her mouth. "Whose texts are turning your face into a tomato?"

"I…uh…no one, just—"

Her hand snaps out and latches onto my phone. She yanks it from my fingers and holds it up to her face. Her little smirk morphs into a devious grin.

"Oh, shit! Girl, I had no idea you were into that kind of thing. Fuck, that's hot." She fans her face with her hand and shoots me a wink. "Tell me everything."

Oh, crap.

Chapter Thirty-Four

My legs struggle for space, crammed into a small chair in the makeshift office space in the corner of Shawn's bedroom. Pushing my forearm onto the desk, I brush aside a collection of empty cans and mugs before pulling my phone from my pocket.

From security cameras in the restaurant, I watch Ava squirm in her seat. Her legs twitch, thighs rubbing together under the table. When her friend grabs her phone, Ava's cheeks turn rosy. Her voice comes through my phone, feathery and sweet.

I can feel Shawn's eyes on me, bearing the weight of his displeasure. He made his feelings clear about hacking into restaurant cameras and the microphone on Ava's phone when I asked him to do it tonight. *An invasion of privacy*, he called it, *kind of sick and perverted*. I don't give a fuck about that. There's no privacy where she's concerned. She's mine and I'll know every single piece of her heart.

I listen as she tells her friend a story of an unconventional romance. In her words, *just a kinky guy she's getting to know*. It doesn't escape my notice that she leaves out any details of consequence. She doesn't tell her friend how I stalk her, frighten her, kill for her. She may not be ready to admit it yet, but the idea of getting me arrested pains her. She may not know why, but she's not prepared to let me go. I'll have to reward her for being such a good, obedient girl.

"You done being creepy, dude?" Shawn's voice yanks my attention away from the beautiful brunette on my screen.

When I level him with a glare, he shrinks, his chest deflating as his feet inch backward. His eyes lower like he's suddenly fascinated by his dirty high-tops.

"Any news?" I ask, impatience bleeding into my voice. Reluctantly, I shut down the video on my phone.

"Well," Shawn breathes out the word with a pained tone, "everyone wants you dead. I mean, *everyone*." He heaves out a dry, anxious laugh. "There are hits out on you from the Rossi and Volkov families. They're offering a *lot* of cash for your head."

My jaw clenches, teeth gnashing together. "Any news that I didn't already know?"

"I found the location of Mikhail Volkov's office."

"Good."

Shawn's mouth opens, then closes. His index finger pops up like he has an important point to make, but he lowers it just as quickly.

I huff out a breath. "Say what you need to say."

He clears his throat and stuffs his hands into his pockets. "Are you going to…uhh…kill him?"

"I'm just going to pay him a visit."

"Yeah, okay. You're going to *'pay him a visit'*." He sticks his fingers up, throwing air quotes around the phrase.

If my eyes could roll further back, I'd be staring at my brain. "Shawn, I don't kill every person I talk to."

"Uh huh." His tone makes it clear that he thinks that's bullshit.

"Fine, I might have to kill him, but that's not my goal. I'm going to try to negotiate with him."

Realistically, at least a few of Volkov's men will die today. I don't expect them to just let me waltz into their boss's office without a fight. I'm not an idiot. If I need to kill all of them, I won't be bothered by it. My moral compass only points in one direction—Ava's. I'll do whatever I have to do to keep her safe.

Another fucking nightclub. What the fuck is it with people and nightclubs? The powerful seem to be enamored with the concept of making money off of them, like they enjoy being immersed in the stench of stale beer and horny tourists. I wipe my palms against my jeans as if my proximity to the building tainted them.

My eyes lift to the gray building before me, Volkov's club, Samogon. At night, it probably looks impressive, a towering edifice of sensuality and sin. In the light of day and without booze's rose colored glasses, the bricks are beginning to crumble. The brackets and poles that hold up neon signs are edged with rust. Like everything else in this city, if you look too closely, you'll see the cracks forming in its foundations. I'm one of those cracks, a piece of the depravity that's corroding the bedrock of this metropolitan nightmare.

I lift my hand to the front door, leaving my other resting on the butt of my knife, and knock. The security camera above the door lets out a soft, mechanical whir, and pivots in my direction. I don't bother to hide my face and instead stare up into it with a grin that begs them to try to fuck with me. Barely five seconds later, the door bursts open, sending a putrid wave of nightclub stench billowing out into the street.

Catching sight of the man who steps into the doorframe, it's pretty clear that they most certainly are going to try to fuck with me. The beefy fucker eyes me, his lips puckering into a sour expression. His eyes flash with recognition and his mouth turns up into a smirk. His two-sizes-too-small t-shirt protests as he yanks his arm back, the fabric threatening to split as his muscles bulge. With no time to block him, I clench my stomach and brace for impact just before his fist collides with my gut.

My ass collides with the pavement so hard I wouldn't be surprised to find it split open beneath me. Pain spreads through my stomach like acid, forcing bile up my throat. My tongue feels like lead as I swallow a mouthful of vomit. Something moves in front of me. My eyes flit upward just in time to watch a beefy body fly through the air, heading directly for me. Nausea suddenly forgotten, I roll to the side to avoid the collision. The harsh pavement scrapes against my cheek as I move, leaving my face stinging.

The giant goon crashes to the ground, his knees cracking beneath him. A sound booms around us, somewhere between a growl and a scream. He moves to stand, his thick legs forcing him upward awkwardly. Before his back straightens, my knife is in his neck. Despite his bulk, the sharpened blade slices through him like butter. The breath gurgles out of him, great globs of blood along with it. His fingers grasp his neck in desperation as his body topples forward.

I step over his twitching body, narrowly avoiding dipping the tips of my boots into a puddle of his blood. I've never been particularly opposed to getting bloodied. It's an expected occupational hazard. Over the years, I've become something of an expert in cleaning it.

Now, something inside of me recoils at the thought of getting some asshole's blood on Ava's floors. The only blood my sweet little bird will ever touch is mine. The thought prompts a flood of images in my mind. I watch Ava's delicate hands clean my wounds, the softness of her skin counteracting the sting of the antiseptic. Her fingertips are gentle as she bandages me.

I let the images dissipate. They whisper away like the fog of my breath in the cold, autumn air. I step into the club, letting my eyes roam around the empty space. Like the outside of the building, the inside is equally unimpressive in the daytime. Daylight pours in from the open doorway. It falls over the black bar top, highlighting the scratches in its surface. It crawls over the red floors, revealing old stains that have seeped into the edges between the tiles.

I walk toward the back rooms, keeping my distance from the walls that seem unwilling to let go of the oily fingerprints of patrons past. I'm certain if I looked lower, I'd find smudges from sweaty asses embedded into the plaster. Out of the corner of my eye, a flash of yellow catches my attention from the end of a small hallway. The *employee's only* sign sits in the center of a metal door. It begs for my attention, leading me toward my target. The camera above it whirs, swiveling in my direction just before the door screeches open.

Two men scramble out, their chests puffed up and eyes sparkling with challenge. Their collective bulk fills the hallway, barring my entry. They widen their stances, challenging the strength of the seams of their jeans. As their arms flex under their shirts, the word *security* printed on the front widens, as if the letters are trying to get away from each other. At the sight of their posturing, a chuckle erupts from my throat.

"Where's your boss?" I ask.

Unsurprisingly, Tweedle Dee and Tweedle Dumb don't tell me where their boss is.

"*Ubey yego*," Dumb hisses. I don't understand the word, but the way the letters smack against his tongue creates a sound that seems equally as harsh as what I assume it means. Dee jams a tattooed hand into his jeans, pulling out a Marakov pistol. He lunges with Dumb on his heels, until there's only inches between us.

His heavy breath puffs against my face. The smell of tobacco and peppermint is so strong that my eyes threaten to tear up. He shakes his head, dislodging a tendril of sandy-brown hair from his eye so that he can glare at me fully. His lips tip up into a satisfied smirk as the barrel of his gun presses into my forehead.

My toe drums against the floor with an audible tapping. "Are you sure this is how you want to play this?"

Dee increases the pressure on his gun, surely forcing a circular imprint into the skin between my eyes. Clearly, this is how he wants to play this. He wants to be the one who kills me and brings my head to his boss. Unfortunately for him, that's not going to happen. My hand shoots up, snatching his wrist and wrenching the gun away from my head. I bend his hand back until his bone snaps and he howls in pain.

I throw my arm forward, yanking his along with it, and wrap my fingers around his. His buddy stands dumbfounded in front of me, eyes wide and mouth gaping. He reaches for his gun, but his twitchy fingers lose their grip, causing it to clatter to the floor. I raise Dee's hand and squeeze the trigger with his finger. The shot penetrates

Dumb's skull. Bone fragments and chunks of scalp fly backward, splattering against the wall.

Dee lets out a pained wail as his knees crumple beneath him. He dangles awkwardly from the arm that's still in my grasp, his face hovering over the floor. I jump back a step, narrowly avoiding the spray of vomit as he pukes his guts out onto the tile. After he heaves up his lunch, he turns his face toward me. My face splits into a grin as I look down at the cowering mess of a man.

"Brother….my brother," he whispers.

"I did try to warn you. We could have avoided all of this if you had just shown me to Mikhail's office." His teary eyes widen as my words sink in. "Don't worry. I'll send you to your brother."

I turn his wrist, feeling the damaged bones shift under his skin, and we squeeze the trigger one more time. I feel the warm wetness as his blood sprays my pant legs and boots.

"Fuck." So much for keeping my shoes clean.

The door to Mikhail Volkov's office pops open with a turn of the handle. The slightly misaligned hinges squeak, but offer no resistance. The man must feel confident in his safety to leave it unlocked. With it open fully, I can see why.

The head of the Volkov family sits behind a mahogany desk with his gun pointed square in the middle of my face. His aim doesn't waver as he rakes a hand though his silver hair. His eyes narrow, more wrinkles appearing at the edges.

I hold my palms up in front of me. "I'm just here to talk."

He nods and places the gun down on his desk. He stands quietly, hiding the discomfort of his aging body. I still catch the slight twitch of his lip as he moves. He runs his palm down his navy blue, tailored suit, pressing out the creases.

He crosses the room to a small bar cart. With a wave of his hand and a quirk of his eyebrows, he offers me a drink. I shake my head, unwilling to chance this meeting coming to an end by poisoning. His hands are unhurried as he pours himself a glass of vodka.

"You killed someone very important to my organization, Mr. Alexander," he says.

It's so rare that I hear my last name spoken that it feels foreign, like it doesn't belong to me. *Ava Alexander*, the name whispers through my mind. It's beautiful, perfect for my little bird.

Mikhail must notice the shock on my face because he grins. "I know the names of my enemies, son."

"I'm not your enemy." I look him straight in the eye, willing him to see the truth of my words.

His eyes flash with surprise for a second before they turn cold. He motions to a large television on the wall that displays the feeds from several security cameras around the club. In one of them, the bloodied corpses of his men lay sprawled over the dirty floor.

He chuckles in a way that conveys no humor. "Is that so?"

"I was given false information on a target," I explain. "I didn't know he was one of yours. I was set up."

He peers at me through narrowed eyes, his mouth pressed into a thin line. "And who is it that gave you this *false information?*"

"Bianca Rossi."

Mikhail spits out a breath, his calm mask slipping at the edges, revealing the rage bubbling beneath it. "Of course," he says flatly, "I expected she would try to kill him." He pinches his chin, rubbing his thumb and forefinger through his neatly manicured beard. "I just didn't think she'd succeed."

He tips his chin toward me, his mouth pulling up into a knowing smirk. "Are you to blame for the chaos in her business these days? I've heard rumors of missing girls and dead customers."

I don't acknowledge the question, since he and I both know the answer. "I have no issue with you or your family," I state.

"No, I suppose you do not."

"But," I let the word hang in the air for a moment, "I will if your men keep coming after me. I'm sure you understand that anyone who does will die."

Mikhail nods solemnly even as his mouth twitches. In that

moment, a silent understanding builds between us. He doesn't care about collateral damage unless it impacts his bottom line. There's a cold indifference in his eyes that mirrors my own. We're similar monsters. Save a select few, the lives lost are meaningless to us.

"I will make you a deal, Mr. Alexander," he says, flashing his teeth in a demented smile. "Kill the bitch who leads the Rossi family and we can put this all behind us."

I nod in response and step back out into the nightclub. I leave quickly, avoiding the corpses I left in the hallway, and hoping that Mikhail doesn't change his mind and shoot me in the back.

Chapter Thirty-Five

"Kill Bianca Rossi?!" Shawn's voice screeches through my phone, worsening the ache that began to form behind my eyes the moment I left Nocturno. "Dude, are you nuts? Do you know how well-protected she is?"

I pinch the bridge of my nose and push out a steadying breath. "I'm fully aware of the situation, Shawn."

"Oh, super. You have a death wish and I get to come along for the ride!" His tone is harsh, but I hear the distinct quiver of fear in his words. "And what about the woman you're stalking? You could get her killed! She's not a part of this shit. She's innocent."

The sound that barrels out of my mouth can only be described as a growl. "I would never let anything happen to Ava. I'll fucking die first."

"Oh," he whispers, "I, uh, didn't think...didn't know you were—"

"Well, I fucking am!" I shout. "I'll protect her."

"Yeah, okay."

Frustration prickles in my gut as I stare at my laptop screen. Despite hours of research, I've found next to nothing on Bianca, certainly nothing useful. It's not surprising, though. People like us, those who live and work within the seedy underbelly of this city, are ghosts. We hide in the shadows, imperceivable to those who live in the light.

"Just get me everything you can on Bianca. I want to know where she eats, where she sleeps, everything." I end the call. The ache in my head deepens to a throbbing pain.

Initially, I hadn't planned to kill Bianca. I'd only planned to make her life hard enough that she'd leave me alone. It doesn't seem like I have a choice anymore, not if I want to keep Ava safe. If both Mikhail and Bianca keep coming after me, it'll only be a matter of time before they find her.

An image flashes in my mind of the face of the woman I couldn't save. Mom's lifeless eyes stare up at me. Looking into the airy blue of her irises was always like looking up at the sky on a sunny day. Now they're cloudy and unseeing. Her beautiful raven hair is no longer silky, but matted with blood. Her cheeks are smeared with it.

"Goddammnit!" I slam my palms on my desk hard enough to shake the wood and send pens scattering to the floor. I won't let it happen again.

Go to her, the beastly thing inside my chest screams. I push myself away from my desk, my body moving of its own accord. *Protect her*. I shove my arms into my jacket sleeves with enough force to nearly rip open the seams. *Keep her*. My car keys are suddenly in my hand. *Make her yours*. My car rumbles to life beneath me. The tires squeal, skidding against the pavement and picking up speed.

Gravel crunches under my boots as I step toward Ava's front porch. Little chunks of rock skitter across the driveway, landing in a patch of dirt and dead grass. I inhale deeply. The emotions that have a death grip on my heart seem to loosen as the perfume of autumn fills my lungs. Greedily, I suck in air until the nauseating tang of exhaust fumes and garbage that saturates the city is replaced by the scent of wood and earth.

The porch groans under my weight, its beams crying out as if they're warning me that they might not hold on for much longer. As I stare down at the aged wood, my mind wanders. It conjures images of the home I'll have built for us away from the stench of the city. My mouth tips up into a smile as I think about my little bird sipping her morning coffee on a porch that isn't about to collapse.

The door handle doesn't budge when I turn it. "Good girl, keeping yourself safe," I whisper.

I let myself in with the copy I took of her key. When I push open the door, I'm hit with an immediate sense of relief. I inhale deeply, pulling her sweet scent into me. She smells like home. A melodic hum travels through the house, leading me right to her.

I step lightly, avoiding the floorboards that creak as I follow the sound of her close-lipped music to her office. She sits cross-legged in her desk chair, her fluffy pajama pants bunched up around her knees. Her hair is pulled into a messy bun, save for a few tendrils that have fallen out. The strands bounce around her face as her head bobs to the melody she's making. She presses her palms to her headphones and belts out a line from whatever terrible pop song is playing in her ears. The sound isn't unlike a cat being strangled, but I'm enraptured, anyway.

She's in another world, her eyes furiously scanning over a stack of papers in front of her. *Where have you traveled to today, little bird?* I ask her silently. In my mind, she whips her chair around, a smile breaking across her face. She jumps up from her chair and throws her arms around me before launching into a wild story about dragons and faraway battles.

Soon, I remind myself as I drag my body away from her office, *she'll love me soon*. My chest pinches with every step I put between us. When did her love start to matter to me so much? When did it change from wanting her to simply want me, to wanting her to love me? Needing her to love me?

"Shit," I huff under my breath.

As much as I want to, I won't disturb her when she's working. I know how much she loves her job and I'll never take that away from her. My feet shuffle reluctantly beneath me, hauling me up the stairs and into her guest bedroom. I lay down on the small bed, letting my legs dangle over the edge of its tiny frame. The moon peeks through the window, creating a line of silver light across the floor.

Hidden in the shadows of Ava's house, the tension in my body eases. My shoulders loosen and my headache drifts away. My little bird won't be alone tonight. I couldn't leave her alone if I wanted to. My body wouldn't let me. Even if I tried to claw my way out, I couldn't. My fingernails would gouge new grooves in her old windowsills, but my feet would remain rooted on the floor.

But I don't want to leave her. She's at risk, especially now that I'm planning Bianca's death. There are too many things that could go wrong. I wonder, does she feel my protection when she can't see me? Does it free her? Does it suffocate her? Imagining her struggling to breathe, my dick strains against the confines of my jeans. She looks so beautiful with my hand around her neck, her cheeks turning rosy and warm. She'll look even more beautiful when she's choking on my cock.

The patter of clumsy footsteps floats up from the first floor. My little bird's bare feet slap against the wooden floors as she moves. I could leave the room, following the sound of her footsteps to her, but the temptation to see what she does when she thinks I'm not around is too great. It claws at me, demanding that I remain in the shadows. Before her feet hit the stairs, my body is moving. I dash down the hallway and into her bedroom.

The puffy down comforter sits askew on her bed, half of it dragging on the floor. The fluffy, purple fabric muffles the sound of my body dropping to the floor. I shove it aside and roll under her bed. At least it's bigger than the tiny thing in the guest room. Bits of dust flutter up from the floor, swirling around my face. My nostrils tickle and I shove my palm over my nose and mouth to block a sneeze.

The floor is rough against my cheek and I can feel chunks of lint and sock fuzz sticking to the stubble on my chin. I rub my fingers over my face, scrubbing them away. When Ava's feet appear beside me, my muscles freeze and I force my breathing to slow. She huffs out a frustrated sound just before her shirt drops to the floor. Her pants come next, dropping into the bundle of fabric. The sight of her bare legs makes my mouth water.

The bed creaks above me, the mattress dipping slightly as she climbs onto it. Her panties flutter toward the floor. I whip my hand out, snatching them before they land on the dusty surface. For a moment, as I lift her panties to my face, I expect some part of me to feel bad about it, as if there's a dormant part of my brain that still cares about society's indoctrinated moral code. That part of me should cringe at the wrongness of hiding under a woman's bed with her underwear lodged in my nostrils. And yet, I couldn't fucking care less.

I suck in her sweet scent, nearly groaning as the delicate zest of her arousal hits my tongue. My jeans become an oppressive binding, crushing my hardening length. I run my palm along it, wishing I had enough space to pull it out.

"What the Hell am I doing?" she groans.

Yes, baby, what are you doing?

The bedsheets rustle and she lets out a pleased hum that makes my dick pulse with need.

"Touch me," she whispers, "just like that."

The soft sounds of her pleasure reach my ears and my breathing becomes as heavy as hers. I had wanted to see what she'd do when she thinks I'm not watching. Now, as I'm considering tearing through her old box spring to get to her, I'm wondering if this was a bad idea.

She whines softly, "I need more."

The bed springs shift and groan just before I hear the drawer in her nightstand squeak open. Her hand fumbles around in the drawer, making objects clatter together and paper rustle. My mind scrambles, trying to remember the exact contents of that damned drawer, but I can't think straight. I can barely think about anything other than the images being conjured in my head by the sounds she's making.

Her breathy moans fill the room and I envision her delicate fingers circling her clit. The cry that falls from her lips paints a vivid picture in my mind; her fingers sliding inside of her, her hips bucking as she forces them deeper.

I fist my hands, gripping them until I feel my fingernails digging into my skin. *What are you thinking about, little bird?* The thought pops into my head and spirals into something dark. The sudden realization that she may not be thinking about me crashes into me like a freight train. My body tingles as jealousy pumps its poison through my veins.

"Gray," she purrs. "Fuck, master, right there."

The organ in my chest expands, pumping so fiercely that I can hear it pounding in my ears. She's fantasizing about me. My cock aches with desire. Precum leaks from me, making my boxers damp and sticky against my skin.

Ava screams my name as the orgasm tears through her. Her body quivers, sending little quakes of movement through the mattress. Her scream drowns out the sound of my groaning as I nearly come in my pants right along with her.

Something falls to the floor with a wet thwack. Turning my head, my eyes triple in size at the sight of a purple, silicone dildo laying beside the bed. The small toy is nowhere near big enough to prepare her for my cock. I imagine her pained expression when I push into her for the first time and my dick hardens to the point of pain.

I still, listening to the sound of Ava's breathing. She snores softly above me, her breaths even and deep. My hand dives out, wrapping around the dildo and pulling it toward me. Little specks of dust are adhered to its surface, stuck in her arousal, but I don't care. I would eat dirt if it was coated in her release. A low moan vibrates in my throat as I suck the tip into my mouth. Her sweetness coats my tongue and my hips jerk, grinding into the box spring. I clean the silicone toy with my lips and tongue until there's nothing left of her on it.

"Fucking perfect," I whisper, my need for her satisfied for now by the flavor that lingers in my mouth.

Something in my chest softens knowing that in her most private moments, she wants me. My anxious, flighty little bird. She's so afraid of my affection, but she can't stop herself from dreaming of it. A plan begins to solidify in my mind. It's time for me to step up, to make her mine in earnest. She'll never be ready if I keep giving her time.

Are you ready for me, my sweet, broken girl?

I'll banish the thoughts that her monster of a father instilled in her. I'll destroy the walls she's built around herself to keep her safe. She doesn't need them anymore. She doesn't need a fortress to keep the monsters out. She has one of her own. I'll be her monster. I'll keep her safe.

Chapter Thirty-Six

A soft hum sounds in my bedroom. I press my head into the pillow, practically stuffing the fabric into my ear, but the sound doesn't stop. If anything, it seems to get louder. The low hum shifts, taking on a gentle melody. I flop my hand onto the nightstand, sending my fingers crashing into the alarm clock. With a grunt, I slam the snooze button. I don't know if it's early, but it feels too early for me to be awake.

The humming stops, replaced by a masculine chuckle. I rip my eyes open and force my body upright, nearly slamming my head into the headboard. My head whips around the room, seeking out the source of the sound. When I find it, I let out a shriek.

Perched on my window bench, with a book in one hand and a mug in the other, is Gray. A very freaking shirtless Gray. The muscles in his stomach ripple as he crosses one leg over the other. He lowers the novel to the bench beside him and pulls off his reading glasses to lay them on top of it.

God, why does he have to have glasses? The feral thing inside of me instantly pops her head up and licks her lips. *Men who read are hot,* she purrs, *and men who read with glasses are double-hot.* I ignore her and pretend my cheeks are heating at the sight of him.

A panty-dropping smile breaks across his face and points to a mug sitting on the windowsill. "I made you coffee."

I tuck the sheet under my armpits and clench them tight, ensuring every inch of me below my collarbones is hidden. My jaw drops into my lap as my eyes pan over his just-woke-up hair, his gray sweatpants, and his bare feet. How long has he been here? My stomach begins to bubble with anger. He's just barged in and made himself at home in *my* home? And he's been reading in *my* book nook? And he made coffee?

"Just make yourself at home, why don't you?" I hiss.

"You are my home," he says.

His home. He keeps saying that. He states it without fear, like it's just some trivial fact and not a declaration that most men run screaming from. A warm emotion flutters in my belly and I immediately tamp it down. I stomp on those butterflies like they're moths eating my favorite sweater.

I spit out a frustrated growl. "How long have you been here?"

He turns, grabbing the mug from below the window, and my eyes catch on the movement of his abs. My mouth waters, which is obviously because of the smell of the fresh coffee and not from anything else. He places the mug into my hands and I immediately gulp down a mouthful of its caffeinated goodness.

"Oh, little bird." He chuckles. The bed dips under his weight as he sits. "I've been here since before you screamed my name last night."

Coffee erupts from my mouth, spraying over my comforter. I cough and sputter, tasting hazelnut creamer in my nose.

I shake my head, feeling my cheeks heat. "I didn't—"

"Don't lie to me," Gray interrupts, grabbing the mug from my hand and placing it onto the nightstand.

Slamming his hands down on either side of me, he cages me with his arms. Warmth radiates from his body as he leans in close. I force myself to be still, ignoring the misguided instinct that begs me to push my body towards his. His enticing scent surrounds me and I suck in a breath through my nose, filling my lungs with that smell that uniquely belongs to him. The romance novels are right. Bad guys smell really freaking good.

A shiver runs through me as his breath ghosts across my mouth. His full lips are only inches from mine and I can't stop thinking about how soft they are. I watch them change, curling into a smirk. It's only then that I realize I've leaned in closer, nearly pressing my mouth to his.

I clench my hands at my sides, ignoring the way my fingers ache to touch him. I don't want to want him the way I do. I don't want to crave his attention, his psychotic devotion. I shouldn't want any of it, but I do. The butterflies in my stomach flutter and flap like they're trying to bust out through my belly button.

Gray wraps a tattooed hand around the sheet and yanks. I try to reach for it as it falls, but his arms keep mine locked at my sides. Cool air hits my skin, immediately tightening my nipples into hard buds. Gray rakes his eyes over me. His tongue darts out, licking a line over his bottom lip. I feel his gaze like a physical touch, caressing my breasts and trailing down my abdomen.

My eyes drop toward my belly. I stare down at it, wondering what he sees when he looks at me. Surely, he notices the softness of my stomach, the creases in my skin, the scars that mark it. Something tightens in my chest. It presses against my lungs, making it hard to pull in air. My eyes sting and my vision begins to blur. I blink away the tears, even as I wonder why they're coming.

I've never felt ashamed or particularly self-conscious of my body. Men have seen me naked before. A pretty good number of them, actually. I've never felt nervous showing my body. Not until now, until Gray. He doesn't look at me with the simple appreciation that men do. His eyes burn me, heating my blood until I think I might boil alive from the inside out. Looking into his eyes is like a rabbit staring into the eyes of the wolf that's about to have its dinner. His eyes are feral, hungry, frightening.

Gray makes me vulnerable in a way that no man has before. He breaks down my shields and exposes me. I didn't invite him in. I didn't let him get close to me willingly. I never let them get close enough to truly see me. He didn't wait for an invitation; he forced himself into my life. He dug into my life, learning everything about me that I never would have told him. He saw my scars.

"Look at me," he demands. His thumb digs into my chin until I tilt my head back, meeting his gaze. "Don't hide from me."

He tears the blankets from my legs, tossing them away from the bed. I shiver against the shock of cool air as the wad of fabric flutters to the floor.

I gasp at the feel of his hand on my ankle. The rough skin of his palm wraps against my flesh as he drags it slowly up my leg. He presses his nose into my neck and sucks in a breath through his nose. "Fucking perfect," he purrs against the sensitive skin below my ear. "I love that you've started sleeping naked. You never did before."

What?

My limbs freeze and my spine snaps to attention. I try to clear the fog in my mind, to think through the haze of arousal that's settled in my brain. How many times did he watch me sleep? How long has he actually been watching me? Weeks? Months? How many times has he been inside my house while I lay unconscious in this bed?

"Oh, yes, precious," he smiles against my neck, "I've been here more times than you know." He breathes out a chuckle that makes goosebumps rise on my skin. "You and I, we've shared your most private moments together. For so many nights, I've been your shadow, watching you sleep, watching you read…" He nips at my neck and I choke out a moan. "Watching you rub your fingers against your needy little clit, wishing it was my hand down your pants."

This is sick, a panicked voice inside of me screams as liquid heat pools in my belly. *This is wrong*, it screeches as my core heats. *This is insane*, it yells as wetness drips down my thighs.

His hand moves higher up my leg, trailing a lazy line toward my bare sex. I shift, trying to clench my thighs together to keep some distance between us. He stops me, wrapping his hand around my upper thigh. He squeezes hard enough to bruise and my flesh dimples beneath his fingers.

"Absolutely fucking not, little bird," he growls. "You're going to open these legs for me and let me see how wet you are."

He wrenches my thighs apart and leans in. My legs jerk as his nose brushes against my core. He closes his eyes and sucks in a breath through his nose. "You smell so good. You smell like mine."

The scrape of his stubble against my pussy makes me groan. I look down, meeting his hungry eyes just before his tongue darts out and flicks my clit. My teeth slam down on my lower lip, holding back the pornographic sound that tries to jump from my mouth.

Desire pours through my body, lighting my nerve-endings on fire. I struggle against the feeling, as if by sheer willpower I could grab onto my sanity and bind it to myself.

"I could eat your pretty cunt all day," he rasps against my folds, "lick you until I drown in your cum. But you haven't earned that privilege today."

God, yes, drown in me, the horny creature inside of me mewls. *Wait, what?*

Suddenly, I'm in the air, my body flipping before I tumble back toward the bed. The air rushes out of me with a grunt when my stomach collides with his legs. I wiggle and push, but a strong arm bands around my waist, keeping me locked against him. My breath comes in short pants, fanning against the mattress before huffing back into my face. Gray wraps his hand around my ponytail and yanks. A tingling burn spreads through my scalp as he pulls my head back.

I release a yelp when his hand slams down on my bare ass. "You will stop lying to me," he demands, punctuating each word with a stinging smack. "Stop denying what you feel for me. Stop pretending you don't want me, that there's nothing between us."

His open palm lands on the top of my thigh and I let out a screech. Hard, stinging slaps land on my skin, hitting every part of my backside. I pinch my lips together to keep the cries in my throat from screaming out of me. Each smack feels harder than the last and I'm not sure how long I can hold them inside.

Fire spreads from his palm, licking my skin as he strikes me. My ass burns and my eyes blur with tears. They dribble down my face in wet streaks before pooling into a damp patch on the sheet. I dig my fingers into the edge of the bed and pull with all my strength, but all I manage to do is wiggle in Gray's lap. His dick hardens, pressing against my stomach and the breath rushes out of me.

His breath whispers against the back of my neck and I freeze. "I know you feel it," he murmurs.

My voice gasps out of me in a hoarse croak. "Feel what?"

He hums against my ear, forcing a choked moan from my lips. "That you're falling for me, Ava," he whispers.

My stomach somersaults. I open my mouth to scream, to tell him that he's wrong, that I'd never fall for someone like him, but the words don't come. The only sound that makes its way past my lips is a strangled sob. A fresh wave of tears sting behind my eyes, blurring my vision. I pinch them shut, willing the tears not to fall.

"This is wrong." The words whisper out of me so softly that I'm not sure he'll hear.

"Does it feel wrong?" he asks, rubbing soothing circles over my sore cheeks.

I gulp, my mouth opening and closing like a fish on dry land. Gray's hand collides with my ass and I shriek as the fire on my skin relights. "I asked you a question," he growls. "Does it feel wrong when you're with me?"

"No."

No, it doesn't feel wrong. It feels anything but wrong. It feels…it feels…I don't know what it feels like. I don't know what this is. My heart aches in the softest way, in a way that I can't understand. It feels like I'm…I'm…

Safe, the little voice inside of me whispers.

The sound of a hand colliding with my skin echoes through the room and I belt out a scream. Pins and needles assault my pussy with stabbing pain as he slaps between my legs. Once, twice, then three times before he stills. My clit pulses beneath the heat of his palm and arousal trickles down my thighs.

"That's it," Gray says, "stay right here with me." I cry out when his fingers brush against my clit. His hand moves lower, making my core throb with need. He traces his fingertip around my entrance and I buck into his hand. My hips move erratically, grinding and gyrating, anything to make his finger slip inside of me.

"I'll give you what you need, little bird." Gray nips at the back of my neck. "But I won't give you what you want."

Gray lifts me, rolling me onto my back. I press my head into the pillows and stare up at him. The morning sun falls through the window and streaks over his skin, deepening the shadows beneath his muscles. I trace my eyes over his tattoos, following the shapes that whirl and writhe over his skin. He presses his pelvis between my thighs. I choke out a breath as I feel his erection pressing into me, barred only by the thin fabric of his sweatpants.

"Please," I whimper, grinding my throbbing clit against him.

He leans in, his hand wrapping around my throat as his lips crash into mine. He swipes his tongue over the seam of my lips and my mouth falls open on a moan. He swallows my cries as his tongue slides against mine. The kiss consumes me, shooting lightning through my veins until my skin crackles with need. When he pulls away, my lips are swollen and tingling.

I arch my back, pulling myself up to reach him again. His hand on my throat stops me and I huff out a whine. He stares down at me, his lips curling into that devilish grin that makes my pussy drip.

"I'll always give you what you need," he says, "and right now, you need to submit, don't you?"

Do I? My mind flits back to each time he's taken control away from me, each time he forced me to submit to his will. I recall the way my body sagged with relief and my mind became blissfully quiet. I'm not naïve; I read enough books to know what sexual submission is, but that's not meant for women like me. I'm too broken, too afraid, too damaged.

No, I shouldn't want this. I shouldn't want him. I should want a normal life, the kind of life that he can't offer me. My chest tightens as I imagine the life I should desire, the white picket fence and Sunday dinners, the gentle lovemaking and soft kisses. That's what I'm supposed to want, isn't it? If it's what my life should be, why does the thought of it make my heart ache?

I've been controlled by men before, hurt by them. Do I really want to let Gray take control? Do I want to be at his mercy? My pussy answers for me, clenching around nothing as my mind floods with thoughts of his punishing touch. A garbled sound of pleasure croaks from my throat when his hand tightens around my neck.

"You need to let go, precious," Gray murmurs. "You need someone to protect you, to take care of you, to free you from the things inside your head that hurt you. Do you want that?"

"Yes," I whisper.

"That's my girl. You have me now. You're mine. My most prized possession, my perfect little pet."

Mine. Perfect. Prized. Gray's words seem to sing inside of me. They wrap around my heart like a soft blanket. The starved, wounded thing that lives inside of me curls into it, sheltering itself in its warmth.

He releases my throat and I suck in a shaky breath. Gray crawls up my body, caging me in with his knees on either side of my head. "Now," he looks down at me, eyes shining with desire, "you're going to take my cock in that sweet little mouth." His finger traces over my lips and his tongue darts out to wet his own. "You're going to be a good girl and make your master come."

He pulls the drawstring of his sweatpants. The fabric slips down his hips and my mouth waters. Dark tattoos curl around his muscular torso, snaking over the line of his Adonis belt. The dark lines stand out against his pale skin, making him look otherworldly, monstrous. *My monster*, the thought purrs through my mind.

When he reaches into his pants and frees his hard length, my mouth falls open. His cock is longer and thicker than any man I've ever been with, probably any man I've ever seen. I pinch my lips together because there's simply no way that's going to fit in my mouth.

"Open your mouth," he demands.

Anxiety churns in my belly and I turn my head into the pillow. Gray grabs my face roughly. His thumbs push into the hollow of my cheeks until my jaw opens and a pained whine squeaks out of me.

"Stick out your tongue," he says as he slips his hand into my hair and fists it tightly.

When I let my tongue fall from my lips, he runs his dick over it. I swirl my tongue over him, catching a bead of precum from the tip. The taste of him hits my tongue and a throaty moan spills from my mouth. He responds in kind, a husky groan vibrating through his chest. His grip on my hair tightens, setting off little sparks of pain that skitter across my scalp, then he shoves himself into my mouth.

Pain radiates through my jaw at the sudden intrusion and my lips quiver. He presses forward, forcing his cock to hit the back of my throat. I gag around him and he moans. He guides his cock in and out of my mouth slowly, letting me gulp in a breath before pushing back in. I swirl my tongue around him, tasting him. Wetness pools between my thighs, my pussy begging for attention. I try to wiggle my hand out from between us to touch my aching clit. As if sensing my intention, Gray's legs tighten around me, trapping my arms.

"That's my good girl," he rasps as his hips thrust forward, his pace increasing. "Look how well you're taking my cock, pet."

He shoves himself into my throat, cutting off my air. He pumps shallow thrusts into my throat, but doesn't pull out enough to let me breathe. My face heats and my lungs tighten. Tears leak from my eyes as panic begins to set it. I can't breathe. I need to breathe. My legs flail between us, kicking and quivering. Spit dribbles from the corners of my mouth, pooling over my collarbones.

"You're okay, baby," he purrs. "You're doing so well."

My lungs burn and my vision begins to fade, the edges blurring and darkening. Gray lets out a long groan. The masculine sound demolishes any semblance of sanity I have left, zipping through my body and sending shockwaves straight to my clit. His body tenses and his legs shake. His hips stutter as he pumps his release into my mouth. He pulls out quickly and I snap my jaw open, needing to spit, and breathe, and scream. Gray's palm covers my mouth and his fingers clamp around my nostrils.

"Swallow it," he growls.

I force my throat to cooperate, gulping down his cum with heavy swallows. He releases me immediately and I cough and sputter, sucking in great gasps of air. Gray smiles as something between a sob and a scream passes my lips. He brushes the tears from my cheeks and sucks his finger into his mouth, tasting my tears.

"I love your tears. You're so beautiful when you cry for me."

Chapter Thirty-Seven

Ava looks up at me, her eyes sparkling with arousal, confusion, and fear. Her cheeks are blotchy and tear-stained. The sunlight streaming through the window catches on the lines of spit that coat her throat, giving her skin an unworldly shine. My little bird is perfect. I release her, crawling down her body until my knees rest between her thighs.

I trail my fingertips gently down her stomach and over her mound. I run my fingers through the strip of hair above her pussy, gently tugging on the coarse strands. My thumb presses against her clit and she gasps. Her body quivers with need and she inches her hips closer to my hand.

"I-I uhh," she stutters.

"I know, precious. You're confused, aren't you?"

Her eyes widen and she jerks her head in a small nod.

"You don't understand why you love the way I hurt you and yet," I trace my finger around her opening, feeling her arousal slick my fingers, "you're so wet and needy from it."

I push a finger inside of her and she bucks into my hand. I insert a second and she cries out.

"You were a very good girl just now," I say, "but you broke my rule, little bird."

She sinks her teeth into her bottom lip, chewing on the soft skin until it pinkens. Her forehead crinkles and her eyes dart between my fingers and my face. She tries to pull away, but I wrap my hand around her hip, holding her in place. My fingers slide in and out of her slowly, making her writhe and wiggle.

"I told you that you aren't allowed to come unless I say you do. But you're so fucking desperate for my cock that you made yourself come thinking about me last night."

Her face reddens with embarrassment and a new flood of her arousal coats my hand. She sputters out a few syllables that most certainly don't form words. A smirk tugs at the corners of my mouth. My shy girl gets so wet when I force her to see the way she wants me.

"You want to come, baby?" I ask.

Her eyes light up like Christmas lights as she nods furiously.

"Say it."

"Yes," she whimpers.

I let my fingers still inside her. "Beg me," I growl, "Beg me to let you come."

She exhales a whine and grinds against my fingers. "Please, Gray."

"What's my name to you?"

"Please, master," she murmurs.

I pinch her clit and she moans, her back arching off the bed and pushing her perfect tits into the air. My hand slides up her body until I have one in my hand. I grasp it firmly, kneading her soft flesh with my fingers. "Please what?" I ask.

She sucks her lip into her mouth and stares at me, pleading with her eyes, but not saying a word. I pinch her nipple hard between my fingers until she lets out a yelp.

"Please, master, make me come!" she screams.

I pull my fingers from her cunt before slamming them back in. She's so wet that they slide in and out of her with ease. Her slick coats my fingers and drips into my palm. I lean my face in, inhaling the scent of her arousal. I suck in greedy breaths through my nose until I can almost taste her. My cock hardens again as it hits me—sweet summer strawberries and the flavor that belongs uniquely to her.

She releases a low moan as I flick my tongue out and swirl it around her clit. I suck the bundle of nerves into my mouth and pump my fingers into her, hard and fast. She clenches around my fingers as her pleasure builds. My teeth scrape lightly over her clit and she screams out her orgasm. I slow my fingers, watching her pant and shudder as she rides out the aftershocks.

She cries out when I suck her clit back into my mouth, rolling my tongue over the sensitive bud. I plunge my fingers into her wet heat, hooking them inside of her to hit the spot that makes her legs shake. She closes her eyes and grinds her hips in unison with my fingers.

"Eyes on me," I rasp against her cunt. "You're going to look at me while you come on my fingers."

She tightens around me, her body pulling my fingers deeper. A shiver runs through her, tensing her limbs. "That's it," I purr, "come for me again, precious."

I watch pleasure color her features, her eyes half-lidded and her cheeks red. She stares down at me as she screams her release. She whines as I pull my fingers from her, her face scrunched up in a pained expression. The sheets drag across the mattress as she pulls away from me, inching herself back toward the headboard. Her eyes widen as I grip her hip and drag her back toward me.

"We're not finished, little bird." I reach behind me, grabbing what I hid at the foot of the bed. When I pull her purple dildo out from behind my back, she lets out a shaky whimper. She clamps her thighs together as I move it toward her.

"Y-you can't," she stammers. "It's…it's…dirty from when I… used it." She looks down at her lap, a blush crawling up her face.

Putting a hand on each leg, I pry her thighs apart. She fights against my hold, trying to push her legs back together. I look down at her pussy and groan. It's pink and raw, glistening with her cum. I press my thumb against her clit, rubbing slow circles around it until she stops fighting and lets her legs fall apart. Her eyes don't leave the toy in my hand, which she looks at with a wary expression.

"It's clean," I say, twisting it back and forth so that she can inspect it. "I washed it before you woke up. I'd never put you at risk, not even with small things."

Her expression softens into something tender, something I don't fully recognize. My heart thumps faster in my chest and my lungs feel too full. Something stirs inside of me, clawing at my chest as if it's reaching for her. It feels wrong and yet I don't want her to stop looking at me that way. I shake my head, refocusing my attention between her thighs.

She shudders as I swipe my finger through her wetness, dragging it across her clit. I press the toy to her opening, making her breath hitch. Inch by inch, I push it into her, watching her mouth drop open on a whispered moan. Ava writhes on the bed, her face distorted in both pleasure and pain. She moans deeply as I drag my thumb over her clit and thrust the toy into her. I quicken my pace, rubbing circles over her sensitive nub and sliding the dildo in and out of her quivering cunt until her back bows off the bed and she sobs out her pleasure.

She eyes me expectantly, telling me without words that she's satisfied and sore. Instead of pulling the toy out of her, I turn my hand, angling it toward her g-spot and continue thrusting.

"Please," she whines. "I can't. I can't."

"You can," I demand, slamming the toy against the spot that makes her scream, "and you will."

Her legs shake and her hips twitch as she mumbles and cries incoherent sounds.

"This is what happens to bad girls who don't ask permission to touch themselves. You're going to come for me one more time."

I push her to the edge, rapidly fanning my fingers against her clit and undulating the toy inside of her until she shatters. I lay down next to her and pull her into my arms as she comes down. She curls into me, resting her head on my shoulder and laying her arm across my stomach. She fits so perfectly in my arms, like she was made to be mine.

"Good girl," I whisper into her hair, "you did so well for me."

Ava snuggles against me, her breathing slowing into a soft stream that fans across my neck. I can't stop my face from breaking into a smile at the way she melts for me. I've never held a woman the way I'm holding her now, the way I always want to hold her. I've never wanted to. With other women, the expectation of cuddling always felt like a chore. It's different with Ava; with her, I need it. Maybe even more than she does.

"Gray, I have to ask you something." Ava's voice is quiet against my neck, wavering with the slight shake of anxiety.

"Anything." I stroke my hand through her hair, hoping that whatever answers I give her won't make her move further away from me.

"Did you…" She huffs out a shaky sigh. "Did you kill my father?"

My smile widens. I hadn't planned to tell her, but I knew my smart girl would figure it out.

"Yeah, I did."

"Why?" she asks, lifting herself onto her elbow to look at me.

"To set you free."

Ava's eyebrows knit together, forming creases on her forehead. I reach out my hand and smooth them with my finger. "I don't under-stand," she says.

"I know what it's like for you." I trace my finger along the edge of her face and she doesn't pull away. She leans into my touch with that soft look in her eyes. "I know how the memories of what he did haunt you."

She flinches at that. Her eyes lower to my chest like she can't meet mine. I press my finger under her chin and tilt her head up. "I know because I'm the same. That's why I am the way I am, Ava."

She shoves her hand into the pillow, twisting the fabric between her fingers. She tugs her lip into her mouth with her teeth.

"I wasn't always a monster. I became one because I had to. I was a normal person once, a kid who wanted to be a teacher, actually. I came home from college during winter break and that's when I found my mom." A heaviness builds in my throat and I swallow it back. "She was dead, and my dad had killed her. I killed him. I freed myself from him, but it changed me." My lungs deflate, emptying the stale air that it feels like I've been holding in for years. "I've never told anyone that before."

A tear rolls down Ava's face. I track its descent, watching it slip down the slide of her nose and onto her pink lips before she brushes it away with the back of her hand. My mouth pops open and I suck in a sharp breath.

She's crying…for me. If I needed any more evidence that she's falling for me, this is it. The tears that drip down her beautiful face are mine. She is mine. Since the moment I first saw her, I knew that she'd love me, that I could *make* her love me. I knew that my obsession couldn't remain one-sided, that I could give it to her, transmit it like a disease. That's how I feel for her. It's a disease. It's a madness that seeped into my veins and spread through my body. It's been eating away at me, corroding the iron shell around my heart so that I can rip it from my chest and hand it to her.

A sigh seeps past my lips as I stare into the teary eyes of the woman who's mine. "I'm not a good man," I say. "I can't offer you anymore than what I am, but I can give you *everything* that I am. Every fucking part of me is yours, Ava."

"Thank you," she whispers just before her lips touch mine. Bells, whistles, and party horns scream in my head as Ava kisses me for the first time. My hand slides into her hair, gripping the strands in my fingers and pulling her into me. I part her lips with my tongue and taste her, and a bit of myself that still lingers. My teeth scrape over her soft lips and I swallow her moans. We pull apart breathless, our kiss having sucked all of the oxygen from the room.

"Tomorrow night at seven," I say against her lips.

"Huh?"

"Tomorrow at seven, I'm going to pick you up and we're going on a date."

Ava stiffens in my arms. Her eyes bounce around the room before settling on my chest. "I don't know if that's a—"

I press my finger to her pouting lips. "I wasn't asking. I'll be here at seven and you will either be at the door, waiting for me like a good girl, or I'll be dragging you to the car by your hair."

An adorably meek whimper squeaks through her closed lips, but she nods her head.

"That's my girl. I left something in the kitchen for you. Wear it."

Chapter Thirty-Eight

For hours after Gray left my house, I continued to walk past the black cardboard box on my kitchen table. When I needed more coffee, I walked past the box. When I needed a snack, I walked past the box. When I needed water, I walked past the box. Every time I looked at it, the butterflies in my stomach flapped their stupid little wings and my heart sped up.

Now, staring down at the sleek gift box, my blood rushes through my veins and pounds in my ears. The last rays of the afternoon sun peek through the windows. Its orange glow falls over the table, hitting the silky, red bow at the center of the box and turning it copper. I trace my fingers over the soft ribbon as a shaky breath huffs out of me.

I try to ignore the memory of the last *gift* Gray left for me, but the harder I try, the more the picture takes shape in my head. I swallow hard as a wave of nausea hits me, making my stomach clench and my mouth water. The more I avoid the images that flood my mind, the clearer they become. Blood. The smell of rust. The mangled, severed hand of the man who wanted to help me escape Gray's obsession.

"I'm sorry, James." The whispered words seem to linger in the quiet of my kitchen. They stick in the air like an echo that I can't hear, because the moment they left my mouth, I knew they weren't true. They feel hollow. My heart constricts painfully in my chest. I didn't want him to die. I hate that he died because of me. He didn't deserve it. But I can't bring myself to feel regret for the fact that he couldn't keep Gray away from me.

"I'm a terrible person," I tell the beautiful box with its beautiful ribbon. "I'm awful," I say as my heart begins to flutter at the sight of it. "I shouldn't be excited to get a present from a murderer."

The word *murderer* tastes sour in my mouth, sliding off of my tongue like wet sandpaper. A realization settles in the pit of my stomach and all the air leaves me in a great whoosh. I don't see him that way anymore. He's become so much more to me than the monster that crept through the dark parts of my home. He's embedded himself in me like a splinter that dug in deep. I can't get him out. I don't even want to. Something inside of me cracks and a piece of the protective shell around my heart breaks away.

The cardboard sighs as I pull the lid away from the box. I delve my fingers into the red tissue paper, peeling it away from what's inside. Something soft brushes against my fingertips. I rub my palm over the smooth fabric before pulling it from the box. My eyes widen as I take in the cashmere sweater dress in my hands. It's perfect. The comfortable fabric falls to my knees and the deep plum color perfectly offsets my pale skin. Heat rises in my cheeks when I look at the tag. Gray cut off the price, but the designer's name alone tells me that the dress costs more than I make in a month.

Peering into the box, I find one more gift nestled at the bottom. I pull out the beautiful, brown leather boots and squeal. They're exactly what I would have chosen for myself or they would be if I could afford designer shoes. They look warm and cozy with a heel that's short and practical.

He knows me in a way I didn't expect him to. Obviously, he followed me around enough to know what I like to wear, but this is more than that. He chose something that would make me comfortable. Has anyone ever done that for me before? Has any man ever sacrificed the way he wanted me to look for something that would keep me warm and keep my feet from hurting?

The butterflies start up again, flapping their wings until my stomach feels like it might float away. Is this the feeling heroines describe in romance novels? This all-consuming feeling like a rope around my heart, dragging me toward Gray?

One thing is for sure. I'm too far gone for this man to pull away now.

Chapter Thirty-Nine

"You have arrived at your destination," a robotic voice announces in the car. I didn't need to use the GPS to get here, but it seems to make Ava less nervous. When the navigation system lit up, her fingers loosened their death grip on her seatbelt. I know she has feelings for me, but that doesn't mean she isn't still afraid. The sick, demented creature inside of me delights in it. It loves seeing her eyes widen in fear. It loves listening to her sharp intake of breath whenever I get close to her.

Walking around the car to the passenger side door, a smile peels across my face. At exactly seven o'clock, my obedient girl was waiting at her front door for me. She twisted her fingers in the hem of her dress, her eyes squarely locked on her boots. Seeing her in clothes that I provided for her did something to me. My chest inflated and my cock immediately stood at attention.

"Spin for me," I said. Her eyes lit up as she twirled around. Her boots thunked against the old porch beams and she nearly tripped over her own feet, but she didn't stop. She spun around like a little girl in her first princess costume. At that moment, my heart sank, falling straight down to my stomach. She never did get to be a princess. She wasn't given plastic tiaras and fairy wands. She was given bruises and broken bones.

My jaw clenched and I made a promise to myself, a promise to her, even though she didn't know it. I promised to make her feel like a princess every single day for the rest of our lives. My good little princess will want for nothing.

I pull open the passenger door and Ava looks up at me, causing my lungs to seize in my chest. Her doe eyes are lined with chocolate brown liner and her lids are dusted with gold. A glossy pink is painted over her plump lips, making them look wet. I nearly stumble over my own feet thinking about those lips, wet and dripping with saliva while she chokes on my cock.

I grab her hand and help her from the car, watching her cheeks flush into a rosy pink. Her eyes find mine and hunger flicks through her gaze. My little bird likes it when I'm sweet to her just as much as she likes it when I'm not.

She lifts her head in the direction of my house and sucks in a breath. "I didn't really look at it before," her eyes drift down to her feet, "the, uh, last time I was here." Her head swivels left and right. "Is this all yours?"

I look around at the expanse of my property, nearly twenty acres of forest with my home at its center. "Ours," I correct.

Ava rolls her eyes and she steps through the dried grass toward the front door, the crackle of leaves muffled beneath her boots. She doesn't understand yet that everything I have is hers, or maybe she simply doesn't believe me. She will someday; I'll make sure of it.

"It's gorgeous," she gasps as she takes in the exterior of the house.

A grin spreads across my face as I stare at my home. The exterior lights cast a soft, golden glow over its stone face. Ashen concrete stretches into the sky, edged by large stone pillars. Square planter boxes filled with small spruce trees line the front entrance, creating a private space on the large porch.

The house itself seems out of place for this area. It looks like something built for the California countryside with its concrete walls and the floor to ceiling windows that cover the second floor. Though it looks like it, the house wasn't built to withstand hurricanes and wildfires. Its reinforced walls and bulletproof windows were built to withstand people like me. It was built for my protection, and now, Ava's.

Ava steps beside me, her hand brushing against mine. I wrap my fingers around hers, letting her warmth radiate through me. I never realized how cold I was before I felt the heat of her body next to mine. Had my fingers always been numb? Had they been frozen the first time she put her hand in mine? My hand tightens around hers. My tendons lock into place as if even the parts of me that live beneath my skin need her.

She looks up at me, her eyes narrowed. "I thought you were taking me on a date?"

I wrap my arm around her waist and pull her into my chest. Her breath hitches as I drag my lips over the shell of her ear. "Do you really think a public setting would protect you from me?" I whisper against her skin. "Or maybe you were hoping I'd touch you in public?"

"I, uh, no," she stammers, her ear heating beneath my lips as a flush darkens her skin.

I scrape my teeth against the spot below her ear that makes her squirm. "I will never let anyone else see you like that, little bird." She shivers as I run my hand up her thigh. "No one will ever see the way you grind your hips when you're desperate for release. Or the way your face looks when you come. No one but me. Do you understand?"

She leans into me, pushing her ass against my growing erection as a soft moan falls from her lips. My hand snakes up her body. My palm trails upward over her stomach and between her breasts before stopping at her neck. My fingers tighten around her neck. "Tell me you understand," I demand.

"I understand." She closes her eyes and her fingers twitch against mine. "Master," she whispers.

I place a kiss against her temple. "Good girl."

I lead her into the house without saying any of the other reasons that I planned our date this way. She doesn't need to know that being in public with me could put her directly in the sight of a sniper's rifle. She doesn't need to know that there's a bounty on my head, nor that that bounty could extend to her if Bianca found out what she means to me. Once I've killed Bianca, she'll be safe. Until Shawn gets me the information I need to finish the job, I can protect her.

"No flowers?" she asks as she hangs up her coat on the hook by the door. "Aren't you supposed to be wooing me or something?"

"You don't want flowers." I chuckle. I point toward the wrapped package on the kitchen counter before beginning to pull things from the refrigerator and cabinets.

"Is that for me?" Her voice is a whisper, barely audible over the clank of pots and pans.

My head bobs up and down. Uncertainty slithers in my gut as I watch her peel the black ribbon from the package. Unease gnaws at my insides as she unfolds the parchment from around her gift. I watch her from the corner of my eyes, because I can't seem to lift them from the countertop.

"Oh my God!" she squeals. "This is the newest romance book from Hannah Rafferty. I didn't even know it was out yet." Her fingers softly brush over the cover before she opens the book and a shriek bubbles from her mouth. "It's a signed copy!" She hugs the book to her chest like it's the greatest gift she's ever received, and all the air I'd been holding in my lungs puffs out.

Suddenly, her arms are around me. She tucks her head beneath my chin and presses her face into my chest. "Thank you," she says.

I melt like ice cream in the fucking sun. My arms mold around her body, pulling her closer. I press a kiss to the top of her head and inhale the delicate scent of her shampoo.

"I don't have to woo you, little bird," I sigh, "I *know* you."

Her arms loosen from around me. She sits down at the counter and opens her book. Some foreign emotion curdles in my gut as I move around the kitchen. I pull two steaks from the refrigerator and pat them down with a paper towel. My fingers fumble with the seasonings, leaving a pile of salt scattered across the counter. My usual finesse is dulled, sloppy, like cuts from an unsharpened blade.

My knife slips through potatoes and carrots, creating grooves in the wooden cutting board beneath.

Thump, thump, thump.

Is that the sound of the knife or the furious beating of my heart?

Thump, thump, thump.

My eyes flick to the kitchen table. Fuck, why did I put out candles?

Women love candles, honey, Mom's voice sings through my mind. *They're romantic. Oh, and when you have a date with a special girl, make sure you give her a little gift like flowers or chocolates.*

Yes, that's why. Women love candles. I wipe my hands down my pants and curse at the streaks of smeared potato starch marking the denim. What is wrong with me? What the fuck am I feeling right now?

Just remember, it's normal to be nervous on your first date, Mom whispers in my head. Is that what this is? I've faced off against mobsters. Bombs have gone off mere feet from my body. I've been shot at by ten men at the same damn time. Through all of that, I never felt nervous. But here and now, with my woman in my kitchen, I'm drowning.

A trickle of butter dribbles from Ava's mouth. I watch its descent down her lower lip before her tongue darts out to catch it. I imagine wiping it from her lips with my tongue and inwardly curse myself for not making her sit in my lap. My eyes roll up her face, tracing the delicate curve of her nose and the soft line of her cheekbones.

"Aren't you going to eat?" she asks.

I nod, immediately popping a piece of steak into my mouth. She smiles around a mouthful of mashed potatoes and makes a sinful noise that has my dick hardening under the table. She stabs her fork into a piece of steak and brings it to her plush lips. They part around it and her eyes close as the meat touches her tongue. I never thought I'd be envious of a piece of cutlery, but as I watch her suck the juice from her fork, I would kill to be it.

"Tell me about what you're reading," I say.

"What?" Her eyes pop open a little wider than normal.

"Tell me about what you're reading for work this week."

"You," she hesitates, sucking her lip into her mouth, "you want to hear about my work? About the books?"

"Yeah, baby, I want to hear about the books." I chuckle.

Ava launches into a story about a battle between two warring clans of werewolves. Pure joy sparkles in her irises as she tells me the story of fated mates torn apart by a centuries old feud. As she talks, I carry our dishes to the sink, watching her toes tap furiously under the table like she can't contain her excitement. Her hands flail wildly around her as she describes the way a magical mate bond sparked to life inside the hearts of two warriors who met on the battlefield.

I place a plate of strawberry cheesecake in front of her and her eyes light up like a Christmas tree. She scoops a piece onto her spoon and dips it into her mouth. She lets out a sinful groan and shovels another spoonful between her lips. I watch her pink tongue pop out and lick the creamy cake from the spoon. A catalog begins to form in my mind of the gags I'll buy her that will force her to keep that tongue out for as long as she wears one. I imagine the way she'll beg when she's only able to loosely form words. The way that her saliva will drip over her pouty lips as she whimpers in need.

"Gray?" Her voice parts the haze in my mind.

"Sorry, what did you say?"

"What is this?" she asks, her voice quivering. "This thing between us?"

"This is the beginning," I say.

She huffs out a breath. "Of what?"

"Of us, of our life together."

She lets her spoon drop to the plate. She watches it land with her eyebrows pulling together.

"I found you, little bird. I found the only person in this world that means something to me." I grip the edge of my chair, feeling the wood splinter under my fingernails. "And I won't let you go. I can't let you go because I can't fucking breathe without you."

Her eyes rocket upward to meet mine, sparkling with unshed tears.

"After my mom died, after I became a killer, I wasn't capable of love. I'm not built for it. But with you, everything is different. I'm different." I swallow back the dryness in my mouth. My heartbeat pounds in my ears so loudly that I can barely hear myself speak.

"I love you, Ava."

Chapter Forty

"**I** love you, Ava."

Grayson's voice seems to echo around me. Or maybe inside of me. His words pound against my heart, scratching massive cracks in its protective cage. My jaw slams shut and my teeth grind together until a dull ache begins to form in my temples.

No one could ever love you, my father's voice screams in my mind. *Worthless, useless girl.*

My fingers twitch, clenching around the hem of my dress. Everything in my stomach suddenly feels like lead, the weight of it sinking me further and further into the chair. He can't mean that. He can't love me. It's not real.

I suck in a breath when Gray's hands land on my cheeks. His palms press against the sides of my face and force my gaze upward. His lips tip down into a grim expression and his eyes harden. I let myself be captured by their icy depths, following the dizzying pattern in his irises. The sharp lines jut inward toward his pupil, like shards of ice in dark water.

"Absolutely not, precious," Gray says, tightening his grip on my face. "You're not retreating into yourself."

He grabs my waist and yanks me into his arms. I wrap my arms around his neck as my feet leave the floor. Gray wraps his hands around my thighs and forces them around his waist.

"You're not hiding from this," he growls. "I fucking love you and I know that you love me back."

My head bumps against his shoulder as he walks, the steady thumping of his footsteps rocking me into him. I lean into him, nestling my face in his neck and surrounding myself with the smell of him. His grip tightens on my thighs and I sigh into his neck.

When he stops moving, his grip loosens around my legs and I slide down his body until my feet hit the soft carpet in his living room. Gray lowers his body, letting one knee land on the floor before looking up at me expectantly. My gaze drags along the hard line of his jaw and I ignore the impulse to reach out and touch his chiseled features.

"Put your hands on my shoulders," he says while grabbing one of my feet and lifting it into the air.

With one leg off the ground, my balance immediately falters and I grip his shoulders to keep from toppling over. The zipper on my boot lets out a metallic hiss, the leather loosening from around my calf. He yanks the boot off and lets it thud to the floor. My sock follows, fluttering onto the carpet by my feet. My breath catches in my throat when I feel his lips press against my ankle.

My fingers tighten on his shoulders as his mouth traces a line from my ankle to my knee. Seeing this man on his knees in front of me does something to me. My entire body heats until I feel like my skin is aflame. Liquid fire pools in my core and begins its slow descent down my thighs. He repeats the process with my other leg, the scrape of his stubble against my bare skin making me gasp.

He stands up and looks down at me with a devilish smile that makes my knees feel like jelly.

"Take the dress off," he demands.

I ball my hands around the hem of my dress, my eyes falling to my feet. My toes wiggle amongst the soft strands of the carpet. My mind begins to run through an internal checklist that I didn't ask for. *Shaved legs? Check. Perfectly rectangular landing strip? Check. Plucked h—*

"Take it off or I'll cut it off."

My eyes shoot upward and I yank the dress from my body, my arms catching clumsily within its sleeves before tossing it onto the couch. Gray pulls me toward him, forcing me to stumble into his chest. His hands roam over my hips and belly with soft, teasing touches. His fingertips slide into the waistband of my panties, his featherlight touch sending a shiver through me.

He pinches the silky fabric between his fingers and groans out a masculine sound of approval. "Bra and panties, too."

I unclasp my bra and drop it to the floor before pushing my panties down my legs. I kick them away and watch them flutter onto the carpet. Even without his hands on me, Gray's gaze touches me like a physical thing. It teases its way down my body like the softest caress. Heat rises in my face and I'm certain my cheeks have turned red. I hold my fingers at my side stiffly, trying to force them not to fidget. A soft thwack sounds in the room as a small blue pillow lands at my feet.

"On your knees, precious," Gray commands.

My legs wobble as I sink to my knees on the pillow. Suddenly unsure of what to do with my hands, I wrap my fingers over the tops of my knees. Gray moves in front of me, drawing my eyes toward him. He unbuttons his black dress shirt, revealing the dark tattoos and rippling muscles beneath. My mouth pops open as he peels the shirt down his arms. The bunching and tightening of his muscles draws me in and I can't help but lean closer. He looks like a dark god, and on my knees in front of him, I feel like I should be praying.

He reaches out, placing a finger under my chin and lifting my gaze until our eyes meet. "I need you to be a very good girl for me and not run away," he says.

Alarm bells scream in my head. I sink my teeth into my bottom lip, trying to ignore the way my legs begin to twitch beneath me. Very slowly, he moves his hands to his belt. The clinking of the buckle rings in my ears and I cringe. He pulls the leather through his belt loops and the fabric whispers a taunt in my ears.

He's just taking it off, a panicked voice yells inside of me. *He's just taking it off and then he's going to put it away. No, no, not put it away. He's going to throw it away. He's going to throw it far, far away.*

Gray takes a measured step toward me. He holds his hands out, pushing the leather closer to my face. My eyes bounce from the belt to his face, which is drawn with a concerning expression that I don't understand. A giggle bubbles out of me from nowhere as I shift uncomfortably.

"W-what are you d-doing?" The words creak out of me.

Gray's eyes soften and something that looks like pity flits across his face. "I'm taking back what was taken from you," he says.

Gray steps closer, his feet nearly touching my knees. My eyes lock on the black leather in his hands as it moves inches closer to me. Lamplight shines on the strap, highlighting the wrinkles and grooves in the leather. It looks soft and worn, but I know that's not the case. There's no such thing as a belt that whips softly.

A shiver zips down my spine and my blood sloshes through my veins like ice. I watch the belt come closer as Gray stretches his arms out toward me. Something inside of me screams. It thrashes and claws at my heart, making every beat painful. My knees squirm out from beneath me and I topple, my ass thudding against the floor. I flip myself onto my hands and knees and crawl, not bothering to try to get myself to my feet. My fingers grip the carpet and I yank myself toward the couch.

The velvety lounge calls to me, offering some semblance of safety if I can just get myself behind it. If I can hide, I can survive. My arms and legs move automatically, propelling me forward. My knees slip against the soft carpet, sending me careening forward. My chin crashes into the floor, making my teeth slam together painfully. I right myself quickly, tucking my arms under me. *Can't stop. Can't stop. Can't stop*, a mousy voice chants in my mind.

Strong arms band around my waist and pull me back. I thrash and scream, my arms flailing wildly, my elbows colliding with hard muscle. A cry spills from my lips as my arms are wrenched behind me, pressed between me and Grayson with the weight of my own body. My ass crashes down into Gray's lap. I squirm, wiggling my limbs, but can't move. I distantly hear whispered assurances as an ache erupts in my hips. He forces my legs apart, draping one leg over each of his.

I watch the belt descend over my head, its tail tucked into the buckle to make a circle of leather. My breathing becomes ragged, each breath feeling like it's being ripped from my lungs. The belt touches my shoulders and scratches against the skin of my throat. My vision blurs as tears burn in my eyes. They pour down my cheeks and dribble over the leather.

"P-please, Gray," I sob. "Please, don't. Please, m-master, please."

Gray wraps his arm around my waist, holding me tight to his body. He runs his nose along the column of my neck and I shiver. I pinch my lips together, but it doesn't stop the needy whine that crawls up my throat when his lips touch my neck.

"Do you trust me?" Gray murmurs against my neck.

I shouldn't. I know that I shouldn't. My mind fights against the concept of trusting the man with a belt around my neck, but my head bobs up and down. It's as if my body answers for me because it can't deny the safety I feel in his arms.

"That's my good girl." Gray nips at my neck, making me shiver with need. "We're going to take back your fear, little bird. You don't need it anymore. I'm going to protect you. I won't let anything happen to you."

I scream as the belt begins to tighten around my neck. The leather tightens against my skin, forcing my scream to morph into a whine. My face heats as I swallow shaky gulps of air. The tears streaming down my cheeks feel like acid. My fingers twitch behind me. I flex my nails, gouging and scraping them against Gray's stomach. He doesn't flinch, but cinches the belt tighter around my neck. Black spots float over my eyes, distorting my already blurred vision further.

The room around me seems to darken. My mind floods with pain and fear. Memories tear through me and I can't stop them. Visions of my bloodied, broken body flit through my mind's eye. My father's voice cracks like a whip inside of me, lashing at my organs. *Pathetic girl, you deserve this. It's your fault. You make me do this to you.*

Like a physical wound, the memories tear me open, baring my broken spirit. Can he see it? Can Gray see it? Can he see the damaged thing that lives inside of me? When the memories tear me open, can he see the black, gooey thing that used to be my soul? Does it disgust him?

Disgusting, just like your whore mother.

A loud thwack bursts through the room and my pussy alights with fiery agony. I look down, my vision clearing just in time to watch Gray slap his palm between my legs again. A scream explodes from my mouth as he hits me again.

"Get out of your head, little bird," Gray demands. His voice softens and he kisses my hairline. "I need you to stay right here with me, baby. I know you can do this."

The belt tightens around my neck and my stomach churns. I swallow back the bile that crawls up my throat and pant against the acidic burn. Gray presses his palm between my legs and my core tightens at his soft caress. His finger brushes against my clit and it pulses. I choke out a moan as he circles the sensitive nub. A dizzying combination of fear and desire swirl inside of me, making the world feel tilted and uneven.

"Just like that," he purrs against my neck. "You're doing so well, precious."

The leather drags across my skin, pulling it painfully. I suck in tiny gasps of air that burn my lungs. The feeling of his finger rubbing over my clit makes me want to cry out, but I can barely muster a whimper. Gray slams his fingers inside of me and my mouth drops open in a silent scream. His fingers make a wet sound as he scissors his them inside of me. I would be embarrassed if I could feel anything beyond the floaty high of oxygen deprivation. My face would heat if it wasn't already on fire.

Gray pumps his fingers inside of me and circles my clit with his thumb. My core tightens, my inner walls clenching around him. Some tiny voice inside of me tries to tell me that this is wrong, but I can't hear it. I don't want to hear it. I don't fucking care anymore if this is wrong. I just want him. No, I need him.

I open my mouth to tell him, but he hooks his fingers inside of me and the only sound that comes out of my mouth is a choked moan.

"That's it, baby," he purrs, increasing the pressure on my clit. "You're going to come for me just like this, aren't you?"

My vision begins to fade, the edges darkening. I wait for the anxiety to grip me in its icy fingers, for fear to wash over me, but all I feel is warmth and my own desire. This want inside of me is like nothing I've ever experienced. All I want is to please him, to be possessed by him, owned by him, *loved* by him. I grind my hips into his palm, forcing him deeper.

Gray's teeth sink into my shoulder and I groan. My hips stutter, jerking against his hand as I barrel toward my orgasm.

"Come for me." Gray's growled voice in my ear shatters me. I come hard, panting and rocking against his hand. I don't even realize the belt is no longer around my neck until I hear myself scream. He slows his movements, coaxing me through the aftershocks of my orgasm.

I wince as Gray releases his grip on my arms and legs. He rubs his hands over them, soothing my aching muscles. He lifts me into his arms, cradling me to his chest. I wince when his fingers brush over my neck. My skin is raw and aching. He touches me gently, soothing the sting.

He peppers soft kisses across my face. "I'm so proud of you, baby. You did so well."

I melt under his praise, pressing my face into the crook of his neck and inhaling his familiar scent. He places something around my neck and I hear a small metallic click behind me. Reaching my fingers to my throat, my fingertips brush over metal. It feels warm, like it had been in his pocket for a while. I trace my fingers over the delicate chain, feeling them dip into a small hoop at the center of my neck.

Gray runs his fingers through my hair and presses a kiss to the top of my head. "You were made to be mine," he says.

His. My heart flutters. I was made to be his.

Chapter Forty-One

I pull Ava in close and she melts in my arms. Her body molds to mine because we fit together perfectly. I pull the delicate chain from my pocket, watching the way the gold sparkles in the light. It's light, having barely any weight to it. But in my hand, it feels like lead, as if the weight of its meaning gives it physical mass.

She cringes as I smooth my fingers over the chapped skin of her neck. I gently place the chain around her neck, using the tiny hex key to lock it into place. I comb my fingers through her earthy, brown locks, untangling the silky strands before pressing a kiss to the top of her hair.

"You were made to be mine," I say.

Ava sucks in a shaky breath and lifts her head from my shoulder. Her face is damp with tears. I run my fingers over the salty streaks that glisten on her cheeks. She's so beautiful when she cries for me, so perfect when she lets go. She looks up at me, her eyes glittering with unshed tears. But there's something else that gleams in her glassy eyes, some emotion swirling in her irises. It looks like devotion, like love.

The light catches on the o-ring at the center of her neck. It reflects onto her chest, making her shine like gold. The tightness in my chest loosens seeing her just as she should be, shiny and adorned with precious metal. She's gorgeous with my collar around her neck, just like I knew she'd be. The sight of her collared and vulnerable in my arms sends my blood rocketing south. My erection juts out, straining the stitching on my zipper.

My blood pumps through my veins, a single repeating word thumping inside of me. *Mine, mine, mine.*

Pressing my thumb under her chin, I angle her chin toward mine. I press my mouth against hers, reveling in the pillowy softness of her lips. I kiss her softly, communicating the way my heart beats for her without words, because there are no words that can express my feelings for her. There is nothing I could say that would convey the depth of my obsession.

A primal, hungry sound resonates in my chest because I'm fucking ravenous for her. I groan as she parts her lips, slipping her tongue into my mouth. She kisses me in a way she never has before, wild and uninhibited. She kisses me like she's starving for me, her tongue tangling with mine and her teeth scraping over my lips. I suck her tongue into my mouth and swallow her moan.

I pull back and wrap my hand around her throat. Ava's lips part on a whimper and she trembles in my arms. She seeks out my kiss, jutting her head forward and leaning into my palm.

"There's no going back, little bird," I breathe over her lips. "I'll never let you go."

Her eyes widen, becoming glossy and wet. "I don't want you to," she says, her voice husky with lust.

I tighten my grip on her neck, feeling her pulse thud rapidly beneath my fingers. "What do you want?"

"I want you," she murmurs.

My own pulse kicks up, my heart so pumping furiously that I can feel it smashing through the walls I've built around it. The desperate creature that hides inside of me perks up. *She wants me*, it says, *not to fuck, not to come. She just wants* me.

It's not the first time I've heard 'I want you'. Women have said it before. They've thrown it around like an easy phrase, something that says they want me at face value. A big cock and a hard face, that's all I've been to them. They wanted to fuck the bad guy, like I'm some mountain to climb. The way the words whisper out of Ava, the vulnerable quiver in her voice, it means more. My perfect, broken girl. My missing piece. She's the only one who's seen the most monstrous parts of me and still wanted me.

Her fingers claw at my chest, her fingernails streaking my skin with pink lines. She grips my shoulders, pulling me closer. "Please," she whispers, "I need you."

"What do you need, precious?"

Her teeth sink into her pillowy lip. She rolls the skin between her teeth, keeping her mouth pinched firmly closed. She leans forward, pressing her neck further into my palm until a whine gasps out of her.

"Still so shy." I chuckle. "Words, little bird. I need you to use your words and tell me what you need."

Her throat bobs under my hand as she swallows. "I need you to fuck me."

I scoop Ava into my arms and she wraps her arms around my neck as I stand. Ignoring the urge to sprint, I take measured steps, carrying her through the house and up the stairs to my bedroom. *Our* bedroom, actually. Last night was the last one she'll spend in her house, the last night she'll spend without my arms around her.

I now move with haste, my long steps eating up the space between us and the place where I'll make her fully mine. She lets out a squeak as I toss her onto the bed. Her ass bounces on the mattress before she settles on her back. I step towards the foot of the bed, my fingers already tugging at my zipper. Ava stares up at me with wide eyes, her fingers twisting in the blankets beneath her.

"I, uh," she stammers, "I have an IUD, so…"

"I know, baby," I say. "Your doctor keeps thorough records."

She swallows hard, her lip quivering and a look of fear flitting across her face. My tongue darts across my lower lip. She's so pretty when she's frightened. Her chest heaves, her breasts rising and falling with each shaky inhale. Her nipples pebble, hardening into dusky, pink buds. Every inch of her is perfect and all mine.

I push my jeans down my legs, my boxer briefs being tugged

down along with them. Ava's eyes follow every movement of my hands as I undress. When I shove my pants off of my feet and stand, she gasps. My cock juts out, hard and aching. She traces it with wide, fearful eyes, like she's only just remembered how big it is.

"You want your master's cock, little bird?" I ask.

She swipes her tongue over her plush lip, nodding furiously.

"Spread your legs for me. Let me see that pretty pussy."

Her face heats, a beautiful, rosy flush coloring her soft cheeks. She parts her thighs, spreading her legs wide across the bed. I groan at the sight of her pink cunt glistening with arousal. It drips out of her, coating her thighs. I grit my teeth, summoning all of my willpower to stop myself from diving forward and plowing my cock into her wet heat. Desperation skitters through my veins, making my heart rate kick up. I won't fuck her yet. I can't. I made her a promise and I won't break it.

My voice croaks out of me, low and dangerous. "Beg me for it. Beg me to fuck that tight little cunt of yours. Beg me to make you come on my cock."

"Please," she whimpers, her fingers curling in the blankets and twitching with need.

I palm my dick, slowly stroking my hand over my length. My needy girl watches, her eyes following the movement of my hand, and a husky moan falls from her lips.

"You can do better than that, precious," I instruct.

Her legs quake and she pants out a desperate sound. "Please, master."

Goddamnit, that phrase almost undoes me. My grip tightens around my cock until the tip darkens to a nearly purple hue. Forcing out a huff of air, I try to calm myself. Seeing her spread before me, desperate and wanting, makes the monster inside of me peak its head up. It doesn't want to wait. It wants to mount her like an animal. It wants to rut her and mark her with my teeth.

"I'm a very patient man," I tease. "I can wait until you beg me properly, but by the look of that sopping wet pussy, I don't think you can."

Reaching my hand toward her, I let my fingertips graze over her dripping center. Her breath hitches at the contact and she shivers. I pop my fingers, coated in her arousal, into my mouth. Her sweet honeyed taste hits my tongue and my dick jerks like it's trying to jump toward her.

"I think my little slut is aching for her master's cock, desperate for me to claim her, desperate for my cum."

Her teeth sink into her lip, her head bobbing furiously in agreement.

She yelps as my palm collides with her inner thigh. I smack my hand down again, enjoying the feeling of her soft body jiggling with the force of it. I pinch the skin between my fingers until she hisses.

"Then fucking beg me," I snarl.

She leans her head back, her breath coming in short pants. The angle of her neck makes her collar catch the light. It glitters against her chin, her skin glowing like a jewel.

"This collar around your pretty neck," I trace my finger over the gold chain, "it means that you belong to me, my little pet. So when I say 'beg me', you will beg me like a good, obedient girl. The time for shyness is over."

She moans at my words, loving the harsh treatment I'm showing her. She lifts her neck, pushing it into my hand. "Please, master," she pleads, her words so rushed that they nearly blend together. "Please fuck me. Claim me. Ruin me. I need you. Please, I'll do anything."

My chest expands at her admission. Her need for me soothes something in my chest. *Mine*, the word hums inside of me, filling every part of me.

"That's my good girl," I purr.

A look of shock flits across her face as I shove her knees toward her chest. I kneel between her thighs, my fingers ghosting over her clit. She rocks her hips, seeking friction that I'm not ready to give her. Not until I'm inside of her.

Pressing the tip of my cock at her dripping entrance, I watch her face contort with an intoxicating mixture of anticipation and fear. I push into her slowly, inch by inch, until I'm half seated inside of her.

I groan at the feel of her cunt gripping me. She feels like everything I've ever wanted, like a paradise I don't deserve. Her wet heat envelops me, her inner muscles squeezing around me.

She lets out a pained whimper, wiggling her hips and scooting back on the bed. I grab her hips, digging my fingers into her skin and not letting her move away from me. Holding her body firmly to me, I shove in another inch, making her cry out.

"Too big," she cries. "It hurts."

I rock into her slowly, reaching down to rub slow circles around her clit. "I know it hurts, baby, but you can take it. You're doing so well."

Her panted breaths fan against my neck as I sink my cock the rest of the way into her. A feral growl bursts from my mouth as her tight walls squeeze around me. She shivers against me, her pants turning into the most delicious moans as I move.

She writhes beneath me, gasping out her pleasure. I pull out slowly before plunging back in. Ava reaches her arms around my neck, digging her fingernails into my shoulders. The bite of pain shoots through me and I quicken my pace, pounding my cock into her.

"Such a good girl," I pant. "Look how well you're taking my cock."

My thumb dances over her clit and I drag my dick over the spot inside of her that makes her squirm. My girl needs more. I need to make her shatter, to fuck her until the only name she knows is mine. I grab her leg, tossing it over my shoulder and slamming my cock deep inside of her.

She screams out a moan and rocks her hips into me.

"That's it," I coo. "Sing for me, little bird."

I increase the pressure on her clit, pinching and rolling the sensitive bud between my fingers. Her eyes roll back as her inner walls clench around me. She's so close, her body tightening and quivering. My own release is barreling toward me, but I need her to come first. I need it like I need the air that I'm sucking into my lungs in great gasps.

"You're mine," I growl, wrapping my hand around her throat. "Say it. Tell me who you belong to."

Ava releases a husky moan. "I belong to you, master," she pants. "I'm yours. I'm yours."

I jerk my hips, the tip of my cock rubbing against that special spot deep inside. Her pussy spasms around me.

"Please," she gasps, her eyes closing, "I'm…I'm going to…"

My fingers tighten around her throat, threatening her ability to scream. "Eyes on me," I demand.

Her eyes pop open, the mossy-green orbs glassy with tears. My heart sputters as wetness drips down her cheeks. So fucking beautiful.

She clenches down on me with a whimper. My lips peel up into a feral grin. Like such a good girl, she's trying so hard to hold herself back. She doesn't want to come without my permission. Her obedience has my hips stuttering and my balls tightening.

"Pl-please, please," she begs.

I pinch her clit and slam my hips forward. "Come for me."

Ava's mouth drops open on a scream as her pussy flutters around me. My muscles tighten and a tingling sensation shoots up my spine. My rhythm falters as my orgasm crashes through me. My fingers dig into her soft hips as I pump her full of my cum, marking her from the inside out.

Mine, mine, mine, the feral thing in my chest sings.

Chapter Forty-Two

Gray slides out of me and I wince, my muscles sore and my pussy aching in the most delicious way. A strong arm wraps around my waist and rolls me onto my side. Gray presses his chest to my back and I melt into him with a sigh, letting the warmth of his body wrap around me. He pulls a soft blanket over my legs and tucks it around me. His lips meet the back of my neck and he winds his hand through my hair, gently brushing his fingers through the messy strands.

My eyes drift closed as an unfamiliar feeling washes over me, loosening my muscles. It feels odd and new, but nice. Is this what peace feels like? Comfort? My mind flits back in time, wondering if any man has ever made me feel this way, satisfied and safe. They haven't. Not a single one. At least, not until him. I've been used to it, prioritizing my own orgasm because no one else would, but it's totally different with Gray. He wrings them out of me, over and over. He demands them.

As I lay in the bed, surrounded by his scent, the warmth of him beside me grows stifling. I curl my fingers into the blanket, yanking it up higher on my body and tucking it around my neck. My stomach begins to churn, a familiar anxiety squirming in my belly. What happens now? He told me I was his, but does he still feel that way? Have I served my purpose now that he's had me?

"I," my voice catches in my throat, forcing me to cough the words out, "should probably get—"

A yelp jumps from my mouth as Gray flips me onto my back. He climbs on top of me, trapping my waist between his powerful thighs. His fingers bite into my wrists as he yanks them over my head and presses them into the pillows. I look into his hard eyes and a pathetic sound crawls up my throat.

"Absolutely fucking not, little bird," he growls. "You're not going anywhere. I know what's happening in your head right now, and it's going to stop." He runs his nose along the length of my neck, inhaling deeply. "You are mine. Tonight, tomorrow, and every night for the rest of our lives."

The butterflies in my stomach flap their wings wildly, pushing against my belly as if they could reach out and touch him. My eyes sting with tears and I blink rapidly to force them back. The panicked girl inside of me breathes a sigh of relief. *He wants me*, she whispers. *He loves me.*

Loosening his grip on my arms, he stares down at me, his eyes soft. There's a gentleness in his voice that takes me by surprise when he speaks. "Here's what's going to happen." He rubs soft circles on my arm with his finger. "I'm going to get you one of my shirts, you're going to put it on, and then we're going to go downstairs. You're going to pick a movie and I'm going to make us some snacks."

I open my mouth to speak, but he levels me with a look that has my mouth zipping closed so hard that my teeth clack together.

"I'm going to hold you and we're going to watch that movie *together*. Then, we'll go to bed *together*. You're not going back to your house tonight." A smirk teases at the side of his mouth. "In fact, you're not going to live there anymore, because once I sleep next to you, I will never be able to sleep without you again."

My eyes widen, releasing a tear that slides down my cheek. He brushes it away, his thumb tracing down the line of my jaw. "Tell me you understand, Ava," he says firmly. Emotion flickers across his face, his mouth pulling down and his eyes closing. "Tell me you want this," he whispers, "that you want me."

My heart bangs in my chest, thumping so loudly that I'm sure he can hear it. Do I want this? God, yes, yes, I do. I reach my hand up, pressing my palm to his cheek. The words fly from my mouth easily because there's no other option for me. Nothing else will ever be like it is with him. There's no one else who could make me feel the things he does. "I want you. I want this."

"Tell me you love me, little bird." The plea in his voice slams into my heart, splintering anything that remains of its protective cage. I feel the pieces scatter within me, laying me bare and vulnerable before him. I can't deny it any longer. I can't pretend that I don't feel the way I feel in his arms—safe, loved, cherished.

My voice cracks with emotion as more tears dribble down my cheeks. "I love you so much that it scares me."

His mouth collides with mine before I can say anything else. We fall into each other in a clash of tongues and teeth. His arms wrap around me and I sigh into his mouth, feeling like I'm finally home.

I nestle into the couch, listening to the rustling of plastic packaging that spills out from the kitchen. Gray hums a happy tune that vaguely reminds me of something from my childhood, but that I can't quite place. A smile creeps across my face as I flick through movies. Indecision wars in my mind as I flit back and forth between a romantic comedy and a thriller. I pull a fuzzy throw blanket around me and snuggle into the pillows.

Realizing that I can't possibly risk my amazing mood with a sad ending, my decision happens in a split second. Rom-com it is! For the first time, I'm not concerned with my choice of film. I'm not worried that Gray will be upset that I chose the *'girly'* movie instead of something with gunfights and cowboys.

The smell of chocolate wafts into the room and Gray glides in behind it. He sets a tray on the coffee table and I grin at the steaming mugs of cocoa and enormous bowl of popcorn.

"Did you pick something?" he asks.

"A rom-com. Emily said it's really cute. Oh, uh, Emily is my best friend, but you probably know that already, don't you?"

He nods, his mouth splitting into a smile that could make the devil's panties wet. "You're so cute, baby." he chuckles.

The couch dips beside me before Gray pulls me into his lap and starts the movie. He wraps his arms around me and nuzzles into my neck. His breath tickles over my nape and a needy sound bubbles up from my throat. My skin pebbles with goosebumps as his lips whisper over my neck. My core warms, heat shooting straight to my center. I clench my legs together, feeling the wetness starting to slick my inner thighs.

"Watch the movie, precious," Gray purrs against the shell of my ear.

His fingertips dance over my exposed thigh, making me pant with need. A moan slides off my tongue as his teeth scrape against my shoulder. My pussy clenches and my clit jumps, begging for his attention. He circles a finger around my entrance and an aching pain shivers through my muscles.

"I'm so sore," I plead.

His chest rumbles with a masculine hum. "I know you are, and you're going to be sore every day." He pushes a finger into me and I moan. "I'm going to fuck this perfect pussy every day with my tongue, my fingers, my cock." He hooks his finger, rubbing that spot inside of me that makes my legs shake.

"And I'm not going to stop when it hurts," he says before sinking his teeth into my shoulder. A shudder runs through me and I moan, rocking my hips into his hand, forcing him deeper. He licks the aching spot where his teeth were, soothing the sting. "Because I know how much you love it when I hurt you."

My insides melt at his words, my nerve endings lighting up at his rough treatment. Maybe it's wrong. Maybe I shouldn't want this, but I don't care. My body heats, my blood boiling in my veins.

"Please, master," I gasp, "more."

"Shh," he chides, "I said watch the movie."

His finger finds my clit, his thumb rubbing over the sensitive bud in that way that makes my breath catch. I cry out as he forces two more fingers into my pussy. His large digits fill me, stretching my insides, making me feel so full that I could burst.

Wanton, needy sounds tumble from my mouth and I writhe in his arms, my inner walls tightening around him. My head lolls, dropping to his shoulder as I roll my hips. His hard length presses against my ass and my mind goes blank. I become something other than myself, some entity made only of need and arousal.

Suddenly, all that matters is pleasing him, obeying him. I try to focus on the movie playing on the TV screen, but my eyes blur in and out of focus. The sounds around me are meaningless, unintelligible syllables that float around the room with no purpose. All that exists for me is him, his body pressed against mine, his fingers inside me.

My core tightens, my body winding up like a spring. My inner walls begins to flutter around his fingers as my body careens towards release.

"That's it," he growls against my ear. "Come for me, little bird."

His words purr through me and I detonate. I scream out his name as my orgasm explodes through me. Stars sparkle in my vision, blanketing the room in shining darkness. His movements slow, his fingers coaxing every last bit of pleasure from my body. I sink into him, gasping and panting.

Gray kisses my temple and wraps his arms around me. "Such a good girl," he coos.

Exhaustion crashes into me, turning my eyelids to lead. I turn in his lap, burrowing into his arms like it's the safest place in the world for me to rest. To me, it is. He feels like safety, like home. I drop my face into the crook of his neck and inhale the scent of him. His smell surrounds me, sweet vanilla and leather dancing in my nostrils. I let my eyes close, the movie left forgotten on the screen.

My eyes rocket open as a thunderous crash explodes through the room. Gray's arms band around my stomach, his grip bruising. He shoves me down, pinning me to the floor with his hand on my back.

"Stay down!" he yells.

He crouches beside me, his arm darting underneath the couch. When he pulls it back, my eyes widen. His hand is wrapped around an enormous military-looking gun. He keeps a gun under his couch?! Is it even called a gun if it's that big? When does it go from a gun to a firearm?

"Do not move from this spot," he commands, sliding past me toward the source of the sound.

I press my face to the floor. Long carpet fibers tickle my nose as I peer out through the space between the floor and the couch. Looking toward the front door, a gasp gets lodged in my throat. The heavy metal door is off its hinges, sitting at an odd angle. It teeters on its side before crashing down, the weight of it vibrating the floor beneath me.

Smoke billows into the room, flowing over the floor in a thick, gray wave. It wafts closer, pushed by the cold breeze that streams through the busted door. My eyes begin to sting, my vision blurring as tears burn in my eyes. I suck in a breath that scorches my throat. My airways constrict as the acrid vapor coats my tongue and fills my nostrils. Coughing and gagging, I fight back the bile that climbs up my throat.

Pop, pop, pop.

The sound of fireworks echoes through the room, bouncing off the walls and smashing into my ears. Who's setting off fireworks in the house? And why? Wait, it's not fireworks. It's gunfire. My stomach tightens, panic clawing inside my belly. A ringing sound buzzes in my ears and a wave of dizziness washes over me.

Something flits past my eyes, a hazy figure of toned muscle and dark ink. Gray careens over the couch toward the door, gun trained on whatever is coming for us. The muscles in his forearms bunch, veins protruding as he propels himself through the air. The sight is nothing short of monstrous as he bounds over furniture, his face drawn and smothered in smoke. *My monster*, the voice inside of me sighs.

I don't dare to move from where I lay pressed to the floor, my breath fanning over it, rustling the strands. Bullets fly overhead, zipping through the air with alarming speed. They careen through the room, forcing wood to splinter and artwork to plummet to the floor. The sound of shouting reaches me, but the words are fuzzy like I'm listening to a conversation from underwater.

Something grabs against the back of my t-shirt, yanking me upward. My feet falter as I whip myself around, sending me careening forward. My chest slams into a hard body, my face crashing into their shoulder.

"Gray!" I cry, my ears blurring with tears of relief.

Only the face I look up into isn't Gray's. A man stands before me, his hand firmly wrapped around the fabric of my shirt. Not-Gray tilts his head down at me, his broad jaw twitching under a smattering of dark facial hair. The corners of his mouth jump, forming a grin that sends a shiver through my body. My eyes meet his and what I see has me jerking in his hold. Dark pools like muddy water stare back at me, full of terrible promise.

"Got you, *cara*." His voice slides over me, viscous and sticky. Even over the ruckus around us, I can hear the darkness in it.

His arm bands around my chest, pulling me toward him. He laughs as I kick my legs out, crashing my bare toes into his shins. Something inside of me snaps. A switch flips, demanding that I lash out and free myself. I wrap my hands around his arm, my fingernails tearing into him until drops of blood bloom on his olive skin. Bending my neck awkwardly, I sink my teeth into his arm. His blood coats my mouth, the sickening, thick liquid sliding over my tongue.

"*Merda*! You little bitch!" he yells. He fists my hair, forcing my head back, making my scalp burn and tears drip down my cheeks.

My feet abruptly leave the floor and I'm tossed into the air. My breath leaves me in a great whoosh as my stomach collides with his shoulder. Cold air hits the back of my thighs along with his hands. They grip me, pinching my skin in his fingers. Everything in my stomach jostles with his steps, forcing bile up my throat.

With each of his large steps, we move closer and closer to the busted doorway. Closer to the outside.

"No, no, no!" I scream, kicking my feet against this stomach. "Gray! Grayson!"

Where is Gray? I lift my head, my vision bouncing with the movement of the enormous body I'm attached to. My eyes scan the destruction, searching for him. Smoke wafts up from the chunks of wood and stone that litter the floor. The kitchen counter is cracked, pieces of marble pulverized into sand and falling to the floor. Blood coats the floor in spatters, and pools under dead men. Their unseeing eyes stare up at me, glossy and red. I swallow a mouthful of vomit.

Amidst the rumble, half cloaked by the remnants of the kitchen table, a shirtless body lays on the bloodied floor. I know that body instantly. He lifts his head, blood streaming down his face from a gash in his head. Our eyes meet and he groans my name. His body is motionless, but his fingers inch across the floor, reaching for me. Tears burn in my eyes and fall down my cheeks as I scream his name.

I pound my fists into the back of the asshole who's holding me. Clawing at his shirt, I rip threads from the fabric. *Get to Gray.* It's the only thought in my head. *I have to get to him. I have to fight.*

White hot pain explodes against my temple, and I cry out for him as the world goes black.

Chapter Forty-Three

"Ava," I croak.

I swallow hard, my throat burning. The taste of gunpowder lingers on my tongue. Pushing my palms against the floor, I move to stand, but my muscles won't hold me. My stomach hits the ground, jagged bits of wood digging into my gut.

With useless limbs, I watch Ava's unconscious form disappear into the night on the shoulder of my enemy. Pain explodes in my chest as my heart shatters. Wetness flows down my face as a face appears in my vision.

Mom, her beautiful face marred with blood. *Save her*, she whispers, *save her because you couldn't save me.* My vision darkens, causing black spots to dance across her face. My body falters, unconsciousness pulling me under.

I'm coming for you, little bird.

Chapter Forty-Four

"Ugh." A groan creeps up my chest and tumbles from my mouth. The sound reverberates through my head, bouncing off the inside of my skull like a tennis ball. That is, if the tennis ball were shot out of a freaking canon at a hundred miles an hour. My pulse pounds in my head. With each beat of my heart, pain stabs behind my eyes. My tongue feels like sandpaper and pain lances my throat as I swallow.

What happened to me? My memory feels like a broken thing, each section unconnected and strewn about in a random order. Clenching my eyes closed, I sift through the pieces. Gray, I remember Gray. Despite the pain in my head and limbs, my body tingles at the memory of his hands on me, his cock inside of me, forcing the pleasure from my body.

I remember being held by him and the smell of chocolate. Cocoa! Yes, he made us cocoa. I recall the way his smile lit up his face when he delivered a tray of snacks and hot chocolate to the couch. Hot chocolate that I never drank. But what else?

I lift my hands to cradle my throbbing head. Something scratches at my wrists and my hands won't move. A vision appears behind my eyes. It plays out like a movie on an old screen, grainy and dim. An explosion, gunfire, blood. Rough hands grabbing me, the taste of blood in my mouth. Gray, my beautiful monster, blood coating his face, his hand reaching for me.

Fuck. I should have drank the cocoa.

Fear shivers through my belly, making my muscles clench and my stomach churn. Steeling my nerves, I pry my eyelids open. The sight of the room I'm in hit me like a ton of bricks, and I swallow a mouthful of bile, narrowly avoiding vomiting down the front of my shirt. Overhead lights dimly illuminate concrete walls. The yellowed light bulbs cast an eerie glow over the rough stone, highlighting the damp, moldy patches that creep up from the floor.

Plastic bins are stacked in the corner of the room. They remind me of the ones Mom used to keep old papers in, tucked away in the basement. Hers were nicer. I'm not sure why, but they were definitely nicer. These are stacked haphazardly and messily labeled with permanent marker. I try to focus my eyes, to read the chicken scrawl on the side of the boxes, but without my glasses, it's no use. Not that it truly matters, but I'd like to know what kind of old junk I might die next to.

I will not die here. I will not die here. I will not die here, some stupid, encouraging voice chants in my head. It sounds an awful lot like mine, but it can't be. Though given that it feels like I've suffered a blow to the head, maybe it is. Maybe a head injury has rewired my brain into believing it can be optimistic.

Focus, Ava! It screeches inside of me.

I inhale a shaky breath, cringing as the sour taste of mildew slides over my tongue.

"She's awake," a gruff voice sounds from behind me. "Tell the boss."

I whip my head behind me, wincing at the pain that shoots through my neck at the abrupt movement. Standing at the far end of the room, their backs pressed against the wall, three men stare at me. Their eyes rove over me. Like a physical thing, their gaze touches me. It prods at me, reminding me that the only thing covering my body is Gray's shirt. One of the men steps forward, his boots stomping across the floor until he's standing only inches away. He steps in front of me and I breathe a sigh of relief that he's no longer at my back.

I tilt my head up, craning my neck to look at him. There's something familiar in his dark eyes. My eyes travel down to his neck where brightly colored tattoos peek out from beneath his shirt collar. Then downward, to where his muscular arms are crossed over his chest. The skin of his forearm is marred, marked with angry, red scratches and a nasty looking bite mark. Then I remember. I pinch my lips together, trying to keep from grinning at the damage I caused him. He notices the direction of my eyes and his lips turn down into a scowl.

"Not this time, *cara*," he grumbles.

He reaches a hand toward my face and I flinch, expecting the worst. I pinch my eyes shut as his fingers trail down the side of my face, his touch gentle. My stomach quivers in disgust at the feel of it. I move to push his hand away, but pain slices into my wrists. My eyes pop open and I force my head down to look at them. It's only then that I realize I'm bound. A rope wraps around my wrists, tying me to the wooden chair beneath me. Unable to break free, I do the only other thing I can, the thing that I'm best at. I make myself small. Shrinking back into the chair, my shoulders draw inward and my chin presses toward my neck.

A deep chuckle rumbles through him. "We're going to have a lot of fun together, *bella*."

The lust in his voice makes my insides shrivel. I can feel the tears burning behind my eyelids, but I refuse to let them fall. I won't let them watch me break.

Click, click, click.

The measured steps of high heeled shoes echoes through the room. Tall, Dark, and Scary rips his hand away from my face, quickly stuffing them into his pockets. He steps away from me, his eyes cast downward. A tremor crawls up my spine. Who can make a man like this afraid?

A feminine laugh jingles through the small space, its tone delicate and sultry. My eyelids shoot open. Standing in what seems to be the only doorway in the room is a woman. Confusion muddles my brain as my eyes pour over her. This is the boss? A woman?

Her designer pumps clacks against the concrete as she steps toward me. She taps a manicured, red fingernail against her hip before picking a piece of invisible lint from her white pencil skirt. She cocks her head, her dark hair rustling over her silky blouse. It falls over her shoulder like a wave of silk that dips between her breasts. With her thin frame and fitted clothes, she looks like a supermodel. I shrink further into my chair. Her chocolate eyes meet mine and I freeze, my muscles tensing as if they sense the danger within her gaze.

A ghost of a smile twitches at the edges of her red-painted lips. "So, this is who Grayson has chosen? This mousy little thing?" Her lip curls as she drags her fingers through a lock of my hair. She drops it and wipes her hand over the front of her skirt.

"What do you want with me?" The words grate over my dry tongue, but at least my croaked voice hides the way my voice wavers.

"Oh, *topo*," she chuckles, "surely you know who you've been in bed with." A smile peels across her face, her lips rocketing up into her pronounced cheekbones. Crinkles form beside her eyes, showing some of her age, or at least what's not hidden by Botox. "Or has he not told you what he is?"

I sink my teeth into my lower lip. *Say nothing*, a voice whispers through my head, *give her nothing*.

"I wonder if I have you to thank, *topo*," her voice holds an air of humor that isn't reflected in her eyes, "since it must have been you that had Grayson distracted enough to fall into my trap."

My brow furrows in confusion and her smug smile widens.

"I set your boyfriend up to take the fall for killing a rat that snuck out of my house." She looses a heavy breath, her fingers digging into the fabric of her skirt. "But of course, it didn't all go according to plan given that he was meant to die during that job. I was going to leave it alone, let it play out, thinking that those Bratva assholes would have killed him straight away. That is, until my men saw him coming out of Mikhail Volkov's club."

Her words swim around in my head, morphing my thoughts into a confusing jumble of nonsense. A painful knot forms in my stomach. The ache climbs up my esophagus, making my throat clench. There's so much that I don't know about the world Gray lives in. There's so much that he hasn't told me. My fists clench behind my back, the motion making the ropes scrape against my sore wrists. I've read enough books about villains and mafia men to know better. I should have asked these questions. But those were just books. They weren't real. But this? This is definitely real.

"God," the woman's scoff pulls me out of my thoughts, "you really are dense. I'll spell it out for you, very slowly since I suspect you need that. My family has been at war with the Volkovs for years. Grayson was the perfect weapon to bring them down a peg. That's all he's really good for, anyway."

My eyes narrow on her, heat climbing up my face as anger begins to simmer in my veins. She inches forward. I try to move away, but I'm locked in place. Her fingers wrap around a lock of my hair and she yanks my head to the side. Hot breath ghosts over my face as she whispers in my ear. "And so here you are, my little bit of revenge."

My head snaps back as she releases the strands from between her bony fingers. My muscles scream at the odd movement, but I mask the pain on my face. I won't let her see it.

"He'll come for me," I spit between gritted teeth.

Her laughter roars through the room. "Oh, that's just precious! Do you think he loves you, *topo*? Men like Grayson aren't capable of it. But it really doesn't matter because he'll be dead very soon." She lets her voice trails off before she mutters, "if he isn't already."

Dead? My eyes widen and ice shoots through my veins. My fingers twitch at my back, splinters of the tough rope jabbing under my fingernails. *No, no, no, no,* that little voice inside of me screams, *he won't. He can't. Not now that he's mine. Not now that I love him.* I blink against the salty tears that burn in my eyes, refusing to let her see them.

"Now," she purrs, "be a good girl and I'll make sure my men play nice with you."

A throat clears behind us before a masculine voice says, "Bianca, you're needed upstairs."

My eyes droop as the bitch sashays out of the room, a wave of bone-deep exhaustion finally hitting me. At least now I know her name.

Chapter Forty-Five

Dried blood cakes my face, sealing my eyelids closed. It cracks as I peel them open and pieces of gore flutter across my face, drifting onto the floor. Morning light pours from the windows, setting a scorching pain ablaze in my head. Despite the agony blooming in my skull, I don't blink. I don't close my eyes.

You deserve this pain, the creature in my chest seethes, its claws dragging down the walls of my heart. *You let them take what's mine. You let them hurt her.*

My lungs tighten painfully, each breath stabbing into the soft tissues inside of me. It hurts because I know it's true. She'd be safe if I had left her alone. If I hadn't walked by that goddamned coffee shop. If I hadn't seen the sadness swimming in her eyes. If I hadn't felt that desperate need to explore it. If I had been a good man.

The remnants of an old memory whisper through my mind. My mother's soft voice rings through it. *Someday*, she says, *you'll find a girl who's very special to you. She'll become your whole world and you'll love her more than anything. Your heart will beat just for her. When that happens, cherish her. Protect her and never let her go.*

Her words seemed so insignificant at the time. After her death, they meant nothing. Her dreams for my life became an impossibility. Because monsters don't get happily ever afters. Liquid drips down my face and I reach my hand up to wipe it away. I must be bleeding again.

I hold my hand in front of my eyes, but I don't see blood. My tongue darts out, testing the fluid in the only way I can think to. Salt hits my tongue and a shiver creeps through my limbs. Tears. They're fucking tears. A sound jumps up my throat, a sob spilling from my mouth.

"I'm so sorry, Mom," I whisper into the air. "I'm so sorry I didn't save you." My hands clench, my resolve hardening every muscle in my body. "But I will save her."

Wood clatters to the ground as I shove my shoulders upward. Digging my fingers into the rubble, I crawl out from beneath the remnants of my house. They don't matter, these broken objects around me. They aren't my home, she is. Chunks of wood and metal slice into my palms as I drag my body across the floor. I ignore the pain that explodes through my skin. It doesn't matter. Any pain I feel now is nothing compared to the suffering I'll cause to the ones who took my little bird from me.

Anyone who has so much as looked at her will die at my hands. I'll drag out their deaths, watching them writhe and cry in agony before I even consider ending their worthless lives. Until I get her back, no one in this city is safe. I'll burn this fucking place to the ground to find her, and when I do, we'll fuck in the cinders.

A grin peels across my face as images flash through my mind. My woman, smiling in my arms, her face smudged with ash. She'll look so beautiful with firelight sparkling in her eyes. She'll dance for me, her full hips swaying in her dress made of smoke.

With a kind of clarity that borders on madness, I sprint to our bedroom. Ignoring the screaming of my muscles, I shovel through the closet. Clothes fly across the room, fabric fluttering to the dirtied floor until I find my stash of tactical gear. I slip the bulletproof vest over my head, even as my body groans in protest at the movement.

My joints ache as I move hastily towards my office. Once inside, I drop my body into my desk chair and switch on the monitors that connect to the security system. The screens blink to life, bathing my face in bright, artificial light. My vision becomes fuzzy and the room tilts around me. My stomach churns and I drop my head beside the desk to vomit into a potted plant.

I swallow down the acrid taste of bile that lingers on my tongue and return my attention to the monitors. I know this feeling, but I don't have time to deal with a concussion. Not while she's in the hands of my enemies. My fists clench, my fingernails digging into my palms. The bite of pain grounds me. For Ava, I'll endure. I won't rest until she's safe in my arms.

Flipping through the security footage, sharp claws grip my heart, shredding the weak organ. Ava's face fills the screen and I suppress the pitiful whine that tries to climb up my throat. I watch my little bird, her teeth sinking into her pouty lip as she grinds her pussy against my hand. My cock hardens as I watch her mouth drop open in pleasure.

Mustering up all of my willpower, I fast-forward through the video of my perfect little pet, sated and sleeping against my chest. I can't linger on those images. If I do, I'll lose myself in her visage. So, I skip forward to the moment the front door exploded open and my enemy invaded our home.

My fingers wrap around the edge of my desk, the wood groaning under my grip, as I watch the bastard who put his hands on my woman. He grabbed her, his fingers dimpling her delicate flesh and bruising her milky skin. I smash my fist into the keyboard, jacking up the volume just in time to hear him call her *'cara'*.

"Bianca." Her name growls out of me, grating against my tongue like a cheese grater. White hot anger boils in my gut, burning away the last of the nausea. I'll make good on my promise to Mikhail. Bianca Rossi will die at my hands.

"Find out where the fuck they are!" My fists crash into Shawn's desk, sending empty cans of some God awful energy drink clattering to the floor.

"I'm working as fast as I can, man," he says as his fingers pick up speed. They clack against the keyboard as traffic camera footage flits across his computer screen. "I tracked them from your place through the south side of the city. I lost track of them somewhere around Belmont, but they were definitely moving north. I suspect they were moving away from the city to wherever Bianca's compound is." He huffs out a shaky breath. "I'm sorry, man. I just can't find where that is."

"Get me the location of every single one of her businesses. Warehouses, storage facilities, whorehouses, fucking jerk-off booths. I don't give a shit. Just find them and get me the addresses."

His voice cracks with uncertainty. "Some of her men are still combing through the city. I've been watching their cars and they're searching. They're coming for you."

I choke out a humorless laugh and Shawn inches back in his chair.

He looks up at me, concern swimming in his eyes. "W-what are you going to do?"

"I'm going to get my girl back."

Chapter Forty-Six

Lifting my head, the tendons in my neck cry out in protest. I peel my eyelids open, fighting against the crust of sleep that glues them shut at the corners. The room swims around me for a moment before everything comes back into focus. Was I asleep?

Even the dim illumination from the overhead lights feels too bright. I blink, trying to force away the full ache that pounds behind my eyes. I open my mouth, sucking in a calling breath. The persistent itch in the back of my throat makes me cough out the exhale. My tongue slides out to wet my cracked lips, but it only leaves a dry, sticky feeling on them.

I'm so thirsty. How long has it been since I had something to drink? It must have been at dinner with Gray. I didn't drink the cocoa he made us. My heart drops into my stomach. I wish I had tasted it.

I wiggle my fingers, hoping to shake away the ache in my hands. The rope chafes against my wrists with each movement, scraping my skin raw. With my arms locked in place, a throbbing pain stabs between my shoulder blades. How long have I been like this? How long have I been here?

I'm certain that it's been hours since they took me, maybe even an entire day. My mind wanders, pulling me from the dank basement. It pulls me back into my own bedroom, to my cozy book nook. The soft blanket in my lap warms my bare legs. I stare out of my favorite window, watching leaves fall from the old trees beside my house. They flutter to the ground in a whirlwind of red and gold. I never realized how much I've always relied on windows to tell me the time.

Thump, thump, thump.

The sound of footsteps drags me back to the present. My eyes refocus, damp walls and cracked concrete filling my vision. A heavy door squeaks open, broad shoulders filling the rusted, metal frame. Tall, Dark, and Scary is back, another man hot on his heels. Scary's eyes find mine and he smiles. A chill rushes through me because it's not a warm smile. There's no kindness in his eyes as they crawl over my body.

He turns to the man behind him, who instantly straightens his spine. He's a bit shorter than Scary, but no less frightening. His navy blue shirt is pulled tight over his muscular chest. The poor fabric looks like it might burst if he were to flex his huge arms. He reaches a hand up, brushing it through his short-cropped hair. Anxiety pours off of him as he steps into the room.

"What are we doing here?" he asks.

Scary rolls his eyes. "Relax. We're just looking." He tips his stubbled chin in my direction. "She's a pretty thing, isn't she?" He licks his lips and I suppress a gag. "Nice wide hips. I bet she's got a fat ass, too."

The anxious one's eyes roam over me quickly before returning to his shoes. "We can't touch her," he mumbles. The tightness in my chest loosens and I breathe a sigh of relief.

He stuffs his hands into his pockets, a sound of displeasure rumbling in his throat. "The boss doesn't let us fuck the fresh ones. Besides, I heard she was promised to someone, anyway."

Promised to someone? a panicked voice screams inside of me. My stomach churns and I tilt my head back, swallowing a mouthful of bile. *Promised to someone?* My lungs inflate painfully, cold, damp air clinging to my insides. Spots dance in front of my eyes and the ceiling lights suddenly seem to brighten. *Promised to someone?* My head falls to the side, my chin crashing into my shoulder just before the room goes dark.

I crack my eyes open and my gaze immediately flicks to the door where the men are. Except they aren't there anymore. My eyes whip around the room, searching for them, but there's no one here. The door they came in is closed and I'm alone.

"No, no, no, no," I whisper. "Did I fall asleep again?" My breathing turns ragged, air panting in and out until I feel lightheaded.

"You can't keep falling asleep here," I whisper-scream into the empty room. "You have to stay awake. Alert. Awake and alert, Ava. Awake and alert!"

A metallic screech sounds through the room as someone shoves the door open. I steel my nerves, preparing for the worst. I can't even fathom what the worst might be, but I need to be ready for it. I straighten my spine and tense my body until my muscles begin to shake. Locking my eyes on the doorway, I watch the door push into the room. A dim light just beyond it flickers, casting little chunks of moving light over someone.

Flicker. Blue jacket. *Flicker.* Dark hair. *Flicker.* Tan skin. Only small bits and pieces of the person in the doorway reach my eyes before they step into the room.

My eyes widen in surprise when a man that can't be a day over twenty pushes into the room. The yellowing lights shine over his face, making his skin appear dull and sickly. His dark hair is slicked back from his face, copious amounts of hair gel making it appear hard and shiny. Thick eyebrows sit furrowed over his chestnut eyes.

He's conventionally attractive with his clean-shaven face and strong nose. His pressed, navy blue suit is perfectly tailored, highlighting his slim waist and broad shoulders. His brown loafers tap against the concrete as he steps toward me. Pressing his hand to his chest, he smooths the wrinkles in his vest.

The smell of expensive cologne clogs my nostrils as he moves closer, a welcome change from the stench of damp that clings to the walls of the dirty basement. His considerable height forces me to tilt my head back to look at him. His lips twitch up, a gentle smile forming on his face.

"You must need to use the bathroom by now, huh?" he asks, his voice lilting upward as if he were speaking to a small animal.

My bladder twinges, a familiar ache having built within it in recent hours. I wiggle in the chair, hoping to push the feeling down and pretend it doesn't exist. Only now that he's said it, it's all that I can think about. God, I really do have to pee. Not trusting my voice not to crack, I nod my head in agreement.

My nerves spring to life as he steps behind me. Fear swims in my gut and my body tightens in preparation. Fingers circle my sore wrists and a gasp jumps from my mouth. I pinch my lips together, refusing to let any other sounds escape. The coarse rope tears at my skin and I grimace. It loosens and my hands fall limp at my sides.

"You can stand up." The hairs on the back of my neck rise as his breath ruffles my hair. "There's a bucket in the corner over there."

My heart sinks and a pained sound squeaks from my throat. A bucket? A freaking bucket!?

The man's voice hardens, becoming something low and sharp that jabs into my gut. "It's that or nothing, *cucciola*."

I stand, gripping the back of the chair as my legs wobble beneath me. Pins stab into my calves and thighs as I hobble towards the corner of the room. My eyes drawn down to the floor, where sure enough, a gallon bucket sits. The cheery yellow plastic taunts me, reminding me of better days, of rare weekends when my father went fishing and Mom and I were free. She'd pack sandwiches, sodas, and plastic pails that we'd lug to the beach in a heavy tote bag. The sun shone brightly on those days, sparkling off the sand where I'd build my castles. Those were the days that I dreamed, that I dared to hope for something more for my life. On that beach with my toes in the cool water, I could be more than just a scarred girl. With my bathing suit hiding the bruises on my back and stomach, I was normal.

Mom, I sigh inside of myself, *how did I end up here?*

A throat clears behind me, dragging me away from the glistening water. It yanks me back to the dark room with musty air and a bucket for a toilet. Tears prick my eyes as I lift the long t-shirt and squat over the plastic pail. I won't let the tears fall, not while he's watching me. I won't let them drip from my eyes while his gaze burns against my bare legs. I won't let him see me break, even as the sound of my bladder releasing bounces off of the concrete walls of my cage.

My cheeks burn as I wiggle my ass over the bucket, trying to dispel any remaining droplets of urine from my skin. I walk back to the chair with my eyes on the man, trying to keep my legs steady and my back straight. He nods toward the uncomfortable surface, telling me to sit back down. My fists clench at my sides and my steps falter.

I stare at the chair like it's the thing that kidnapped me and locked me in this room. My thighs and bum throb from lack of movement. As my eyes flick between the chair and the man, his eyes change. There's something within their depths that frightens me more than any of the men I've seen so far, something cold. Gingerly, I sit back down. The man looks down at me and grins. A shiver creeps through my shoulders at the sight of his smile. It looks wrong on his face, like it isn't meant to be there.

He shoves a small plastic water bottle into my hands. I crack it open and guzzle it down with one word repeating in my mind. *Survive, survive, survive.*

"Aren't you a lovely little creature?" he purrs, eyes roaming over my face and body. The look in his eyes makes the water in my stomach feel like sand, heavy and sickening. My jaw clenches as he peruses my form. Goosebumps rise on my skin, but it isn't from the cold air that drifts through the room. Every hair follicle on my body stands at attention, sensing the wrongness within this man. My legs quiver, receiving the signal from my brain that tells them to run, but they can't move. I'm frozen in place under the weight of his gaze.

He grabs my face, his fingers digging into my cheeks until my teeth scrape against the inside of my mouth. "You're going to be my birthday present," he growls. "Did you know that?"

Unable to move or speak with his grip bruising my face, I remain silent and motionless.

"You should be thanking me. Mother wanted to sell you, but I convinced her to let me keep you." His lips tilt into a proud smile that doesn't reach his eyes.

Mother, the word rings through my head, demolishing any question about who this man is. This is Bianca's son. This is the one they said I'm promised to. My eyes blur, fat tears falling down my cheeks before I can stop them.

His palm whips across my face, agony blooming in its wake. Liquid dribbles down my upper lip, salt and copper splashing over my tongue. A gag lodges in my throat as I taste my blood.

"Thank me, you ungrateful whore!" he screams, peppering my face with spittle.

"T-thank you," I sob.

He shoves me further into the chair, roughly tying my wrists behind my back. The wood grinds into my shoulder blades, making me yelp. His hands trail over my hips and stomach before stopping on my breasts. Nausea swirls in my belly as he gropes my chest. His fingers clamp around my nipples and I scream in pain and disgust.

He lets out a scoff and withdraws his hands from my body. "I can't touch you like this," he complains, wiping his palms down his suit pants. "You're dirty and you stink. I'll have the men clean you up before my birthday party tomorrow night." His fingers grip my chin, forcing me to look at his face. "And you will be fucking grateful."

He stomps out of the room, leaving me to sob into the empty space.

Chapter Forty-Seven

"Any luck?" Shawn's voice crackles through my phone.

"I'm at one of her warehouses now." Frustration ripples through my body, increasing my grip on my phone until the plastic creaks. "I've hit three of her businesses already and no one had any fucking answers."

"Shit," he breathes. "Okay, that's okay. Those were her customer-facing businesses, right? Brothels and stuff? It makes sense that no one would know much there. Did you, uh…dispose of the clientele?"

"They're all dead."

Shawn sucks in a heavy breath. "Right, right, of course they are. Just, you know, do what you have to do to get her back safely."

"I am," I seethe into the speaker before cutting off the call.

Dim, evening light peeks between the buildings at the edge of the city, the fading sun casting a red glow over the old bricks. Bits of gravel scatter beneath my boots as I walk through the alley. I watch them skitter across the ground, lodging themselves in the cracks in the concrete. Within those cracks, tiny tufts of green peek out. Maybe weeds are the only things that survive in this shithole.

As I round the corner, my eyes crawl along the warehouse,

marking points of entry. The crumbling bricks wouldn't be hard to get through with the pipe bomb in my pocket, but that's not ideal. Looking further along the building, I notice a small side door. It looks weak, its edges rusted and worn. That's how I'll get inside.

A cold wind lashes at my face, assaulting me with frigid air and the stench of the city. I tug my hood over my head and stuff my hands into my jacket pockets.

Is she cold? The thought whispers through my mind, slicing into the soft tissue like a razor. The organ in my chest pounds against my ribcage as if it could bust free and find her itself. It's almost winter and the near-freezing air has a sharp bite. Her bare legs flash through my mind, bitten red by wind and frost. *She must be cold. I have to bring her home.*

The thought of bringing my little bird back to me propels me forward. It's the only thing that allows me to ignore the pounding in my head and the ache in my bones. My boots pound against the pavement, my limbs moving me even while my mind is stuck on the image of her. Her mossy-green eyes swim in my vision as my body reaches the door. The soft curves of her hips dance before me as I pull the bomb from my pocket and duct tape it to the rusted door hinges. I light a match and watch the flame sparkle like the gold collar I locked around her shapely neck.

The fuse sparks and sizzles, shooting tiny embers into my hand. I pivot quickly and dive behind a nearby dumpster, hoping it will shield me from the majority of the blast. The explosion rings out through the alley. The sound smashes into my ears and floods my head with a dizzy haze. Chunks of metal and stone whistle through the air, some embedding themselves into the brick while others crash to the ground.

I press my body into the side of the dumpster, letting the ringing in my ears quiet. The next sound that reaches my ears stretches my mouth into a grin. The screams of injured men echo through the alley, their agonized wails dancing in my ears like a symphony. I stand, stepping through the cloud of smoke that billows from the doorway.

The stench of burning flesh and metal clings to my nostrils. The heat of a small fire warms my face. Moving forward, metal and debris crunch under my feet. I walk through the haze until my boot bumps into something soft. I look down at the floor, blinking against the smoke that blurs my vision. The two guards once stationed at the doorway have been thrown back several feet. Their bodies lay crumbled on the floor, limbs dangling at odd angles. Their blood pools on the floor from the shards of metal that pierce their skin. One of them is silent, either dead or in shock, but the other is screaming.

Pulling a handgun from my waistband, I aim it between his eyes. The man looks up at me, his face tear-stained and bloody, before he rattles out a shaky sigh. Something that looks like relief crosses his face, slackening his features and quieting his screams.

"A quick death is too kind for you," I fume, releasing my grip on the trigger.

I move forward into the warehouse, stepping over his mangled body and leaving him to bleed out from his wounds. He deserves an agonizing death. They all do for taking what's mine. His fingers crack under my weight and his screaming renews, the sound roaring through the building. I hope they're all listening, suffering with the knowledge that death is coming for them.

The smoke begins to clear and two things become immediately apparent: I've got everyone's attention and I'm severely outgunned. Nearly a dozen men snap to attention, their eyes and guns trained on me. I throw myself behind a metal barrel as the bullets start to fly. My body crashes to the floor with a thud that reverberates through my bones, but at least I'm not dead. Gunfire pummels the barrel, each shot pushing the metal to its breaking point. With my fingers pressed against my seemingly single-use barrier, I will the rusted metal to hold on until they need to reload.

Seconds drag by as bullets spray overhead, crashing into walls and sending objects tumbling across the floor. A mist of brick dust fills the air, clogging my nose and coating my tongue. The sound of gunfire pounds in my ears, reigniting the fiery pain behind my eyes. Until now, I had almost forgotten about the head wound. *Women love scars*, the creepy creature inside of me purrs. *Ava will know how hard you fought for her.* All of this, everything I do, is for her. I'd lay their corpses at her feet if I didn't think it'd make her sick.

Click, click, click.

My lips twitch into a smile at the telltale clicking of their spent weapons. It's my turn now.

I spring up from the floor, sending the barrel crashing against the concrete. I have less than two seconds while they reload to assess the situation. My eyes scan the room, making a mental note of its layout and exit points. There's a back door, but it's mostly blocked by crates and boxes. High on the walls, a few small windows light the space, but they can only be accessed by a ladder. The warehouse itself is large, but sparsely packed. That means a couple of things: Bianca doesn't give a shit about OSHA regulations, and more importantly, there's nowhere to hide.

My eyes pan over the faces of ten men who are rapidly loading their weapons. Actually, eight men. Two of them would barely fit the description of the word. Their faces twitch with panic and sweat trickles down their foreheads. Those are my targets. The rest of them have been in the game a long time, at least as long as I have. They won't give me the information I need like the younger ones will. I draw my arm in a line in front of me, placing a bullet between the eyes of everyone except those two. I hate to make their deaths so quick, but it can't be helped.

The two twenty-something-year-olds hands fidget in their pockets, their fingers frantically searching for fresh clips while they try to keep their eyes on me. Springing forward, I eat up the distance between us in seconds. The shorter of the two twists his baseball cap around on his head and races for the back door. Wood cracks against the floor as he topples crates and climbs over boxes. Splinters of wood crackle under my boots as I step toward him, but he doesn't look back. I slam the butt of my gun into the back of his head and his body hits the floor with a muted thunk.

I pivot on my heels, turning back to face the second one. His shaky hands have moved from the pockets of his cargo pants to the one in his sweatshirt. Does he even have another clip? Our eyes meet and a tear dribbles down his pinkened face. I move toward him, watching his clumsy feet fumble backwards until his back meets a brick wall. His eyes widen, more tears streaking his cheeks, as I approach him. My fist collides with his nose and his head cracks against the wall before his body crashes to the floor.

Groans fill the room as Baseball Cap and Sweatshirt come to.

"What the fuck, man?" Baseball Cap yells. He wriggles in his chair, yanking his arms against the rope I've used to bind him. "Do you even know who you're messing with?"

A sigh rolls out of my mouth and I tap my gun against his shoulder. "Have you ever been to Bianca's compound?"

"Fuck you," he seethes before snapping his quivering lips shut.

I press my gun into the soft part of his shoulder and squeeze the trigger. His howl echoes through the room, followed by a trickling of liquid. The scent of urine wafts up from his body and I step around the puddle that's formed beneath his chair.

"Have you been to Bianca's compound?"

"N-no! No!" he sobs. "I-I've never been there."

I tap my gun against his forehead. "Last chance. Have you ever been to Bianca's compound?"

"I swear," he screams, "I haven't! I haven't!" Tears stream down his face, dripping onto his bloodied shirt.

"You're of no use to me then." I pull the trigger, sending chunks of his skull and brain matter splattering against the wall and the face of the guy next to him.

Sweatshirt sobs as I approach him, his face streaked with blood and tears.

"Please, please, please," he whispers.

"Have you ever been to Bianca's compound?" I ask, tapping my gun against his kneecap.

A glob of spit trickles from his mouth as he sucks in a breath. "I-I don't know. I don't know."

He screams as the bullet shatters his knee, spraying the chair and floor with blood and bone.

I shove my gun into his stomach. "Have you ever been to Bianca's compound?"

"I th-think I d-dropped someone off there one time. I don't..." He retches, turning his head to vomit on the concrete. "I don't kn-know the address."

"Explain to me where it is," I demand, digging the hard metal into his gut.

His breath whistles a choppy tune through his gritted teeth and sucks the snot back from his nose. "I-it's outside the city. N-north. It's north. B-big white house. Lot of land. I-think it's on...umm..."

My hand creeps lower, the gun moving from his gut to his one good knee.

"Fitz!" he yells. "Fitzgerald Road!"

"Good," I breathe. "That's very good."

I lift my arm and fire, putting a bullet between his eyes.

Chapter Forty-Eight

Strong arms wrap around my waist and I curl into them. Pressing my face into the crook of Gray's neck, I inhale deeply, pulling the smell of him into me. He smells like safety, like home. Pressing my palms against his chest, I let the warmth of him seep into me and my body calms. My bones seem to settle, their achiness drifting away in his presence. My limbs stop shivering as if they know they don't need to anymore.

His breath dances over my neck, caressing me like the gentlest kiss. His lips touch my skin and I gasp. My skin heats as he kisses a lazy trail down my body. His fingertips whisper along my body, tracing my hips and tickling my thighs. My core tightens as his teeth scrape over my stomach. I push my hips forward, desperate for the feel of his mouth against my aching sex, but strong hands push me back.

"Please," I whisper.

He looks up at me, his icy blue eyes full of hunger. A strand of black hair falls across his face and I try to reach my fingers out to brush it away. Only, I can't move them. I wiggle my fingers, the motion making something tug against my wrist. Why can't I move my hands?

Gray nips at the soft skin of my calf, yanking my attention back to him. I moan as his tongue darts out, licking a line from my leg to my ankle. His teeth sink into my ankle and a yelp jumps from my throat.

"That hurts," I cry.

He doesn't move. He doesn't turn his head or look at me.

"Gray?" A twinge of panic colors my voice, making it high and rasped.

I cry out as a sharp pain zips up my leg.

"Please, stop!" I whimper, feeling his sharp canines dig into my skin.

They're so sharp, too sharp. Why are they so sharp?

My voice is hoarse, my scream crackling with fear. "Gray, please, look at me!"

He tips his face up and my breath gets lodged in my throat. Blood coats his mouth, thick and dark. It pours from his lips and splatters against my legs.

I yelp, my eyelids shooting open. The chair beneath me jostles and I force my body to still so it doesn't topple over and dump me onto the hard floor.

"Just a dream," I breathe. "It was just a bad dream."

A stinging pain shoots up my leg, making me screech. Searching for the source of the ache, I look down at myself. Blood trickles from tiny wounds on my legs. I trace their dripping pattern down to my ankles. There's something nestled against my right foot, something small and light. Squinting my eyes, a dimly lit shape comes into view. The thing moves, fur shifting and tiny eyes blinking.

A disgusted sound jumps from my mouth when I realize what's crawling on my skin is a rat. Its tiny teeth are jammed into my flesh, gnawing at my skin. I shoot my leg out in front of me, dislodging the disgusting creature. It sails through the air with a terrible shriek and thunks against the wall.

Claws skitter against the floor and I yank my feet up in case it decides to come back.

"Shit!" I cry.

Tears stream down my face, dribbling onto the collar of my shirt. My legs tremble and I suspect that if I wasn't sitting, I'd have already sunk to my knees. I sob into the emptiness of the room, my head swimming with painful and beautiful memories of the man I've only just begun to love.

Looking around the cold, concrete room, my sobs deepen. My entire body shakes with the force of them. I pinch my lips together, like keeping the sounds of my sadness inside might keep me from breaking. I might die in this room. If I don't, if I'm given to Bianca's son, I'm certain that I'll wish I had.

"It can't end like this," I whisper. "I can't end like this."

I cry until there's nothing left in me, and when my eyes finally close, I hope I see Gray again. Even if I can only see him in a nightmare, I want it. I'll love him in that dark, hopeless place if it means I get to love him for just a little longer. I'd do anything for just one more night. Just one more kiss.

I'd do anything to go home.

Chapter Forty-Nine

I shove open the door to the backroom of Club Gara and stumble inside. My legs are unsteady beneath me, my feet dragging like they're made of lead. I jut my hand out, using the wall for balance. Looking around the room, I see no signs of the previous damage made by Volkov's men. Every edge and corner is pristine and new, decorated in sleek reds and dark woods.

Malik tips his head up, looking at me from his seat on a new velvet sofa. His mint green suit looks out of place against the cherry red fabric. He closes the book in his hands and drops it onto the cushions. Smoothing out the wrinkles in his suit, he stands. His leather loafers tap against the patterned tile floor as he walks toward me.

"You've redecorated again," I note.

Malik's eyes roam over me, rising from my feet to my face. "You're injured," he says in a voice laced with concern, "and you're covered in blood."

"I need your help." The words spew from my mouth, feeling foreign as they dribble off my tongue.

When was the last time I asked someone for help? Memories of suburban neighborhoods flood my mind and my lungs tighten. The child that still lives somewhere deep inside of me stirs, his pleas for aid whispering through my mind. Every one of them went unanswered. I shake my head, forcing him to step back inside of me where no one can find him.

Malik's dark brows shoot up into his hairline. "You're asking me for help?" His eyes narrow, honing in on the wound on my forehead. "This must be truly serious, *habibi*."

"Please." The word whispers through my gritted teeth.

He wraps a large hand around my forearm, his gold rings digging into my aching muscles. He moves us forward, leading me toward a small table in the corner.

"Sit," he says, his hand pressing against my shoulder to force me into a chair.

He pushes a bottle of water into my hand. I look down at it, my mouth suddenly feeling dry and sticky. I immediately gulp it down, quenching the thirst I hadn't realized I had.

"Layla," Malik calls, "*ak'l law samahti*."

The young woman I've seen here before dashes out of the room, her long skirt billowing behind her. The gold stitching its edges shimmers in the light, casting little specks of amber that glitter across the floor. *I should buy Ava a skirt like that.* The thought bursts through my head unbidden, making my heart sink into my stomach.

"Tell me what happened." Malik's voice drags me from my thoughts.

"Bianca," I spit her name like it's poison, "she's taken my woman and I need to get her back."

Something crosses over Malik's features, memories flashing in his eyes. "How did this happen?"

My hands ball into fists and the plastic bottle in my palm cracks into pieces. "Her men showed up in the middle of the night. They blew the door off my fucking house and knocked me out."

The back door creaks open and Layla walks in. I avoid looking at her skirt, my eyes inspecting the wood grain on the table. She places a tray of sandwiches down in front of us along with two more bottles of water. Malik clears his throat and waves his hand toward the food.

"You need to eat," he says.

Grabbing one off the platter, I stuff the corner into my mouth. The bread and beef slide over my tongue and my stomach lets out a loud gurgle, reminding me that I haven't eaten since Ava was taken from me. There didn't seem to be a point to it. The moment she was gone, food ceased to have value. Everything that I eat without her tastes like ash.

"I'm certain they took her to Bianca's compound," I mumble around a bite of food.

Malik rasps out a sigh. "No one knows where that is."

"I know where it is."

His eyes widen and he quirks an eyebrow. "Are you certain that—"

"Look," I grumble, "I know where it is, and if we go in together, maybe we can find her. Fuck, maybe we'll find your sister, or maybe we'll die." I slam my palms against the table, toppling sandwiches and bottles. "But I'd rather be dead than live without the woman I love. I'll die long before I have to live with the knowledge that I didn't try to save her."

"My sister." Malik exhales heavily, his eyes glistening with unshed tears. "That was many years ago, Grayson. I fear we won't find Rana there. *Inshallah,* I will see her again, but it won't be in that place."

My stomach plummets to my feet and my fists clench at my sides. Malik has no reason to help me, not if he won't find his sister. I straighten my spine, willing my body to harden for what comes next. I'll go to Bianca's compound alone and I'll get Ava out, even if I can't make it out with her.

"I'll help you," Malik declares.

My mouth drops open. "What?"

A deep chuckle rumbles from his chest. "I'll help you. We'll bring your love home." Emotion flashes in his eyes and his body tenses, making the table groan under the weight of his grip. "And we'll kill Bianca for what she's done to us."

Chapter Fifty

My limbs tremble and shivers wrack my body. A dull ache thrums in my jaw from the constant chattering of my teeth. The cold, damp air around me seems to have seeped into my bones. It's spread through my body, icing my veins and making my skin so cold that the rats don't even seem interested in what I have to offer anymore. In the dark, they scurry around the edges of the room, chittering to remind me that they're there.

This morning, two men I hadn't seen before came downstairs. At least I think it was morning. I don't actually know what time it is or how long I've been down here. My only concept of the passing of time comes from how much pain and numbness I feel in my arms and legs, and whether or not I have to pee. I assume it was morning, because I definitely did have to pee. At least these men were kind enough to turn their backs to me while I sat on the bucket and cried.

They gave me water and some kind of protein bar that tasted like cardboard and peanut butter. It wasn't enough to stop the constant cries of my empty stomach, but it lessened the ache in my belly. With eyes filled with pity, they informed me that the birthday party for Bianca's son, who I now know is called Nico, is tonight.

They said they'd be back later to '*clean me up*' and a ripple of disgust crawled through my gut, threatening to resurface my breakfast.

As the door closed behind them, a plan began to stitch itself together in my mind. Maybe not an entire plan, but the ghost of a plan. A plan of a plan? I don't know and it doesn't really matter. The only thing that matters is getting out of here, and I need to do it before they come back.

Run, a voice whispers through my mind. My eyes well with tears because for the first time, the voice doesn't belong to my father. It belongs to Gray. *Run as fast as you can, baby*, he says.

I squeeze my fingers into my palms, letting my nails bite into my skin. "I have to fight." Shoving out a quivering breath, I vow to the skittering rats and shadowy corners of my musty cage, "I will fight. I will get out of here."

I won't let you go, Gray promises in my mind. *I can't let you go. You're mine.*

My heart thumps out a wild beat in my chest, ratcheting up my pulse. "Okay," I whisper, "think about this, Ava. The damsel…" I cringe, the word tasting bad on my tongue, "…she's locked in the basement, tied to a chair in the lair of the enemy. Where have I read this before?"

Memories of words and passages swim through my mind. I search through each of them, plucking out the pieces that don't fit. Closing my eyes, I remember all the worlds I've been to, the places I've seen. I recall every battle, every trial, and every heartbreak. A picture begins to form behind my eyes of a woman bound and trapped, her eyes sparkling with defiance. She looks down at her ripped gown, scheming a way to get out of the ropes that bind her.

"Elodie!" The name explodes from my mouth and I pinch my lips together. Craning my neck, I push my ear toward the ceiling, hoping no one heard my outburst. After what feels like several long minutes, when the room is still silent, I let out a heavy sigh.

"Elodie was trapped in the dungeon of her enemy, where her mate couldn't get to her. What was that book called? *The Thieves? The Thieves of Something?* Well, that part doesn't matter. What matters is how she got out." I speak to myself with quiet words, letting the familiar cadence of my own voice calm me.

"She toppled her chair over and it smashed into splinters on the floor." I look down at the chair I've been bound to, focusing on the edges and grooves in the wood. It doesn't appear to be an antique, but it's not brand new, either. Wiggling my ass in the seat, the chair rocks slightly, like the connections between the legs and the floor are uneven. I shimmy my hips and the wood groans uncomfortably.

"Good, good," I mumble, my head bobbing with excitement.

I suck in a heavy breath, feeling my lungs expand against my ribcage, before forcing it from my mouth. Pressing my bare feet into the floor, I straighten my spine. The chair rocks beneath me as I sway my hips. The legs tip out from under it, and for a moment, I'm weightless, my body falling through the air.

Pain crashes into me, jolting a yelp from my throat. Despite the chill of the concrete floor, heat radiates through my side. Blood leaks from the inside of my cheek and I press my tongue into it, feeling the indentations of my own teeth in my flesh. The coppery liquid tastes like freedom on my tongue. I yank my arms forward, ready to burst from my prison, but my arms don't move. They don't fucking move!

Kicking my legs backwards, they collide with the legs of the chair—the very solid, unbroken chair. Tears leak from my eyes, pooling between my face and the hard floor.

"Didn't work," I wheeze. "Didn't work."

My arm is trapped beneath me, my elbow crushed under a wooden arm. Tingles crawl up the ensnared limb and tiny pins stab into me. Seconds tick by, turning into minutes as I lay pressed against the floor.

"Okay," I choke out. "It's okay. It's okay. Your arm is going numb." I grit my teeth and force my words out between them. "It's good. This is good. You can pull your arm out of the rope and you won't even feel it."

A sob gets caught in my throat as I wiggle my wrist and begin to pull. Fear whirls like smoke inside of me. Its tendrils crawl down my throat, choking me. I cringe as images of my hand, mangled and bloodied, drift through my mind. Even through the numbness, I feel the rope rake over my skin, scratching and ripping.

I know it hurts, baby, Gray's voice purrs through my mind, *but you can take it. You're doing so well.*

I pull and pull, twitching my fingers and thrashing my hand until it pops free. Almost immediately, the numbness begins to recede, leaving behind a burning pain that makes me wince. Drawing in a steadying breath, I look down at my hand. My skin is red and torn. My eyes follow the lines that make up the bleeding cracks along the top of my hand.

Watching my blood drip onto the concrete, I hiss, "It's not that bad, Ava."

I fight with the remaining rope, my fingers slick with blood and sweat. Perspiration leaks from my palms, burning like acid as it spills into my cuts. My other hand pulls free and I gasp out a cry of victory.

A chill seeps into my hands as I press them to the concrete, making my bones quiver. My legs feel like jelly, wobbling and shaking as I stand.

"What now?" I ask the empty air. My throat tightens and uncertainty creeps beneath my skin. Gripping the hem of my shirt, my fingers twitch.

Weak, my father begins to murmur inside of me, *pathetic little—*

Everything, Gray's voice booms over the painful memory. I let the sound fill me, reaching into my arteries and injecting them with strength.

"Okay," I breathe, "I need a weapon." My eyes dart around the room before focusing on the plastic containers stacked in the corner. I push up onto my toes, keeping my steps quiet as I cross the room.

"I need a weapon. The damsel always finds a weapon to defeat the enemy with."

Up close, I can read the words scrawled across the front of the ugly cornflower blue bins.

"Christmas? Fucking Christmas?!" I groan, smacking my palm against my forehead.

I yank the first bin off the top of the pile, wondering what the heck I'm supposed to do with holiday decorations.

"What were you expecting," I scoff, "a bin of swords and daggers?"

I run my fingertips over the plastic, feeling the rough edges and aged grooves. Pressing my fingers under the lid, it pops off easily. An old, dusty smell wafts out, tangling in my nostrils and making me want to sneeze. Tinsel crinkles and crunches as I sift through the bin.

Under the first layer of tree garland, my hand lands on something more solid. It's light with a smooth surface, like glass. Lifting the small bauble from the bin, my eyes widen. The globe sparkles, the yellow ceiling light glinting off its surface. A hand-painted sleigh glides over the ornament, driving through a snowy field. It's pretty, but ultimately useless.

I drop it back into the bin and the tinkle of broken glass floats out behind it. Pushing the box aside, I stuff my hand into the next one. My fingers fumble around, feeling rough fabric and bits of string. As my hand nears the bottom of the decor heap, something hard pokes into my palm. I wrap my fingers around it and yank.

My lips twitch into a smile at the sparkling, metal Christmas tree topper. I squeeze the star in my hand, clenching with all my strength. Rather than bend in my fist, the metal bites into my hand. Its edges are ragged, time and use having sharpened them.

"Perfect." I chuckle.

A metallic zing sounds as I scrape the edge of the star against the floor. Over and over, I scratch it over the concrete, forcing little bits of metal to flake off. The flecks scatter across the floor like silver glitter. I press my finger to the tip of the sharpest point and gasp. A bead of blood wells on my fingertip, marking the metal with a festive holiday red.

Looking up from my makeshift weapon, the heavy metal door looms before me. Its rust tinged edges haven't changed since I arrived, and yet they look different, more ominous than before. A shiver dances down my spine. If this were a book, perhaps the coppery borders would be foreshadowing, the author is warning me of the blood that's yet to come in my story. I grasp the handle and a chill zips through me. I pull and twist, but the door doesn't budge.

I suck in a breath, hoping the air will quell the anxiety gnawing at my insides.

"Okay," I whisper, "I just have to wait until they open the door and then, I'll attack."

My heart sinks into my belly. I don't know how to attack. I've never attacked anyone before in my life. I've always been too quiet, too afraid. For my entire life, I've stood motionless in the face of conflict. Even when my safety was at stake, something deep inside of me demanded that I be still. Even as fists and boots crashed into my body, that little voice would cry out from the depths of my soul, begging me to be immovable.

Today, she isn't calling for my stillness. Today she's louder, more forceful. *Fight*, she demands inside of me, *fight and survive.*

I ball my fists at my side, blood trickling over the antique tree topper and dripping beside my feet.

"Okay, Ava, just think about the books. The small, unassuming woman needs to defeat the bad guys. She has no real weapons, just something she grabbed along the way. You've read it somewhere, I know you have."

I wade through a sea of words, feeling the prose of each manuscript that's been in my hands flood through my mind. I pull on the threads of each story, searching for answers. Inside of me, the sounds of battle ring out. Swords clash and cannons boom, but those aren't the stories I need. I push them away, sifting through the tales that live within me.

Somewhere in the expanse of my memory, I see a tiny piece of broken metal sparkle in a woman's hand. Around her, machines beep and hum in a familiar rhythm. From her fingers, I can feel smooth metal and raised buttons. Her fear quivers through me, tightening my lungs and making it hard to draw breath. The air around her feels thin, like it isn't enough to live on. Her vision is hazy like she's looking through fogged glass. No, not just glass, her helmet! It's her freaking space helmet!

"Olivia," I whisper as her world comes into full view. "I remember! She was a doctor, kidnapped by alien rogues. She had to fight them to get control of their ship and steer it back to her lover."

Crouching down next to the door, I let myself fall into her story. "She had a chunk of metal that she broke off from the ship's command deck. She used it to stab the alien guards, one in the jugular and the other in the femoral artery. She stabbed one guy in the neck right where you would take your pulse and the other in the crease between his abdomen and leg." My nose scrunches. "Gross, but okay."

Seconds drag into minutes as I crouch beside the door. My fingers ache and the Christmas tree topper digs into my palm, but I don't loosen my grip. Sweat drips down my spine, making my skin feel sticky and my shirt cling to my back. My heart pounds a rapid beat in my ears. It thumps like a war drum, calling me to action.

It feels as if hours pass before I hear movement outside the door. I flex my muscles, balancing on my toes and loosening my knees. Tilting my ear, the sound of muffled voices hums through the door. Hearing only two distinct tones between them, I huff out a relieved breath. Two men. I can take on two men, can't I? Lengthening my spine, I imagine myself as a wolf. I envision sleek, gray fur that will protect my soft flesh, lean legs that will propel me forward, and sharp teeth that will cut through skin and bone. The door beside me begins to slide open, letting out a shriek.

"*Merda!*" a masculine voice yells. "Where did the bitch go?!"

Pressing my toes into the concrete, I spring forward and slam my shoulder into the partially opened door. It flies backward before crashing into something, presumably one of the men, given the grunt that sounds behind it. Something heavy thumps against the floor before another man bounds into the room. Yanking my arms behind my back, I hold the metal ornament against my lower back in a bruising grip. Slowly, the man steps toward me, his enormous form casting a shadow across the floor.

Be meek, I tell myself. *Be unassuming. Be quiet. Let him get closer.*

He closes the distance between us and I crane my neck to look at his face. It's not a face I've seen before, though it's no less chilling than the others. A thick, white scar streaks across his face, stretching from his eyebrow to his mouth. His lips peel up into a frightening smile as his hand reaches out toward me.

"Don't fucking touch me!" I screech.

I shove my feet against the floor and jump upward, my body crashing into his chest. He struggles, trying to fling me off of him as my arms band around his neck. The metal star scratches against the skin of my palm. I feel the sharp sting of its edges cutting into me, but I don't let go. I pull my arm back and slam it forward, lodging the star into his thick neck.

A choked scream gurgles from his open mouth before I yank the metal from his skin. Hot liquid sprays over my face and I jump to the floor. I swallow down a gag as blood pumps from his body, squirting across the room with each beat of his heart. He crumples to his knees, a pool of red forming around him. The tang of copper fills the room, so thick that I can taste it on my tongue. With a muted thunk, he falls to the floor, forcing a spray of blood to erupt from beneath him and splash onto my toes.

My bare feet slide against the blood-soaked concrete as I step over his body. Through the doorway, I see another man. He lays on the ground just beyond it, his hand pressed against a leaking wound on his forehead. I surge forward, tossing my body into the air. The breath wheezes out of him as I collide with his stomach. His eyes flit to the bloodied Christmas ornament in my hand, emotion flashing across his face. His lips quiver and my own twitch, the edges tilting upward.

"None of you will ever touch me again," I assert.

I slam my hand down, jamming the metal star into his groin. A ragged scream jumps from his open mouth, the sound of his pain reverberating against the concrete walls. Flinging my hand back, I jerk my festive weapon from his body. I pinch my mouth shut as blood spurts from his wound, coating my face and arms. It sprays against the walls, making the room look like a scene from a horror movie. Wiping my face with the bottom of my shirt, I move to step around him.

"I'm getting the fuck out of here," I tell his shuddering body.

Lifting my eyes, I look at the staircase ahead of me and tighten my grip on the tree topper. I try to ignore the fear that claws at my insides, cramping my stomach and making my lungs feel too tight. Sucking in a shaky breath, I imagine myself as a brave woman. A woman like Elodie, like Olivia, like all of the women whose stories have filled me with hope. The Christmas decoration in my palm becomes a sword, sharp and unyielding. The ragged t-shirt clinging to my body becomes the armor I wear into battle.

"You cannot stop," I remind myself. "You have to keep moving. You have to get out."

I place my foot on the bottom stair and immediately jerk it back as a thunderous sound booms through the stairwell. The ceiling quivers, sending chunks of dirt and plaster into the air. They rain down on me, embedding into my hair and sticking to my blood-soaked skin.

Pop, pop, pop.

I dive behind the door as the sound of gunfire peppers the air. Above my head, men scream. Their shouts leach through the walls, slamming into me and making my heart stutter.

"Maybe I'll just wait here for a bit."

Chapter Fifty-One

I press my hand against a tree, feeling the rough bark scrape across my palm. The jagged pattern in the wood pulls a memory to the forefront of my mind. I recall the bark of an old oak tree, the way it pressed into my skin the first night I watched my little bird. In my mind, she sits with a book in her hand, her nose scrunched up as she reads. Her eyes find me in the darkness, those green gems staring into my soul before she even knew I was there.

"Tell me," Malik's voice comes from beside me, dissipating the memory, "what's the plan?"

Clenching my jaw, I look toward Bianca's compound. The evening sun casts a red glow over the large estate. It rolls over the white mansion, painting the wood red. The entire building screams of wealth. I scoff at the gaudy stone pillars that stand at the corners of the oversized entryway. Of course Bianca would build a house that looks like a Roman temple.

Too bad for her that the only worship that will take place here tonight is a practice older than Rome. The red sky speaks to me like it's beckoning me, demanding sacrifice. It dares me to spill blood here, to make the ground match the crimson sunset.

I follow the path of dim light as it climbs up the stone stairs and over the front door. Two men stand before it, their posture rigid. They each hold a semi-automatic rifle in their gloved hands. Their eyes scan the tree line, their gazes flicking over us without seeing.

"I'll take the front door," I say. "You take the back. We take out the guards quietly before we go inside."

"That's all?" Malik chuckles.

"Just get in the building. Take out everyone you see and find Ava."

He nods, a smirk tilting the side of his mouth. Leaves rustle softly beneath his feet as he moves further into the trees. Pulling my hood over my head, I stuff my hands into the pockets of my jacket. I wrap my fingers around my gun and take slow, casual steps toward the house. At the sound of my footsteps, the guards perk up. They raise their weapons in my direction, tilting their heads toward me.

A smile splits my face and I let out a loud chuckle as I make my way up the steps. "You guys get a look at the babe Bianca brought in? Tony said—" I really fucking hope there's a guy named Tony here "—she's got a fine ass on her."

One of the men snorts out a laugh and brushes his fingers through his short-cropped hair. "*Fra,* I saw them bring her in. I was hoping for a turn with her," he says, jutting his hips forward and humping the air, "but she's apparently off limits. Nico's fucking birthday present, they said. Lucky prick!"

My mouth snaps shut, my molars grinding together as red tinges my vision. I smack my hand down on one of the guard's shoulders and bark out a laugh. My fingers dig into his clavicle and his chuckle turns into a grunt. Whipping the handgun from my pocket, I slam it against his temple and squeeze the trigger. His blood splatters across the pristine walls of the white house. The other guard gasps and raises his gun toward me, his blue eyes wide with fear. I pivot on my heels and shoot him between them.

I smash my shoulder into the ostentatious, white door, rattling its gold handle as I shove myself inside. My bloodied boots slip on the white marble floor, sending me careening into a large wooden table. It rattles as my hips collide with its edge, sending an ugly vase crashing to the floor. The sound of shattering ceramic echoes through the foyer, bouncing off the high ceilings. Across the room, five men jump to attention, their hands fumbling for their waistbands to draw their guns.

"One chance!" I shout. "Where *the fuck* is my woman?"

Eyes narrow and mouths drop open before someone yells out, "It's him! It's Grayson. Fucking shoot him!"

I drop to the floor, kicking my leg toward the leg of the table. As it topples to the floor, I hope it's as expensive as it looks because cheap tables make terrible shields. Sticking my hand into my pocket, I pull out a pipe bomb and spark my lighter, holding it against the fuse until it begins to sizzle. Wrenching my hand back, I throw it over the table toward the center of the room. It clangs against the marble floor and I brace for impact, wrapping my arms around my head.

Within seconds, an explosion rocks the foyer. Metal debris explodes outward, impaling the beige, paisley wallpaper and fragmenting ceramic busts and baubles. I look up as the ceiling groans. A chandelier shudders before crashing to the floor, scattering crystal chunks across the room. I press my palms to my ears, shifting them around to alleviate the ringing that's blaring in my eardrums. As it begins to fade, screaming, groaning, and gunfire take its place.

I whip my head around as a booming laugh sounds beside me. Malik runs toward me, his long legs bounding across the room. As he nears, he lets them slip from under him. With surprising fluidity for a man of his size, his body sinks to the floor. He glides toward me with a grin plastered to his face. His clothes squeak against the marble as he slides in my direction like a muscular luge sled shooting across the ice.

His shoulder collides with my hip and he chuckles. Tucking his hand beneath his chin, he looks up at me with a smirk. "This is exciting!" he chirps, inserting a fresh clip into his gun.

"Go find her!" I shout over the chaos. "I'll hold them off here."

His smile fades, replaced by a solemn look that forces his mouth into a line. "Cover me."

Popping my head up from behind the table, I spray bullets into the group of men on the other side. More men have filed into the room, replacing their fallen associates. Splinters of wood fly from the table as their bullets smash into it. When I duck back down, Malik is gone.

Pushing my arms out beyond the safety of my wooden barrier, I fire into the crowd. Amidst the popping of gunfire, I hear the thunk of bodies as they hit the floor. At each thwap of a corpse crashing to the ground, the creature inside of me perks up. I can feel its feral grin stretching across my face as they die. It claws inside of me, its talons ripping into my heart. *Ava is mine*, it screeches. *Bring her home. Bring her back to me and kill everyone who's touched her.*

Chapter Fifty-Two

With my body crushed against the metal door, I listen to the chaos above me. Gunfire pops like fireworks, the sound exploding through the ceiling. Shouts and yells drift through the wood and insulation, filling the basement with the haunting echoes of anger and pain. My hand aches from my grip on the Christmas star. Its jagged edges dig into my palm, but I don't loosen my grip.

Thunk, thunk, thunk.

I tilt my ear toward the doorway as the sound of heavy footsteps drifts from the stairwell. My heartbeat quickens, my pulse pounding in my ears. My steady breaths turn into choppy pants. I squeeze the weapon in my hand, holding it in front of my body like a shield. As the sound moves closer, I lift myself onto my toes, preparing my legs to lunge forward.

From the doorway, a shadow lengthens across the floor, its imposing frame drifting toward the ceiling. I pinch my lips together, holding my breath inside as it moves forward. Broad shoulders breach the doorway and a man steps into the room. His head swivels around as if he's searching for something. Something that I hope isn't me.

As he steps under a dim overhead light, I can tell that he's not one of the men who's been here before. I'm certain I would have remembered him if he had. He's tall and broad, his muscular chest pressing against the confines of his shirt as he moves. His hair is dark, neatly trimmed and close to the scalp, highlighting the small gold hoops in his earlobes. He turns his head, giving me a glimpse of his strong jaw and shapely nose. He's a handsome man, but his face does nothing to alleviate the anxious churning in my belly.

When his gaze swivels in my direction, I don't hesitate. Shoving my toes into the floor, I leap at him, jutting the ragged metal star toward his stomach. He stumbles backward, his eyes popping open in surprise. His feet jump back several steps and he lifts his hands in a sign of surrender.

"*Shway, shway,*" he says. His heavily accented voice is soft, its tone not unlike one someone might use to calm a scared kitten. His gaze jumps to the bloody metal in my hand. "Be calm, tiny killer. I'm here with your love to…" His voice drifts off as he looks down at the two bodies lying on the floor, "…to rescue you."

I narrow my eyes. "My *love*? Are you talking about Gray?" My heart pounds erratically inside my chest, its beat forceful but unsteady. "Are you here with him?"

His lips lift, a warm smile taking over his face. "Yes, *habibti*! Grayson has come for you."

All of the air leaves my lungs in a whoosh and I bite my lip to suppress the smile that wants to crawl across my face.

The man looks down at me, his eyes moving from my toes to my face. Then they flit between me and the bodies laying beside us. "I didn't realize you and Grayson were," he pauses, pursing his lips like he's deciding on the right words, "in the same profession."

My eyebrows shoot into my hair. "Wait, you think…"

I look down at myself and gasp. My clothes are dirty and discolored, the fabric both wet and crunchy from the various stages of the blood that's soaked into it. I lift my hands, noting the crusted blood beneath my fingernails and the ragged cuts that span from my wrists to my fingertips. Wiggling my toes against the floor, I feel the slickness of viscous fluid between them.

A dry laugh creeps up my throat. "I'm a fucking book editor."

His face breaks into a wide grin and he howls a laugh that fills the room. It's an infectious sound, warm and deep, like the clang of a brass bell. I can't help the giggle that bubbles up from my chest in response. He reaches out his hand toward me, opening his palm as if asking me to take it. I wipe my dirty palm down the front of my shirt and stare at his large hand.

"Come with me, *ya helwa*," he says. "I'll protect you until Grayson can."

My hesitation melts away when I look into his eyes. His wide smile causes wrinkles to form around them. There's a warmth in his irises that reminds me of autumn leaves and hot chocolate. In their depths, there's something kind and hopeful. I place my hand in his, letting the tightness of his grip and the warmth of his skin ground me.

Pulling me behind him, he moves toward the stairs. I slide to the left, my head popping out from behind the bulk of his body. The staircase emerges before us, the wooden steps cracked with age and caked with dust and plaster. My stomach clenches. Somehow, this incredibly ordinary thing, a simple staircase, looks as daunting as a mountain. At its top, light peeks out from under the door. For a moment it flickers. Is it just my imagination or does it look like the flicker of tiny flames ready to swallow me up?

"Stay behind me," the man says, his hand pressing me back gently.

"Wait," I whisper into his back, "what's your name?"

"Malik," he chuckles, "my name is Malik."

I step carefully, keeping my body safely tucked behind Malik as the rough steps scrape the soles of my bare feet.

"Okay." I suck in a lungful of air before pushing it out from between my teeth. "Here we go."

Chapter Fifty-Three

My makeshift barrier rocks in front of me, teetering on its bullet-torn edges. The smell of gunpowder and copper drift through the air, so potent it clogs my throat and sticks to the roof of my mouth. I duck down as a metal projectile rips through the right side of the table. The wood splinters and cracks, shooting a chunk of mahogany into my face.

"Shit," I spit through gritted teeth.

Wiping the blood from my cheek, I peer through the ragged hole in my failing barricade. Corpses litter the floor, their limbs cocked at odd angles and their blood still dribbling onto the marble. The formerly elegant fabrics of overpriced curtains are torn and stained. Cracks splinter the high windows of Bianca's palace. My eyes follow a path of viscous pink goo that drips down the glass.

Pulling my head back, I stuff the barrel of my gun into the hole and fire until my clip empties. I reload, readying myself to take out more of the fuckers. Just as I put my gun back up, movement at my left catches my attention. I swivel my upper body, training my gun toward the motion.

My heart sinks at the sight of Malik, standing alone with his shoulder pressed to the ugly floral wallpaper. Lowering my weapon,

I watch his mouth jump up into a toothy grin. A growl rumbles in my chest.

"What the fuck are you smiling about?!" I scream. "Where is she?!"

A squeaked gasp sounds behind him and a mass of earthy, brown hair peeks out from behind his back. I jump up, suddenly uncaring that bullets aimed in my direction are zipping through the air. Without permission from my brain, my body careens forward, narrowly dodging the chunks of metal. The chaos around us seems to dissipate as my vision narrows, honing in on brown hair and green eyes.

I nod at Malik and something passes between us, an understanding without words. Our eyes blur with tears that we won't shed today—mine of gratitude and his of something else. His smile is wide, but tinged with sadness. He steps away, anchoring himself behind a stone pillar before opening fire on Bianca's men.

Ava looks up at me and my chest tightens. Her eyes are wide and glossy. Blood covers her face and neck. A tear trickles from her eye, streaking through the crusted red fluid. I pull her into me, wrapping my arms around her shivering form. I inhale the sweet smell of her beneath the blood, sweat, and gunpowder that coats her skin. The creature thrashing in my chest calms at her nearness.

"You're always so beautiful when you cry for me," I whisper into her hair.

She presses her face into my chest and sobs a laugh. A shiver runs through her body, the movement rippling through my ribcage as her shoulders quake. I run my fingers through her matted hair, feeling dried blood flake into my palm. Her scalp is dirty but smooth. Bits of dust, plaster, and clotted blood are embedded in her hair. I breathe a sigh of relief when I don't find any injuries. Dropping to my knees, I take her face in my hands. I run my fingertips over her skin, searching for the source of the blood. Her lip is split, the cut having already bruised and scabbed over, but I don't find any other wounds.

I look down to where her bare feet shiver against the floor. More blood coats her toes, streaks of it reaching up her legs. Wrapping my fingers around her ankle, I feel her pulse quicken beneath her skin. I trace them up her leg gently and she gasps. Tightening my jaw, I try to ignore the way that little sound races through me, traveling from my ears to my dick. How many days has it been since I heard it last? How many days since I thought I'd never again hear the sound of her surprise or the anxious thump of her heartbeat?

I search for injuries by running my palms up her bare legs. Her skin is cold and caked with blood and dirt. Scrapes and small puncture wounds mar her beautiful legs. My stomach knots and fingers twitch against her. My pulse quickens as images flood my mind of all the ways they could have hurt her.

"Where are you hurt?" I rasp, pushing the words through my teeth.

Ava's eyes widen before her gaze returns to her feet. "I'm fine. It-it's not my blood."

A tremor zips through her hand, drawing my attention to the thing she's squeezing in her palm. Light reflects off the metal between her fingers, highlighting its ragged, blood-tipped edges.

I stand, biting down on the smirk that tries to slide across my mouth. "What is that?"

She shifts her feet anxiously, her weight teetering from one to the other. Her teeth sink into her bottom lip as the corners of her mouth perk up. "It's a…uh…" her eyes meet mine and her eyebrows furrow, "Christmas tree topper."

I smile, a chuckle building in my chest. "Did you get your pretty hands dirty, my clever little bird?"

She nods, a blush forming on her cheeks so deep that it shows even through the caked blood. "I killed two guys with it," she whispers.

"Fuck," I groan, pinching her chin between my fingers and angling her mouth toward mine, "that's hot."

She rears back, trying to pull her face away from me. "I, uh," she stutters, "I haven't brushed my teeth in like…days."

I grab her hip with my other hand and harden my grip on her face. "I don't give a fuck about that. Don't deny me this. You have no idea what it's been like for me without you." A breath gets caught in her throat, tears forming in her eyes as she looks at me. "You can't understand what it's like to spend years with a shriveled up organ in your chest, a useless heart that doesn't beat."

Pulling her closer, I crush our bodies together. Her breasts press against me and I stifle a groan, reveling at how perfectly she fits against me. "Only to find the one person in this world that makes it function." I swallow thickly, emotion clogging my throat. "Then to have that person taken away…"

"Fuck!" I pinch my eyes closed, feeling the sting of tears behind my eyelids. "If something had happened to you, Ava. If I had lost you, I…"

My lungs tighten, my pulse slamming in my chest. "I was prepared to die here today if it meant I could follow you in death. So now, I need you to kiss me."

Her mouth crashes into mine, her lips parting on a whimper. I feel the tears on her cheeks spread across mine as she kisses me. Her arms wrap around my neck and the tiny weapon in her hand scrapes against my nape. A desperate sound vibrates in my chest as I think about how ferocious my frightened little bird has become, how beautiful she looks with blood on her face. She moans into my mouth as my tongue slips against hers. My dick hardens against my zipper at the taste of her. The tang of copper dances over my taste-buds, along with a flavor that's uniquely hers.

A throat clears behind me. "A little help, *habibi*?"

My body protests as I pull away from her, my lungs seizing as if the air is thinner when it isn't coming from her mouth. My legs move, but my eyes linger on her swollen, pink lips. She runs her tongue over her bottom lip and I clench my fists, summoning all of my willpower to keep me from tackling her to the ground and fucking her right here amidst the gunfire and death.

"Stay here," I demand.

Her lips squeeze into a pout. "I can help."

Wrapping my fingers around her elbow, I push her behind the gaudy stone column. It may look hideous, but it should withstand a few bullets. "I know you can, baby," I sigh, "but you will stay right the fuck here." My words come out growled, my heart thrashing at the thought of putting her in any more danger. "And you," I turn my eyes toward Malik, "stay with her."

He nods, placing his body in front of her like a shield. His stance widens as he unstraps a tactical rifle from his back. With the confidence that he'll protect her in my stead, I turn my back on them and move toward the thunderous sound of gunfire.

An uncomfortable feeling wriggles in my gut, a slithering feeling of unfamiliarity. I owe Malik a debt for what he's doing today. I'm not unaccustomed to owing debts. It's often a necessity of my job, but I know Malik. The only way he'll let me repay this is through friendship. And in that, I'm entirely out of my depth. An image flits through my mind—Ava and Malik sitting in our living room, laughing. Would she enjoy that? Would she gush about her favorite books with him? Would she fascinate him with tales of love and war? Jealousy churns deep inside of me, souring my stomach. No, those stories are for me. No matter what he's done today, those moments when her eyes light up are mine, and mine alone.

I step toward the spray of oncoming bullets and press my body behind another piece of overstated furniture. The mahogany bar cabinet twitches as metal slams into it. Glass crunches under my boots and the oaky scent of whisky wafts up from the floor. I click my tongue against the roof of my mouth. What a waste of good liquor.

I force out a heavy breath, steadying my pulse. The rapid drumbeat in my chest lessens, dulling to a steady thump. *Av-a, Av-a, Av-a,* it beats her name against my ribcage. I almost lost her, my heartbeat. I almost fucking lost her. My nails dig into my palm as I clench my fists at my side.

Digging my hand into the pocket of my cargo pants, I pull a bomb out. The smooth metal is warm beneath my fingertips. Muzzle flash sparks through the room, lighting the room and sparkling against the steel pipe. I run the fuse between my fingers, a smile spreading across my face. No one will survive this. No one but the three of us will walk away from here.

Sparking the fuse, I toss the bomb over the bar. It sails through the air and lands in the center of the crowd of Bianca's men. With a resounding boom, it detonates. The vibration of the blast reverberates through the room, making it wobble. I cover my head as wood and plaster rain down from the ceiling. Shrapnel and nails rocket through the room, shattering windows and impaling flesh. A shrill song of shrieks and moans drifts through the room.

Gunpowder and smoke fill my nose, wrenching a cough from my throat. Pressing my hand over my mouth and nose, I wait for the smoke to clear. When it does, I peer through the open cracks on the bar in front of me into the room beyond. Mangled bodies cover the floor, their limbs sprawled out around them or missing entirely. The ringing in my ears subsides and silence slithers through the room.

I stand, huffing my relief out from my lungs. I turn around, a smile pulling at my lips as I look toward my little bird. She steps out from behind the wall of Malik's chest. A shy grin lifts her face, spreading little cracks through the dried blood caked on her cheeks.

Her eyes widen and she throws her arm out in front of her, pointing in my direction. "Look out!"

Pain explodes in my head. I stumble back, my thighs crashing into the wobbling bar. My boots squeak against the slick marble floor as I whirl around. My eyes narrow, honing in on a figure at the other end of the room. I recognize him immediately. His dark, slicked-back head and prominent cheekbones give him away—he looks exactly like his mother.

Nico steps forward, belting out an angry screech and points his gun between my eyes. Dropping to the floor, I nestle my body behind the bar. It explodes in a shower of splinters, but I manage to avoid the barrage of bullets he sends my way. Popping my arm out from behind the rubble, I shoot in his direction. I hear the ping of metal and the crash of glass before the click of my empty gun.

Click, click, click.

"Come out and fight me, motherfucker!" Nico growls as his gun clatters to the floor.

I stand, pulling a knife from the sheath at my ankle. He yanks a blade off of a nearby corpse and wipes the crusted blood across the leg of his suit pants. He stomps toward me, his eyes flashing with anger and determination. Stopping just shy of a foot from me, he moves left. I move with him. Like a twisted dance, we circle each other with our knives drawn, waiting to see which of us will make the first move.

As impatient and cocky as his mother, it's only a moment before Nico lunges forward. He jumps toward me, his arm outstretched and slashing. His blade slices across my bicep. A stinging pain zips up my arm as it rips through my jacket and into the skin below.

"Not so tough now, huh, Grayson?" he chortles.

I swing my leg out. It connects with his knee and sends him crashing to the floor. Rushing behind him, I bend over his body and ready my knife to slice across his thick neck. He thrusts his head upward, forcing his skull into my chin. My teeth crack together and I stagger back.

Nico jumps to his feet. His knife rips through the air toward my face, sending a puff of air whistling through my hair. I rear my head back, narrowly missing the slice of his blade. As his arm falls, I whip my knife out, connecting it with his side. He grunts and totters to the side before regaining his footing.

Our eyes flick to the ceiling as it howls out a loud groan. A slimy grin peels across Nico's mouth and he shoves my chest with his elbow. My balance teeters, my feet sliding backward toward the sound. The plaster above us ripples. A line tears through it just before a massive wooden beam plummets toward me.

The sound of a frightened scream blasts through the room. "Gray!" Ava cries as I dive sideways, avoiding the bulk of the falling wood. White hot pain lances my hand and my grip on the knife loosens. My body thunks to the floor where chunks of the rubble dig into my back and legs. The blade clatters to the floor beside me. I reach my hand out toward it, my fingers desperately searching for the handle. Nico's boot collides with it first, sending it sliding across the marble.

The air rushes from my lungs as his body lands on mine. His elbow crashes into my sternum and his knees pin mine together. A humorless laugh barks out of him and he presses his knife to my throat.

Fuck.

Chapter Fifty-Four

I gasp for air and choke on my breath. Malik's arm wraps around my waist, pulling me closer to the shield of his body.

"*Shway, shway,*" he whispers against my hair. "You must be strong now."

I grit my teeth. Strong? How can I be strong when the man I love, the only man I've ever loved, is about to die? Tears prick my eyes and roll down my cheeks.

"Please," I sob, "you have to help him."

He shakes his head and his chin rustles my matted hair. "I can't." There's a quiver of sorrow in his quiet voice. "Grayson asked me to protect you above all else. His life means nothing without you, *ya helwa.*"

Tears fall from my eyes, blurring Gray's form. Nico's knife is at his throat, red beads forming beneath the metal.

Nico's voice booms through the room, rough and angry. "Did you think that you could come into my home and take what belongs to me?" His fist collides with Gray's stomach, jolting a ragged cough from his mouth. "That mousy bitch is mine now and I will fucking have her!" He lifts his upper lip, baring his teeth in a sneer. "Maybe I'll fuck her in front of you while you die on my floor."

No, no, no! My own voice screams inside my head. *This isn't right. This isn't how it ends!*

I clench my fists at my sides. The Christmas tree topper digs into my palm, but I don't loosen my hold. Instead, I let the bite of the metal ground me. It reminds me that I'm real. That this is real. And that I'm strong. I'm so fucking strong.

My body begins to move before I tell it to. My arms wriggle and my feet lurch forward. Malik's arm tightens around my waist, halting my movement.

"No, *habibti*," he murmurs.

I whirl around in his arms, forcing him to face me. The growl of a feral animal spews from my mouth. My arm juts out, jabbing the ornament toward his neck.

"Let me go," I snarl, "or I'll kill you just like I killed those men in the basement."

Malik looks down at me, a knowing look shining in his eyes. He releases me with a chuckle and flashes me a toothy grin. "Yes, tiny killer, I believe you would."

Pivoting on my heels, I face the mayhem in the room. The previously luxurious looking furniture is toppled, broken, and caked with blood and soot. The tall windows are smeared with red, allowing only small slivers of moonlight to peek through. An enormous wooden beam lays against the floor, the mass of it blocking me from getting to Gray directly.

My bare feet pad against the dirty floor. Pain spikes in my heel, but I refuse to look down. Skirting around the beam, I move toward the nearest wall. Nico's angry voice rumbles through the room, but the words are meaningless when they reach my ears. They don't matter. He doesn't matter.

I squeeze the small weapon in my palm and slide my back along the wall, steadily inching closer to them. I keep my eyes forward, my gaze entirely focused on the man on the floor. A pained groan bubbles out of Gray's mouth and my lungs seize. It's now or never.

If I don't move now, he'll die. And I can't let him die. My mind reels, visions of my life before him flooding through me. It was quiet and comfortable. I lived through the books I read. Within them, I found love, I fought battles, I saved lives and rode dragons. But it wasn't real. None of it was real. Yes, I lived within those pages, but I never really lived. Not until Gray found me. My life was safe and I fucking hated it.

I lunge forward. Blood splashes against my ankles as my feet slap against the floor. Debris lodges between my toes, cutting into my skin, but I don't stop. Hot liquid drips from my palm as the ragged metal digs into me, but I do not stop.

You are stronger than this, someone whispers in my mind. The voice doesn't belong to my father and it doesn't belong to Gray. It's mine. *No one can hurt you anymore. You are stronger than them.*

My heart slams in my chest and I scream out a war cry. Nico's head turns toward me, the knife in his hand lifting from Gray's neck. Shoving my toes into the floor, I launch myself at Nico's back. I wrap my arm around his shoulder to anchor myself to him. He howls and thrashes beneath me, trying to buck me off. Pain bites into my arm as his fingernails drag across my skin. I wrap my legs around his waist and lift the Christmas tree topper above my head.

Gray looks up at me, his eyes sparkling with pride. His mouth lifts into a wide smile that makes his eyes crinkle. He dips his chin in a subtle nod and I slam the ornament into Nico's neck. Yanking it back, I jump from his back, barely avoiding being covered by the blood that spurts from his wound. He gasps a yelp as his knees give out, sending him crashing to the floor.

Nico writhes against the floor, using his hands to grip his throat to stop the bleeding. Gray jumps up, his hands wrapping around Nico's and pulling them away from the wound. I stand over Nico's twitching body, watching a pool of red form beneath him. "You will never own me," I spit. "My life is *mine* and no man will ever control me again." My eyes flick to Gray. "Not unless *I* decide to let him."

We watch in silence as the spurting of Nico's wound becomes a slow trickle and then stops altogether.

"It's over," I breathe, finally letting the metal star fall from my fingers.

"Not quite, little bird," Gray grumbles as the sound of clattering wood and metal rings out around us.

Movement drags my eyes toward the room's entrance. Chunks of wood that used to be furniture topple over, revealing a very angry Italian woman in a white pants suit lumbering toward us. Bianca's eyes hone in on the bleeding corpse of her son, and she lets out a horrific scream. "Nico!"

She rushes toward him, the hem of her white suit pants collecting blood and soot as it drags against the floor. Gray shoves my body behind his as she nears. I stare at the wall of his back and listen to the choked sobs that tear out of Bianca's chest. Gray steps toward her and I follow on his heels. At the thunk of his boots on the marble, Bianca whips her head toward him and points her gun at his head.

In a movement faster than my eyes can track, Gray's foot collides with the woman's chest. The gun clatters against the floor as she falls back into the rubble. His fist wraps around the collar of her designer jacket, hauling her to her feet. She spits and curses, her fists smacking against his chest, but he doesn't move.

"You made a very big mistake, Bianca," he seethes. "You took something that doesn't belong to you."

She kicks her leg out, jabbing her heel into Gray's knee. He winces, but doesn't loosen his hold on her.

"You killed my son!" she screeches.

A laugh bursts from his mouth. "*I* didn't kill your son." He cocks his head in my direction. "She did."

Bianca's eyes rocket toward me and for the first time, I don't shrink back at the anger in her gaze. I killed three men today and I'm not sorry about it. Just like if I were reading a novel, I fell into a role. Her son was a rabid dog and I was the skilled veterinarian that put him down. A giggle climbs up my throat. That sounds like the beginnings of a meet-cute story waiting to happen.

"Close your eyes, Ava." Gray's voice pops the bubble of my thoughts.

The confident woman that lives inside of my chest lets out an angry huff. Crossing my arms over my chest, I glare at him. "I can handle this," I growl. "I won't be meek anymore."

He nods, understanding flashing in his eyes. "I know, precious," he sighs, "but right now, I need you to close your eyes."

Though my fingers tense against my arms, my eyes slip closed. Bianca's pained wail blasts my eardrums and I stumble back from the sound. The audio track for a horror movie I never want to see plays in my ears. Bones crack. Pained moans and shrill cries echo around me. Drops of liquid patter against the floor. The wet squelching of something I can't even attempt to name fills the room.

Arms wrap around me and I yelp.

"You're safe now, little bird."

Chapter Fifty-Five

I pull Ava into my arms, reveling at the feeling of her body pressed against mine. Her skin is cool, the result of spending several days half naked in a basement, but she doesn't feel cold in my arms. Maybe the warmth that seeps from her body and into mine is just my imagination. Is this what love does to me? Is that what makes her feel like sunlight pressed against my chest?

Pressing my nose into her hair, I inhale deeply. Beneath the scent of copper and ash, the sweet smell of her lingers. I suck it in greedily, needing it like I need the oxygen in my lungs. She wraps her arms around my shoulders, her face nestling into the crook of my neck. Her tears wet my skin as I carry her from the room.

Malik leans against the splintered door frame, brushing bits of plaster from his jacket sleeves. When he sees me, he nods. I don't have the words to express my gratitude for the risk he took today, so I simply nod back.

I point my finger toward the ruined foyer and the rooms beyond. "Torch it."

"Gladly." He chuckles. He looks down at the woman in my arms and his mouth tilts up into a proud grin. "I'll see you soon, tiny killer."

"Bye, Malik," Ava mumbles against my neck.

Stepping outside, a cold wind whips at my face. I pull my jacket around Ava and move toward the tree line. Leaves crunch beneath my boots and I breathe in the earthy scent of decay. I've always appreciated autumn for the way that it kills. The season means more to me now than it did before. I look down at the woman in my arms and the way her hair falls against my shoulder, the colors of it like warm earth and fallen leaves.

At the edge of the woods, I turn back toward the house. The crackle of flames drifts through the night air as fire licks at the wood of Bianca's former home. Embers lift from the house, floating toward the sky like fireflies. A black wall of smoke moves toward us and the acrid tang of gasoline coats my tongue. Ava sputters a disgusted sound and presses her nose into my neck. She's not used to it, but I don't mind the scent. It smells like destruction and vengeance, like an ending and a beginning.

The flames rise higher, engulfing the enormous house and warming the wintery chill around us. Pulling Ava from my arms, I place her on her feet. She wiggles her toes in the dried leaves and sighs. Tears drip down her cheeks as she tilts her head toward me.

"You came for me," she whispers.

I place my fingers beneath her chin, stroking the smooth curve of her neck. "And you killed for me." No, that's not right. I shake my head. "No, not just for me. For you, for us. You're so brave, baby, so much braver than you ever let yourself believe."

Wrapping my arms around her, I pull her into my chest. "I will always come for you. There's no place in this world that you can go that I won't find you."

She presses her palms into my chest, her fingers kneading the fabric of my jacket. She opens her mouth, but doesn't speak. My eyes track the movement of a tear that glides down her cheek, settling on her wobbling lower lip. Need burns in my gut and I lean down to taste the salt of her on my tongue. She gasps out a sob as I lick a tear from her cheek.

"I-I almost, almost," she sputters, "I almost died. They were going to…going to…"

"Shh, it's okay now. You're safe now," I whisper, rubbing my palms over her arms. "Nothing like this will ever happen again."

"How can you know that?" she whispers.

I step back from our embrace and latch my hands around her shoulders. Shoving her forward, I press her back against a tree. Her back hits the rough bark and she lets out a whimper that makes my dick jump to attention. She shoves her hands into my chest, her fingernails scraping over the fabric of my shirt. Pressing in closer, I invade her space and shove my knee between her thighs. My fingers wrap around her throat and I squeeze just hard enough to pinken her cheeks and make her pant for air.

"Because no one in this world is allowed to hurt you ever again." I run my palm up her thigh, feeling her legs quiver as I near her center. "No one but me."

Her eyes widen, fear and lust evident on her face. The demented creature that lives inside of me purrs, loving the way she fears me.

"You're mine, little bird."

My fingers whisper over her skin, trailing over her body to her chest. I grip the collar of her shirt between my fingers and wrench my hands apart. The fabric shrieks as it rips apart. Its frayed edges dangle at Ava's shoulders. She shivers as I run my palm over her soft stomach. Her breath becomes shallow and ragged. Her breasts bounce as she sucks in shallow pants, drawing my eyes to her chest.

The cool night air blows by us, hardening her nipples into stiff peaks. Dipping my head, I swirl my tongue over one of the rosy buds, wrenching a gasp from her lips. She shudders as I scrape my teeth over the sensitive skin.

"Do you need me to show you why I'm your master?" I pinch her other nipple between my fingers and tug. "To show you why you chose me?"

She hisses as I sink my teeth into her flesh, rolling her nipple between my teeth. I groan at the sweet taste of her skin and the spice of her sweat. Need builds inside of me and that feral thing in my chest claws at my ribcage, needing to be closer to her, to devour and claim her.

Her hands fall to her sides and she twists her fingers in the scraps of her ruined shirt. She bucks her hips, drawing a whimper from her lips when her core grinds against my leg.

"That's it, precious," I breathe against her chest and press my knee harder into her core. "You want me to prove to you that you're mine?"

"Uh huh," she pants.

"Good, then I will." I pull my mouth from her nipple and she whines at the loss. Gripping her chin between my fingers, I force her gaze to meet mine. Her half-lidded eyes shine with a delicious combination of lust and fear. "We both know how much you love being mine, obeying me, submitting to me. I knew you would from the moment I first laid eyes on you."

I grind my pelvis into her hip, forcing her to feel how hard I am for her. Her eyes widen and needy little sounds sputter from her mouth.

"You see, I may have chosen you at first, but tonight, you chose me." I run my nose over the side of hers, my breath ghosting over her lips. "Because you need this. You crave this."

I run my finger over the gold chain at her neck. The firelight dances over the metal, sending sparks of light glittering against her milky skin. "You love this collar, don't you?" I ask. "You love being my perfect little pet."

"Yes." The word is barely a whisper, but it rings in my ears as clear as a bell.

Pulling my knee from between her thighs, I shove the scraps of her t-shirt aside, revealing the naked flesh beneath. Soot and blood from the tattered fabric smear across her skin and I suck in a breath. She's gorgeous this way—her skin coated in the evidence of her freedom. The red and black slicks look like the strokes of a paintbrush on canvas. It's a masterpiece given to her by the dead. It shows the way she fought, the way that she didn't freeze in her fear. She never will again.

"Open your legs," I demand.

Leaves crackles beneath her as she shuffles her feet, stepping her legs apart by mere inches.

A yelp jumps from her lips as I smack my palm down on her

inner thigh. The flesh pinkens into a perfect rosy handprint and I grin. "Wider. Open your legs and let me see what's mine."

She steps her legs apart further, giving me a glimpse of her wet center. Moonlight and fire glimmer off of the arousal that coats her thighs, making it look pearlescent against her pale skin. I cup her dripping cunt and her lips part on a husky moan.

"You're so wet for me," I groan, pressing a finger inside of her and reaching my thumb toward her clit. Her eyes roll back as I circle the bundle of nerves. Pressing a second finger into her tight channel, I pump my fingers and feel her clench around them. She bucks her hips, grinding her cunt into my hand.

I press my lips against her ear. "And so needy for my attention."

Ava wraps her arms around my neck, gripping the fabric of my jacket tightly between her fingers. I trail my lips down her neck, nipping and sucking on her soft skin. She whimpers, her hips writhing against my hand seeking her release.

"What do you need, precious?" I scrap my teeth over the sensitive skin below her ear. "Do you need your master to fuck you? To remind you who owns your body?" I pull my fingers from the tight grip of her pussy and she whines. Pressing my palm against her sternum, I kiss a line across her chin. "Who owns your heart?"

Her voice is hoarse and desperate. "Please."

I open my zipper and let my cock spring free. Air fills my chest at the way her eyes widen and her tongue darts out to wet her lower lip. Her hungry gaze follows the movement of my hand as I stroke it over my hard length. Wrapping my hand around her thigh, I squeeze the supple flesh in a bruising grip and wrap her leg around my waist. An excited hum vibrates in her throat as I line myself up to her entrance.

I pause with my cock only inches from her dripping center. "Tell me what I want to hear, little bird."

"Please, fuck me, master," she begs. "Please."

"That's my good girl. I'm not going to be gentle with you." The flash of trepidation in her eyes makes me groan. "I need to remind you that you're mine."

I thrust forward, slamming my cock deep inside of her. Ava

screams and clenches around me. My tenuous grip on my self-control shatters and I pump into her wet heat with hard, fast strokes. The feral being inside of me purrs at the feeling of her cunt squeezing around my length. It relishes in the tears that dribble down her pink cheeks and the way her face pinches with pain.

"Fuck," I grunt, "you feel so good. Such a *good little slut.*" I punctuate each word with a hard thrust.

I want to make this last, to make her come over and over until she can't breathe, but I can't. I can feel my body barreling toward orgasm. Every part of me knows that I almost lost her. My organs clench and my muscles twitch, all of them reaching for her. Tomorrow, I'll give her more. I'll drown her in pleasure until the only name she remembers is mine. But tonight, I need to claim her. I need to pummel into her and force my seed so deep inside of her that she'll be marked forever with my essence.

Her body tenses and her moans drift through the air like a song. Reaching between her legs, I stroke my fingers over her swollen clit. She jerks in my hold, her body quivering with need. I pinch the bundle of nerves between my fingers and she cries out.

"Tell me you're mine, little bird," I demand, angling my cock to hit the spot that makes her writhe with pleasure.

"I'm yours," she pants. "Please, please, I'm going to—"

"Not yet, precious." She screeches as I smack my fingers against her clit. "Tell me you need me."

"I-I need you."

I drag my cock against that sensitive spot deep inside of her, feeling her muscles squeeze me like a vise. "Tell me you love me."

Her breath whispers across my face with her whimpered words. "I love you so much."

I drag my fingers over her clit and pump into her with rough, even strokes. "Then come for me."

Ava screams out her release into the night. The symphony of my little bird's song reaches my ears and I quickly follow, pumping her full of my release until it drips down her luscious thighs. I scoop her into my arms, elevating her ass with my elbow to ensure that she keeps most of my cum inside of her. The organ thrashing in my chest is like a feral animal that settles with the knowledge that she's marked by my scent.

Ava nestles into me, sighing happily and pressing her head into my shoulder. I press a kiss to the top of her head and wrap my jacket around her.

"Let's go home." She sighs.

Home. My heart expands within me, its beat thumping out her name. I carry her away from the burning ruins and a warm feeling ignites within me. After all of this, everything she's been through here, she wants to go home with me. *You are her home,* the beast within me sighs.

Epilogue
Six Months Later

I shrug off my sweater, letting the soft fabric slide down my arms and pool around my waist. A warm breeze drifts by and I inhale the scent of wildflowers and earth. I rub my fingers along the hem of the picnic blanket beneath me. Speckles of sunlight peek through the trees and I watch their tiny beams float down toward my hand.

A smile pulls at my lips when the light catches my ring. The teardrop-shaped ruby glitters above the ashy gray band. Blood and soot. That's how he found me in that house, and that's all that we left behind. We sealed our vows the same way, standing in City Hall the next week, caked in blood and soot. It shocked me that I didn't bawk at his impromptu proposal or that he'd wanted me to wear the tattered, dirty t-shirt that I had worn during my captivity. It seemed fitting that my new life should begin in the ashes of what I left behind.

The chittering of a small animal draws my eyes toward the trees, where green leaves and tall pines reach upward toward a blue afternoon sky. It's beautiful here.

"Hungry?" Gray asks, gesturing toward a generous spread of cheese, meat, and crackers.

My stomach lets out a gurgling rumble and I laugh. "Starving."

My eyes follow the movement of his body, watching the way the muscles in his forearms bunch as he moves. He piles salami and cheddar on a cracker and moves it toward my mouth. I open my lips to accept the tasty treat, letting my tongue brush over his fingers as he feeds me. He pulls his fingers from my mouth, a heated look flashing through his eyes.

His voice takes on a deeper tone, hinting at something dark. "Do you know why I like it here?"

"Idummoo," I mumble around bites of food.

He runs his hand up my thigh and I swallow thickly. My skin tingles in the wake of his touch and my core tightens at his closeness.

He leans in, his breath ghosting over my lips. "This place is very special to me."

My gaze flits around the clearing, taking in the trees around us and the large patch of earth. We sit in the center of what's almost a circle. The forest around us is lush and green, but this particular area is only dirt. The tree cover is so vast that the sun must not be able to come through enough for grass or flowers to grow here.

Gray places his thumb under my chin and angles my face toward him. When our eyes meet, my stomach flutters and my nerve-endings spring to life. Goosebumps break out over my bare legs, their bumpy pattern creeping under my skirt. There's something dark within his gaze, something predatory.

"This," he says, waving his hand in a circle around us, "is where all the bodies are buried."

My breath catches in my throat and the blood in my veins turns to ice. Is he telling me that we're having a picnic in a graveyard? A graveyard of his victims? I dig my teeth into my lower lip to stop it from wobbling. He can't be serious. I shake my head because surely, he's kidding.

A devilish grin slides across his face. "Oh, yes, precious." He grabs my hips, forcing my body in front of him until my knees bump his. He opens his legs, pressing his thighs on either side of mine and trapping me between them. My steady breaths turn into choppy pants as I draw in much needed air.

His fingers trace along the line of my jaw, his eyes never leaving mine. "Everyone I've killed, every man who's ever touched you…" his voice trails off, his grip tightening on my chin. "They're all here, buried beneath the dirt."

He dips his head and kisses a line along the column of my throat. I moan at the feeling of his lips on me and the scrape of his teeth against my sensitive skin. His hand wraps around my throat, the other grabbing my hip in a bruising grip and I choke out a gasp. His fingers tighten around my neck, making me work to suck in air. Fear skitters through my veins, tightening my stomach and pinching my lungs.

"Are you afraid of me, little bird? I can feel your pulse racing." His tongue flicks out, licking a line across his lower lip. "Is my little wife afraid of me?"

"Yes," I whisper, not trusting the strength of my voice.

An approving sound hums in his throat. "Good. You should be."

He releases his grip on my neck and I suck in a greedy breath, filling my lungs to capacity. I yelp as he grabs my waist and yanks me into his lap. My stomach collides with his thigh and all the air puffs out of me. He lifts my skirt, baring my panty-clad ass to the creatures of the forest. The rip of fabric echoes through the trees just before I feel the breeze glide over my naked core.

Warmth pools in my belly as Gray's fingertips dance along the tops of my thighs. I wiggle my hips, trying to force his fingers to the place that I really need them. Without my permission, wanton, needy sounds fall from my lips. I gasp as his hand cracks down on my behind and a jolt of pain zips through my body.

"So impatient," he chides.

My heartbeat quickens at his commanding tone. Need courses through my body, dampening my thighs and making me desperate for his touch.

"Please, master," I beg.

His open palm smacks down on my ass harder and I groan at the sting. He rubs a slow circle over my stinging skin before cracking his hand down again. I wince as he slaps the tops of my thighs several times in quick succession, making my skin burn. Pushing my thighs apart, I silently beg for him to turn his attention toward my aching pussy. My clit pulses with every slap of his hand against my bare skin.

He runs a finger over my slick folds, his touch barely grazing the sensitive flesh. "Do you want me to touch you, little wife? To fuck you here above the corpses?"

Embarrassment floods through me, heating my face, but I can't deny that I want that. I want him. I want every monstrous part of him and every shadow that lives in his heart.

"Yes." The word croaks out of me.

Gray chuckles. "Will my little bird sing for me?" he asks, tracing his fingertips around my entrance. "Will you scream so loudly that the ghosts will hear you in their graves?"

He plunges a finger inside of me and I scream, "Yes, yes!"

Arousal courses through my body and I can already feel myself tightening around him. I rock my hips into his hand, pushing him deeper. His palm cracks down on my sore ass and I moan.

"Fuck," he groans as he pushes a second finger into me, "your needy cunt is gripping my fingers."

He scissors his fingers inside of me, adding a bite of pain to the pleasure. My muscles tense at the dizzying combination.

"I need more," I cry. "Please, fuck me."

He withdraws his fingers and I whine at the loss. Every second without him inside of me, my desperation grows. He flips me off of him and onto my knees. My balance teeters and my body wobbles, but his hand on my waist steadies me. His gaze finds mine and I nearly orgasm from the look in his eyes alone. It's filled with so much need and hunger, like a mirror of my own desire reflected back on me.

I watch, fascinated, as he unzips his pants and pulls out his cock. He runs his hand over his length and my pussy clenches around nothing. A bead of arousal drips from the tip and I lick my lips.

"Ride me," he commands.

My knees wobble as I position my thighs on either side of his. I hover over him, pressing the tip of his cock to my center. Pressing my hands against his shoulders, I steady myself, preparing to sink down onto him slowly.

His fingers dig into my waist and he yanks me down, forcing himself inside of me in one swift move. Pain and pleasure erupt in my core as he stretches me. I cry out at the feeling of him inside me. My fingers fumble against him, grasping at the fabric of his shirt. My fingernails dig into his skin and he moans low in his throat.

I begin to move, my hips grinding into him and pushing his cock to that spot deep inside of me that makes my core spasm. He fists my ponytail in his hand and tugs. The bite of pain in my scalp makes me cry out and tears drip down my cheeks.

"That's it, precious," he purrs. "Make yourself come on your master's cock."

His words reach my ears and twist around inside of me, tightening my core. I press my knees into the ground, pulling myself up and down on his hard length. He reaches a hand between my legs and I moan as his fingers find my clit.

His circles the sensitive bud and my insides clench. My movements become choppy and my legs uncoordinated as I careen toward my release.

"Fuck," I pant. "Please, master. Please let me come."

His fingers pinch around my clit and he slams his hips upward. "You want to come, little wife?" My muscles tighten around him as he teases the bundle of nerves between his fingers, rolling and rubbing it. I clench my muscles tight, trying to hold back the orgasm that threatens to explode through me.

"Please, I-I need to come," I cry. "Please!"

Gray rolls his hips, dragging his cock over that sweet spot deep within me and I sob out a moan.

He dips his head and his breath pants across my shoulder. "Come for me," he growls before sinking his teeth deep into the flesh at the crook of my neck.

My screams bounce between the trees as my orgasm tears through me. My pussy flutters around him and stars speckle my vision. His rhythm falters, his hips slamming up into me with abandon. Groaning and gasping in my ear, he fills me with his release.

His strong arms wrap around me and my head lolls, flopping against his shoulder. He runs his fingers through my hair and for a moment, the world quiets. The leaves in the trees, the wind in the air, even the spirits that surely haunt these woods seem to be silenced. The only thing that exists is us and the furious beating of our hearts.

"I love you, Ava," Gray murmurs against my hair. "You're my everything."

Yes, the little voice inside of me hums, *I am <u>everything</u>.*

Acknowledgments

Many years ago, I had this crazy idea that I wanted to be an author. As I got older, I decided that it simply wouldn't work. I thought surely it would be too difficult and that the market would be too hard to break into. Years after I had that first crazy idea, I had another—I was going to write that book.

There are so many people who joined me on this journey, and I'm so thankful for each and every one of them.

I want to express my deepest gratitude and love for my family, whose unwavering support kept me going during the most difficult parts of this process. To my boyfriend, who listened to me talk for hours about this book and whose creativity fueled so many ideas.

A heartfelt thanks to my beta readers, Mom, Kim, Daphne, Emma, Mara, Ophelia, Sara, and Cera, whose invaluable input strengthened so many aspects of this story. A huge shout-out to Michelle, whose insight as a sensitivity reader greatly helped me in editing this book.

A special thanks to my editor, Hannah, who not only fixed every misused em-dash in this book but also hyped me up every step of the way. Your feedback not only made this book better, but also gave me the courage to share this story with the world.

This book wouldn't be the same without the beautiful cover design and graphics by Valerie of Turning Pages Designs and the striking character art of ViiMorte. Your work brought this story to life in a way I never expected.

Finally, to the readers who picked up this book and let Grayson and Ava's story live in their hearts, thank you.

About the Author

J. F. Page is an up-and-coming author with a love for romance. Her stories drag her readers into dark and strange worlds, where passion and magic reign.

Spanning contemporary dark romance, dark paranormal romance, and more, she loves to keep her readers guessing as to what she'll do next.

When she isn't dreaming up stories about handsome villains with questionable morals, she can be found in her home in New Hampshire, hiding in her book nook and sipping on peppermint tea.

Find out more about her upcoming works at www.jfpageau thor.com